The Perfect Blend

Rachel Lynn

Also by Rachel Lynn

<u>The Cin Cin Series</u>
First Crush
The Perfect Blend
A Second Sip (Coming soon!)

Copyright © 2024 by Rachel Lynn

ISBN#: 9798335034142

All rights reserved.

No part of this publication may be reproduced, distributed, or transmitted in any form or by any means, including photocopying, recording, or other electronic or mechanical methods, without the prior written permission of the publisher, except as permitted by U.S. copyright law. For permission requests, contact the author.

The story, all names, characters, and incidents portrayed in this production are fictitious. No identification with actual persons (living or deceased), places, buildings, and products is intended or should be inferred.

No portion of this book may be reproduced in any form without written permission from the publisher or author, except as permitted by U.S. copyright law.

Cover Design by: Ryan Kidd

First Edition. 2024.

FOR AMANDA, MY BRAVE AND TRUE FRIEND. THANK YOU FOR YOUR COURAGE, BRAVERY, AND THE LIGHT YOU SHINE WHEREVER YOU GO.

Contents

Roman and Andy's Playlist	XI
Prologue	1
Chapter 1	13
Chapter 2	23
Chapter 3	31
Chapter 4	42
Chapter 5	57
Chapter 6	70
Chapter 7	79
Chapter 8	94
Chapter 9	107
Chapter 10	119
Chapter 11	131
Chapter 12	144
Chapter 13	155
Chapter 14	169
Chapter 15	182

Chapter 16	194
Chapter 17	210
Chapter 18	225
Chapter 19	232
Chapter 20	242
Chapter 21	253
Chapter 22	260
Chapter 23	270
Chapter 24	282
Chapter 25	297
Chapter 26	304
Chapter 27	310
Chapter 28	318
Chapter 29	326
Chapter 30	338
Chapter 31	346
Epilogue	360
Acknowledgements	366

Roman and Andy's Playlist

Scan the Spotify code below to follow along with Andy and Roman through Italy.

Prologue

Andy

He's the most gorgeous man I've ever seen.

From my spot at the bar, I have the perfect view of the room. I see him before he sees me, which gives me precious, precious, minutes to reel in my open mouth. I watch him walk in, tension agitating the most perfect set of broad shoulders in existence.

Everything else seems to fall away: the thumping of the bass music blasting behind me, the loud laughter from the girls to my right, and the burn of vodka resting on my tongue.

Everything is gone. All there is, is him.

The lights flash over his strong jaw, full mouth, and perfectly straight nose. His black hair falls in disarray over his forehead in messy curls, as if he's been plowing his fingers through it. But it's his eyes—green as jade and sharp as an asp—that have my breath catching in my throat.

He scans the room, sucking in a deep lungful of air. I haven't been able to move, praying to all the gods and devils this man looks my way. I already know it'll be knee-weakening, soul-crushing if he looks at me.

It's like he can hear me, like I'm shouting my thoughts down some form of invisible bond, because he turns, and levels those gemstone eyes in my direction.

I see it. The minute this weird gravitational force hits him.

His eyes rove down my short dress, my long legs bare for the taking. I feel his gaze like fingertips sliding up my thighs, over my hips, across my belly before skirting up my ribs, over my breasts, into the valleys of my collarbones and around my neck.

The moment his eyes meet mine, all the air is sucked from the room.

I watch his chest move with another deep breath and then he's crossing the room toward me, his long legs cutting between the dance floor. I feel pinned by his stare, the bar and my back becoming one entity.

His eyes are dark, locked on me, as he weaves through couples grinding and writhing on the dance floor and suddenly... He's before me.

So tall. So very, very tall.

He smells like leather and spices, vanilla and a green forest canopy. His weekender hits the floor by my feet. We don't say anything. We just stare. My tongue is thick, my mind is cloudy. He's more stunning up close and he's zeroed in right on me.

He bends his dark head, bringing it close to mine.

"Hello." His voice is as smooth as rich dark chocolate and as deep as the ocean.

I swallow thickly. "Hi."

His lips twitch, and I feel that little muscle tick travel all the way to the base of my stomach.

"Drink?"

I don't care that he's monosyllabic. This is already the most exciting encounter in a club I've ever had. I rattle the full one in my left hand. He takes the glass from my hand and sucks against the straw, right where my mouth just was. My eyes widen in surprise as he holds my gaze and takes another pull.

I'm nearly panting as he licks his lips. He rears back, cool air licking between us.

"This is shit," he yells over the music. "Let's get you something better."

He doesn't ask me to move as he leans his big body over mine and across the bar to get the bartender's attention. His chest is warm against mine and I can see two thin, gold chains dangling around his neck. His right hand drops harmlessly to my hip, but I feel it like a brand against the thin fabric of my dress.

My lust-addled mind is telling me to lean forward and lick the neck of a perfect stranger. I'm nearly salivating to get a taste of him when another drink is pushed into my hand.

"To good taste," he murmurs, clinking his drink against mine.

I take a sip. I have to give it to him; this is way better. I glance over my shoulder and watch the bottle of Clase Azul being put back on the very top shelf.

"Are you saying that I don't have good taste?"

He shrugs a shoulder. A dimple appears on his left cheek when he grins.

He rattles my old drink at me. "I don't know. *Am* I?" he parrots.

I laugh. "I think you are. I think it's awfully bold to judge a girl off one drink. Maybe it's an off night."

He leans against the bar, caging me in on one side.

"Something tells me you don't have off nights."

I lick my lips. "Is that right?"

He hums deep in his chest. "You seem like the type of girl who usually knows what she wants." He tips his head in the direction of my drink. "Shitty drinks included."

"Oh, really," I sass, "and who made you the authority on good alcohol?"

He laughs like I've just told the funniest joke he's ever heard.

"Trust me. I didn't ask for it."

"So, what are you asking for then?" I wave my hand over him. "*You* seem like the type of man who usually gets what he wants."

"Is there much of a difference between us then?" he asks.

"I know what I want. I think you *get* what you want." A cocky little smile spreads across his face. "There's a difference between the two."

"Not always," he says. His eyes dart to my mouth. "But yes, usually."

His voice makes me shiver.

"So," I begin. What are you—"

He holds up a hand, stopping me.

"Want to dance?" He nods back towards the crowded dance floor.

"You want to dance?" I yell over the music.

He grins. "Am I going to get what I want or what?"

My mouth pops open. The fucking *nerve*. When he takes my hand, I don't fight him. The victory in his eyes makes my knees weak. He passes his bag over to the bartender for safekeeping and drags me to the floor. His hands are on me and rational thought flees as he draws me close. He's warm and strong beneath my hands as I run them up his chest and around his neck. His eyes are depthless when I meet his gaze.

Dancing has always been fun. It's never felt like foreplay, but that's what this is. His body moves and rolls against mine. His mouth is by my ear, on my neck, brushing against my bare shoulders. I move with him, desperate to keep up as his hands sink low on my back. One song rolls into two and then into three before we come up for air.

"Are you up for an experiment?" he asks, eyes following my hands as they trail down his chest.

"Depends." I'm not the type of woman to back down from a challenge and right now, I'm ready to throw my entire moral and belief system out the window to keep him in front of me. "What is it?"

He rakes a hand through his inky hair.

"My life is currently being... upended." He exhales harshly. "This is my last weekend of freedom and I don't want to think about what's waiting for me on the other side of this."

"I see. So, you came here to what? Forget?"

His dark eyes roam over me.

"Something like that," he murmurs.

"And what's your experiment?" I'm nearly purring at the warmth of his chest against mine.

"No names, no stories, no personal details." He rolls his bottom lip between his teeth. "I take you home and do every disrespectful thing that's rolling around in my head right now."

I gulp. I've gone home with a few guys before, but always after getting to know them at least a little bit. I've never done something like this, especially with a man so intense he makes my knees weak. He watches me for a long moment, tracking every movement of my face as I decide.

"No details?"

"None, other than you telling me all the ways you like it."

I shiver. This could be the best or worst decision of my life. I decide to roll the dice.

"Then let's go."

His eyes widen in surprise. He keeps his gaze locked on mine as he brings my hips hard against his. I can feel him against my thigh and I gasp at the thick length of him.

He takes my hand and leads me from the floor. He drops a fifty on the bar to cover my tab and grabs his bag back from the bartender. He threads his fingers through mine and then we're moving through the throng of dancing bodies and out into a sticky July night.

"How far?" I ask, struggling to keep up with his quick strides.

"Not very." He slows his pace to accommodate my heels.

To the crowds moving past us, we probably look like a couple heading home for the night. My body is nearly vibrating as he pulls me against him when we cross through a heavy bout of traffic.

I dig my phone out of my clutch one-handed and send a text to my best friend, Willow. I let her know I'm safe and share my location, just for good measure. I know she's on the other side of the world right now, but it's a habit we started when we're so far apart from each other.

We walk in tense silence and it's long enough for me to question my life choices. Is this crazy? I hardly know the man towing me through the streets of New York. We reach a high rise, the outside glossy and glassy. It reflects the city lights back to us and there, all the way at the top, are balconies. I wince. Heights have never been my favorite thing, and seeing the world from so high up has sweat collecting on the back of my neck.

We ride the elevator in silence before it opens on the very top floor. He sucks in a deep breath like he's nervous for what he'll see, too. We step into the white marble foyer and he drops his bag. We wander into the living room, his hand still wrapped around mine.

It's scarce, cold, empty. I shiver, running my free hand up my other arm as goosebumps explode over my skin. There's furniture, but just the necessities. I can smell the disinfectant, the nearly sterile atmosphere surrounding us.

"Is this your place?" I ask hesitantly.

"Yes." His voice is tight.

"You haven't moved in?"

He shakes his head. He lets go of my hand long enough to cross to the stocked bar cart on the other side of the dining room and pour us each a drink. He brings the bottle of whiskey with him, setting it down on the glass top table with a loud *clink*. New York shimmers and pulses below us, red brake lights and street lights twinkling like stars.

"Where is all your stuff?"

I'm nervous now. Serial killers have apartments like this, with no personal details and hospital levels of cleanliness.

"It's on its way. I just landed tonight." He gestures toward his weekender. "I thought I said no details."

"You did," I agree, wrapping my arms around myself. "This is just... weird."

He sighs. "I know, I apologize. My life is... hectic. If you're uncomfortable, I'll call you a cab and send you home. We can forget the whole thing."

I turn to look at him. He does look like hell, or what I imagine he'd look like struggling. He's devastating to look at. I can't fathom what he's like when he's on his game, calm and put together. There's a touch of wildness in his eyes, a hint of desperation that has me reaching for my drink and knocking it back.

"No," I say, much more confident than I feel. "I want to stay."

His eyes flare. He grabs a chair from the kitchen table and pulls it out. He drops into it, legs spread, knees far apart. He clutches his drink on his thigh, the other arm draped across the table. It's a masculine, dominant position. He jerks his chin in my direction.

"Take off your dress."

My cheeks heat, even as my fingers reach for the zipper at my back.

"Bossy," I tease, inching it down.

His tongue runs over his lip.

"You have no idea, sweetheart."

I step out of my dress, kicking it in his direction. He must see something in my eyes, the challenge in the set of my shoulders because he grins. It's a flash of white teeth against dark skin, brightness in the shadows around us, and I know I've stepped into the deep end.

He's going to make me beg for it, work for it, bring me to the edge and then leave me there. As I walk to him, I can read every dark promise in the set of his eyes and mouth as his rough hands glide up my thighs.

His mouth brushes against my navel. He bites the elastic of my underwear and pulls, letting it snap back against my skin.

A wave of pleasure rolls through me and I grin, because whoever this stranger is, he just met his match.

When he does finally get me naked, he's voracious, insatiable. His mouth is filthy, sinful, as he whispers in my ear and slides between my legs, working me up over and over and over again. He praises my every move, every whimper and moan. His fingers play me like a well-tuned instrument. He knows my body better than I do.

He has me on every surface. The kitchen table, the cold marble floor, the couch, the shower, and finally his bed.

When I think he can't go again, he sinks himself between my legs.

His voice is soft as velvet, deep as night. His eyes are hypnotizing. He locks my hands over my head and thrusts into me with near violence, never tearing his eyes away from mine. It's intense and more intimate than I'm used to. For a man who wants to know nothing about me, he's learning things quickly.

He's unraveled me faster than anyone else ever has before.

His body is lithe with muscle, powerful, rigid. I've never seen anyone built like him, the dark tattoo snaking over his shoulder, the ripple of muscles in his abdomen and chest. He lifts me like I'm nothing, tosses me around like a feather.

He's tender, caring, attentive but *demanding*. He has me on my knees for him, and I go willingly, my own pleasure mounting at the wildness in his eyes, the way he's unhinged as he works my mouth.

We don't sleep. We don't rest. We keep our promise, no details, no names, no backstories. It's the wildest night of my life, but every time he touches me, I feel him sink further into my DNA.

We fall asleep wrapped around each other in the hours past dawn. The city wakes up around us, soft gray clouds hiding the sunrise. He holds me close, like I'm precious to him. He wakes me when the sun is fully risen, fingers moving down my stomach.

In the light of day, I can see how gorgeous he actually is. His hair is so black it's nearly blue. His eyes are clearer, but they're still unnerving to meet when he looks at me. Stubble lines his hard jaw and his lips are swollen from my mouth.

There's an unspoken agreement between us: one last time and then I go.

He pulls me on his lap and I let him watch me as I rock on his lap. He looks at me like a miracle, like some form of goddess he's lucky enough to worship. My orgasms leave me shaking, breathless, quaking on top of him, and watching him break apart in the sunlight is seared in my mind forever.

I'm off-balance as I get dressed and gather my things. I slide my phone back into my bag, head fuzzy and disoriented. I know I don't know him, but somehow, I feel like I do. He's looking at me much the same way, like last night was more intense than he thought it'd be.

He walks me to the door, bare-chested and in black joggers that hug an impressive set of thighs. I know there's still a bruise on the left one from where I sank my teeth into him.

I don't know what to say. I feel like we've said everything and nothing all at once. He stares at me blankly, and I take it as my cue. I open the door, but he slaps his hand against it, shutting it.

"Tell me something real," he whispers from right behind me. "Something. Anything." There's a tinge of desperation in his voice.

My heart is racing against my ribs. I lick my dry lips. Something real? A million details come to mind, but none seem right enough to tell him. I lift my eyes to him. I can't think of one thing, so I give him several.

"I'm terrified of heights. I only like scrambled eggs, not over easy. Lunch is my least favorite meal of the day. My best friend and I drink wine every Wednesday when she's home, and it's the highlight of my week. I miss her when she's gone—and she's almost always gone. I live alone. I think I've always been alone. Lilac is my favorite color and I hate peas. Music is my therapy, but I haven't been able to sing in years and you… you unnerve me." I meet his gaze. He's breathing harshly enough that I can feel his warm breath on my shoulder. "I don't even know you, but I know I'll never be able to forget you."

He's speechless, and I leave him with that. I slip out the door and run. I run home, hands shaking, heart pounding. I call Willow and tell her everything. I can barely breathe. I can still feel his hands and mouth and chest vibrating against mine.

Life has a way of ripping the rug from underneath your feet, blindsiding you in the cruelest and most impossible ways. He's still thrumming in my veins Monday morning when I head to work.

I can't stop thinking of him, my perfect stranger.

It's like a record scratch when I walk into the conference room and find him there, hunched over the table next to my boss, Mr. Bendetti.

My eyes are playing tricks on me, I know it. Of every place in the city he could have turned up, it can't be here. I'm hallucinating, I tell myself. I haven't been able to stop thinking of him, so my mind is playing tricks on me. It's not him. It *can't* be him.

But it is, I realize, gut sinking to my toes. His jade eyes meet mine and I feel it like a blow to the gut.

It's him.

The signet ring that was so cool on my neck flashes in the light and the full mouth I nearly drowned in is frowning at the corners.

I can barely hear him speaking to me over the roaring in my ears, the pit in my stomach. I can't stop looking at him. His hair is different, brushed off his face. His suit is immaculate, all clean lines and trimmed perfectly to him.

I catch a few words: my son, Roman, just arrived, Italy.

He's staring at me and I watch the emotions flick over his face: disbelief, joy, hunger, sadness, misery, and then they're gone. His mask slides into place, his cool and indifferent eyes meeting mine and I know.

I just slept with my future boss. My current boss' son. I feel the damn break inside me, a light shuttering out.

"It's good to meet you, Alexandra," he says, crossing the room and offering his hand. So indifferent, so cold. "My name is Roman."

He takes my hand like he doesn't know every line of my body, the sounds I make, the way I move. Numbly, I put my hand in his. That painful zap of electricity moves up my arm. He drops my hand quickly, as if I've stung him.

"Andy," I nearly choke. "My friends call me Andy."

I watch him whisper it, taste it, roll it around in his mouth. His eyes gutter.

I force myself to smile, force the light into my eyes. It's easy to do, considering I've done it for most of my life.

I sink into my seat, realization slipping into place.

The man of my dreams, my nightmares, is the one man I can never, ever have.

Chapter 1

Andy

Three years later...

I tap my foot against the gray and white tiles under my feet, watching the security line inch forward. I pat my pockets for the tenth time, feeling for my passport, wallet, and phone.

Our flight to Italy leaves in three hours, but I'm always early when flying out of JFK. I've learned from experience that nothing ever goes to plan, and I'm not necessarily someone who thrives in chaos.

The line moves up another few inches, and I pull my boarding pass out of my bag. I've flown plenty of times, but the anxiety of being trapped inside what is essentially a Pillsbury can of biscuits still makes my throat feel tight.

It's been a while since I've been overseas and knowing there's a nearly nine-hour flight ahead of me, where I hover over the deepest parts of the ocean, makes me thankful for the Dramamine and anti-anxiety medication in my carry-on.

I need to get it together.

I need to get it together for when *he* gets here. I need every wit, sense, and element on my side for the next three weeks.

I'm traveling to Italy with none other than Roman Bendetti.

Roman, who has haunted the corners of my dreams for the last three years.

Roman, who has done nothing but rile me at every turn.

Roman, who has driven me crazy every second of every hour of every day.

The man I want, but can never have.

Anxiety flutters beneath my breastbone. My mouth is parched, my tongue clumsy with nerves.

I pull my phone from my pocket and shoot off a text to my best friend, Willow.

> **ANDY: Do I really need to do this?**

> **WILLOW: It'll be fine. Think of how much you love Italy. That should outweigh your dislike for Roman.**

> **ANDY: Doubtful.**

> **WILLOW: Let me know when you're through security. They added *27 Dresses* to the in-flight movie list.**

I snort. *27 Dresses* has become somewhat of a staple in my adult life. It's become my go-to comfort movie when I need a little cheering up. 2008 James Marsden hits differently with his floppy brown hair and crystal baby-blue eyes. A girl can dream about a grand profession of love and a guy loudly cheering her on.

Willow has spent more time in an airplane than anyone I know, and she's never had a single issue in her thousand flights across the globe. Though, that number is infinitely smaller now that she's settled happily in New York with her hot and sexy architect designer fiancé, Wes.

She travels sparingly these days, which is great for me. I missed her when she was away. New York never felt complete without her—nowhere ever does. When she does travel now, however, Wes is in tow.

Their home is full of pictures of them in vineyards around the globe, hiking waterfalls, lounging on white sand beaches. They are disgustingly, blissfully, mind-numbingly in love and I could not be happier for them. Seeing Willow settled, content, fighting her demons and working through her trauma, only makes mine feel like quicksand beneath my feet.

I feel like Kate Winslet in *Titanic*. You know the line: outwardly she's everything she's supposed to be, but inside she's screaming? Yeah, that's how much of my life feels. Perfect smile, impeccably dressed, finishing school level of manners and etiquette but inside...

The TSA agent calls me forward and I step up to the podium and hand him my passport and boarding pass. He flicks his eyes between the picture in my passport and my face for an unnervingly long amount of time before finally passing my documents back under the safety screen.

"Have a good flight."

I move through the line, toeing off my Vans and stuffing my belongings into one of those gray plastic bins. I try not to think about how many other people's shoe germs are coating my things as I step through the metal detector.

Once my things pass x-ray inspection, I slip my shoes back on and head to the first-class lounge in terminal three. I've never flown first-class before, but I don't know why I was expecting anything different from Roman Bendetti.

He's a man who screams class and luxury.

Thankfully, this wasn't a ticket I needed to purchase for myself.

I text Willow that I've made it through security and she shoots me back a thumbs up emoji before typing out:

> WILLOW: Everything is going to be fine, Andy. Roman will make sure you're safe.

I wish her message actually reassured me. Last year, when her relationship with Wes went sideways, it was Roman that she called for help. Roman who took care of her and picked her up and helped her find mental clarity. Roman, the man who hasn't looked at me with anything other than barely controlled contempt over the last three years. Roman, who doesn't seem to have an issue extending kindness to anyone that isn't me.

When Mr. Bendetti approached me about the idea for this trip back over the summer, I laughed. I had laughed so hard I nearly cried, but when his smile didn't come, I realized he was serious.

"My son can be... brusque," he had said, Italian accent still thick despite his many years in the States. "I need to be able to work with these vineyards and owners. To create a strong, friendly alliance."

I didn't miss the emphasis he placed on the word *friendly*.

"Can't you send someone else?" I blurted. "Anyone else?"

"You are my client relations manager, Andy. There is no one better to oversee these dealings than you. I am hoping you'll be able to smooth out Roman's rough edges."

"What about my clients? I need to be available for them if they need something," I'd said a little desperately.

"I will take care of it. There is nothing more important than this. I need your complete focus while you're there. The future of Cin Cin rides on this."

There'd been no arguing after that. I was going to Italy, hogtied and screaming for my life. I spent half my childhood in Italy with my nonna before she passed and going back now does excite me. The last time I was there was in college, shortly after her death.

I spin her emerald ring around on my finger, an anxious habit I developed somewhere along the way. It will be good to go back and see the places she saw and walk the streets that were her playground. Emotion clogs my throat. It's been years, but the grief of missing her hasn't abated.

I flash my boarding pass again at the attendant standing guard over the first-class lounge. He waves me inside and I beeline toward the coffee bar. I fix myself a cup and take a seat at the window. The sun sets over the city of New York. Warm, golden light coasts over my skin and I watch the planes land and take off, lost in thought.

I think of all the people coming and going, the destinations that await them. Somewhere in the sky are two best friends embarking on an adventure that will seal them together for life. Somewhere else, someone is heading home for the first time in years or saying goodbye to someone they thought they'd never have to live without. A thousand emotions linger above my head in a perfect sunset sky.

I pull up the email Roman sent that morning detailing all our stops along the way.

Our itinerary is lengthy, starting in Rome before we move north to Tuscany and Umbria. From there, we'll travel to Veneto and then to Piedmont before ending in Cinque Terre. Three weeks all in. Three weeks with the man who haunts every part of my life.

I've done my best over the years to avoid Roman Bendetti like the plague, but like any sticky and annoying object, he seems to cling to me wherever I go.

"Alexandra."

God.

That fucking *voice*.

Smooth as silk. As dark and soft as midnight.

It's been years, but my reaction is always the same. I close my eyes; I steel my spine. I try not to shudder at the velvet in his voice. I shouldn't still have such a visceral reaction to the way he says my name, but I do. I feel it like a caress. I know what those fingers feel like against my thighs and between my legs. I know the taste and shape of his mouth.

I know it *all*.

I desperately wish I didn't.

I dig deep, building the parapet up around my heart and my mind before spinning in my seat. I let my cool and indifferent mask slip into place. Roman Bendetti will never know the riot of chaos he still causes in my chest when he looks my way.

"Roman."

His bag is slung over his shoulder and his Ray-Bans dangle from his fingers. Even for an overnight flight where no one can see him, he's dressed in charcoal slacks and a white button down, sleeves rolled to his elbows.

"Sorry to keep you waiting. Have you been here long?"

God, sometimes it's so painful talking to him. So strained. This is the man who made me come in under two minutes with just his tongue.

He *knows* me, and maybe that's the problem.

"No," I finally say. "Maybe half an hour?"

He frowns like it is too long to be kept waiting. He'd only texted me once this morning with the document that contained the places we were staying, the contacts of our host, and the car services that would be taking us from place to place.

He takes the seat next to me and pulls his laptop from his bag. He settles in, tapping out email after email and I watch him. I always feel like I'm watching him, waiting for him to look at me. Waiting for him to say *something*, anything.

I know you're probably thinking this is the most pathetic attempt at moving on you've ever seen and I've *tried*. I have tried. Believe me. I've tried to date a few men since my night with Roman.

I've sat through my handful of painfully awkward dinners, with my mind wandering and my heart dormant in my chest. I've faked smiles and good times and collapsed in on myself like a dying star when I returned home, still aching for a man that doesn't want me back.

I've gone to clubs and bars to meet someone new. I've flirted and kissed and teased and felt… nothing. The sex has been subpar but then again… Roman raised the bar so high there was no one who could top it.

And there have been… moments.

Moments where his mask slips, and I see the man who worshiped me so thoroughly stars appeared behind my eyes. When we went to Shimmer last year, he'd stalked his way onto the dance floor. He'd held me like he did that night, hands firm, mouth on my neck, hovering by my ear. Flustering me to the point of no return. The thick, hard length of him pressed against me had my mouth going dry and I could feel him trembling with restraint.

He'd danced with me for a long time, hands roaming. It was only when I had breathed his name that he stepped away from me abruptly, as if he'd realized what he'd been doing. After he stalked off the dance floor, I raced home, heart aching with tears in my eyes.

Then again when we went to the Harper's beach house for Memorial Day that first time. I woke early, anxious, restless, and headed to the beach for a run. I've never been much of a runner, always opting for my Hot Girl Walks instead, but that morning I ran. He, too, was out for a run. Shirtless, bronzed, dripping with sweat. Mouthwatering.

Panting, he'd given me some pointers and we'd finished our run together, arms brushing. When we'd gotten back to the house, he stopped to ask me,

"I know what I'm running from. What about you?"

He'd left me with that. I wanted to say I was running from him. Running to him, away from him, I'm never quite sure. He takes care of my friends. He takes care of me when I drink too much. I know he waters my office plant when I forget. I know he's the one sending me coffees in the morning when I'm running late. He does it quietly, hiding deep within the shadows.

It's these little morsels that keep me hanging on, desperate for any crumb I can get.

We're called for boarding and I gather my things. I slip a Dramamine and an anti-anxiety pill out of my pill organizer and gulp them down with my cold coffee. Roman watches, but says nothing.

He leads me onto the plane, the comforting smell of his cologne dragging me forward. The flight attendant shows us to our seats, and there's no mistaking the hungry little look she gets on her face when Roman's muscular back is turned as he stows his bag overhead.

When she catches me staring, she flushes.

I have no right to be jealous, to try and claim something that's never been mine. She offers me an apologetic smile before clearing the aisle and letting me take my seat beside him. The seats are large, curved, and recline back all the way to form a small bed. The care kit that's waiting for me on my seat comes with PJ's, an eye mask, toiletries, a neck pillow, and a few pieces of dark chocolate. I settle in and clip my seatbelt low over my waist.

"Are you going to be all right?" His voice is tight with... worry.

I glance at him. He's eyeing me like a specimen under a Petri dish.

"What do you mean?"

He grounds his teeth together, like he's hesitant to say.

"You're afraid of heights," he says quietly.

I'm struck dumb. My foolish, idiotic self gave him so many little pieces of me that night. I'd nearly forgotten I told him that.

"I'm okay," I reassure. I show him my little pill organizer. "I'm hoping to sleep most of the flight and forget the fact that I'm about to be thirty-thousand feet above the ground in a metal tube full of bolts and screws and probably duct tape."

"Duct tape?" he asks, alarmed. "Alexandra, they don't repair planes with duct tape."

"Do you moonlight as an airplane repairman in your free time?" I snip. "How would you know?"

"These planes are serviced regularly," he grounds out. "There's no duct tape."

"Either way, I'd rather not think about it if there is or not."

He nods, the motion stiff. God, he must hate this. Being stuck with me for weeks on end. He's never told me he's regretted what happened between us, but I know he does.

The rest of the plane is boarded and the flight attendants rehearse their safety rules as we push back from the gate. It's a clear night, nothing but stars twinkling overhead as we taxi the runway and head for takeoff.

I'm white-knuckled against the seat as the plane tilts and the ground fades away. It's a turbulent takeoff and I'm practically green by the time we level out. I've never thrown up on a plane, and today is not the day for me to start. My knee bounces in place and I squeeze my eyes shut. How many years has it been since I've been on a plane? My work usually always keeps me in New York unless I need to travel for a conference, but most of those are drivable.

"Breathe." The command is soft but firm from where it comes by my ear. "Inhale, Alexandra. Now."

My body rises to the command, and I suck in a sharp breath. He waves the flight attendant over who was eye-fucking him earlier and asks for a ginger ale. When she tells him in-flight beverage service hasn't started yet, he glares.

"I would much prefer to make this trip without her throwing up. So, if you could please get one for her, I would greatly appreciate it." His smile is saccharine when it comes.

Flustered, she brings me a ginger ale. Roman pops the tab and shoves it into my hand.

I take a sip, bubbles bursting over my tongue.

"Better?" I hear him ask.

I nod. "Better."

He relaxes back against his seat. I press my warm skin to the cold glass of the window and close my eyes.

Every time I take one step away from him, he pulls me right back where I started.

Chapter 2
ROMAN

For the last three years, I have been haunted.

Every waking hour, I can feel the phantom tendrils of all my life decisions peering over my shoulder with wide and curious eyes. It feels very Ghost of Christmas Past with the way it plays all of my decisions on a loop over and over again before my eyes.

The woman that's made every day utter torture with her presence sleeps soundly beside me. I watch her lashes flutter over her cheekbones, her head pressed against me as we head east over the Atlantic. During her waking hours, she's content to cut me to the quick with that viper tongue of hers. In sleep, she reaches for me like she's doing right now.

From the moment I met her, Alexandra McNeil has been the bane of my existence. I have never wanted to simultaneously fuck, throttle, and take care of someone so much in my life. I press my head back against my seat, exhaustion tugging at me.

It's been a long six months. Fuck, a long three years, really. Taking over my father's business is nothing like I thought it would be. It's thrilling in a way I wasn't expecting, but Christ, am I tired.

My phone never stops ringing. My emails are always piled high and demanding attention. My free-time has dwindled to the hours I spend in the gym and the few minutes before bed where I watch an episode of

How I Met Your Mother or the highlights from one of the professional division league games back in Verona.

My dating life has dwindled into nothing, except for the few dates I scrounge for my galas and dinners and press related events.

None of them mean anything, and none of them go anywhere.

No one is *her*. No one could ever be her.

And dammit, have I tried.

I have tried to get the taste of her out of my mouth, remove the way her skin feels from my hands. I have begged whoever is listening to take the imprint of those perfect golden eyes out of my mind, the impression of her full mouth, that sultry little laugh she does.

No one listens.

No one *ever* listens.

This feels like a test. One I'm destined to fail. One that leaves me wondering what my father was thinking when he told me who he wanted me to go to Italy with. It's like he knew. Like he wanted to test my commitment to the company, to him, to the CEO position that is staring at me down the barrel of a gun. My last test, my last flex of willpower. If I can make it through three weeks with the woman who has managed to undo me, nothing is impossible anymore.

Our itinerary leaves very little free time, but I know her. I know Andy will tug me off course, just as she's always done. She'll flick those whiskey eyes to me, ask for something, and I'll fucking give it to her because when have I ever been able to say no?

She wants to go to a club? I'm there, fighting off the dick bags who like to get handsy.

She wants to go away to a strange man's beach house? I'm there, even though I know that Brooks Harper is one of the best men in New York.

She wants to drink herself into a stupor? I'm there, holding back her hair and force-feeding her pretzels.

She wants to outrun her problems? I'm there, teaching her how to do it without getting shin splints.

She forgets to eat breakfast in the morning? I send her her favorite: a blueberry bagel with cream cheese.

It's the only way I can show any sort of defiance for this very beautiful cage I'm currently ensnared in.

Giving up my dream, my future in the professional division of soccer in Verona with the Gladiators, has gutted something in me. Cin Cin has always been my father's dream, not mine.

Nicco, my younger brother by only a few minutes, seems to have been spared from a massive life change of his own at the moment. I don't know the ins and outs of his deal in the company— that's stayed between him and my father. Whatever it is he's meant to do for Cin Cin, I have a feeling that it will be coming for him soon.

The four years I spent in the league were the best of my life. The friendships I made, the challenges, the pitfalls, the triumphs. They were all I ever wanted.

None of us knew my father's business would take off the way it did. It started with his father before him, Salvatore. According to Dad, Grandpa Sal always had a glass of wine in hand. He was something of a connoisseur when he was alive and amassed quite an impressive selection of wines. He fell ill before I was born, but no matter what the doctors said about his alcohol intake, Grandpa Sal never stopped drinking. His tastes changed as his body withered, and my father started making wine in their small Tuscan home to find something that would make his father happy.

When that didn't work, he started calling his friends and neighbors who owned surrounding vineyards and wineries. Before long, my dad had realized a new dream: to find the wines people were looking for.

He was never able to find the one Grandpa Sal had been craving before he passed, and now I think it's his mission to save the people of the world and their wine choices.

I understand why he did it, what drove him to this point. I think, in his grief, this was the only thing he latched on to. He built a business, called everyone he knew, everyone who ever owed him a favor, and began. His business grew, expanding into Spain and France. The move to New York came right after I was born.

All for the American dream.

My mother supported all of it. She worked late with him, going over ledgers and books and shipping orders. He bought a small office in the middle of Manhattan and worked around the clock. It only took a few lucky chances, a few big named clients, before he was sprinting full speed ahead.

From there, it was all a fever dream.

I was technically an American citizen, but my mother applied for dual citizenship in Italy for my brother and I. All our family was still there, and so my life was split jumping the pond several times a year to go back home.

In the last few years prior to moving back, I started learning more about my inheritance. Sitting in on meetings, reading reports. I remember the days leading up before I had to leave for New York.

My teammates threw me a going away party crazy enough to raze Verona to the ground. I don't remember much of that night, if I'm honest. Italian newspapers and articles circulated, their headlines all about my early retirement. I've been recognized a few times in New York and only in certain circles. I haven't been back to Italy since then, and I'd be a damn liar if I said I wasn't feeling apprehensive about going home.

I didn't even tell Matteo and Christian, my two best friends on the team, that I was coming.

If I did, there's no way they'd let me leave without getting back on the pitch.

I wasn't sure I'd ever be ready for that.

I tell myself all the time my punishing diet and gym regimes aren't because I'm holding out hope I'll be able to play again at that level. At best, I could maybe play in a men's league somewhere in Central Park.

Andy doesn't know, and I need to tell her, just in case. I've only shared my history with one person: Willow. It was a moment of weakness, but one I was glad I made. As far as I knew, she never shared the details of our conversation with Andy. Her trust only adds to all the reasons I like her as a person. Seeing how happy her and Wes are rubs something raw in me.

There was a time, a weekend, where I thought I could have that.

I glance back at Andy's sleeping face. It's a rare moment of honesty and trust between us, and I'm the reason there aren't more of those.

When she walked into that office three years ago I... Fuck.

Fuck.

I've never had the air knocked out of me so forcefully in my life. Of all the places she could have turned up, of all the people she could have been, she had to have been the one who managed our customer relations.

She had to be the one my father chose.

She had to be the one that *I* chose.

It was the wildest, most passionate weekend of my life.

My tastes are... particular, and Andy rose to every single one of them. Every. Single. One. She was bold and brave and sexy and mind-meltingly perfect for me.

I spent that whole weekend dreaming about her, wondering if I could go back to that bar and bribe the security guard for the copy of her I.D. swipe when she arrived. I was going to go back on my word. I was desperate for details, desperate for more. She hooked me.

When I introduced myself, she told me to call her Andy...

It suited her. She's spunky and kind and sexy and a little wild and the name felt good in my mouth. Too good.

Which is why I will only ever call her Alexandra. I see the ire in her eyes, the irritation. She snaps at me. Her anger is the most I can have, and I'm a greedy mother fucker. I'll take all of it. Every drop.

She stirs against me and bolts up right in her chair when she realizes she's been using my bicep as a pillow.

"What time is it?" she asks, rubbing her eyes.

She's cute when she's sleepy. She's cute when she's mad and excited and happy and drunk. She's cute all the time and it's the *worst*.

Her hair has slipped from its ponytail and hangs haphazardly down her back. Her sweatshirt is oversized and worn in, dwarfing her hands and the mouth-watering curves I know are hiding beneath its baggy shape.

I calculate the time change in my head. "Around two. New York time," I whisper, not wanting to disturb the sleeping passengers around us.

She glances at the screen on the back of the seat in front of her. We took off at eight sharp, and there's three hours left until we touch down in Rome. She brings up the flight pattern and the little animated plane that's inching further and further toward land.

"You haven't slept?"

I shake my head. Honestly, I was worried. After seeing how green she was on the takeoff, I wanted to make sure I would be up if she needed me. It's not my first sleepless night, and something tells me it won't be my last.

"I don't really sleep on planes," I lie.

I always sleep. I pick my window seat, burrow against it, and pass out.

"Oh," she says softly.

She sips her water and fidgets in her seat. She twists the ring she always wears on her right middle finger around and around.

"Who gave you that?" I ask, watching it gleam in the soft lighting. I've always wanted to know. It's an antique, that much I can tell on my own.

"I haven't told you this?" she asks, almost in surprise.

I shake my head. The things I've learned about Andy over the years are courtesy of office gossip, my father, Willow, and overheard conversations.

"It was my nonna's," she murmurs, brushing her thumb across the gem. "She left it to me when she died."

Of course. I knew about Andy's ties to Italy, to her family. I should have known.

"It suits you," I say before I can stop myself. Her eyes widen the smallest bit. I clear my throat. "Are you excited to be back? It's been a few years, hasn't it?"

She nods. "I am. She was born in Sicily, but lived all throughout Rome and Tuscany in her twenties and thirties. That's still where my birth father's family is. Apparently, the Matranga clan is large and well spread out. I wouldn't be surprised if I run into a cousin somewhere."

"Are you close to them?"

She's thoughtful for a moment. "When I was small, yes. But when Nonna died, things sort of slipped away. She was the last tether to my dad and my relationship with his siblings. Things sort of faded after that."

"I'm sorry," I murmur, because I am.

She shrugs. "They were a good few years. I wouldn't trade them for anything."

We fall silent. The flight attendant comes over and offers another round of drinks. I re-up on my whiskey and Andy opts for peppermint tea. I hoard it, just like I do with every morsel of information she's fed me over the years.

She flips through her movie options before landing on one that makes her dance in her seat. She pops her headphones in.

"What's that?" I ask as the opening scene plays.

She removes her left ear and glances over at me.

"It's called *27 Dresses*. It's one of my comfort movies."

I could give a shit about a rom-com, but I'm invested in her happiness. I queue up my own screen and match the timer bar to hers. Her lips twitch, but she says nothing. We hit play at the same time and settle into our seats.

We fly in the darkness, laughing quietly together as Rome inches closer and closer.

Chapter 3

Andy

We land in Rome at nine a.m.

I've been awake for too many hours and I'm disoriented, exhausted, desperate for a coffee and a soft bed. Roman is stoic as he navigates us through the airport. He's careful to walk beside me, his jade eyes swinging across the airport like an on-duty bodyguard. His hand drops to the small of my back. It's a ghost of a touch, but it makes me shiver as he steers me toward baggage claim and customs.

The airport is large with several designer stores wrapped around its circular build. There are small markets for snacks and books and more wine than I was expecting to see. Even though it's early, I can hear the telltale sound of a cork popping out of the bottle. My smile is small as I think of Willow, knowing it's her favorite sound in the world.

I shoot her a text, letting her know we've landed.

We make it to customs and I sway in line, awaiting my turn to show my passport. Roman stands behind me, tap, tap, tapping away on his phone. We make our way to the front of the line and a very disinterested agent takes my passport. He asks me my purpose for visiting Italy, how long I'm staying, and why.

I must give him the right answers because he stamps my passport and waves me along so Roman can step forward and repeat the process. His eyes find mine in the crowd. There's lightning in his stare and I feel it roll through me like a shockwave.

His face is grim as he strides toward me and we head for the exit. He brings his phone to his ear. His Italian is flawless. Though, I reason, it would be considering he's lived here for most of his life. I groan inwardly. Roman is sexy all on his own, but coupled with the rich timbre of his voice, the perfect inflection, he's frying my last brain cell as we speak.

We step into the sunshine and my eyes land on a small Italian man, probably in his mid-sixties with a handwritten sign that says BENDETTI. Not Bendetti and McNeil, just Bendetti, like I'm his.

"Sergei!" Roman's voice has a note of happiness in it I've never heard before.

"*Signore!*" Sergei whoops, smacking his hands together and tossing his sign to the side.

I watch, dumbfounded, as Sergei lifts all of Roman's six-foot three frame into the air. Sergei is smaller than Roman by a good six-inches, but he manages to hoist him like he's nothing.

Roman is laughing as Sergei sets him down and it occurs to me that I've never heard Roman laugh before. It's rich, lovely, full of joy. His laughter notches itself under my breastbone.

Sergei places a hand to Roman's cheek. His Italian is fast. Faster than my rusty ears can translate. Roman's voice is low, deep, as he answers. Sergei's dark brown eyes meet mine and his entire face lights up.

"*Buongiorno,* Alexandra. My name is Sergei." He air kisses each of my cheeks. I blink in surprise, returning the motion clumsily. "I will be helping you navigate Italy while you are here."

"It's good to meet you, Sergei. Please, call me Andy. Almost everyone does." My eyes flick to Roman. He frowns at me.

"As you wish, Miss Andy." He grins, eyes sparkling.

I chuckle. I think of Wes, knowing he was named for the character in the *Princess Bride*. It was his mother's favorite movie. Roman's curious eyes cut my way, but I ignore him.

"Are we ready to go?" Sergei asks once our bags are stowed in the trunk of the car.

"If my Lord Commander wishes," I snipe, sauntering past Roman.

His answering growl makes the hair on my arms stand on edge. I smirk, sliding into the backseat. Sergei's laugh is too joyful as he takes the wheel.

"She keeps you on your toes, no?" he calls.

Roman folds his big body beside me, leaving the front passenger seat open. His eyes are not happy.

"So it would seem," is his tight retort.

Sergei's snicker is gleeful as he yanks the wheel hard to the left and sends us into traffic. There are no traffic laws here, I'm realizing. Cars swerve around each other, beeping and honking as we move into the heart of Rome. I keep my gaze out the window, careful not to look over at the man silently glowering beside me.

I love the architecture here. The sweeping windows, the worn brown stone of the buildings, the curves and arches of the Colosseum. We're only here for a night before we move north to Tuscany, but energy pumps through me. Whether Roman wants to join or not, I fully intend to stow my things where we're staying and explore.

I watch the city roll by, the sweet scents of gelato swirling through my open window. It's a balmy seventy-five degrees and I watch tourists and locals make their way in and out of *gelatarias*. I'm suddenly starving, my stomach announcing itself loudly to the rest of the car.

"We are almost there, Miss Andy," Sergei calls from the front. "We will get you some breakfast, yes?"

I nod, thankful for his offer. We bump over cobblestone before finally pulling over in front of white marble building. There's a covered entryway with a green and white checked awning. A red carpet leads up the steps into a revolving door. Roman is out of the car before I can turn.

He opens my door for me and offers a hand while Sergei wrestles our bags out of the trunk. I take his hand, that delicious little zap moving up my arm. It's been years and that hasn't faded. I think he still feels it, too. Like now. He draws his hand back so fast it's a blur.

Hotel Gardenia is quaint, but full of a luxury I've only experienced with my grandparents on my stepfather's side. George's parents are made of money. Literally made from it. There was a time it excited me. That was when I was too young to realize all the ways they tried to manipulate me and my life with it. There was a time when the new back-to-school clothes, concerts, ballet, singing lessons, and travel I was afforded in my youth swayed me.

Not anymore.

The interior is full of creams, golds, and rusty-reds. The front desk is an immaculate slice of rose quartz with small varnished gold lamps. It smells like citrus and linen and I already know the bedroom of a lifetime will be waiting for me.

Roman checks us in, his voice smooth and almost bored as he gives our names. The girls behind the counter blush, gawking at him as he slides his black AmEx across the counter. While everyone else is looking at him, no one is looking at me. Which means it's the only safe time for me to check him out, ogle his thick legs and ass, the dip in his back I could ski off and the thick forearms that drive me to distraction.

Roman thanks them and I shake myself from my daze in time to accept my keycard from him.

Sergei follows us up to our rooms and I quirk my brow. Is he Roman's valet? Driver? Assistant? We ride the elevator up to the sixth floor silently, the old school elevator grates allowing me glimpses into each floor we pass. When Roman hauls the door open, we move down the hallway to the right.

"It's a shared room," Roman says, pressing his keycard against the digital lock. "We can keep the door between us locked, but I'll be next door if you need me."

He doesn't offer me any other sort of goodbye, and I glare at him from the hallway. I stalk to the door beside his and let myself in. I'm seeing red as I push inside but it leaves me in a *whoosh* when I see where I'm staying.

The room is gorgeous with its Parquet flooring, four-poster king bed with gauzy white curtains and thick duvet. There's a marble fireplace against the far wall and a gorgeous white and gold filigree armoire to hang my dresses in. There's a small terrace adjacent to the bed with a little iron table and chair. I fling the door open, letting the noise from the streets below filter in.

Sergei clears his throat and sets down both of my suitcases.

"Okay, Miss Andy?" he asks.

I nod, grinning. "Yes, everything is great. You don't need to call me 'miss', Sergei. Just Andy is fine."

His smile is genuine when it comes. "Okay, Just Andy." He goes to leave when I stop him.

"I'm sorry for asking but... How do you know Roman? You seem like old friends?"

"*Si, si.*" He nods vigorously. "I drove for Mr. Roman when he lived here before. I have been close with his family for years."

Curious. Why would Roman need a driver before?

"I am sorry, Just Andy but if you want to know more, you must ask Mr. Roman himself. He is very...*privato, si?*"

"*Si*," I answer, knowing Sergei's loyalty is already pledged.

"I will come to collect you tomorrow morning. Have a good night, Just Andy." He tosses me a wink before slipping out, leaving me alone.

Having Sergei for the duration of this trip may just be a blessing in disguise.

I wander into the bathroom and take the most luxurious shower of my life. The shower is attached to a porcelain clawfoot tub and I decide that I'll take a bath in the morning with a steaming cup of coffee with the most ludicrous number of bubbles. The vanity is laden with creams and soaps for my use and a thick, fluffy robe hangs on the back of the door.

By the time I dry myself off, I'm starving and itching to walk.

I dig in my suitcase for an athletic dress, a crossbody bag, and my sneakers. I twist my honey-blonde hair into a knot on top of my head. I'm forced to do my makeup, because the bags under my eyes are deep enough to use for souvenirs.

I tuck my keycard into my crossbody and step into the hallway. When my door shuts, Roman's opens.

His head pokes out, hair dripping water into the blue and white carpets in the hall.

"Where are you going?"

I stride past him. "Pizza. And a drink. Why? Would you like to come?" I huff, sarcasm dripping off each word.

"Sure. Give me a second."

I pause at the end of the hallway, slowly turning. I feel like I'm in a horror movie where the main character has just realized the serial killer is right behind them. Roman's door opens again and he steps out, tucking his phone and wallet into his back pocket.

"I know the perfect spot."

He takes the lead, and I let him. He's in dark jeans and a heather gray t-shirt and a pair of black and white Nike's. His hair is wet, drying against the nape of his neck. I stare at the shifting muscles in his back as he hauls the elevator screen open and we step inside. Jazz music plays as the floors descend, and I can't figure out if I'm hallucinating or not.

We step into the lobby, the girls fawning over him as we walk by. I might as well be invisible when I'm next to him. I quietly laugh to myself. If that isn't hitting the nail on the head, I don't know what is.

We step outside, the early afternoon sunshine warm on our faces.

"This way."

Roman walks with confidence and heads turn as he passes. I quicken my step to keep up with him as we walk for a few streets. The smells are amazing. I catch trills of laughter and music as we walk and I'm itching to step inside each shop and look around. I could spend weeks here, months, and never tire of it.

Nonna shared so much of this place with me when I was young, but now, it's only after she's passed that I really soak it in. I was blinded by grief the last time I walked these streets, and I feel as if I'm seeing it with new eyes.

I know our itinerary is loaded with meetings and work, but I vow to myself I'll steal a few moments for myself in each place we visit.

Roman rounds the corner and stops, letting me catch up to him. I nearly smack into his back, because the plaza opens to the Trevi Fountain. I've been only once with Willow, and we were tipsy and giggling too hard for me to remember much of anything. It's packed with tourists, but I don't mind the crowds.

I drink in the stone carvings, Oceanus standing tall in the middle. The water is crystalline and happy as it bubbles into the pool below. Someone nudges me from the back, and I bump into Roman. His arm sweeps behind me, pulling my back to his chest. He blocks most of the crowd, letting me soak it all in.

I pull my phone from my bag and snap a few pictures, struggling to get above the hundreds of heads in front of me. I feel him sigh and then my phone is gone. He extends his arms over his head and snaps away, changing the angles to get the full shot.

"Thank you," I say, unbelievably flustered at such a small act of kindness.

The steel in his eyes softens. "You're welcome. Come on."

His hand closes around mine and he tugs me through the crowd. I'm not dumb enough to think this trip will change things between me and Roman, but damn if there isn't a small little kernel of light blooming in my dark heart already.

Roman stops outside a little pizza place and grabs the closest table on the street. There are dozens of lunch places around us and I wonder what made him pick this one. He snaps his menu open.

"Why here?" I ask, opening my own menu.

Only his eyes flick up to me over his menu. "What?"

"I'm not complaining because I'll eat just about anything right now, but why here? There's a dozen places we could have chosen. Why this one?"

He glances around the piazza.

"See the guys standing out front of that place over there, handing out menus?" I follow his gaze and nod, finding the men trying to lure tourists inside. "That's the fake shit. No real Italian restaurant will stand in the streets and beg for guests. It's a tourist trap and an easy one. Plus," he says, "I lived here. Trust me, Alexandra. I won't steer you wrong."

I snap my menu shut. "Then by all means." I wave my hand at him. "Lead on, My Lord."

His eyes blaze. "Such a brat," he mutters.

I smirk as he orders for us. I can't suppress the thrill that races up my back at the grit in his words. When the waiter asks for our drinks, I order myself an Aperol Spritz. Roman goes for a glass of red. It was my drink of the summer last year, but I'm down to repeat it while I'm here.

We sit in silence, watching the square. Roman answers emails on his phone, and I send a few more pictures to Willow. Her responses come in droves.

> WILLOW: The Trevi fountain?! Didn't we go there? Wait, weren't we drunk?

> WILLOW: Why are your pictures taken at such a high angle? Did you grow on the flight over?

> WILLOW: Hot list #261: Italian men in the summer.

> WILLOW: Wes wants me to take it back, but I refuse.

I can't help it, I laugh.

"What?" Roman asks, eyeing my phone. "What's so funny?"

"Willow," I answer just as our pizzas and drinks are set down. My mouth waters at the steam and melted goodness before me. I help myself to a piece, dragging it onto my plate to save all the stringy cheese. "Well, technically, I guess it's Wes. Willow wants to add Italian men in summer to our Hot or Not list, and Wes wants her to take it back."

He rips into a slice, licking sauce from his lip.

"What's a hot or not list?"

I fill him in on our tragic night out back in college and the list that's come from it. There's too much interest in his eyes as he stares at my phone.

"Let me see it," he demands.

"No." I polish off my first slice and reach for another.

"Has Wes seen it?" he asks, eyes narrowing.

"Yes." I sip my drink. "But he was already half in love with Willow then and it was our mutual call to let him see it."

He jerks his head toward my phone. "Ask her if I can see it."

"No," I say again.

"Who else has seen it?"

"No one but us," I state. "And I would like to keep it that way."

There's suspicion in his eyes. "Why? What's on it?"

I try to curtail my blush. It's a random list with no rhyme or reason, but there are things on that list he'll know are from me and me alone—because of *him*. I can't afford to give him any more pieces of myself than I already have.

"Don't worry about it, Roman. It's just a thing between girlfriends."

He's smart enough to let it drop.

We finish lunch in strained silence.

When he asks me if I want to walk more, I say, "Is Chris Pine the hottest of the Chris'?"

He sighs, turning toward me.

"What is that supposed to mean?" he asks, exasperated.

"You said, "Do you want to walk more?" and I said, "Is Chris Pine the hottest of the Chris'?" The answer to both of those questions is an obvious yes."

His answering growl sends the most gleeful smile across my face.

We wander the streets of Rome. He finally buys me gelato after I press my face into the glass of six other *gelaterias*.

I order hazelnut and vanilla and he orders chocolate and raspberry. I'm shocked to my core when he scoops both onto his spoon and offers me a bite. I close my mouth around the plastic, knowing his mouth was on it just before. He doesn't look at me as I try it.

It feels easy to be here with him. For the first time in a long time, my guard is down. We sightsee and hit all the tourist spots. He doesn't complain when I stop to take pictures.

By late afternoon, my energy is flagging. Even with the two espresso shots we stopped for, I'm dead on my feet. His chuckle is deep, barely there, as he hails a taxi. He barks the address to our hotel and I slump in the backseat.

When the driver drops us off and we make our way inside, he stops me outside my room.

"Sergei will be here at nine a.m. sharp," he says, leaning against his door. "We can meet for breakfast at eight in the lobby. We'll drive to Tuscany and meet with Gilbert at his estate vineyard."

He's all business again, like he doesn't know how to be alone with me. Even his hands are shoved deep into his pockets. I nod, offering him a salute.

"Yes, sir."

His jaw ticks. Whatever sharp retort he wants to say doesn't come. He lets himself into his room, leaving me alone in the hallway for the second time that day.

My guard is back up, and that's where I tell myself it'll stay.

Chapter 4

ROMAN

I MEET ANDY IN the lobby after a fitful night of sleep.

She's already waiting for me, her bags packed. She hasn't seen me yet, so I let my eyes rake over her. Her jeans are cropped and ripped at the knee. Her Nike's are green and white and match the tight green t-shirt she's wearing. Her hair is loose and wavy in the way I love. I'm dying to sink my hands into it, to feel just how soft and silky it is for myself. Wrap it around my fist and give it a sharp tug.

"You're here," she says, turning to face me. "The girls were kind enough to save their most special table for you." Her smile is sweet, but her words are acidic.

I glance back at the girls at reception and they wave, dissolving into a fit of giggles.

There's a high chance they know who I am, but they're too shy to say it.

I gesture for Andy to lead the way. Her ass looks amazing in those jeans and I'm desperate to palm it. Worst part is, I've had that sweet little ass in my hands, I know how good it feels. I felt it clench and flex as she rode me.

I clear my throat. The concierge takes our bags and stows them for us until we leave. Andy steps out into the morning sun and her honey-blonde hair turns into spun gold. She's beautiful. She's always been beautiful and the words tangle in my mouth. I'd love to tell her, just once, how beautiful I think she is.

"Let me hear how good your Italian is," I say when we're settled and ready to order.

She wrinkles her nose. "I'm rusty," she pleads. "I'll embarrass you and myself."

"We'll be here for three weeks," I remind her.

She rolls her eyes. "Yes, you don't need to remind me that you're in purgatory, Roman. I'll order the damn breakfast."

Whoa, what? Purgatory? Is that really what she thinks? It's purgatory only because I can't touch her, taste her, hold her hand when we walk.

Our server comes and Andy opens her mouth. She starts slowly, tongue tripping over the words but by the end she's got it. Her Italian is soft, raspy. I feel it straight down to my cock. It twitches painfully in my jeans and I shift in my seat.

Triumphant, Andy hands her menu back.

I want to ask her what she meant, why she thinks I'm in purgatory but think better of it. I don't want to know. I can't know. I can't know why her chocolate-brown eyes get so sad sometimes. Why she looks at me the way she does. Instead, I pretend I don't see it. I know it hurts her when I do, but I have no other option.

A steaming pot of coffee is set down on the table and I watch Andy move. She elegantly shakes out her napkin and drapes it carefully across her lap. Her posture is stiff, formal, as she pours us each a cup. Her spoon gently runs against the lip of her saucer to remove the excess coffee and creamer. She brings the cup to her lips, sipping daintily from the flower-painted porcelain. Bewildered, I can only stare.

She must feel it, because she looks up. It's an elegant setting, there's no mistaking that, but there's no need to stand on formality with me.

"What was that?" I ask.

"What was what?"

I mime shaking out my napkin and gently lifting my cup to my lips, pinky up.

"*That*," I say.

"I went to finishing school," she says with a shrug. "I had table manners drilled into me at a very young age."

"Finishing school?" I parrot. I set my tea cup down with a loud *clink*. "Why would you need to go to finishing school?"

"You'd need to ask George's parents."

"George?"

"My stepfather." The words are curt, brusque.

I work my jaw back and forth. I can see she's uncomfortable, so I decide not to press for more details. I have three weeks to unravel her.

Our breakfast is delivered and Andy spears a piece of cantaloupe before popping it into her mouth. Her French toast is thick and covered in cinnamon, powdered sugar, and fresh berries. She dumps the little carafe of syrup on top and cuts off a square. I frown down at my spinach and egg omelet with wheat toast and a side of orange juice.

She doesn't even glance up as she cuts off a giant chunk and passes it over to me. I pop the whole piece into my mouth. The bread is sweet and fluffy and the tartness from the strawberries has my mouth watering.

"I'm getting what you get next time," is all I say as I cut into my eggs.

Andy's smile is triumphant, if not a little cocky.

We check out of the hotel just as Sergei pulls up out front. His normal red beater is gone. After I saw what he was working with yesterday, I made the arrangements for another car for him. We'll be doing a lot of driving, and I want Andy safe.

"Good morning *signore*. Just Andy, you look lovely."

She smiles at him and I'm jealous of all the careless ones she tosses out.

"Thank you, Sergei." She squeezes him on the shoulder as she takes a seat in the back.

I'm jealous of those easy touches and casual smiles. Jealous of each one she hands out to everyone who isn't me. She does look lovely. I want to tell her that, too.

"Took advantage of that amazing bath," she calls, twisting back to the trunk as he loads our bags. "So many lotions and soaps to choose from."

"Only the best here. Most everything is made from the fresh olive oil we get from the groves. Does wonder for the glow." He gestures to his face. "My wife still looks like she is twenty. Lucky me." He wiggles his eyebrows at her and she rewards him with a laugh.

I pop my neck. Andy in the bath, covered in bubbles, her skin slippery and soft. I tip my head back to another perfectly blue sky. I strike a bargain with God. If he can get me through these weeks, I'll do whatever He asks me to do.

It's a three-hour drive, and Sergei wastes no time swinging right into traffic and moving northbound. I hear the little whine Andy lets out as we drive through Vatican City, the Sistine Chapel looming in the distance. We're flying back out of Rome, and I mentally calculate if we can extend the trip a day or two so I can get her there.

Sergei scans the radio for a while, but service is spotty as we move out of the city. He dangles a cable back to Andy. We've never swapped music before, but I paid attention to the songs she quietly sang at the Harper's beach house when we set around the fire.

"Just Andy, you want to play some music? Tell me what is popular in America."

Andy's delicate fingers close around the cable as she plugs her phone in. There are a few quick taps and then music is filtering through the car.

"Ah, I know this one. Harry Styles, *si*? My daughters are always talking about him."

My phone vibrates and I glance down. Since Nic and Brooks' brothers commandeered the BEACH CREW group chat, Wes, Brooks, and myself were forced to start a separate one where there were less memes, no names, and no TikToks being shared 24/7.

> BROOKS: Safe travels, daddy Roman.

> WES: Gross. But yeah, safe travels.

> ROMAN: We just left. Sergei is singing Harry Styles. It's going to be a long drive.

> BROOKS: Dude has good music. Don't knock it.

> ROMAN: Not knocking it. There's just not enough coffee in the universe to grant me the patience I need for this drive.

> WES: Unrequited love chaffing a bit, Roman?

> ROMAN: Shut up, Wesley. Don't you have a kid's playroom to draw?

> BROOKS: Oooh, sick burn.

> WES: You're both unbearable.

I choke down my smile as we push further into the countryside. I've always loved Tuscany with its rolling, sweeping hills and undulating skyline. I'm anxious for Andy to see it. Plus, the further from the city we get, the less likely it is that anyone will know me. It's been a few years, and I'm not conceited enough to think that anyone still cares about me and what I gave to the league, but I was pretty damn good at one point in my life.

Best striker in the league, or so the news outlets said.

I hardly remember.

Sergei and Andy carry most of the conversation. Her music taste swings in drastic ways and I can hardly keep up with the change in genre.

When Sergei runs out of things to say and settles into the drive, I listen to Andy's soft humming in the backseat. Sometimes she sings and it's just loud enough for me to make out. Most of it is mumbled, hummed, but her voice is beautiful. Chills crawl up my back.

I know from one of the many morsels I've stolen over the years that Willow and Andy are big karaoke fans and now I understand why.

"*Voce di un angelo*," Sergei murmurs. "Very beautiful, Just Andy."

"Why do you keep calling her that?" I grumble. I catch her smirk in the rearview mirror.

"That is what she asked to be called. Just Andy. I do as she says."

"It's perfect," Andy calls from the back. "Don't change it for Scrooge McDuck up there, Sergei."

He nods, smug, fingers flexing on the steering wheel. This is going to be a hellish three weeks if they keep ganging up on me like this.

Andy presses herself to the window with just over an hour left of the drive. The landscape sweeps out and falls away, the hills rising and falling over each other. The sun glints through the valley as the road dips and twists before us. We're all silent as the cypress trees whizz by us. Vast stoney estates sit on perfect hill tops, their vineyards sloping toward the sun.

It's probably the most beautiful place I've ever seen in my life.

Finally, Sergei pulls up to Gilbert Mattero's estate and pops the SUV into park. Mattero Family Wines has been in business for close to one hundred and fifty years, with some of the oldest Sangiovese vines in all of Italy. I know my father is keen on getting some of his fruit. Now it's my job to sell it.

Gilbert meets us in his driveway, gravel crunching under his boots. They're stained purple with grape juice. I see the bodies stooping and standing in the vines and realize they'll be harvesting while we're here. It's been a long time since I've been in a vineyard harvesting grapes, but it's good, honest work. Sorting through grape clusters is incredibly important to the outcome of the wine.

Andy steps out of the car and Gilbert's sun-drenched face smiles.

"Ah, you must be Alexandra." His blue eyes crinkle as he kisses her on each cheek. "Antony has nothing but good things to say about you. I feel as if I know you already."

Andy is gracious, as she always is.

"Please, call me Andy. Thank you, that's incredibly kind. Mr. Mattero, your place is..." She trails off. I see the sheen of silver in her eyes. "This is unreal."

Gilbert preens, pride rolling off his chest.

"This estate has been in my family for generations. Please, no formalities. We are family here. Call me Gilbert. Come, I'll show you around. Roman." He dips his head toward me and shakes my hand. "*Merda*, you look just like your old man. It is good to see you, boy."

I smile tightly. "You as well, Gilbert."

He looks exactly as I remember with his deep brown skin, salt and pepper hair, and big blue eyes. He's a stocky man, but he always was. His hands are rough with use and permanently stained purple from all the grape must.

Sergei takes our bags to the guest house out back. Gilbert tucks Andy's hand into the crook of his arm as he leads us down into the heart of the vineyard. My eyes rake over the Sangiovese clusters, the long bunches nearly black in color. I twist one off and pop it into my mouth.

Sweet juice bursts over my tongue. I chew for a minute before spitting it back into my palm. I search through the pulp for the small seeds.

"Up to par for you?" I hear Gilbert say. One of his bushy gray eyebrows is raised.

I show him the seeds in my palm. "Brown." I shrug. The seeds being brown means the grapes are ripe and ready to go.

I dump the grape onto the ground and brush my hands on my jeans. Andy has the oddest expression on her face but says nothing. Gilbert continues his tour, leading us further down the hill.

He takes us into his underground tunnels. The air is damp and cool, lampiers burning where they sit on the wall. The barrels here are kept at perfect temperatures for extended aging. There are a few unlabeled bottles stacked on a shelf in the corner, their surfaces cloudy with cobwebs and dust. I'm itching to get my hands on a bottle and see how his wines have aged.

I squint against the glare of the sun when he finally leads us above ground. We crest the top of the next hill. He points to various points in the distance, explaining each to Andy. She nods thoughtfully as he explains the weather patterns and the mountain structures around us.

The guest house sits down the next slope. It's close enough to the house to feel like it's part of the property but far enough away to offer a veil of privacy.

"Tomorrow, we harvest our Cabernet." He gestures to the block furthest from us. "We'll have rain by Friday." He squints up against the blue sky, as if it's speaking to him.

What day is it? I'm jet-lagged within an inch of my life. I check the screen of my phone. It's Tuesday. By Friday, we'll be in Umbria and out of the storm if his premonition is correct.

"Can I help?" Andy asks.

Gilbert seems surprised by Andy's offer and honestly, so am I.

"It is an early morning, *bella*. I would hate to burden you."

She squats down to the vine in front of us, her fingers sliding against the grapes. She studies it for a long moment.

"Willow and I helped with several harvests when we were here in college. I'd be happy to help. It's been a while since I've gotten my hands dirty."

I swallow the strangled groan in my throat. Watching her delicate fingers stroke against those clusters... Fuck.

I need to get it together.

"I will never say no to more hands." He claps once. "Dinner will be around seven. Take the day, explore, sleep, rest, whatever it is you need. I have a few special bottles for us to drink tonight."

Andy thanks him again before he heads back to the main house. We're left alone, just the two of us. We stare at each other.

"What's the plan?" she asks, squinting against the sun.

"What do you mean?"

"I mean," she says, sighing, "what's the plan? We work harvest, ask him for his grapes? They won't hold in transit across an ocean."

I shake myself. "Of course they won't. The plan is to have the grapes crushed, processed, aged, and bottled here but under the Bendetti label. My dad wants a few vineyards with varying varieties. Gilbert makes his own wine and does very well. His tasting room is over the next hill. It'll be hard to convince him to part with even two rows of his Sangiovese, but I'm going to try."

The vines are old, gnarled and twisted with age. The oldest vines have very little clusters, but I know what a gold mine the fruit hanging from it is.

"What if he says no?"

"Then he says no," I say simply. "There are plenty of vineyards, plenty of properties to visit. If the north fails, I'll go south. If I can't get what I need here, I'll go to France. And Spain. And Portugal. Wherever I need to."

"Determined, aren't you?"

She says it like it's something good, something to be proud of. For me, I need it to mean something. I need to know leaving my dream behind has meaning to it.

If I fail at this, then what was it all for?

***

Andy and I wander down to the guest house in silence. A thousand words are burning on my tongue. Why finishing school? Where did she learn to sing? Why did she stop? What's her favorite karaoke song? How can I get her to sing again?

The cottage is gorgeous, but then again, all of Gilbert's property is. The kitchen and living room are cozy with their wooden floors. The fireplace sits in front of a sofa and loveseat with a large coffee table bisecting the two. Andy trails her fingers over the tile-topped kitchen table. The kitchen is small but functional with a tiny stove and fifties-style fridge. There's dried rosemary and lavender hanging over the sink, a copper kettle open and waiting to be used.

Over the kitchen table are two large windows. Andy leans across the bench seat in the back and throws them both open, flooding the room with sunshine and cool air. I duck under the thick wooden beam in the ceiling and watch her open the back door. There's a small stone patio outback. I already know where I'll find her tomorrow morning. She seems to seek out the light and the table and chairs waiting for her are the best place to do it.

She brushes by me, her perfume tickling my nose. I love her smell. It clung to my sheets for days after she was there. Soft, sweet, sexy. Sandalwood, vanilla, brown sugar. Good enough to eat.

She takes the steps two at a time. The first bedroom has my bags in it. The iron bed frame hugs the right wall and is dressed in blues and creams. There's a closet, a chest, and a TV mounted to the wall, but other than that, the space is sparse. She wanders down the hallway and opens her bedroom.

It's eastern-facing, promising her dappled morning sunlight. She lets out a delighted sigh as she trails her fingers over the rosy-pink bedspread. Her room has a reading chair and a small side table perfect for a cup of tea. Curtains fall to the floor in a soft sage green, spilling into a primrose and white area rug. It's a feminine room, soft and graceful. Just like her.

The bathroom is small and we'll have to share the space, but I don't mind. We'll each have our own sinks and I have no plans to be anywhere near this room when she takes her shower. If I had it my way, I'd be in New York. But even that doesn't feel far enough away.

I head to my room, giving her her space. I feel her eyes trail after me, but I don't stop. I head into my room and throw on my running gear. Being this close to her...

I step outside, content to run the length of the vineyard as many times as I need to. I push through my jet lag, needing to burn off this anxious energy before I do something stupid. Before I open my mouth and say something I can't come back from. When I get back from my run, Andy is gone. There's a note on the table waiting for me.

Boss, I went up to the main house to help with dinner. Don't worry. Find me when you're back.

She's such a brat. My hand flexes by my side. What I wouldn't give to bend her over the couch and punish her for that smart mouth of hers. It's an effort not to. I stomp up to the shower and turn the water on cold. Getting myself off to the image of Andy isn't new for me. It's not something I'm proud of, but the girl comprises every fantasy I've ever had. The sounds she makes, the way she anticipates what I need. The night we danced at the club, her hips tight and working against mine.

It doesn't matter that the water is colder than the arctic, I fist my cock until it aches and I'm coming on the white tile walls in a few harsh breaths. I drop my head into the spray, feeling an odd mixture of guilt and relief.

I towel off and get dressed, tossing on a collared shirt and chinos. I slip into my shoes; finger comb my hair and make the quick walk up into the main house.

There's laughter waiting for me as soon as I open the door. Music is blasting and I hear Andy's unmistakable cackle as I step inside. Gilbert and his wife, Alana, are pouring wine and laughing as Andy sets the table.

She's changed, trading her jeans and sneakers for a pretty sun dress that brushes just below her knees. Her hair is loosely braided back from her face, a few loose pieces framing her delicate neck. Her face is flushed from wine and laughter and I feel my chest squeeze.

She's perfect. She is achingly perfect. Her doe-brown eyes are dancing when they meet mine and I can count on one hand the number of times she's looked at me like that.

"Andy was just telling us about your adventures with your friends," Alana says, passing me a glass of red. I swirl and sniff, picking up on the earthy and spicy notes of the Sangiovese. "Not surprising Nicco would be the first to throw himself into a freezing ocean."

I grimace. "That's my brother for you."

Gilbert chuckles. "I hope he never grows up. He has spirit, your brother."

Alana peeks in the oven, her silver hair falling over one shoulder.

"Just a few more minutes."

Their dining room is drenched in sunlight. Over the hills, the sun dips behind the horizon. Varnished gold dances across the walls, the worn oak table top, and the many glasses and plates Andy helped set. She moves into a beam, her skin flushed and glowing.

I'm a desperate man.

I sip my wine, shove my hand in my pocket, and turn my back on her.

"The vineyard crew will be joining us, I hope you don't mind," Gilbert says, cutting up a fresh loaf of bread.

"Not at all," Andy says. "They can give me some pointers for tomorrow."

Alana pulls her eggplant lasagna out of the oven and sets it on the table. Bowls of salad, bread, meatballs, and olive oil are scattered between candles and fresh flowers. It's a feast fit for a king.

The vineyard crew arrives, covered in dirt and grape pomace. They grin wildly as they step inside.

"Marco, Adam, Elio, meet Andy and Roman. They're here to talk grapes and help us harvest in the morning."

We exchange pleasant hellos, but Adam's eyes are molded to the curve of Andy's waist and I'm ready to snap his neck when Alana touches my arm.

"Breathe, Roman," she whispers. "You're practically vibrating."

I blink and it's gone. I grind my molars together so hard I think they might crack.

"Of course," I reply smoothly. "Apologies. How can I help you?"

It's a fine enough evening, even if the crew is besotted with Andy at the end of the night and Adam promises to stick close to her in the morning in case she needs help. I limit myself to two glasses of wine, even though I'm dying for more. Gilbert's wines are rich and vibrant and have the potential for long aging—cellar and bottle.

We help clean up, soft music humming in the background. The vineyard crew are dead on their feet and Gilbert sends them off with the promise of a good breakfast in the morning. Andy scrubs every pot and pan clean for Alana, refusing to leave until the kitchen is tidy. I admire that about her. The way she takes care of those around her.

I've watched her do it with Willow for years, but her kindness extends to everyone she meets. I could stand to be more like her. To open myself up a little more. There was a time I was like that. A time when I would have laughed and made jokes and made an ass of myself, but that man feels like he's locked a thousand leagues below the ice.

Finally, Alana and Gilbert shoo us from the kitchen. Andy sighs in contentment as we wander the dimly lit path back down to the guest house. The air is cool, ripe with late-summer flowers and earth.

"I could live here," Andy says, surprising me. She hugs her arms around herself. "Living in a kitchen like that. My own vegetable garden outback. A full wine cellar. A view like this."

The sky is endless overhead. So far from the city, the stars have nothing to hide behind. My tongue feels thick, useless, in my mouth.

"A man that loves me." She says it so softly I think I mishear her. "A family to come home to." She shakes her head, biting her lip.

I reach for her arm. She shivers when my hand wraps around her bicep. I turn her toward me, heart erratic in my chest.

"A man that loves you?" I ask, voice rough.

"Yes," she whispers.

"Do you have a man, Alexandra? One you haven't told me about?"

She blinks at me in confusion. "No," she says slowly, "but there has to be one out there somewhere, right?"

Fuck. I feel the dagger twist right through my heart.

"Right," I grind out.

When she pulls away from me, I let her go. I stand, rooted to the spot, as she walks away from me, her dress swinging against her legs.

I scrub my hands down my face, sighing.

I have no right to be jealous, not when I've been destined to only watch her go.

Chapter 5

Andy

The sun has barely risen as I step into the vineyards, blowing warm air into my cold hands. Fog rolls through the valley, moist, damp air clinging to my skin. I didn't exactly pack for cold weather so I shiver in my t-shirt. The afternoon promises to be sunny and warm with the temperatures climbing into the seventies but for now, it hovers just over forty-five degrees.

Gilbert has been up and moving for hours, judging by the look of him. He has a cup of coffee in his hand as Alana sets up a table with fresh bagels and muffins. Each of us has a thermos full of coffee to take with us when we head out. Pruning shears sit on the end of the table with a few small plastic bins for us to put the clusters in once we harvest them.

I pluck a muffin and a cup of mixed fruit from the table and lean against the stone wall in the garden. Despite the size of the meal we had for dinner last night, I woke up to a rumbling stomach. The muffin is moist and loaded with sweet blueberries as I bite into it. I groan, calling my compliments out to Alana. Her laughter is like wind chimes: musical and soft.

There was no sight of Roman when I woke this morning, so I showered and dressed as quickly as possible. I'm just bringing my coffee to my lips when I see him cutting through the fields.

He looks like Mr. Darcy, stalking up the hill with the fog clinging to his ankles. Of course, I could only mean the 2005 adaptation of *Pride and Prejudice*, directed by our lord and savior, Joe Wright.

My mouth goes dry at the sight of him in his backward baseball cap and black sweatshirt. He's in jeans and sneakers. He's *mouthwatering*. I never get to see him dressed down without his suit of armor on.

He offers a small smile to Alana and accepts her cup of coffee, and then his eyes find me. I can practically hear his eye roll as he crosses the yard to where I stand.

"Is that all you're wearing?" he asks gruffly.

"Good morning, Roman," I say instead, sipping my coffee.

He huffs. It's as close to a laugh as I ever get.

"Good morning, Alexandra. Now, answer my question. Is that all you're wearing?"

"So bossy," I mutter, and then freeze.

I watch his eyes darken. I watch the light in them blink out and then they do the most miraculous thing, they drop to my mouth. He sucks on his teeth and I feel dizzy all of the sudden. All of Roman's attention is a thing to behold and when he gives it to me...

Jesus.

"I didn't think I would be so chilly," I finally say, voice breaking.

He looks at me like he's starving. I want to tell him I am, too.

He sets his coffee down next to mine and removes his hat. He tugs his sweatshirt over his head. He's wearing a navy-blue thermal underneath that hugs his arms like a second skin. I catch a sliver of his toned stomach as his shirt rides up his abs.

He was fit when we slept together three years ago but now... He's roped in muscle.

"Here. Arms up."

I obey, just like I always do. He tugs his sweatshirt over my arms and head, sliding it into place. It smells divine. It's warm from his body heat and I shudder as it falls to mid-thigh. I turn my head, sniffing the collar.

I hear him groan. "Alexandra," he bites out. "Knock it off."

"What?" I ask innocently. "It's not my fault you smell so good, Roman."

He shoves his hat back on his head and I swoon. I need to text Willow as soon as I'm clear of him. Backward baseball hats need to move high up on the list.

Alana hands him a loaded plate and we lean against the garden wall together to eat. Gilbert gives us about fifteen minutes to wake up before he assigns us our blocks. He has Roman and I spread out on either side of the vineyard. Adam is paired up with me and the Cabernet.

He gives me an easy smile. He's good-looking enough with his blonde hair and hazel eyes. He's fit from his hours outdoors but just like with everyone else... There's nothing there. No spark, no pull. Not when Roman is standing beside me.

"If he bothers you, call me, Alexandra. I'm serious," he warns, grabbing his shears and plastic containers.

"Okay, okay," I grumble, nudging him out of my way to get my supplies.

He stops me with a hand to my chin. He squeezes, bringing my face up to his. It's a possessive touch, one that makes my stomach flutter. There's no laughter in his eyes as he looks at me.

"Will you call me?" he asks again.

I bat his hand away.

"Yes, boss. I'll call you if I need you."

He flinches, but drops his hand.

"Fine. Good."

He stalks away, broad shoulders fading between the rows of grapes. Guilt gnaws at me. I shouldn't have said that. I should have just accepted the help, but accepting anything from Roman feels too dangerous.

"Come on, gorgeous," Adam calls. "Let's get going."

Adam walks me through the clusters and what I'm looking for. Anything that has rot, mold, or has turned to raisins gets left behind. He tells me they only want the best bunches, and though hand harvesting takes much longer than using machines, it ensures they get the very best grapes in the vineyard.

He shows me a few rough clusters. He clips them at the stem and lets them fall to the ground, moving on down the row.

"Happy harvesting," he calls, moving further up the row and leaving me on my own.

I fish my AirPods from the pocket of my leggings and pop them in. I find a random playlist on Spotify and hit play. Troye Sivan pumps into my ears and I get moving.

It's tedious work, but I don't mind it. I inspect each cluster like I'm studying diamonds under a microscope. My pace is slow, but I know I'm being thorough. When I fill up my little bucket, I walk back toward the end of the row and dump it into a larger bin. Once it's full, Gilbert comes by on a buggee and picks it up and drives it over the hill to the winery for crushing.

I repeat the process over and over again, slowly clearing my way through the grapes. My thighs are screaming and my lower back seizes on the last plant before I stand.

Adam is done five rows by the time I finish my third.

He hands me a water bottle and grins, sweat clinging to his neck and forehead.

"How's your back?" he asks.

I wince, stretching. "Sore, but okay. I like this type of work. Beats staring at my computer all day."

He nods thoughtfully. "I tried to do the office thing for a while, but it didn't work out. The craze of L.A. was not for me. I moved here on a work visa two years ago and just decided I didn't want to go back."

"Family doesn't miss you?" I ask, draining half my water bottle in one go.

His lips twitch. "They do, but they come and visit. No complaints about having a son living in the heart of Italian wine country. Or," he says slyly, "was that your way of asking me if I'm attached?"

"Oh," I blurt. "No, I just—"

"Because I'm not," Adam says quickly. "Attached, that is. How long will you be here? Would you like to grab dinner before you go?"

I'm spared from answering. I hear his footsteps behind me and I shiver, the heat of him rolling against my back.

"Alexandra."

There's no humor in Roman's voice and I know I'll find him glowering when I turn.

Adam glances at him, unperturbed.

"Think about it and let me know." He glances back at me once, his eyes flicking to Roman before he abruptly picks up his pace and vanishes over the hill we're on.

I turn to face him. "Yes?" I reply, syrupy sweet.

"Did that *boy* just ask you out while you're wearing another man's sweatshirt?"

I glance down at myself. I didn't want to risk taking it off and ruining it, so I've been sweltering in it for the last few hours. I wiggle out of it, throwing it back at him.

"I believe he just did."

Roman swipes his sweatshirt from mid-air.

"Are you not cold anymore?"

The morning sun blazes overhead. The fog burnt off hours ago, leaving behind a sticky humidity that has coated my skin.

"I'm fine. Thank you for lending it to me," I say brusquely. "I have more grapes to cut."

"Gilbert wants to talk," he says, stopping me in my tracks. "We've done enough for the day. His guys have the rest."

I glance at my phone. It's pushing eleven a.m. I nod, the motion jerky.

"Sure. Where is he?"

Roman leads me out of the row of vines. A little four-wheeler sits waiting for us.

"Do we have to take that?" I eye it speculatively.

"The winery is two hills over. It'll take us forty-minutes to walk it." He swings his big body over the seat and turns the engine over.

The only place for me is behind him.

He reads the trepidation on my face.

"I won't let anything happen to you, Alexandra. I promise."

I know he means it. It's one of the few things I *do* believe. Roman Bendetti would take a bullet for me.

I straighten my shoulders and stalk across the space between us. I try not to think about it as I wedge myself against him, my thighs flush against his, my breasts crushed into his back. He reaches behind him and blindly fishes for my hands before wrapping them around his waist.

"Hang on." His voice sounds strained over the engine.

I interlace my fingers on his stomach and he gives it some gas. We shoot down the hill, the wind tearing at us. I feel his low rumble of laughter vibrate against my chest. We bump along the dirt, grapes flying by us at an alarming speed.

"Roman!"

I shriek when we hit a bump and the tires leave the ground. He's really laughing now as he straightens us out, practically fishtailing us in the green grass leading up the hill. I press my face right into the center of his back and squeeze my eyes shut.

"Oh, God," I mutter. "I'm going to die, aren't I?"

"Ye of little faith, sweetheart," he calls over his shoulder.

Sweetheart.

The endearment sears through me like a brand. I can still picture him sitting on the chair in his kitchen when he called me that for the first time. It's just as damaging the second time around.

We bump along for a few more minutes before he skids to a stop. He has to pry my fingers apart to get off the four-wheeler. There's a wildness in his eyes I've never seen before.

"You okay?" He's actually smirking at me. Confident, cocky, arrogant, self-assured.

God, he's so hot.

I hate him.

I swing my leg over the seat and ignore the mirth in his eyes.

"Fine, thanks," I call over my shoulder as I make a beeline for the open barn door in front of me. He jogs to catch up with me.

"We were perfectly safe," he reassures, knocking his elbow against mine.

"Sure. We just left earth for a few seconds on a five-hundred-pound death machine. No big deal."

He grips my arm again, stopping me in my tracks.

"Alexandra," he says, almost in exasperation. "You have to know I would never let anything happen to you."

I cross my arms across my chest. "Sure."

He purses his lips. "Sure?"

"Yes, I know. I know you'll keep me safe, Roman. It just... scared me for a second, okay?" I brush by him. "I'm not a fan of motorcycles or four-wheelers. I try to avoid them when I can."

"Okay," he says, utterly taken aback. "I'm sorry. I'll see if Gilbert will let me drive his truck back."

I nod, throat tight. I can't explain my anxiety or all the reasons why. He reaches out first this time, squeezing my hand.

"Thank you," I manage.

I rip myself away from him, before I do something stupid like lean into him for comfort. I walk into the barn, the smell of yeast and grapes assaulting my senses. Gilbert stands at the base of a tank, hands on his hips. I watch the juice drain out of the de-stemmer and crusher before pumping into a tank.

"Looks good," he says, turning toward us. "Great harvest this year. Really, really good."

"That's wonderful," I say. "You work hard out here, Gilbert. You and your crew should be very proud."

He seems speechless for a moment. "Thank you, Andy."

"I know you know why we're here," I say. "I know you know what Mr. Bendetti wants to do. I know you're probably hesitant to share your hard work and labor with someone who may not do it justice, but, Gilbert, I need to tell you about my best friend."

"Oh?" His surprised eyes meet Roman's.

I feel his curiosity against my back, but Roman doesn't stop me from talking. We never discussed his pitch or what he would need from me when this happened, but for Gilbert, this feels right.

"Willow is the most dedicated, driven, loving person you'll ever meet. For her, wine isn't just a drink but a story. It's your story, your father's, your grandfather's. It's your legacy, your time and effort. Your energy. The blood, sweat and tears that go into every bottle. Willow is a gifted storyteller. She immerses herself in her wines. She makes people care; you know? It's the reason she's the best sales rep Cin Cin has ever had. She extends the same dedication and love into the tasting room staff. I can promise you with all my heart that no one else will take care of your wines and love them the way Willow and Mr. Bendetti will—apart from you and Alana of course.

"I know these grapes are special. I know what it will cost you to part with a few rows of it, but I would ask you to consider it. Making Willow happy, making Roman happy," I say, stumbling over the words, "means everything to me when it comes to this project. I can promise you I'll be available whenever you need me and if it helps you for me to come back out and share the progress, I'd be happy to do so."

Gilbert gapes at me. "Well, Andy. You drive a hard bargain."

Roman steps up to my back. "It means a great deal to us," he murmurs. His hand lightly brushes against my waist. "Everything my father has done has been for his family, including this. I think he regrets never being able to find the perfect wine for his own father, before he passed. I think this is his way of making it up to him."

"Did you bring her to wear me down, Roman?" he accuses, jabbing a finger in my direction.

Roman holds his hands up in surrender.

"I brought her because she's the best person to have in a situation like this."

I can practically taste the honesty in his words.

He sighs. "Let me talk to Alana. I'll have an answer for you by tonight."

***

True to his word, Roman drives Gilbert's truck back to the guest house. I know he wants to talk to me about what I said, but I don't give him the chance to. I march straight up the steps and into my room. I collapse across the cover, dirty clothes and all. With the jet lag and the early start to the morning, I'm so tired I don't know which way is up. It's pushing six o'clock in New York and I groan at the sunlight filtering into the room.

The exhaustion wins despite the light shining across the floors.

I sleep through lunch and nearly dinner.

I dream about Roman. I dream about his hands and mouth and his deep laughter. He's been weaving in and out of my dreams for so long, it doesn't surprise me anymore when he appears. I've grown used to the ache that comes with it.

When I wake, the sun is nearly gone from the sky. I'm disoriented as I sit up. My shoes are off and there's a blanket draped across my waist. Neither of which were my own doing. I bolt from bed, shower with top speed and jump into a pair of leggings and a t-shirt and haul ass across the property.

I'm panting as I fling open the kitchen door. Roman looks up from his laptop, eyes wide.

"Did I miss it?" I gasp, leaning against the frame.

Alana's expression is puzzled. "Not at all. We weren't going to start without you."

I cross to the kitchen island and take the stool next to Roman. "You should have woken me," I hiss.

"I tried," he rumbles. "You sleep like the dead, girl."

I deflate, my adrenaline crashing. "Thank you for tucking me in." The words are begrudging at best, but he rewards me with a half smile.

"You're welcome."

Gilbert brings the chicken in from off the grill. Alana finishes dicing tomatoes and cucumbers for the salad and we fix our plates before taking a place at the table. We eat, chatting about easy things until there's nothing else left to address but the elephant in the room. Gilbert leans over and takes Alana's hand. She nods encouragingly at him and I drain the white wine from my glass.

"What are your projections?" Gilbert finally asks.

I know Roman was waiting for this, so I let him do what he does best. He grabs his laptop from the kitchen island and pulls up an Excel file. He walks Gilbert and Alana through the cost per ton they'd be willing to pay— which is an absolutely outrageous amount.

He walks them through the numbers, what the tasting room would need for the first year and what they'd charge. He makes sure to add any specificities they want known about the wine and ensures that Willow will take care of it.

"Ideally, we'd like a few reds for next year. I was thinking perhaps the Sangiovese from some of the younger rows and some Cabernet. The old vine Sangiovese would be bottled and aged until you're satisfied with it and then we could bring it on to the portfolio."

"You realize the time, right?" Gilbert asks. "It'll be three years, at least, before that goes into the bottle."

Roman's answering smile is all teeth. "I'm a patient man, Gilbert. Just like my father."

Gilbert's eyes swing to me. "What do you think, Andy?"

I pour myself another glass of wine and take a moment to gather my thoughts.

"I think you won't find anyone else who will take care of your wine the way we will. I think if there's issues, you call me and I come running. It's no small feat parting from what's so deeply rooted in you both but I promise we'll take care of it."

I can feel the pride rolling off Roman. Under the table, he reaches over and squeezes my knee. I nearly choke on my wine at the contact of his hand.

Gilbert sighs. "Then we have a deal, Roman."

They shake over the table. Alana is beaming.

"The world will know us, Gil," she whispers in excitement. "They'll know what you can do. Finally."

Her words strike a chord with me. Gilbert does well locally, but he has so much more potential than he gives himself credit for. The world *should* know what he's capable of. We toast to new beginnings and I can practically feel the ease settle in Roman's shoulders.

After we conclude the business dealings, Alana asks me to help her plate dessert. Roman and Gilbert step out into the twilight, the bistro lights on the patio glowing faintly above their heads.

"It's a good thing you're doing," Alana says, handing me a small stack of plates. I lay four of them out and grab silverware from the drawer by the sink. "He works hard. He deserves the recognition."

I hold my glass aloft. "He does a wonderful job. We'll do it justice, I promise."

"Of that I have no doubt." She grabs her homemade tiramisu from the fridge and cuts off four healthy slices.

I can't take my eyes from the window. Roman's head is bent, that little half smile playing on his lips. My heart stutters as his eyes meet mine through the glass.

"He's different than I remember," Alana says beside me. "He was always so charming as a boy, but the last few years have changed him. He's had to give a lot up to be where he is now."

"What did he give up?" I blurt.

Her mouth twists. "It's not my story to tell. You'll have to ask him yourself." She pauses, weighing her words. "He's different with you. Protective in a way I haven't seen before."

I scoff. "He's probably worried I'll botch this whole thing for him with my big mouth," I tease.

Alana tsks under her breath. "That's not it at all. I see the way he looks at you, Andy. Like he's begging to get a little closer."

I feel the color rise to my cheeks. "I don't know what you mean," I say quietly. When I look up again, he's already staring at me.

"Don't you?" she asks, voice tender.

I clear my throat. "We work together. He's my boss. I'm his employee. It's all it can ever be."

Her words are even and clear when they come.

"We'll see about that."

Chapter 6
ROMAN

ANDY AND I WALK in the dark, the lights burning from the guest house at the end of the path. My entire body is buzzing, burning. We did it. *She* did it. I don't know if I would have been able to sell Gilbert all on my own. I glance at her, the dreamy expression on her face, as her eyes roam the skies.

"Thank you," I say abruptly. Fuck, not smooth at all.

She shrugs. "No problem."

I stop walking. She doesn't understand what she just did for me. What she *always* does for me. She finds a way to fix it, make it work. My confidence in this trip cranks up a notch. The success of this project settles right on those perfect shoulders and I grimace, because I know that's why my father sent her. To close the deal when I fuck it up.

It takes a moment for her to realize I'm not by her side anymore. She glances back at me. There's a wrinkle between her brow that I want to press my lips against, smooth away with my thumb.

She takes another two steps before I close the gap between us. Her gasp is soft against the fabric of my chest and I do something I've wanted to do every day for three years— I hug her. I haul her body against mine, my arms wrapped tightly around her shoulders and back.

It takes her three agonizing breaths to respond, but then her arms slip low around my waist. She nuzzles against me, head burrowing into my chest.

Fuck. Fuck. *Fuck*.

This was a bad call.

My body has taken over. My hand moves up and down her back and she's nearly purring against me. I squeeze my eyes shut. Why did I do this? Why? I'm a glutton for punishment, apparently.

"Thank you," I say hoarsely. Her fingers pass over my lower back and I bite back my groan. I need to step away even as I'm dying to lift her and wrap her legs around my waist. "I appreciate the help."

I give myself one more second to breathe her in, feel her heart pounding against mine before I rip myself away from her. There's confusion in her eyes and I hate it. I hate that I put it there, over and over and over again. There's nothing confusing about what I feel for her, what I want from her, what I *need*. No, those things are easy. It's everything else that's complicated.

I watch her shake herself, drawing back those strong shoulders and elegant neck.

"You're welcome, Roman." Her eyes flick over me with forced indifference.

She's walking away from me again and God, am I tired of it.

"Did you mean what you said?" I call, halting her once more. "About wanting to make me happy?"

She mumbles something under her breath.

"Yes," she finally says. "You're going to be my boss, right?" The words are nearly choked. She turns her face away as she says them, as if she can't bear to look at me. "Your happiness translates to the rest of the staff and our jobs so, yeah. I want this to work. I want you to be happy." Her eyes focus down on the stone path beneath her feet.

"Is that all?"

Her head whips to mine. I know I shouldn't have asked that. I should have kept those words locked up tight— just like all the rest of them. Her eyes are closed, shuttered off. Ah, my strong and brilliant girl. Her walls are tall, but I've always been a strong climber.

"What else could there be?" Her voice is so sad, so hopeless.

Willow's words come back to me when I took her to my brownstone.

Do you really have no hope where Andy is concerned?

By the time I pull myself from my thoughts, Andy is already in the house.

I follow behind slowly, the feel of her arms still lingering around my hips and that Goddamn perfume...

I take the steps two at a time up to my room. I can hear her bumping around at the end of the hall. I debate saying goodnight, but decide against it. I'm restless, on edge, so I do what I always do these days when I feel like this: I work.

I hammer out emails, set up conference calls, respond to galas and charity events. All with the word 'yes'. Cin Cin needs all the contacts it can get, which means I have to go make nice with a bunch of people I don't even care about. I hear Andy's door open and close. She rushes past my room and down the stairs.

I fall into my work routine, reading and rereading for the thousandth time all my proposals and pitches for this trip. I triple check my numbers, the tonnage we're asking for and how much the bottling materials will cost us. It needs to be worth it for these farmers to part with their fruit.

It's only when the clock inches toward one a.m. that I realize Andy never came back up the steps.

I'm out of bed in an instant, heart in my throat. Fuck, what if something happened? What if she was hurt? How could I have not noticed until right now? I stride down the hall, knocking once on her door before swinging it open. Her bed is empty and still made from this morning. I check the bathroom, finding it cloaked in shadow.

I race down the stairs. The small living room is empty, but the blanket that usually hangs on the back of the couch is gone. The kettle now sits on the stove, quietly humming from recent use.

There's only one more place she could be.

I stalk through the kitchen, nearly ripping the door off the hinges as I step outside onto the back patio. I find her curled up on the daybed, tucked in the blanket from the living room. There's an open book on her lap and an empty mug of tea on the glass coffee table. I sigh, scrubbing my hands down my face.

Fuck, that scared me. She's not even mine to protect and yet...

"Andy," I murmur, softly enough so she can't hear me.

Her name tastes sweet, like summer strawberries in my mouth. She doesn't stir.

I pick up her book, eyebrows rising at the risqué cover with a woman in a ripped red gown and a man with more muscles than sense. I smirk, already knowing what's in these pages. I stuff the book into my pocket and gently scoop her into my arms.

"Roman?" Her breath is warm on my skin as I adjust her against me.

"Time to get you to bed, sweetheart."

She nuzzles against me, her mouth brushing against my neck. I grit my teeth, shockwaves rolling through me. I know what that mouth can do, the marks it leaves, the pleasure it brings. I manage to wedge myself through the kitchen and up the stairs. She loops her arms around my shoulders, fingers sinking into the hair on the back of my neck. I know she's half asleep, but the little circles she's making with her nails is fraying me alive.

Just that little ghost of a touch and I'm instantly hard and aching. I'd die to sink between her legs again. This time, I'd never stop. I'd never leave the bed. Fuck the rest of the world, she's the only thing I want.

I slide sideways through the door frame to her room and gently set her down on the mattress. The little whine she lets out kills me. She curls against the mattress, looking so small all the sudden. I grab the duvet from the other side of the bed and fold it over her.

"Sweet dreams, Alexandra," I whisper.

I can't help it. I'm a selfish bastard. I brush the hair back from her forehead and press my lips against her cool skin.

She slides her hand out from under the blanket and clasps my wrist.

"Stay," she mumbles, eyes fluttering. "Please stay."

"Baby," I breathe, heart stuttering in my chest. "You don't mean that. Just get some sleep, okay? I'll see you in the morning."

She doesn't mean it. She can't mean it. I can't let myself slide into bed with her. If I do, it'll break me. I'll never be able to stop. I'm hanging by a thread as it is.

She adjusts herself against the mattress.

"I wish you wanted to."

I feel dumbstruck, locked to the floor. The words are burning up my throat. I want to stay more than I want to take my next breath. I want to hold her, kiss her, explore the body I know better than my own.

I back away from the mattress. She shudders, and I can't watch her break because of me. I turn on my heel and storm back into my room.

I don't sleep at all.

***

We spend one more day with Gilbert and Alana. Andy won't meet my eyes in the morning, which means she was more awake than I thought she was. She talks to Alana while Gilbert and I sign and finalize the contracts. Once they're signed, I send them off to my father. This should feel sweet. It should feel like a victory but instead, I can't stop thinking about all the things I've lost.

Sergei comes back to pick us up shortly after lunchtime. We have one more stop in Tuscany to make before we head to Umbria.

"Where will you go from here?" Alana asks. She hands me a packed bag with fresh fruit, cheese, and a few muffins for the ride.

"We're going to see Macki next."

Gilbert laughs. "Good fucking luck," he says between laughs. "You're going to need it."

Benny Macki is the person I'm looking forward to seeing the least on this trip. He's an ass. He's loud, crass, has no filter, and is a real pain in the ass to deal with. He does, however, grow some of the best grapes in the area. I don't even want to let Andy near him when we get there. I wish I could send her with Sergei until we need to move north, if only to spare her.

Alana and Gilbert hug Andy goodbye like she's their long-lost daughter. They exchange information and promise to keep in touch.

"Are you ready?" I ask Andy when my goodbyes are said.

"Ready when you are, Lord Commander." She marches past me and slides into the back seat.

God, I hate that fucking nickname, but I know I hurt her last night. I can see it in her eyes. I roll my shoulders, trying to shake it off.

"There's nothing wrong with being happy, Roman," Alana calls to me softly. "Walls will never get you anywhere."

I offer her a nod and a tight smile before slipping into the front passenger seat. Sergei wordlessly passes the cable back to Andy. She sorts through songs for a while before finally picking something soft and slow, piano driven and haunting. She sings as we drive, her voice a few notches below the volume level Sergei has the radio on.

It's an hour and a half drive to Macki's vineyard and winery, *La Dea*. Her music gets sadder and sadder the further we drive. Sergei sends frantic and curious glances into the rearview, but Andy doesn't take her eyes off her window. She worries the ring around her finger. The scenery dips and ebbs with the valleys as we move into the Chianti region. Olive trees sprout in droves as the landscape pushes up around us.

As we drive, I realize Andy and I can't continue like this. Something needs to change between us to make this trip bearable. Alana's words echo in my mind. Maybe we can never be together, but surely there are no rules about being friends.

La Dea rises from the hillside like Dracula's Castle, all sharp edges and steel. I hear Andy's little gasp. Sergei frowns as he turns up the long driveway. For the rest of the trip, he'll be staying with us. The only reason he didn't stay at Alana and Gilbert's with us was that his sister lives nearby and he wanted to catch up with his family.

Sergei pulls into the circular courtyard at the top of the driveway. There's a wooden sign with an arrow pointing to the left with the word WINERY carved above it. Macki might be an asshole, but he makes a damn good wine.

"About time."

He's glaring at us through the car, ancient hands planted on his narrow hips. I'm out of the car instantly, opening Andy's door for her. She ignores my outstretched hand and slings her bag over her shoulder.

I block her path with my body, caging her against the car. I feel the frustration roll off her.

"We need to talk," I growl low enough for only her to hear.

"Do we?" she snipes. She cranes her head back to glare at me. "You've made it clear where you stand, Roman. This is what you wanted. Now move."

It's not what I wanted. Not by a long shot. I step out of her way, because I don't want to fight in front of Macki and Sergei. Macki sizes Andy up, blue eyes sharp as they run against her. I don't know why I ever thought I need to worry about Andy. She gives as good as she gets.

She crosses her arms over her chest and sends him the most withering stare I've ever seen.

"Can I do something for you?" she snaps.

Sergei's bushy brows rise in surprise.

"You kept me waiting," Macki gripes. His bark is just as bad as his bite. I want to rage at him for the attitude he's throwing her way.

"Did we?" She checks her phone screen. "Pretty sure we were supposed to be here by four o'clock, and it's ten of now."

His old mouth snaps shut. "Fine. Have it your way. Go drop your stuff and meet me in the winery in an hour. Rooms are that way." He points back to the building behind him. "One hour." He stalks away without a backward glance.

"He's pleasant," Andy says demurely.

She grabs her bag and steps inside the castle before us. I know Macki's sons live here half the year when they come back to work harvest. The foyer is massive with a large curling staircase right in the middle of it. There are old oil paintings on the walls of Macki's from generations before. It feels nearly Baroque with the design, decorations, and the suit of armor standing guard in the corner. Benny was always eccentric and odd, so it makes sense his home reflects his character.

A housekeeper intercepts us and brings us to the guest floor.

"Two rooms for you," she says. They sit across from each other in the hall. "Mr. and Mrs. Bendetti, your room is through here." She gestures to the room on my right. "Sergei, you'll be across from them."

Andy holds up a hand. "We," she retorts, gesturing between us, "are not married."

The housekeeper's eyes widen. "You're not? I could have sworn the emails said husband and wife."

Andy blanches but I can't stop the twist coming to my lips. Fuck, I like the way it sounds. She's got the prettiest flush on her cheeks and I want to kiss her senseless.

I can see the fire in her eyes when she opens her mouth but I step in before she snaps at this poor woman.

"It's not a problem," I reassure her smoothly. "We'll work it out. Is there another room available?"

The housekeeper shakes her head. "Afraid not. With Mr. Macki's sons in town, all rooms are occupied." There's real dismay on her face and I offer her the best smile I can.

"Not to worry. Thank you for showing us the way."

Her eyes are wary as she turns to leave us. Andy is motionless in the hallway, a muscle in her jaw pulsing wildly.

"I can find somewhere else to sleep," Sergei offers. "I do not want to cause a problem."

"Not at all, Sergei. Make yourself comfortable. I'll figure it out." He opens the door to his room at my insistence. "Let me talk to *my wife* about it."

Chapter 7

Andy

Oh. My. God.

Ohmygod.

My wife.

My wife.

There is nothing, and I mean nothing, hotter than Roman Bendetti's deep voice calling me his wife. Nothing on earth. I squeeze my thighs together at the uncomfortable rush of arousal building between my legs.

Roman twists the gem-cut doorknob and waves me inside my—*our*—room.

He drags our bags inside and closes the door. He leans against it, sealing off my only exit point. I glance at the balcony to the left of the bed. We're high up, probably the fifth or sixth floor. I'd break more than an ankle if I launched myself out of it right now, but the thought is still tempting.

The room drips in opulence and I feel like I'm in mid-century England with the heavy burgundy drapes, the deep mahogany bed posts, and large marble fireplace. There are two wing-backed chairs and a large couch in front of the mantle, a gold-encrusted table stretching in front of the hearth. There are two armoires, a dresser, and bedside tables.

"Perfect," I say. "I'll take the couch. You can take the bed. Problem solved." I dust my hands together.

"We need to talk," he says again, ignoring me.

I do not want to talk about asking him to stay with me last night. I'm going to blame my momentarily bout of insanity on the romance novel and herbal tea I drank before passing out on the chaise. It's the only logical excuse for asking.

I don't want to think about the way his voice sounded when he called me baby or how his lips felt on my skin. I don't want to think about *any* of it.

"Why do we need to do that?"

He sighs. "Alexandra."

"Roman." I plop my hands on my hips and send him my most menacing glare.

The tension is thick between us.

He rubs his forefinger and thumb into his eyes. "We have two and a half weeks left on this trip," he begins, voice rough. "I don't want to fight my way through it. Do you?"

I deflate, arms dropping to my sides.

"No," I answer honestly, "not really."

He nods in relief. "Good. Then I propose an experiment."

"Oh?" My brows rise at his choice in words.

He blows past it, as if he doesn't remember it but I know he does. I see it in his eyes.

"Yes. We become friends. We... start over."

"Friends?" I ask, trying the word out for size.

Friendship with Roman feels just as dangerous as everything else, but God am I tired of fighting him.

"Yes." He's animated now, really leaning into his new idea. "Yes, we're just two friends who work together, traveling through wine country for a common goal."

"Friends."

His eyes are sparkling. "Up for it?"

I don't have anything else to lose at this point, really. This trip would be much more enjoyable if we weren't so skittish around each other. It would make it enjoyable to be here, to taste wine, to laugh with him. I've been craving this, a chance to be close to him. It's all those thoughts that have me nodding along with him.

"Okay," I finally say.

"Okay?" he repeats, clearly bewildered that I would agree so quickly.

I laugh. "Okay, Roman." I close the distance between us and offer my hand. "Friends."

"Friends it is."

He slides his big hand against mine. His palms are rough against my skin. It makes me shiver. He squeezes my hand, visibly relaxing.

"Does this mean you'll start calling me Andy now?" I ask hopefully.

He runs his tongue along his teeth. "I can't give you everything you want, sweetheart." He winks. He fucking *winks* at me. "Have to keep you on your toes somehow. Come on, we're going to be late to meet Macki and I don't trust him not to bury us in the very back of the vineyard where no one will ever find us."

The one-eighty he does on me gives me whiplash. I think it's the most words he's ever said to me at one consecutive time.

He takes my hand and tugs me from our room. Sergei is waiting for us in the foyer and as a trio, we take the short walk over to the winery.

Roman's hand settles on my lower back as he guides me inside the tasting room. It's just as eccentric as his house, but it works.

A large metal chandelier hangs from the ceiling, casting a warm glow across the room. The bar is made from wood and marble and hovers over a dozen bar stools in matching colors. His wines are displayed behind the bar horizontally, stacked one on top of the other. The room is wide with several tables and couches scattered throughout. The back wall is nothing but glass, offering a perfect view of the mountains in the distance and the vineyards that sweep down western-facing slopes.

"Welcome," Macki says gruffly.

He shakes Roman's hand for the first time and introduces himself to Sergei. He surveys me like I'm a wild animal.

I hold out my hand as a peace offering. Roman looks ready to kill him if he refuses.

"Sorry about that, Macki. Let's start over. I'm Andy."

He slides his weathered skin against mine. "Benny." He surveys me for a moment. "You have a real mouth on you, girl."

My smile is biting. "I know."

He chuckles. "Well, let's get started then."

He gestures for us to take a seat. I pick the end seat, putting Roman in the middle. Five wine glasses are set up before us with a few oyster crackers for a palate cleanser. Macki moves behind the bar with ease as he pours us two ounces of each wine.

He talks in depth about the soil, the elevation, and sun exposure. He explains that though all of the reds are Chianti, which legally needs to be made with eighty-percent Sangiovese, they're categorized differently due to their age, both in the bottle and in oak. We taste through them one by one. As we progress into the Gran Selezione, which requires thirty months in barrel and an additional three in bottle, I can't stop the hum of appreciation that escapes me.

"Ah, you have good taste," Macki says. He swirls his own glass, peering at the wine in the light. "Well integrated tannins, smoked Bing cherries and a dusting of leather. A good vintage. Something that can age for a long, long time."

I snap a picture of my flight and send it to Willow.

> ANDY: Wish you were here to show these guys up.

> WILLOW: LOL! You know how to hold your own, Andy. Don't let them intimidate you.

> ANDY: I finally experienced my first backward baseball cap in the wild and I think we need to restructure our list.

> WILLOW: I agree. Number 1?

> ANDY: You read my mind.

> ANDY: Also, we need to add when he calls you his wife in a very possessive tone because of a room mishap.

> WILLOW: HE DID WHAT?

> WILLOW: CALL ME!!!!!!

I stuff my phone back into my pocket, praying no one notices the flush on my face.

Roman seems at ease, swirling his glass, sniffing, writing down a few notes as he goes. His throat works on another swallow, and I can't take my eyes off of him. He has two days' worth of scruff on his jaw and I'm itching to drag my fingers across it.

Roman asks him how business is and Macki turns suspicious, answering his questions with a brusqueness I've only ever seen from Roman.

"I know why you're here, Roman. The only reason I agreed to take the meeting was because of your father. I'm not interested in selling off my wine under someone else's label."

Roman nods in understanding.

"I get it, Benny. We'd pay you well for it and make sure it gets into good hands."

"It doesn't matter. It's my wine, my labor, my time. Perhaps your father should look into investing in vineyards of his own."

"I think that's his eventual goal, but you know as well as I do how long it takes to produce wine off a fledgling vineyard. We need wine now if we're ever going to get this off the ground. He trusts you. He trusts what you can do and he knows you make good wine. It wouldn't be forever, just for a year or two."

Macki stares at him for a long time before finally saying, "No."

"Look, just think about it. At least let me make my pitch before you turn me down, yeah? We can meet in the morning after breakfast and you can reject me then."

"You won't change my mind."

Roman is persistent. "We'll see about that."

We finish our wine tasting with a glowering Macki. Every wine is delicious. When the tasting room opens for the night, Macki makes himself busy with his customers. His countenance is much different with them than it is with us. Sergei excuses himself to turn in early.

Roman and I walk back to the main house. We're just about to step into the foyer when he stops me.

"Are you up for an adventure?" he asks.

The late afternoon slants across his face. His eyes are glowing, magical, hypnotic. A soft breeze ruffles his hair and I think I'd do just about anything with him.

"Depends. What did you have in mind?"

***

Thirty-minutes later, we're driving toward a little town just north of us called Greve. Roman tells me all about it as we drive. It's a cute little town, known for its art and museums and restaurants. I'm excited to explore with him. I'm excited that he even asked.

His right hand is wrapped around the steering wheel while his left rests on the gearshift between us. I smooth down the skirt of my sundress and try to calm down my racing heart. He let me use the bathroom first when we got back into the room. I managed to splash water on my face and do my makeup while he answered a few calls from New York.

A dress felt like the safest option in case we were headed somewhere nice. I'm glad I chose it, because when I stepped out of the bathroom, he'd changed into gray slacks and a black button down. He's cuffed his sleeves to his forearms, flashing the signet ring he wears on his pinky finger and expensive watch on his left wrist.

That signet ring has haunted me for years. It glints gold against his tan skin, the center onyx-black with a carving of a white rose and a B wrapped through the stem. The feel of that cold metal against my neck while he drilled himself into me will never fade. I press my legs together again, crossing and uncrossing them. His eyes track the motion, and I command myself to sit still.

We drive in comfortable silence before he pulls over on the side of the road.

"That's the Castle of Montefioralle. It was an open-air market back in the 13th century."

"Wow."

The castle is beautiful, with its warm yellow walls and metal statues out front. Roman parks the car and steps out into the twilight. He skirts the front of the car, coming around to open the door for me. He grins at me, and fuck, is it disarming to have his smile flashed my way after being desperate for it for so long.

He takes my hand, weaving his fingers with mine before leading me into the piazza.

"This is the Piazza Matteotti. It's the main square in town, though it's not quite a square. See?" He gestures to the square, which is really more of a long rectangle.

The village before me is beautiful. The portico wraps three quarters of the way around the piazza, shielding it from the scorching afternoon sun. There are dozens of artisan storefronts for us to wander through and a handful of restaurants with outdoor seating to take advantage of on such a nice night. Roman doesn't let go of my hand as we walk, and I'm too afraid to question it in case he stops.

We stop at the Wine Museum and browse around inside. We take the self-guided tour, exploring the history of the Chianti region. Even when he lets go of my hand, he's never far. He leans over me, his chest brushing against my back. His hand rests on my waist, his lips are by my ear.

If this is friendship with Roman Bendetti, what does more look like?

We browse a few other shops, staring at paintings and hand-woven baskets and bags. Everyone is kind, welcoming us into their storefronts with open arms. We wander for a while before our hungry stomachs lead us to a cozy outdoor seating area at one of the restaurants. There are no menus on the table.

"Chef's special," he says, grinning at me again. "Up for the challenge, sweetheart?"

"I'm in if you are."

He shakes his head, chuckling. "Dangerous words."

I shrug, sipping my water.

"I like a bit of danger in my life from time to time." My tone is light, coy, casual, but his eyes darken at the insinuation.

His tongue flicks out against his top lip.

"Those romance novels doing it for you, Alexandra?"

I scoff, blushing. "I have to get it where I can, Roman. A girl can't be too picky these days."

"Is that right?" The words are nearly purred at me.

His eyes rake over my collarbones and neck. I feel his gaze like fingertips.

What are we doing? I clear my throat and adjust my position in my seat.

A waiter comes, relieving me of a response. He explains that it's a prefixed menu tonight due to the festival that starts at sundown. Roman looks at me for approval.

"Sounds good to me."

"Any allergies?" the waiter asks.

"None for me," I say.

"Same. A bottle of Montepulciano, though, if you can."

"Very good, *Signore*. I'll be right back with that."

The lights in the piazza dim and the bistro lights that swing from the portico turn on. A small band takes up residence in the corner across from our seats. I watch the stalls being set up outside storefronts.

"Seems we picked a good night to come," I say, leaning across the table. "I love live music. It's one of my favorite ways to spend my free time."

He takes the kernel of information I offer and runs with it.

"Tell me about the singing," he says, leaning forward. "That night, you told me you don't sing as much anymore. Why is that?"

I nearly choke on my water. He's never brought up that night. Not once. Not if it could be helped. I school my features into passivity before I answer.

"Singing was always just for me growing up. I used to put on concerts in my room when I was little. When my mom remarried George, his parents felt I needed rounding out. Their words, not mine," I say quickly when I see his expression darken. "They put me in all sorts of lessons but singing was really the only one that stuck. I took music lessons for years and that sort of took the joy away from it. When Willow and I were roommates in college, we would go to a lot of karaoke bars and I was able to reclaim a little bit of it for myself."

"I'd love to hear you sing one day," he says, stunning me into silence.

Who is this man? Where are his surly glares, the disapproving frowns? How long has he locked the real him away? His mask is gone and nowhere in sight.

"Really?" I wrinkle my nose. "Why?"

Our wine is delivered. The waiter pours us each a glass. Roman lifts his glass to mine.

"To friendship," he says, taking a sip.

He rolls the wine around in his mouth before groaning deep in his throat.

I gulp, the sound of his groan skittering up my spine and reverberating deep in my bones.

"To friendship," I mutter, taking a large sip of wine.

"But, to answer your question, you have a beautiful voice. Well, from what I can make of it in the car."

"Maybe," I hedge.

The idea of singing in front of Roman flusters me.

"I'll go to a karaoke bar, if it makes you less nervous," he teases.

I scoff at him. "You don't make me nervous, Roman."

He leans back in his chair, draping his elbow across the back of it. His free hand spins his glass around on the tabletop.

"Don't I?" There's a challenge glittering in his eyes.

"Nope," I say sweetly, popping the 'p' hard at the end. "Not at all."

His grin is slow, lazy, as it splits his face.

Jesus Christ, this man is too hot for his own good.

"I'd have to say you're a liar."

I match his energy, leaning across the table. I drop my voice to a hush.

"Think what you want, Roman. It'll only be your fault when you're disappointed in the end."

His answering laugh is husky and dark. I'm saved by our waiter once more. I nearly run after him, thanking him for sparing me from the most intense 'friendly' dinner I've ever been at.

The prefixed menu is composed of wild boar pappardelle, roasted summer vegetables, wafer-thin cuts of salami and ham with assorted cheeses, nuts, and fruit. Roman and I fill our plates, listening to the music float through the piazza.

I can't stop the smile spreading across my face as I try the pasta.

"What's that smile for?" he asks, fighting off his own.

"Just happy," I say before I can think about it too hard. "It's beautiful here. How do you ever get yourself to leave?"

A shadow flickers across his face.

"It's not always by choice."

I hesitate to ask him the questions on my mind, but I remember our truce, our call to friendship.

"You didn't want to come to New York?"

He shakes his head, spearing into his vegetables.

"No, not really. I had a life here. I had... a career," he says evasively.

"What did you do before all of this?" I ask, doubting he'll give me a real answer.

He stares at me for a long minute before saying,

"I was the starting striker for the Verona Gladiators."

I blink, because I must have misheard him. I set my fork down very carefully.

"You were what?"

He sighs. "I played in the professional soccer division here for four years before I was forced to retire early and move to New York and learn the business."

I open and close my mouth, but no sound comes out.

He was a wreck that night in the bar. The grief and sadness in his eyes haunts me even now.

"Forced to retire?" I croak.

"Yes. Part of the agreement I made with my father. He has plans to retire next year and in order to do that, he needs to prepare me to become CEO."

I shake my head in disbelief. "Does he know you don't want it?"

"He does. Well, I think he does," he amends. "He knows I wasn't happy to leave. That's why this project is so important to me. I need it to mean something."

"I understand," I say earnestly, because I do. "Why didn't you ever say anything?"

"I wasn't in the right headspace for a long time. I was angry, plus, we've only been friends for four hours." He tries to lighten his tone into an air of playfulness, but there's a rock in my stomach.

"I'm serious."

He must read something in my expression, because he drops the pretense.

"I was out of my mind. I was grieving my future and terrified and pissed off at everyone and everything. I had to become another person when I took this on. The Roman I was when I played died the day I walked into that office. I had to be a boss, a leader. I had to give up…" He cuts himself off abruptly. "Anyway, I couldn't have spoken about it even if I tried."

It feels all too natural for me when I reach across the table and take his hand.

"I'm sorry, Roman."

He gapes at me before squeezing back. "It's not your fault, Alexandra."

I shake my head. "Maybe not, but I haven't made it easy on you."

"I haven't made it easy on *you*. Thank God for fresh starts, right?" This time, his smile does reach his eyes.

"Is this the first time you've been back since then?"

"Yes. I haven't even told my teammates I'm here. I don't know how to tell them I'm back. I'm not the man they remember. I'd hate to disappoint them."

"They'll be glad to see you," I insist. "No matter who you are now. How could you ever think they'd be disappointed? What you're doing is amazing. You should be proud of yourself."

His chewing slows. "Thank you," he says thickly. "Maybe I'll reach out to them."

We eat in silence for a few minutes, my mind whirling with all of this new information. I remember when Willow came back from his brownstone last year. I had begged her to give me all the sordid details of his home and what they spoke about. She gave me all the details I could want about his place, but when it came to their conversations, she was surprisingly firm on not telling me. Now I know why.

When our plates are clear and the bottle is down to the dregs, Roman stands and stretches. The piazza has transformed into a dance floor and he offers me his hand. I stare at it like it may bite me. He laughs.

"Come on," he goads when he sees my hesitation. "Dance with me."

I ignore the warning bells in my head. I slip my hand into his and let him lead me over the stone streets and into the throng of people. His arm wraps low around my hips, the other clasping my hand to his chest. He's warm against me and the smell of him settles over me. His cologne takes me back to the last time we were this close and I feel goosebumps break out over my body.

His eyes scan the crowd and his arms tighten around me.

"You look beautiful," he says against my ear. "I've wanted to tell you that every day for the last three years. You're beautiful. You always are."

I can barely breathe. "Roman—"

"Just—let me have this, okay? Let me just have this moment." There's a touch of desperation in his voice. I can hardly speak because

I feel it, too. Like this is all just borrowed time. "You're the most gorgeous woman in every room. I can't take my eyes off you. I never could."

I risk looking up at him, heart racing. He's already looking down at me, his eyes heavy on my lips.

"I dream about you, Alexandra. About that night. About us. Do you?"

My answer is immediate. "Yes, I do."

He groans, nuzzling his nose against mine. I'm dying for him to kiss me. To end this agony. He dips his head and ghosts his mouth over mine. It's the barest whisper of a kiss, but it's more than he's given me in three years.

"This was a bad idea," he murmurs.

His fingers splay open, pushing into the small of my back.

"The very worst," I agree breathily.

I stretch up on my tiptoes, sinking my hands into that glorious head of hair.

He dips his head, and I know he's going to kiss me this time and I brace myself for it. For him.

His mouth just touches mine when his phone rings, tearing our moment to shreds.

Chapter 8
Roman

If I didn't need a fucking phone, I would break the damn thing against the sidewalk. But, as it turns out, I'm running a business and always need to be accessible. Andy's eyes are cloudy with lust, her face flushed, her lips parted.

Stepping away from her is physically painful.

I watch her gather herself, watch the realization of what we almost just did settle into place. Her hands are shaking as she runs her fingers over her lips.

"What?" I bark, tracing the motion of her hand.

"Roman." My father's voice is warm, still heavily accented from his years living here. "*Come stai?*"

I rub my eyes.

"I'm fine, Dad. Macki is being a pain in the ass, but it's what we expected."

"The Mattero contract is a big deal, Roman. Congratulations."

"That was all Alexandra," I say quickly. "She charmed Gilbert within an inch of his life."

He chuckles over the line. "That's not surprising. He's always been *testardo*. How are things going otherwise? How is Andy?"

I sigh, because I already know this won't be a quick five-minute phone call.

"Alexandra is fine. She's taking to the lifestyle over here."

"Just as I thought she would."

Andy's walls are locking back into place, and I know that for tonight the moment is gone. We head back to our table and I pay the bill before taking her hand and walking back to the car.

My father fills me in on New York, the tasting room, Willow's current plans for the staff and a few other details. Most of this could have been sent in an email and if this were any other time I'd be happy to talk to him but tonight...

He finally says goodbye as we pull into *La Dea*. It's painfully quiet between us as we climb the steps back to our floor.

"You take the bed," I say when we step into our room. "I'll sleep on the couch."

Her eyes travel up my tall frame.

"You won't fit on that couch. You're too tall."

"I'll be fine," I say dismissively. "I've slept in smaller spaces."

She purses her lips and folds her arms across her chest.

"What? When you were five? Don't be silly, Roman. I'll be fine on the couch."

She grabs her toiletry bag and a bundle of clothes and locks herself inside the bathroom. I can hear the zipper go down on her dress as it whispers against her leg.

"Fucking hell," I curse quietly.

I would have worshiped her tonight. I would have gotten my head between those pretty little thighs and made up for three years of not eating her for breakfast, lunch, and dinner. My cock twitches painfully in my slacks. I drop into one of the wing-backed chairs and rest my elbows on my knees.

"You're up." I can hear the nerves in her voice.

I count to fifty before I stand. Her pajamas are rose silk and illegally short. Her long legs are toned and tanned and my fingers twitch by my side. Her face is free from makeup and her hair is knotted on top of her head. I meant what I said, she's beautiful all the time, but seeing her like this, right before bed, feels like a privilege I don't deserve.

She gives me a wide berth as I grab my bag and head into the bathroom. I hear the covers rustle beyond the door.

I turn on the shower. I need to cool off. I need to calm down. I can't get the image of those long legs wrapped around my waist, squeezing the life out of me. Those little whimpers and moans, her pleas, her cries. How pliant she goes against me, the way her body goes soft when I touch her. I'm ready to come before I even step in the shower. All it takes is three harsh strokes before I twitch, coming against the shower wall.

That's twice now in four days.

I'm no better than a teenager.

Offering friendship seemed like a good idea, at the time. There are lines, I remind myself. Boundaries. It was a beautiful night. Full of romantic music with a beautiful woman at my side. I'll get it together in the morning.

By the time I step out in sweats and a t-shirt, she's tucked against the couch.

"Good night," she calls, voice small.

"I don't like you sleeping there," I say, hands on my hips.

She squirms against the hard back.

"I'm really fine."

I roll my eyes and cross the room. She's over my shoulder before she can protest. I drop her in the center of the bed. She bounces once, those little shorts riding so high I can see the curve of her ass.

"Make a line," I say gruffly, gesturing to the pillows. "You stay on your side; I'll stay on mine."

"Yes, sir," she says, putting the pillows into place.

Because I have no filter and I'm at my wits end, I growl,

"I swear to God, Alexandra, every time you sass me like that all I want to do is fuck that smart ass mouth of yours."

She gapes at me. "What?"

"You heard me."

I cross to my side of the bed.

I can feel her thinking as I lay down and turn on my side away from her. I don't trust myself to lay the other way. She settles back against the sheets, her body as far from mine as can be.

She's silent for a long time before she whispers into the darkness,

"Maybe one day you will."

Fuck.

Her breathing levels out in a few minutes, but I lay awake for a long, long time.

***

Macki is waiting for me in the dining room with his two sons, Gianni and Loren. They're all frowning, which isn't a great sign for me. Andy was still asleep when I rolled out of bed and I crept from our room so as not to wake her.

Sergei reads the paper at one of the little tables by the window, sipping his cup of coffee. He looks refreshed, ready for the day. Which is great, because if this meeting goes the way I think it will, we'll be leaving ahead of schedule.

"Roman, it's good to see you," Loren says.

He shakes my hand. We used to sling mud at each other when we were kids after it rained. Gianni never really ran with us much. He's almost a full ten years older than me.

"You as well, Loren. It's been a few years."

He smiles, and it comes much easier than his father's.

"Grown up a bit since. No more mud pies for me."

"Shame," I say, remembering. "You always had the meanest arm."

He winks. "Still do."

"Are you two done or can we talk?" Macki grumbles. He yanks out a chair and takes a seat. "The floor is yours, Roman. Go ahead."

Gianni and Loren follow his lead, taking the seats on either side of him.

I glance back to the hallway, wishing Andy were with me. She'd know what to do, what to say to charm them into agreeing to this. I can't have her fight all my battles, though. I need to win this one myself.

I open my laptop and flip to the tab in my Excel sheet that I created just for them. I spin the screen for them and begin my slideshow of the tasting room in New York. The words feel tangled in my mouth, uncertain, as I explain the set up. I walk him through the projections for the next five years.

Since the tasting room opened for the sales reps of Cin Cin, people are buzzing about coming to visit. We have mock up menus for flights, food, and programming to focus on each of the wines that are bottled under the Bendetti label. I even tell him that his name will be on the label, so the entire world will know it's his.

"I can just do this myself," he says. "Everything you want to do is what I'm already doing, but I don't have to part with my yields"

"I understand," I say in what is, I hope, my most patient voice. "You do well for yourself here, Benny. You always have. We can just give you an extra reach."

"It's interesting," Loren says. "It would be cool for someone on the other side of the world to drink our wine in their home."

"Then we get shipping," Macki grunts. "We can do all of this ourselves."

Gianni is silent. I wasn't expecting much from him, but I still find myself disappointed at his lack of interest.

"I won't beg you, Macki. I know a lost cause when I see one. Just... Think about it, yeah? If you change your mind, just call me."

I slide my business card across the table. "I'll be in Italy for another two weeks if you'd like to meet again."

He takes the card, but doesn't say anything.

"Take care, Roman," he says, and I know we've been dismissed.

From there, I see no reason to stay. Ever since Andy mentioned reaching out to the team last night, I've been unable to stop thinking about it. A newfound sense of urgency fills me. It feels right, feels necessary, to go and see them.

My phone is burning a hole in my pocket. All I can think about is Christian and Matteo. My teammates. My family. I know my silence has hurt them over the last few years. I yank my phone from my pocket before I can chicken out and text them both.

> ROMAN: Have any free time later today or tomorrow?

Their answers are instantaneous, and I know I don't deserve them. Not after the radio silence I've given them over the last three years.

> **CHRISTIAN:** FINALLY! He returns!
>
> **MATTEO:** Was wondering when you'd show back up, Striker.
>
> **CHRISTIAN:** Are you really here? You're coming back?

ROMAN: I'm here on business for Cin Cin, but some time freed up. Think there's space for me on the pitch tomorrow?

> **CHRISTIAN:** One o'clock sharp, Bendetti. Don't be late.

I check our schedule to see what I can make work. We weren't supposed to be in Umbria until tomorrow to meet with Dominic Mazzaro, but I have a feeling I can convince him to push it back a few days. Taking the weekend to explore Verona with Andy seems like a better option.

I bring my phone to my ear. It rings twice before Dom picks up.

"Hello?"

"Hey, Dom."

"Roman," he says, voice crackling over the line. "Good to hear from you."

"You, too. Listen, I know this is a pretty big last minute ask since I'm supposed to be there tomorrow, but do you think we could move our meeting until Monday?" I explain the situation to him plainly.

He agrees readily, saying he needs the extra time to harvest. We reschedule for Monday afternoon and a weight slips off me.

"Sergei," I call. "Can we be ready to go in a half an hour?"

He shoots from the table, nearly upending it in the process.

"*Si, signore. Dove stiamo andando?*"

I grin at him. "Verona."

His whoop of joy could wake all of Italy. "I will get the car right now!"

He bolts out the front door. I'm just as anxious to get going as he is. I take the steps two at a time back up to our floor. When I step into our room, Andy is already dressed and ready to go in jeans with flowers sewn onto the back pocket and a soft blue t-shirt that clings to her in the most distracting way.

"How'd it go?" she asks when she glances up at me.

I cross the room in two quick strides. Her eyes widen as I grip her face and plant a solid kiss to the center of her forehead. She gapes at me.

"Roman? Did you get the contract?"

I shake my head. I can't stop smiling.

"Nope, he turned me down."

Confused, she splutters, "Then what—"

"I pushed our meeting back in Umbria until Monday. I was wondering if you'd like to spend the weekend in Verona with me?"

Joy breaks out across her face.

"You called them?"

I nod, barely able to contain my excitement.

"Yup. I'm going to scrimmage with them tomorrow."

She launches herself at me, throwing her arms around my neck. I scoop her up, lifting her clear off the floor. My laughter is deep, so full of happiness I hardly recognize it.

"I'm so happy for you!" she says, nearly vibrating with excitement. "Can I watch?"

"Who else am I going to show off for, sweetheart?" I ask, setting her down.

Her blush is so sweet when it comes. She races around the room, packing her things. The urgency in the air has me moving to pack up my own clothes and electronics. Sergei is already waiting for us in the car, engine running. His bags are neatly stacked in the trunk.

Andy crawls into the back and I slip into the passenger seat. Sergei passes the cable back for her phone. I like this little routine we've begun.

It's a three-hour drive to Verona, and I feel a little bad about carting them all over Italy so I can step back inside my dream. My body is itching, thrumming, to run until my lungs burst. Andy's music choices are upbeat and happy.

She sings a little louder for me today and I know with utter certainty it's the only thing I want to hear before I die. Sergei shoots me an approving glance. Maybe things don't need to be one or the other, maybe there can be room for everything.

We arrive in Verona in the early afternoon. I spent the drive finding places for us to stay. I booked us an Airbnb in the heart of the city near Juliet's Balcony. I know Andy is a closeted romantic— her reading materials tell me as much. I thought it would be nice for her to wander toward the balcony and leave a love letter for Juliet.

Our host messages me, letting me know the rooms won't be ready until later. I did send them a reply message apologizing for the late booking but I made sure to explain the situation. It's the only time I've named dropped in the last three years.

Their reply was immediate: We can do it.

Sergei parks the car outside the Airbnb.

"My wife's cousin lives a few streets up. Do you mind if I go and say hello?"

I check my watch. "Enjoy it, Sergei. We can check in a little later. I'll text you the code when it's ready."

He nods, striding up the street.

He could have stayed with us, and he knows it, but I do appreciate the alone time with Andy he's given me over the last few days. Sergei is a good man. I'm lucky to have him.

Andy squints up the street.

"Where exactly are we?"

I smile. "I picked a place near Juliet's Balcony. I thought—"

Her screech of joy is deafening. She takes my hand and yanks me to follow her. I'm nearly jogging to keep up with her. Making her happy is the best job I've ever had.

We walk for a few blocks taking in the sights. The homes are beautiful with their varying colors and large balconies. I know Andy is probably dreaming about coffee and tea at midnight in the city.

"Up to the right," I say, pointing to the little courtyard up ahead.

She's panting when she skids to a halt, neck craned up to look at the balcony that inspired Shakespeare's greatest tragedy. The square is crowded, as it usually is. It's one of the biggest tourist attractions in the city. Below her balcony, the building houses a small museum with costumes and props from the many versions of the movie and souvenirs to take home.

"I know this isn't real and she was never here," Andy whispers, staring at her statue, "but there's something magical about it, isn't there? That all these people travel here to rub a statue, to write letters to someone who would die for love." She shakes her head. "Maybe it's silly, I don't know."

"It's not," I say softly, quietly. "It's not silly."

"I think it's nice to believe in something, don't you? To pour your heart out to someone who can't judge you for it." Her sigh seems sad. "Wistful," she says almost to herself. "A place of almosts and maybes. A place for the *what ifs*."

She walks up to the statue and touches Juliet's right breast. It's meant to bring good luck in love. She squeezes her eyes shut, like she's begging the statue to hear her. My chest feels oddly hollow seeing the pain on her face. I wonder what she's begging Juliet to do for her, but some part of me thinks that I already know. I just don't want to face it.

I don't want to say it.

When she's done, she moves to the wall of letters. She grabs a piece of paper and leans against one of the smoother stones and begins to write.

I'm desperate to know what she's writing, what she's pouring out of her. I grab my own piece of paper and find a secluded corner. There's not a lot of men writing to Juliet, so I'm hoping that means maybe she'll hear me.

Juliet,

Being with her feels like breathing. It feels too good, too natural. I know I can't love her, but I can't let her go. Give me the strength to decide. Do I go? Do I stay? Am I allowed to live in this dream? She deserves more than I can give her as I am right now. Help me become a man who is brave. A man who is unafraid— a man worthy of her.

Roman

I seal my envelope, hands shaking at what I've written. I hand it to one of the secretaries of Juliet. She smiles at me and says,

"*Lei sente tutto. Avere fede.*" Her eyes shine as she takes my envelope from me. "*L'amore conquista tutto.*"

She hears everything. Have faith. Love conquers all.

How she knows what I've written, I'm not sure. Andy's drying her tears as she passes her letter over. The secretary doesn't say anything as she takes her envelope, but her eyes are sad. Andy is abnormally quiet for the rest of our walk.

We pop into the museum and look around before heading up the street toward the Piazzo delle Erbe. We grab coffees from one of the cafes and take in the sights. The market is in full swing, vendors and long lines snaking through the piazza.

Andy pauses at one of the jewelry tables, eyes scanning the silver baubles with interest.

She picks up a ring with a small amethyst stone. It's a beautiful band engraved with leaves and vines.

"*Quanto?*" she asks the jewelry maker.

The woman's weathered eyes are kind as they rest on Andy's face. "*Trenta euro.*"

Andy asks the woman if she's made the ring herself and the woman nods. She explains that everything is handmade and crafted in her small little apartment. Her rings are made from real stones and silver, so it will never fade or tarnish.

Andy reaches into her bag when I slip the money from my pocket.

"Let me," I insist.

"Roman—"

"Please," I say again. "I want to."

Andy's hand falls from her bag and she lets me pay. She slides the ring onto the middle finger of her left hand and examines it. It's beautiful, delicate. It suits her.

I like the idea of coming back to New York and seeing the ring I bought her on her finger. A secret. A nod to our time here. When things go back to being strained, at least this will remain.

She lets me hold her hand as we spend the afternoon walking and exploring. We head over to the Ponte Pietra bridge before heading to Duomo di Verona. From the bridge, Verona spreads out around us. We lean on that bridge for a long time, my arms caging Andy against the stone sides. Neither of us are in a hurry to leave and so we watch the boats drive up and down the canal.

The Duomo di Verona is staggering, awe inspiring with its high ceilings. We study the art pieces and statues side by side. We speak in hushed voices as we do the tour through the main part of the church.

By the time we step outside, our host texts us that our place is ready. We make the walk back across town. We pass the supposed house of Romeo and skirt the crowds outside.

The Airbnb is large enough for the three of us, though Sergei and I are bunking together in the room with the two double beds. Andy drops her things in her room, eyeing the large bed and beautiful view of the city.

There's a communal living room for us to hang out in complete with a full kitchen and dining room. It was an expensive place to book, but it's worth it to see Andy's silhouette on the terrace, all of Italy before her like some kind of queen.

Juliet, I think, *if you can hear me, help me.*
Help me make her mine.

CHAPTER 9

ANDY

FRIDAY AFTERNOON WE HEAD to the pitch. I'm buzzing with excitement, but Roman has withdrawn into himself. I know he's nervous about seeing his teammates again after all this time, but I have full faith that they'll welcome him back with open arms. Sergei is decked out in one of Roman's old Gladiator jerseys, BENDETTI blazing across the back.

I'm dying to ask for one of my own, but I don't. Wearing his name feels like a statement I'm not ready to make just yet. Instead, I opt for black jeans and a burgundy t-shirt that I French tuck and a pair of Vans.

Security is expecting us when we drive up to the player's gate and we're waved through. Roman exhales sharply through his nose when we park and make our way into the back entrance of the stadium. He clutches his bag tightly in his fist and I hurry my steps to loop my arm through his.

He flinches at my touch but relaxes when he realizes it's me.

"It's going to be great," I reassure. "I promise."

"We'll see," he says, voice tight.

A security guard leads us through the locker rooms downstairs. None of the team is inside, but I know they're waiting for him on the pitch. There are clothes and jackets and shoes shoved into each cubby. The room smells faintly of antiseptic and sweat.

Roman walks past a few lockers and then stops dead.

"That's my locker." His voice is hoarse, strained.

There's a brand-new jersey and a pair of cleats waiting for him just inside. There's a small handwritten note on top that reads: welcome back.

The ache that seizes my chest is bittersweet.

He runs his finger down the maroon and black striped kit with something close to reverence. Sergei clears his throat.

"We go to the pitch now, Just Andy."

Roman doesn't make a sound as Sergei and I follow the tunnel at the end of the locker room. I squint against the sunlight waiting for me and step on the pitch. I've been to many sporting events and always wondered what it would be like to stand on the field.

The answer is that I feel small, intimated, by the thousands of seats around me. I can't imagine being down here in the middle of a game with that many people cheering and screaming for you. I'd turn tail and run.

A man across the field breaks apart from the rest of the group and runs our way.

"Sergei!"

His long blonde hair is knotted tightly on top of his head. His beard is groomed and well-maintained but the man is covered in dirt. The wall of muscle slams into Sergei, hoisting him into the air.

"Matteo," Sergei gasps. "*Per l'amore de Dio*. Put me down!"

Matteo laughs, but drops Sergei back to his feet.

"Where is he? I'm dying to see him." He rubs his hands together gleefully.

"Taking a much-needed moment, I think," Sergei says. He nods his head in my direction. "This is Alexandra."

Matteo's eyes are two shades deeper than Roman's. He's quick to smile and I can just spot the dimple on his right cheek as he flashes that panty dropping grin my way.

"Andy," I correct, offering him my hand. "It's nice to meet you, Matteo."

"It's *really* nice to meet you, too, Andy." Matteo brings my knuckles to his lips for a swift kiss. "God, I love American girls. Where has Roman been hiding you all this time? Is this why he hasn't been back?"

"Um—"

"She's been with me, jackass," Roman says roughly from behind me. "She's *mine*, Matteo. Back off."

Roman drops a possessive hand on my hip and pulls me back against him. I gape up at him, at the scowl that's marring his perfect face.

Matteo's eyes sparkle with mischief. He sends me a wink and I stifle my laughter against the back of my hand.

"It's good to see you too, Roman." He grins and opens his arms.

Roman begrudgingly lets me go to embrace his teammate. Matteo mutters something low into Roman's ear and he barks out a laugh.

"Christian!" Matteo bellows back toward the players on the other end of the pitch. He keeps one arm around Roman's broad shoulders. "Guess who showed up!"

It's everything I hoped it would be. The other players take one look at who is standing next to Matteo and sprint the distance between us. Christian is *tall*. His eyes are two twin storm clouds, perfectly gray in color. His dark head buries itself into the crook of Roman's neck as they squeeze the life out of each other.

I can feel the joy radiating off him as he's passed around through all of his old buddies. They grin, clasping him on the arm, cupping his cheek, touching their foreheads together.

It's a beautiful sight. Roman's happiness is palpable and I feel like I'm seeing him for the first time, all his blurred edges taking shape. I choke on the tears at the back of my throat. Roman turns away from his team, glancing back at me. His eyes widen when he takes in my expression.

"Baby," Roman murmurs, closing the space between us. The endearment melts me to my core. There's worry in his eyes. "Are you crying?"

I wave my hand in front of my eyes.

"No," I croak. "No, I'm fine. I'm just... I'm happy for you, that's all."

His smile is soft when it comes.

"I never would have done this if it weren't for you."

I brush him off.

"You would have, I'm sure of it. I'm just glad I get to be here for it."

"Are we going to fucking play or what?" Christian calls, British accent thick. "Or did you forget, Roman?"

Roman growls over his shoulder at him.

"Grab a seat, okay?" He leans close, lips brushing against my cheek. "You better not cheer for anyone else but me," he warns.

I shiver in anticipation.

"Or what?" I can't help but rile him.

It makes him wild, dangerous, just how I like him.

His smile is all teeth. "Do it and find out."

A whistle is blown and Roman walks backward from me before turning and running onto the pitch. He warms up, stretching and jogging up the length of the pitch before circling back with the team.

Sergei and I make our way to the first row of seats that are nearly field-level and settle in to watch.

"That is his old coach, Dante." Sergei points to an older man in his mid-fifties. I watch the delight cross Dante's face at the sight of Roman on the pitch. Cheers go up, and hands roughly shake and jostle him. "They were very close," Sergei tells me. "It was awful when he left, Just Andy. I have never seen him so low."

I hate that for so long I didn't know. Hate that he struggled, grieved, all alone with no one to talk to. He's the strongest man I know, and I feel proud to know him and call him my friend.

I swallow my laughter. A lot changes in a week. If you would have asked me last month, I would have told you that Roman Bendetti was my archnemesis, the bane of my existence but now...

He's quickly becoming the center of my universe.

They break into two teams and Roman takes his place on the line. He looks too good in his jersey, in the tight pair of black shorts that hug his thick and impressive thighs. His hair is loose around his face and I hold my breath in anticipation as Dante blows the whistle and sends them into motion.

Roman is fluid, graceful, as he runs up the field. I don't know much about soccer, so Sergei fills me in. He explains that a striker, or a forward, is responsible for scoring goals or setting up plays and passes to enable another teammate to score.

"You should have heard them cheer for him," Sergei says. "The stadium would chant his name. Roman, the fiercest gladiator in the ring. He had the highest number of goals in a single season. In the history of the club. There's a plaque for him here and everything."

"And they just let him go?" I ask. "He makes it seem like he just walked away and history has forgotten him."

"I think that is what he tells himself to make it easier. The news circulated for weeks. His jersey sold out of nearly every shop in town when he retired. They miss him. Italia misses him."

I watch him jog up the field, snatching the ball from Christian's nimble feet. He kicks it up above his head before sprinting full speed toward the goal. He dodges a handful of other players, rolling the ball under his right foot before feinting right and then left, rolling it up the inside of his foot.

I'm out of my seat before I can stop myself.

He brings back his leg and launches the ball toward the goal. It sails past the goalie, finding its home in the corner of the net. The team explodes on the field and before I can stop myself, I'm jumping up and down and screaming his name.

In the midst of the huddle around him, his dancing eyes find mine as I scream his name until I'm hoarse. He's dripping with sweat and the only thing I can think of is how badly I want to cross the field and drop to my knees in front of him. His smile turns absolutely wicked, because he knows.

He's deadly in a suit, on the field, in every aspect of his life.

Roman Bendetti is everything I want.

They play for almost two hours without stopping. I know he's in good shape, but I'm speechless at his stamina and speed. I'm uncomfortably aroused by the time he's done. I watch him mop the sweat from his brow with the bottom of his jersey, exposing a tanned sliver of his abs.

Roman, Matteo, and Christian walk the pitch together separate from the rest of the team. Their laughter is comfortable, familiar. Roman seems at ease in his skin for the first time since I've known him.

"They all came up together," Sergei supplies. "They started together as rookies and moved into the spotlight at the same time. They are brothers, *sí*?"

I can see it. The familiarity between them. I wish I could change it for him. I wish I could take the business from him, tell him to come back here, live his dream, find his happiness. My throat clogs up at the thought of not seeing him every day but if it made him happy… I'd find a way to live with it. A way to live without him.

"What did you think?" Matteo asks, stopping before our seats.

Christian runs a white athletic towel over his face.

Roman's eyes are nearly black when he looks at me. I can tell he's amped up, on edge.

"I think you made a soccer fan of me," I hear myself say.

Matteo's answering smile is all charm. "It's football here, gorgeous."

Roman bristles beside him.

"Right," I say, flushing at the mischief in his eyes.

"Knock it off, Matteo," Roman growls.

He shrugs, still grinning at me, undeterred.

"We'll play here tomorrow night," Christian says. "I would love to invite you to come. I'll have tickets waiting for you. Roman? Sound good?"

He runs his tongue along his lip. "Alexandra?"

I love that he looks at me first before deciding.

"I'm in."

"Then we'll be here," Roman says.

He mops at his brow again and I nearly faint.

I can't stop staring at him. I can't stop imagining his hands gliding up my thighs, slipping between my legs, those rough fingers working me to a near fever-pitch.

"You sure you can't come back?" Christian asks. "I'll fire whoever you want me to."

Roman's answering chuckle is dry. "Unfortunately, I'm sure."

"What are you doing for dinner? I want to hear all about New York. And," Matteo says slyly, "Andy."

I flush under his gaze. Roman simmers beside him.

"We're staying at an Airbnb not far away. You're all welcome over," I say. "We can cook and you can fill me in on all the dirt I've missed on Roman."

"Careful," Roman warns, and it's just for me.

I ignore him. If I keep keying him up like this, I'm going to have to deal with the consequences but the thought of that is... thrilling.

"No, thank you," I say, voice saccharine. Christian's entire body shakes with silent laughter. "Will you come?"

Roman coughs. "Alexandra." He's exasperated, but I'm enjoying myself too much to stop.

"We'll be there," Matteo says. "Send us the address."

Roman tosses me a warning glance before they head into the locker rooms to change. Sergei leads me to the team store where they sell all of their jerseys and t-shirts. I browse around for a while, looking for anything with Roman's name on it. I debate asking the woman behind the counter but an idea strikes me.

"Hey Sergei," I call. "What's Matteo's last name?"

***

I do buy two jerseys. I ask the woman behind the counter about Roman's jersey and she shows me to a section I missed. The selection is small, but I find a jersey in my size. I buy a t-shirt with Matteo's last name on it and I know I'm playing with fire, but if I'm honest, I'm dying to get singed by him. I hide them both in my room at the bottom of my suitcase until tomorrow.

Christian and Matteo are just as loud off the pitch as they are when they're on it. They arrive with a bottle of wine and a cheese platter. Against their better judgment, they both kiss me on the cheek soundly when they arrive. Roman is nearly vibrating when they do it, his eyes branding my skin on the place where their mouths were.

He crosses the room toward me as Sergei leads them into the kitchen. I hear a cork pop from the bottle and the rustling of glass from the wall behind me.

"Alexandra, are you purposefully trying to rile me up?" Roman asks.

He cages me against the living room wall, his big hands on either side of my head.

"I don't know what you mean," I say, feigning innocence.

His eyes rove over my face.

"I think you do," he murmurs, voice like velvet. "If you want to play, baby, that's all you have to say."

God, do I. I know in my gut I won't be leaving Italy without Roman's mouth on mine. I don't know when it became my mission for this trip, but here we are. I want to unravel him, break him, make him desperate for me in the way I've been for him over these last three years.

"I saw you in the stands," he murmurs, lips brushing my jaw. "Flushed and screaming for me. Did you like watching?"

I squirm against the wall, the heat of him soaking into me. My heart kicks against my ribs in a painful staccato.

"Roman," I breathe. "We're supposed to be friends." He crowds me against the wall. "This doesn't feel very *friendly*."

His laugh is dark where it brushes against my skin.

"I think you're my best friend in the whole world right now," he rumbles, leaning in.

He presses a soft kiss just below my ear.

My fingers dig into the wall behind me, and I wait. He doesn't move, doesn't press closer, but the sight of his body over mine makes my head spin.

Sergei's laughter draws close and Roman tears himself away. He doesn't say it, but I can see the unspoken words in his eyes.

We're not done here.

He leaves me flushed against the wall, my skin burning. Roman's filthy mouth is one of the many things I remember from that night. He was very, very specific with me. He liked to hear me, liked me to plead and beg and agree with him. I know he gets off on control, and I'm more than happy to give it to him.

I take a deep breath before rounding back into the kitchen. Matteo hands me a glass of wine and taps his against mine.

"So, Andy, tell me everything. Who is my friend in New York? This new businessman in our midst." He waves his hand over Roman's frame.

My eyes slide over to Roman where he stands at the island prepping vegetables for dinner. His movements jerk as he chops up fresh tomatoes and I know what he's thinking. He's not been himself in all the time he's been there and I could say that. I could say he's been surly and rude and off-putting. That he's been stand-offish and a little cruel, but I don't.

"Oh, I'm sure you know how he is when he's faced with a new opponent. He's been driven and focused. Maybe a little *too* much," I tease.

The tension fades from Roman's shoulders and he shoots me a grateful look.

"That sounds like our captain," Christian says.

Captain? He certainly left that part out.

"He's learned quickly," I continue. "There's been so many changes since he's come on, and they've all been great. I know he misses it here, but we're thankful for him at Cin Cin."

His eyes soften when he meets mine. *Thank you*, he mouths.

I wink at him.

The thing is, I'm not even lying. Apart from our personal relationship, all the goodness he's brought to the company is real.

"That's not surprising," Matteo says. "Roman has never faced an adversary that he hasn't been able to beat. The corporate world never stood a chance."

"So, tell me what he was like when he was here. I want to know everything."

Roman's head snaps up.

"Not *everything*."

Matteo and Christian exchange a glance, both weighing how much shit they want to get themselves into but then Matteo shrugs and leans forward against the table.

"One time, we were in France..."

"Not this," Roman begs, setting down the knife. "Matteo."

Matteo grins, ignoring him. "We lost. It was a bad game. The refs were dirty and they definitely threw the game in favor of France. We went to the bar afterwards, you know, to blow off steam."

"I'm not listening to this," Roman grumbles.

I laugh, utterly delighted.

"Roman gets inordinately pissed that night and leads the bar in a 'fuck the French' chant that got us kicked out of the bar. We wandered the streets that night, wasted, laughing, cursing the French until our faces were blue. Coach was *pissed*. Made us run drills until we were all barfing on the pitch."

"Roman? My Roman?" I say, gesturing to the man currently grinding tomatoes to make sauce.

My Roman. Well. Can't take that back. Everyone's heard it now.

Matteo's green eyes sparkle.

"Yes, *your* Roman. Then there was the time in Spain..."

Matteo and Christian tell me two dozen stories, each one crazier than the one before. I watch Roman shift uncomfortably under the attention before finally loosening up.

By the time dinner is done and Roman finally joins us at the table, he's laughing. Sergei looks like a proud father, drunker than I've seen him on this whole trip so far.

Roman's fresh pasta falls apart in my mouth. The sauce is sweet and acidic and I help myself to two servings of it before finally setting my fork down. I like seeing him here. I like meeting his friends, getting a glimpse into the life he left behind. The ache I felt earlier returns and I wonder if there's anything I can do to get him back here where he belongs.

Matteo and Christian finally leave around midnight. Matteo promises me there will be tickets waiting for us when we arrive tomorrow and invites us out with the team afterward, win or lose. Roman looks to me first again, and I agree.

Being with him when he's this happy feels like standing in the sun and all I want to do is bask in it.

Chapter 10

ROMAN

I SHOULD HAVE KNOWN that Matteo wouldn't leave us tickets for just any normal seats. I pick up three VIP tickets from the front office. The man working the booth visibly pales when he sees me.

"You're... you're... Roman Bendetti."

He scrambles for a piece of paper and a pen. I cringe, because it's been a long time since I've had to sign anything for anyone. Word spreads that I'm here and before long, there's a crowd around us. Pictures are taken, chants and cheers of my name rise up in the crowd. I sign half a dozen shirts and hats, shielding Andy with my body as best as I can.

Andy presses to my side, her zip-up sweatshirt done all the way up to her neck. When the crowd surges around us, I wrap my arms around her and pull her close. Security comes to take us through the back and we walk the tunnel to the VIP seats closest to the pitch.

The Gladiators work through their warm up drills and the noise in the stadium is deafening as the crowd cheers their home team on. I miss the buzz, the excitement, the adrenaline.

We'd come off the field so keyed up most of the guys went home to their girlfriends or wives for the fuck of a lifetime. There's nothing like the post-game haze. Feeling untouchable, God-like. I felt that way yesterday leaving the field and it was just a practice game. Hearing Andy cheering for me, screaming my name...

God. If I had her here when I played in the league, I'd always be sprinting home to her, pushing her up against every surface I could find and fucking her until neither of us could stand.

"Oh, my God. Roman," she says, tugging on my arm. "*Look!*"

I follow Andy's finger up to the screen above us and there we are.

There I am.

The crowd roars. The banner on the screen reads: WELCOME HOME, CAPTAIN!

"Stand up!" Andy urges, practically shouting at me. "Roman, stand up!"

My legs are numb as I do what she says. I stand from my seat and wave. The noise intensifies around us, chants and cheers ringing in my ears. And then I hear it:

"Striker! Striker! Striker!"

I shiver. I never thought I'd hear that again, thirty-nine thousand two hundred people screaming for me. I swallow down the ball of emotion building in the back of my throat. When I look at the pitch, my team is clapping for me.

I will not cry in front of all these fucking people.

I will not cry in front of Andy.

I give a curt nod toward the pitch, my lips pressed together so tightly they ache. I reclaim my seat, the foundation of my world rocked. Andy's eyes are silver-lined with joy when I glance over at her.

The screen moves off us and I feel like I can breathe. Andy unzips her sweatshirt and grins proudly at me. Seeing her in my team's colors is going to give me a heart attack.

"What do you think?" she asks, twisting in her seat proudly.

I scrub my hand over my face.

"Alexandra," I rasp. "So help me God if you've got my name on the back of your jersey."

She snickers, wiggling her eyebrows at me.

"Want to find out?"

Fucking do I.

She turns, offering me her back. I take one look at the name there and feel my blood pressure skyrocket.

VENETTO. She's wearing fucking Matteo's jersey.

Her eyes are dancing as she looks back at me.

"What do you think?"

"I think you should fucking take it off," I snap.

I hear Matteo's howl of laughter from the sidelines before us. It takes all of my willpower not to launch myself at him and beat the smug look off his face. I have no right, no reason to be jealous but I am. I'm so jealous my vision blacks out. She's *mine*. She belongs with me.

"I thought you might say that." She shrugs, back still to me. She lifts the hem of her shirt and I reach to stop her, but I'm not quick enough. She removes her t-shirt, revealing another jersey underneath, and there I am. Right where I belong. Right across her back.

It takes me a minute to compute it. Seeing my name in big block letters across her shoulders is doing *all* sorts of things for my ego and my libido.

She grins at me. "Better?" She settles back against her seat, stuffing Matteo's jersey in her bag.

"Christ, Alexandra," I mutter.

My hand flexes on my thigh. I have half a mind to pull her right across my lap for being such a brat.

"Just keeping your ego in check, Roman."

I huff. "It's not my ego I'm worried about, sweetheart."

I loop my arm over the back of her chair as the starting whistle blows.

Sergei cheers through the duration of the game, whistling and yelling loud enough to shake the stadium. His Italian is rough, angry. He uses every colorful curse word I've ever heard toward the ref who doesn't call the foul on Christian. Andy is out of her seat, outraged. My lips quirk in amusement.

"Why are you screaming, Alexandra?"

She shrugs. "Solidarity." She jerks her thumb over to Sergei. "What happened?"

I walk her through each play as it happens, the formations the team takes. She nods along with me, eyes trained on the pitch. I like sharing this part of me with her. I like seeing the flush on her cheeks, hearing her yell. I like how she leans into me when I speak, how she asks questions when the whistle blows.

The crowd surges to their feet when Matteo breaks away. He's always been lightning fast and watching him streak down the pitch has me hollering for him at the top of my lungs. He kicks, sending the ball into the top most part of the net. The goalie dives, but it slips through his fingers. The ball spears into the back of the net and the crowd around us erupts.

He runs from the goal; arms raised in triumph over his head. It's almost universal, their decision to race toward where I'm standing. Half the team leaps up onto the rail, rubbing their sweaty bodies all over me and Andy. She's doubled over in laughter by the time they finally make their way back onto the field.

It's the most fun I've had in a long time and when the Gladiators take the game 3-1, I stick my fingers in my mouth and whistle as loudly as I can. The team claps in my direction and I grin at them. I know the energy coursing through them, the adrenaline and hype music that will be blasting in the locker room in the next ten minutes. Coach will be gruff with his debrief, but proud.

A few fans in the seats around us come over and ask for pictures and autographs, and I take my time with each of them. I don't know when or if I'll ever have this chance again. Andy watches it all with tenderness in her eyes. The stadium empties around us as the final stragglers make their way toward the exit.

"I'm sorry, Roman." Andy's voice is small by my shoulder. "Sorry you ever had to leave this."

Her words jar me. I feel thrown off-balance by the devastation on her face.

"It's fine, really."

"If things were different, would you move back? Would you leave Cin Cin?"

Where is this coming from? At one point, I would have said yes. I would have walked away from absolutely everything to get back here. I look at her for a long moment. Now, I would have to give her up. I don't know if anything is worth that.

"I don't know," I say. "Too much time has passed for me to play at this level. I wouldn't be able to keep up."

She shakes her head. "It's why you work out so much, isn't it? Why you have the saddest diet I've ever seen. It's almost like you're waiting for the call to come home."

Fuck. I didn't realize I was so transparent.

"Maybe," I admit. "It's what I'm used to. Maybe part of me hoped I'd be able to come back here, but I'm realizing that won't be the case. It's okay, Alexandra. Really. I've accepted it."

"What if someone else took the company over?" she presses. "Would you leave then?"

I round on her. "Where is this coming from?"

Does she not want me to stay?

"What if I did it? What if I volunteered for the CEO position so you could come back here?"

I blink at her in shock.

"It's not that simple, baby. I appreciate you even offering, but there's too many legal roadblocks in the way now to undo what's been done. My life is in New York."

She turns away from me, leaning her hands on the rail. She stares down at the pitch like it's offended her.

"No one's ever offered that for me before," I murmur. "Thank you for thinking of me."

Her smile is watery when it comes.

"You deserve to be happy, Roman. I watched Willow take back her life this last year. I watched Wes step into himself. And now that I know this," she says, waving her arm toward the pitch, "I want you to be happy, too. I want you to seize a bit of life for yourself."

I stare at her. She's everything I want to seize in this life and the one that follows. The team spills back onto the pitch, yelling my name, effectively breaking the moment between us.

"Ready?" Christian calls.

Andy shakes herself, chasing the shadows from her eyes.

"Ready!" she says, overly bright.

I wonder how many times I missed that. The polite smiles, the perfect manners, the way she's able to force brightness into her eyes, her smile. It's like she turns on a switch for the rest of the world. I want to ask her why she does that, when it started, but we join up with the team and head toward our cars out back and I lose the moment.

Sergei heads out for the night, shaking the hands of each member on the team. He was part of this family once, too. We drop our stuff and opt to walk to one of the clubs in town. We're quite a spectacle all together and we get stopped more than once for pictures and autographs. Christian leads the charge into the bar and it almost feels like they've been waiting for us to get here. We're led upstairs by one of the hostesses to a private balcony that overlooks the dance floor below.

There's a separate bar and lounge here for us to use and it keeps us away from prying eyes unless we want to mingle. The music is loud. I can feel the bass move through my heart, my chest, my limbs. The DJ spins his record around, switching up the music and mixing it with another song.

Champagne bottles are uncorked and then there's a flute being pressed into my hand.

"To the captain!" Matteo yells, hoisting his glass in the air. "Long may he reign!"

Eleven faces stare back at me, all of them as dear to me as family. Andy lifts her glass into the air and it's about two feet shorter than the rest of the glasses raised in toast to me.

"Nah, to you guys. To the best fucking team in the league!"

They roar in agreement, knocking back their drinks in one big swallow.

Their energy is unmatched, and I know it's going to be one of those nights.

A kicked out of the bar night.

There are only so many night clubs in Verona, and they keep taking us back no matter how much we fuck up. We spend too much money to be banished forever.

I can barely keep track of Andy as she works her way through the team, talking and laughing. Raphael, the goalie, keeps her interest for a long time. Raphael is a good man. Humble, kind. Everything Andy could ever want.

She laughs, her head tilted back. My eyes track the delicate lines of her neck and I pour myself another drink.

"Never seen you down so bad," Christian says, sliding up beside me.

I scoff. "I'm not... down bad."

"You really are," he says. "What's wrong? Why aren't you going for it? She's way out of your league, by the way, but all she seems to want to look at is your ugly mug."

I glance over at her and sure enough, even though Raphael is speaking to her, her eyes are on me.

"It's complicated," I say, tearing my eyes away. I can't watch it.

"How so?"

"I'm going to be her boss," I remind him. "Dad's going to retire in the next year or so, and that means the CEO position will be mine. She'll report to me."

Christian rolls his shoulders. "Does she report to you right now?"

"No, not technically."

"Do you cut her paychecks?"

I grind my molars together. I know where he's going with this.

"No."

"Do you make her schedule?"

"No."

"So, what's the issue? If you start dating before you take over the position, it's not breaking any rules."

"I wish it felt as simple as that. I'm a VP in the company. It's crossing too many lines already. We have... a history."

I've never spoken to anyone about that night. Mostly, it's because I'm ashamed of how I treated her afterward. I was so out of my mind I don't remember most of what I said, but I'll never forget the look in her eyes when I was done.

I turn so that I'm facing Christian and say for the first time out loud, "We slept together. Three years ago. The night I landed in New York after leaving here. We said no names, no details, no stories. When I walked into work Monday, she was there."

"Fuck, Roman." His eyes widen.

I nod. "I had to sit through a three-hour meeting with her. I was out of control when we finally left the conference room. I chased her down. I told her..." I exhale sharply. Guilt strangles me. "I told her it could never go anywhere. We had to act like we were strangers. No one could ever know. It was a quick fuck, nothing more. It didn't mean anything. There was no reason for us to let it affect our jobs and we just needed to be adults about it and move on. I'll never forget the look on her face. She looked as if I'd slapped her." I wipe my hand over my mouth. "For sharing a night with someone with no words, it was... the most intimate thing I've ever experienced. It felt like I knew her without even speaking."

"And now you think you've blown it?"

"We've spent the last three years at each other's throats in this toxic little dance. I can't let her go, but I can't ask her to stay."

Christian nods in understanding. "Neither of you have dated anyone else?"

"I haven't even tried," I confess. "Not really. I can't speak for her but... Last year, I started showing up more. Going out with our group of friends back home in New York. I'm tired of staying away."

"So don't," he says, like it's the easiest thing in the world. "You don't think if you told your dad what happened he wouldn't give his blessing?"

"I'm afraid to find out, if I'm being honest. This project is a lot. Nothing can go wrong right now. It'll complicate things. They're complicated now."

I don't share any of the moments we've had in the near week we've been here. Those are just for me.

"Then just exist here, in the now. Worry about it later. You're here for two more weeks, right? No one is staring over your shoulder at every move you make. This is a gift, Roman. Why not let yourself touch a bit of happiness?"

Could I do it? I've already offered friendship and that seems to be going well. Would two weeks be enough? Would we be able to get each other out of our systems and move on once and for all or would we be right back to where we started, all longing glances and tension?

"You're much smarter than Matteo," I say lightly. "Thank you, Christian."

He bumps me with his shoulder.

"Go get your girl."

***

Andy isn't where she last was. In fact, neither is Raphael. Matteo is neck deep in a bottle of champagne, but he's coherent enough to tell me that they left together when I ask him if he's seen Andy.

A weight settles in my stomach.

Fuck. I'm too late.

"Think he was walking her back, but I dunno," he slurs, draining the bottle. "Good luck, captain."

I leave the club without a second thought. I race down the stairs and push through the dance floor to the door. The temperature outside has dropped and I shiver as I make the quick walk to the stadium to grab the car. I don't see them walking the streets, so I'm hoping that means I'll catch them on the drive home.

I break into a sprint when I near the stadium. I rip the driver's side door open and slip into the plush leather seat. I turn the engine over and peel out of the parking lot, anxiously drumming my fingers on the steering wheel.

Please, please, please don't let me be too late.

I can barely breathe by the time I pull up to the Airbnb. There was no sign of them on the streets, which either means she's safe in our place or he took her back to his. I jog up the stairs and punch in the code on the padlock on the door. My hands are shaking so badly it takes me three tries to get it right.

I shoulder open the door and stumble into the living room. It's dark. It feels like a tomb. I cross the room toward her bedroom and knock on the door before swinging it open. I can't wait for her to answer. I need to know.

I step into her room, and there she is, turning down the covers like she's been waiting for me all this time.

She freezes in place, wide eyes taking me in. She's in that little silk pajama set again and I know my decision has been made.

"Roman?" she asks, eyes wide with alarm. "What's wrong?"

"You left with him," I grit out. Fuck, I'm panting. "You left with him."

She stares at me like I'm crazy, and maybe I am.

"I had a headache. I wanted to leave. You and Christian were talking, I didn't want to interrupt. Raphael offered to walk me so I left."

Logical. Responsible. Smart.

"You should have asked me."

She folds her arms across her chest. She lifts her chin in that stubborn tilt that I love so much.

"And ruin your reunion with your friends? No. Plus," she adds, "it's not your job."

I scrub my hands down my face. Not my *job?* Everything is my job where she's concerned.

"Did he kiss you? Did he *touch* you?"

"What?" Anger and confusion war in her eyes. "Roman. No! Where is this coming from? Why are you acting like such a fucking neanderthal right now?"

"Because I want you," I say. The words are guttural, raw. She freezes. "I want you, Andy. I want you so badly I can't think straight."

"You— you want me?" she repeats, almost as if she didn't hear me.

"I do. Since that first night and every day since." I cross the room toward her. She scoots back until her legs bump against the mattress. "New deal. We do what we want for the next two weeks. We can be whoever we want to be. You want to eye-fuck me in public, sweetheart, go right ahead. If I want to get my head between those fucking thighs of yours, you let me do that, too."

I watch her throat work on a swallow.

"Two weeks? And then what?"

"We go home. We go back to our life. Two weeks. No rules. Just us."

"Just us."

I nod. It's the longest minute of my life as she rolls her lip back and forth between her teeth. Finally, she looks up at me and I see it. She wants this.

"Okay, Roman," she says softly. "Two weeks."

My mind goes peacefully, wonderfully blank. Now all I need to do is move.

I grin down at her.

"Then put your hands on the bedpost, baby, and let me touch you."

Chapter 11

ANDY

My body moves on its own.

I do as he says.

I turn around. I place my hands on the bedpost.

Oh, God. What did I just agree to? Two weeks, just us. Nothing else. Two weeks and we go back to real life.

I know I've just broken my own heart. I know there will be no recovery from this.

From him.

Those warning shouts go out of my mind as I feel him step against my back, the warmth of him bleeding into me and then his hands are on me. Those big, rough hands slide up my hips, my ribs, across my stomach.

I can hear my rough breathing, feel the pounding of my heart in the tips of my fingers. I feel the wetness pool between my legs as he brushes his nose up the column of my neck.

"Been thinking about this," he murmurs against my throat. "About you." His hands slide up my arms. He peels the thin little straps of my camisole down my shoulders. "Can't be as good as I remember, can it?"

My moan is breathy as he kisses a slow path down my shoulder. His hands slide up to cup my breasts. He thumbs my nipples through the silk, turning them into hard little points. He pinches me through the fabric and my head drops back against his chest.

"Nah, it is. Isn't it? It's that fucking good, Andy."

I nod, almost delirious as he shoves my top down, baring my breasts. I let go of the bedpost and his hands drop.

"You take your hands off the bed post and I stop touching you," he says. I scramble to get my hands back into place. "Good girl." His hand smooths down my back in a long caress. "You look so pretty like this."

His left hand comes up to sweep across my collarbone before circling my neck. The gold of his signet ring is cool against my fevered skin.

This is what I remember. His dominance. His filthy, filthy mouth. The way he knows me, reads me, teases me. He thumbs my nipples again, rolling them between his fingers. He remembers. He remembers what I like and just how rough he can be.

His hand slips lower, untying the drawstring at my waist.

"Have you thought about this?" he whispers, nipping my ear. "Thought about me touching you like this?"

I nod. "Yes," I say, because I know he likes to hear it.

"When you're alone and you touch yourself," he whispers, "whose name do you cry out?"

"Yours," I moan. "Only yours."

"And those other men?"

"What other men?"

He snarls against my throat.

"God fucking damnit, Andy. Spread your legs."

I do as he says. I spread my legs wide. He doesn't let go of my neck as the thick fingers of his right hand slip beneath the silk. He cups me over my underwear and hisses in satisfaction. He gives an experimental thrust against my back and I feel him. He's hard as steel as he twitches against my backside.

"Roman," I plead.

A satisfied rumble moves through him.

"I won't fuck you. Not here."

"What?" I ask, my mind clearing for a moment. "Why?"

He rubs small little circles over the apex of my thighs and coherent thought leaves me once again.

"Because Sergei is across the room and I want to be able to listen to you scream when I get back inside you, Alexandra."

I rub my ass back against him, desperate for any sort of friction I can get. I can feel myself leaking through my underwear. I've never been this turned on, this ready. He grips the fabric, pulling it tight against me and I gasp.

He pulls the fabric aside and slowly, deliberately, he swipes his index finger up my slit.

"Oh, God," I whimper.

I feel his smile against my neck.

"Oh, you're ready for me aren't you?" He gathers my arousal on his fingers and gently massages my clit. My knees buckle against him. "You walk around this wet for me all the time, sweetheart?"

I nod, because it's true. "Yes. Always. I—" I stop myself.

"You what, baby? Tell me," he urges.

His hand slides down further between my legs and he pumps half a finger inside me. Sweat breaks out along my brow.

"I imagine crawling under your desk at work and getting you off while you're on conference calls." He groans and slides his finger inside me. I clench around him and he rewards me with a slow pump of his hand. "Bending over the conference room table for you. Letting you eat me out on top of it. Our secret. Only we know."

"Fuck," he spits. "You'd let me do that?"

I nod. I'd let him do just about anything. My nails dig into the bedpost as he slides his finger out and makes another slow, tortuous path over my clit.

"You were made for me, weren't you? Just for me." His fingers move faster and I moan.

"Please," I beg. "Please. Waited so long for this."

His smile is wicked. "All the more reason to take my time."

I wiggle against him, grinding down on his fingers. He moves fast, slipping two fingers inside me. My head falls forward and I bite my lip to keep from moaning again. He pumps leisurely, kissing up and down my neck over and over again. My orgasm is building, coiling at the base of my spine. Those slow, languid pumps of his fingers are unraveling me.

"Roman," I gasp. "Let me touch you."

He chuckles and it's dark as night against my skin.

"Needy, sweetheart?"

"Yes," I say, my self control abandoning me.

He teases me for a few more torturous seconds, nibbling on my ear and the place where my neck meets my shoulder. I push back against him and he hisses.

"Touch me, Alexandra," he commands. "Now."

His fingers slide out of me and then I'm turning and in his arms. My hands are in his hair as his mouth descends on mine. His tongue sweeps into my mouth and I'm a goner. I press myself against him as tightly as I can. His arms come around me, sliding down my waist before palming my ass. He lifts me and guides me to wrap my legs around his hips. I squeeze, remembering how much he loves that.

"Shit!" he barks, thrusting between my legs.

His mouth is divine. The ultimate drug. He licks into my mouth like he can't wait to get between my legs. I nibble his lip, tugging hard on his hair. The pain spurs him on and he drops me on the bed.

"Shorts off. Right now."

I scramble to obey. I slide my shorts down my legs.

"Sit up. Bend your knees up and spread them for me."

I can't even think about being embarrassed. I'm desperate to come, desperate for him. I sit back and draw my knees to my chest and then widen them as far as I can go. He stands at the edge of the bed. The raw hunger in his eyes is enough to make me shake as his gaze drops between my legs.

"So fucking perfect." His tongue darts out to touch his lower lip. "And so fucking *mine*."

His knees hit the floor the same time his arms wrap around my thighs. His eyes are burning when they meet mine and then he dips his head.

His tongue moves up my center in one long, languid stroke.

"Oh, fuck," I breathe. "Fuck."

He yanks me to the edge of the bed and spreads my thighs as far as they can go. His tongue was always magic but my memory doesn't do it justice. He sucks my clit into his mouth, moaning at the taste of me.

I press my hand over my mouth to keep from screaming as he devours me. He's staring at me from between my legs, his mouth and jaw glimmering from my wetness. It's the hottest thing I've ever seen.

"Worshiped as you deserve," he says against my skin.

He slips a finger inside me and my eyes roll back in my head. The timing of his tongue and finger sync up and I'm barreling toward my release at lightning speed. The vibrations from his moans are earth-shattering. I curl my fingers into his hair and tug.

"Come, baby. Right on my tongue. Show me who it belongs to."

He gives me one hard suck on my clit and I come, riding his face until my vision falters. I can barely breathe, barely think, as his fingers take me for all I'm worth. I'm shaking when he pulls away. He plants soft kisses up my thighs and stomach. He nuzzles his face below my breasts, his heartbeat galloping against my ribs.

"We have a lot of time to make up for," he rumbles. His hands squeeze my thighs. "We share a room from now on."

"Okay," I breathe. "Yes."

I feel his lips curve against mine.

"So eager to please, baby."

My laughter is hoarse. "Yes, sir."

His head lifts. His irises are blown, nearly all black.

"You want to put that smart mouth to use, Alexandra?"

I lick my lips. "Yes."

He groans, sliding off me. He undoes his jeans, his eyes on mine. I sit up, helping him shove his pants down his hips.

"This is going to be fast," he warns. "You drive me crazy, Andy."

It turns me on to hear him call me that and it's like he knows. His mouth lifts into that lazy grin that drives me wild. His pants drop to his ankles and his cock springs free, falling heavy against his leg.

He's huge. Bigger than I've ever had and so deliciously thick. He slips his hand into my hair and wraps it around his fist.

"Suck," he commands.

I slide my tongue up his shaft, moistening him with my mouth. I flick my tongue over his tip before sinking him deep into my throat.

"Fuck," he groans. His head drops back. "So good."

I grin, bobbing my head faster and faster. I grip the base of him and squeeze in tandem with my mouth, working him into a frenzy. His breathing turns harsh and I know he's close. His hips move, fucking into my mouth with near violence. I'm already worked up again, so much so that I slip my fingers between my legs and rub.

"Oh, baby," he murmurs. His fingers flex hard in my hair. "Yes. Yes. Right now, Andy."

I moan around him and that's all he needs. He jerks once more and comes down my throat just as I find my own release, my thighs closing hard around my hand. I slide off him, spent, delirious, happy.

I hear him zip his jeans back on and then he's lying next to me on the bed. His hands are soft as they brush the hair from my eyes. We don't speak, but Roman and I never needed words. Everything is right there in his eyes.

"Okay?" he finally asks.

I nod, smiling a little. "Yeah."

He hesitates, which is unlike him. He takes my hand in his and rubs his thumb over the ring he bought for me earlier.

"Was it... what you remembered?" he asks, almost shyly.

I grin at him. "Are you asking me how often I think about that night?"

His green eyes meet mine. "Maybe."

We've never talked about it. Not once. I always wondered what he thought of it and if it haunted him like it haunts me. In any other world, we would have texted and called each other. I would have told him how badly I needed to see him again after that night every day. I would have snuck in and out in the middle of the night if I needed to. I would have gone to him.

"It was better," I admit. "God, Roman, I've thought about that night so many times. If I was good, if it meant anything to you, if you were half out of your mind like I was that whole weekend."

His expression turns earnest.

"I did. You rocked the foundation of my life, Andy. I almost went back to the club Sunday and bribed the security guard for the scan of your I.D. so I'd know how to find you."

My heart twists in my chest.

"So why didn't you?"

He brings my knuckles to his lips. "I wasn't sure what it meant to you. I've never... had a connection like that with someone."

"Neither have I." I pause. "I like hearing you say my name," I confess. "It sounds... right."

"Andy?" he asks, and he's smiling. "Not calling you that felt like the last remaining shred of my willpower."

"And now?"

"All my willpower is yours," he says quietly.

I see the emotion in his eyes, the sadness, the longing. I wonder if he's regretting asking for this. Two weeks won't be enough, and we both know it.

"Let's get you cleaned up," he says, breaking the tension.

He scoops me up and carries me into the ensuite bathroom so I can straighten myself back up. I hear my bedroom door shut and then reopen and then he's in the bathroom with me, brushing his teeth. I give him a curious look.

"I told you," he says, breath sweet and minty. "We stay together from now on."

***

I call Willow as soon as we reach Umbria.

Sergei no sooner has the car in park before I'm swinging my door open and launching myself from my seat.

Roman's light eyes meet mine in the rearview mirror in question and I wave my phone at him in a silent response. He calls my name once but I don't stop power walking up the long drive, cypress trees standing tall like silent soldiers around me. My hands are shaking as I put the phone to my ear and let it ring.

It's evening in New York. If I know Willow, and I do, I know her and Wes are sitting down to watch the Yankees game with a nice bottle of wine.

I started my spiral halfway to Umbria. The emotion of watching Roman hug Matteo and Christian goodbye is still lodged in my throat. Roman's eyes were clearer than I've ever seen them when he slipped into the car. I wonder if he found some closure in coming back here. Matteo and Christian both made me promise to take care of their captain, and I assured them that I would do my very best.

I moved deeper into my spiral when an email from my stepfather, George, came through. I barely see him anymore. Once I rebelled in college, they made their disapproval known. Now I only see him and my mother when they need me for something.

Sure enough, the mayor is holding his annual charity ball next month to raise funding for the children's hospital. Images are everything for the McNeil's— something I learned too early on in my life.

It's important, George's email read, that we provide a unified family front and show up for a good cause. His wording made me think that maybe my step-grandparents are under some sort of fire. It wouldn't be the first time and I'm sure it won't be the last.

Though our relationship is tempestuous, we came to an agreement before I left for college. One event once a quarter. No complaints, no eye-rolls. I show up, I play the part of the socialite I hate so much, and I go home. I wonder what my mother had to do to get them to agree to that.

My hands shook as I sent back my response to his email: ok.

After that, my mood was beyond salvaging. I passed the cable to Sergei for his music choices and we listened to Perry Como's best hits for the last hour of the our trip.

I could feel Roman's eyes in the mirror for most of the drive. His gaze has always felt like a touch, lingering on pulse points and the delicate skin of my inner arm and thighs. I squirmed in the back seat for a good long while under his gaze.

Which leads me to my last level of my spiral: I let Roman Bendetti get his mouth between my legs last night.

My future boss.

I know this is a bad idea. I know it is. From the outside, you'd never know his world had just been rocked. He's always so collected, so calm. Seeing him the way he was last night... I shiver. Waking up to his nose brushing up the column of my throat, his hands wandering and squeezing my hips as he brushed a leisurely kiss to my neck was everything I ever dreamt of over these last three years.

He's forever intense, forever cracking away at me. Fear grips me roughly by the throat.

I quicken my pace, nearly sprinting through the olive grove and into a little garden at the back of the villa. A belvedere greets me, the marble columns thick with ivy and strong beneath the curved iron dome.

"Andy?" Willow's voice finally connects over the line.

I slump onto the marble bench, fingers trembling as I brush my hair from my forehead.

"Hey, Will."

"What's wrong?"

Willow is one of the most intuitive people I've ever met. She's so hyper aware of everyone around her. Even the slightest tonal change has her hackles rising. It's not surprising to me that she can read the defeat and the anxiety in my voice from thousands of miles away.

"Have a minute?"

I hear a cork pop in the background. Wes' deep voice echoes over the line.

"Hey, A!"

I grin at the nickname. Wes is one of the best men I've ever met. His friendship has been an unexpected joy in my life.

"Of course. What's going on?"

I sigh. "It's a lot."

"I'm here. Tell me everything."

I do. I tell her about Roman's initial deal of friendship, the '*my wife*' comment, the game, the club, what happened last night. I explain our new deal: two weeks as just Andy and Roman. Just us. No titles, no labels. Just two people in Italy.

I tell her about George and the email and the gala next month. It's been months since I've seen or spoken to my mother—something I know Willow understands quite well.

She lets out a low whistle. "Jeeze, Andy," she finally says. "Are you okay?"

My laugh is watery as I bite at my thumbnail.

"I don't know."

It's as honest an answer as I can give. I *don't* know.

"What do you want to do about Roman? Will you be able to walk away in two weeks?"

"What choice do I have?" I ask weakly. "I feel like if I don't do this, I'll regret it and wonder for the rest of my life but doing it..."

"Also seems dangerous?" she prompts.

"Yes," I murmur. "It feels like I won't be able to walk away but I can't help but feel like so much of this is because of how everything happened, you know? Maybe it's the thrill of 'what could have been' and maybe it's not this intense."

Even *I* can hear the lack of conviction in my voice.

"Andy," she says softly, "I think we both know that's not true."

I slump against the bench.

"Yeah," I say in defeat. "I guess we do."

"Or," she counters, "Roman sees that you two are meant to be together and you figure out a way to make it work when you get back to New York."

Panic has me glued to my seat. Somehow, the thought terrifies me even more that this could maybe be real. That he could feel like this. Want this, the way that I do.

"Andy?" she asks when I fall silent.

"Why is that even scarier?" I whisper.

"Hope is scary," she says. "Makes us do all sorts of crazy things."

"Like agreeing to sleep with your future boss for two weeks, no strings attached, and pray he feels enough to change his life so we can be together?"

She laughs. Damn, I miss her. I'd give just about anything to be curled in my apartment with her, drinking wine on the couch.

"Yeah, something like that."

"God, this is so dumb." I rub my eyes. "It could end in disaster."

"Or your happiness," Wes chimes in. "You deserve a shot at trying to be happy, Andy."

"And if it all comes crumbling down?"

I can practically feel his shrug over the line.

"Then we help you pick it up."

Gratitude riots through me. I have so many good people around me and sometimes I don't know what I did to deserve it.

"We'll handle George as we always do," Willow adds, all business. "I'll see if Brooks can get Wes and I an invite for some back up."

I smile though she can't see it. Brooks Harper has all the power in the world at the mercy of those impressive hands. Securing an invitation should be easy enough for him.

"Thanks. I appreciate it."

"I've got you, Andy," she murmurs.

My heart tugs painfully.

"And I've got you, too."

Chapter 12
ROMAN

Sergei and I unload our bags into the villa. It's a beautiful home with porcelain tiles, warm walls, sweeping staircases and a kitchen custom made for cooking. Through the sliding doors in the living room, I watch the vineyards undulate over the hills before disappearing from sight.

The main house is a go-kart ride away. Dominic Mazzaro rents this property out year round for tourists looking to immerse themselves in the Italian countryside. Getting him to rent this property to me was like pulling teeth. I offered him double his usual price because we're only staying for two days and I've ruined his other renting prospects for the rest of the week.

I stretch my back and groan, wincing at my stiff muscles. It took us over four hours to get here. I'm desperate to lay down and take a nap, but I know there's a lot I need to do before I can get to that.

"Beautiful," Sergei says, staring out at our view.

There's a nice size deck right off the kitchen with a few day loungers and a covered hot tub. I glance up at the cloudless blue sky above us. Dominic's place is far enough removed from Orvieto that there won't be any light pollution to block us from the stars.

An idea crosses my mind.

A bottle of wine, Andy and I under the stars curled up on one of those daybeds. My lips twitch. If I only have two weeks, I'm sure as hell going to make them count.

"I am going to rest. Let me know if Just Andy is okay. I worry about her."

"So do I," I admit.

"Call me if you need anything, yes?"

I nod, watching him take the stairs up to the second floor.

The front door bangs open again and I turn as Dominic strides in.

He's a handful of years older than me, but you'd never know it by the looks of him. His black hair has begun to gray at the temples but it only adds character to the rest of his ruggedly handsome face. His blue eyes are smiling as they meet mine. He pulls me into a tight hug, clapping me twice on the back.

"Good to see you, Dom," I say, finding that I really mean it.

"You, as well. You look good, Roman." He searches my face and nods to himself. "Happier than I've seen you."

"I was able to see some of the team," I say, following him into the kitchen. "It helped. Thank you again for pushing the meeting back."

He waves me off and opens the fridge.

"It rained all weekend here, anyway. Not good weather to see the vineyard. It's still muddy. We will have to take precaution tomorrow if the sun isn't able to dry everything today."

Dom grabs a cold bottle of white wine and pops the cork. He pours each of us a glass and slides one my way over the island.

"*Cin Cin!*" he says wryly.

I grimace, but touch my glass to his.

"Cheers," I echo, and sip.

Dom's mother and my mother were longtime friends. My father exploited every one of our familial connections when he made my travel itinerary back in the spring.

Dom and I grew up fairly close and I always considered him a good friend of mine. When my time in the league took off, it was harder and harder to come out and see him, but we kept in touch. His family winery, *Casa Mazzaro*, has been passed down through the last ten generations. They have some of the oldest vines in Umbria and are known for their white wines. Dom also makes some of the best sparkling wine in the region.

His mother is currently on vacation in the French Riviera. Dom's grandmother, the matriarch of the Mazzaro family, insisted on meeting us since Lillianna was away.

"Where is your travel partner?" he asks.

I'm about to answer when the front door opens again. As always, anticipation roils in my stomach when I know Andy is near. Her sneakers squeak over the tile as she rounds the corner.

Andy is a book I know well. Sometimes, I think I know her better than I know myself. She spins her emerald ring around her finger and I already know she's anxious. There's tension around that usually smiling mouth of hers and those chocolate-colored eyes I love so much are void of light.

When she sees Dom leaning against the island, all of it evaporates. Her hands drop to her sides and the tension in her eyes and around her mouth vanish so quickly I'm left wondering if I was hallucinating.

"You must be Alexandra," Dom says, offering her his hand. "I'm Dom."

"Andy," I say quickly. "She prefers to go by Andy."

The look she shoots at me is grateful, if not a little surprised.

"Hi, Dom," she says. "Nice to meet you."

He grabs another glass from the cabinet and gives her a healthy pour. It feels like a silent test when he slides the glass her way. She swirls and sniffs with comfortable ease before tasting.

Her eyes widen in surprise.

"Trebbiano is hard to find in the states," she says. "Well, at this quality, at least."

His smile is lazy when it comes. "You know your wines," he says, impressed.

She leans her hip on the counter and her perfume wraps around me. My fist tightens where it rests on my thigh. I've been haunted by the scent for years and not once has it failed to drive me insane.

"I spent half my life here," she says quietly. "My nonna was a big fan. Plus, my best friend is a level three sommelier and she's given me half her education by proxy."

"My gain then," he says, all charm.

Andy blushes and it's the most infuriating thing I've ever seen.

I'm ready to hurl my wine glass at his head when he clears his throat.

"My nonna should be here any moment. I apologize in advance," he says, wincing. "She is as opinionated as they come."

"I'd expect nothing less," Andy says.

She takes the stool next to me. Under the counter and away from Dom's prying eyes, I run my index finger over the back of her hand. She jolts, but recovers quickly. Dom peppers Andy with questions and I watch, finger brushing against my lips, as she forces brightness back into her eyes and smile.

Dom's grandmother makes her entrance a few moments later. Her gray hair is braided back from a face that has been deeply tanned and lined from the sun. Her mouth is hard and slashed to the side in a semi-permanent frown. Her dark eyes are stern and assessing as she rakes them over Andy and I. Though she's small in stature, the confidence and authority rolling off her make her seem larger than life.

Andy visibly stiffens beside me as Nonna settles her cracked and worn hands on her hips.

"Nonna," Dom says, leading her closer. "You remember Roman, right? This is Andy. They work for *Cin Cin*."

"I know who they work for," she says, her English broken and rough. Her eyes flick to me and linger. "*Hai bisogno di tagliarti i capelli, ragazzo.*"

I touch my hair experimentally. I don't think it's too long at all.

Andy still hasn't moved.

Nonna's eyes meet hers. They stare at each other for a long, long time.

"*Sposata?*" she asks, waving back and forth between the two of us.

"No," Andy says.

"Yes," I say at the same time.

Andy's wide eyes meet mine. She whacks me in the chest.

"We're not married."

"You stay at the main house," Nonna says, gesturing to Andy with an ancient hand. "Only married couples stay together."

"Dom." I glower at him.

He holds his hands up.

"House rules."

Andy slides from the stool.

"That's fine. I'll stay at the main house if it'll make you more comfortable," she says only to Nonna.

My dreams of drinking wine wrapped around her on the daybed crumble into dust.

"Good girl," Nonna croaks. "I remember, Roman. You were a good boy. You come to take our wine?"

I shake my head. "I want to buy it from you. All the credit of your vineyard will remain on the label, but it will be ours instead of yours."

"Convince me," she says, dismissing me. "Andy, let us go to the main house to prepare dinner."

Andy casts a forlorn look back in my direction and scoops up her suitcase. She follows Nonna like a soldier heading into battle.

***

Dom and I make our way up to the main house a few hours later. Sergei wakes from his nap and joins us on the patio for another glass of wine. I forgot how funny Dom is. He's quick to laugh and sharp as an asp. My face is aching as I step inside Dom's family home. The villa is a sight to behold but this...

The warm stone on the outside of the house is covered in crawling ivy. The travertine entryway spreads throughout the entire first floor of the house and up the large staircase in the middle of the foyer. The kitchen island and counters are made of yellow and white mosaic tiles. Fresh rosemary and eucalyptus hang over the stove, their oils loosened by the water boiling below. The floor-to-ceiling windows offer a panoramic view of the vineyard and the hundreds of Trebbiano grapes waiting to be harvested.

Nonna commands the kitchen, snapping commands at Andy left and right. Andy's face is flushed from steam, her blonde hair curling away from her face. She presses the side of the blade into a fresh clove of garlic before tossing it into the pan on the stove.

It smells like my childhood. I miss Nicco more at this moment than I think I ever have. We used to help our mother make dinner almost every night when my father worked late in the office. I want to text him, reach out to him, but I don't. Showing that side of me... It doesn't come naturally. Plus, I don't trust Nicco to take it seriously. He's more likely to send back a thumbs up than admit any real sort of emotion.

"Set the table," Nonna orders, waving a wooden spoon toward Dom. "Andy, the spinach."

Andy does as she's told and adds the spinach into the pan in front of her. The next series of moments are calm and graceful as she stirs in heavy cream and chicken stock. Nonna drains the pasta in the sink beside Andy, cloaking her in another plume of steam.

"Roman, the bread." Nonna jerks her chin to the freshly made loaf of bread. "Sergei, get the wine."

I grab a knife and begin slicing, artfully arranging it in the little bread basket she's provided. Music pours out of Nonna's ancient speaker and Cass Elliot's soft voice wraps around us. Andy hums along, murmuring the words low under her breath.

"You sing, *bambina*?" Nonna asks, turning to face her.

"I do," Andy says, adding chopped chicken into the pan. "Not as often any more."

"Shame," Nonna says. "Singing makes people happy."

She shrugs. "I suppose so."

"Sing it louder," Nonna barks. She waves her wooden spoon toward her own throat. "Like you mean it."

Andy flushes and turns back to the stove.

"I'd rather not, Nonna, if that's all right."

Nonna scoffs, indignant. "Sing or don't sing, I don't care. There is no use hiding in the shadow, Alexandra, when you were born for the light."

I pause in my cutting. Andy's shoulders tense. I'm tired of not going to her and making sure she's okay. Nonna glares as I abandon my post and cross the room, dropping my hand to Andy's waist.

"Are you okay?"

Andy stirs with agitated movements.

"She looks just like *my* nonna," she chokes out. "She wasn't as stern, but they look so much alike."

I sigh. "Sweetheart, take a break. I got this." I move to take the ladle from her hand but she shrugs me off.

"I can't," she whispers. "I can't."

I hear the tears threatening her voice.

I brush a soft kiss to her shoulder.

"We'll talk later?" I ask.

She nods jerkily before switching off the gas. Andy sets the skillet down on top of the oven pad on the long dining room table. Nonna mutters something unintelligible.

Something is wrong. She was off in the car and when she took off like that, I was ready to chase after her when Sergei stopped me with a hand to the arm.

"Space," he'd said. "Give her her space."

It nearly killed me to do it.

Dinner comes together in harsh commands and more barking, but soon we're all seated at the table together. Andy's eyes remain down on her lap and she eats robotically. The food is delicious. Nonna was always a master class in Italian cuisine and it's exactly as I remember it. Dom opens a bottle of sparkling wine and makes a turn around the table, filling our flutes.

"I know we have a lot to talk about," I say, watching the fine bubbles dance in my glass, "but I have a personal request, business aside."

Dom reclaims his seat.

"Oh?" he asks, interested piqued. "What's that?"

Nonna grunts, eyeing me with contempt.

"I was wondering if you had any unlabeled sparkling wine that I could buy off you."

He tilts his head. "Sure. I have plenty in my cellar. What do you need it for?"

I feel Andy shift beside me as she sips her wine.

I tip my head toward her.

"We have friends back home that recently got engaged. Sparkling wine has a special meaning to them both— well, the first crushing of the grapes. I was hoping to private label something for them as an engagement gift."

"Roman." Andy's eyes flutter shut, almost in defeat.

Her hand finds mine under the table and she squeezes.

"That's a thoughtful gift," Dom says. "We could mock up something while you're here. I can throw it on the labeling machine and have it ready and shipped home to you by the end of the month."

"Thank you. I appreciate it."

Dinner passes in comfortable conversation and more wine than any of us need. After her third glass of white, Nonna's harsh commands soften. We talk about the past, our adventures as boys. Dom regales Andy with every embarrassing story he knows about me and I watch carefully as she laughs at the right time.

She's learning everything about me, but the longer I see the strain linger by her eyes, I'm realizing that maybe I don't know as much as I think I do.

When Nonna stands to clear the plates from dinner, Andy excuses herself from the table. She slips outside, scrubbing her hands over her face. She drops to the marble railing and stares out over the countryside.

"What is wrong?" Nonna asks by my side. She jerks her head toward the patio doors.

"Andy lost her nonna a few years ago. It's been a while since she's been back but you… look like her. I think she's hurting."

Nonna mutters something under her breath. She shoves the bread basket into my unsuspecting arms.

"She is haunted by something," Nonna says, scuttling over to the fridge.

She removes a few cups of chocolate mousse. Dom grabs a port from his wine fridge and pops the bottle.

"What are you going to do about it?" she asks.

"Me?"

"No," she barks. "Santa Claus. Yes, you. What are you going to do?"

"What is there for me to do?"

"*Dio*," she mutters, shaking her head in exasperation. "Are all men so thick in the head?" She bangs her fist against her temple. "Go comfort her. Help her find her voice again. Do not just sit and let it go by you."

She thrusts two cups of mousse my way. Dom nods sagely behind his grandmother.

"She's right."

"Of course, she is," I grumble. "Why wouldn't she be?"

Nonna barges by me and opens the door. She calls Andy back inside. Her eyes are glassy when they meet mine. I hand her a cup of mousse and she takes the small spoon from it and licks the chocolate from it.

My eyes follow the motion.

"Very good, Nonna," Andy calls, setting the cup down. Nonna waves her off. "If it's all right, I'm going to go up to bed."

"Andy," I begin, but she shakes her head.

"I just need the night, Roman," she pleads. "Please. Can you give me that?"

I search her eyes. I hate the idea of leaving her alone when she feels like this, but I respect her too much to press her any harder.

"All right," I say, stepping back.

Relief sweeps over her. "Thank you."

"Harvest is early," I say. "The vineyard crew will be here early in the morning. I was planning on helping Dom out when they get here, but maybe we can talk after?"

She nods. I watch her bid Nonna and Dom good night. She makes her way toward the stairs. I should just let her go, but I never did learn when to quit.

"Andy, wait."

She pauses mid-way up the staircase and I take them two at a time to meet her. I brush the hair from her eyes and press a soft kiss to her forehead.

"Sweet dreams, baby."

Her eyes fill with tears.

"Good night, Roman."

Chapter 13

ANDY

I sleep until lunchtime.

I tossed and turned for a good long while before sleep finally tugged me under but once it did, I slept like the dead. I slide the duvet off my legs and stretch. My head feels clearer today. I move to the windows and draw back the thick white curtains. The vineyards stretch before me and I watch the workers bob up and down the rows as they harvest the Trebbiano.

It doesn't take me long to spot Roman. It seems like I always know where he is, like there's some sort of compass in my chest and he's my true north. I watch him chug water from a bottle, his white t-shirt damp against his chest from sweat.

I owe him a conversation from yesterday. I wanted to tell him, but I didn't trust myself to say the right things. When he offered to buy all of Dom's sparkling wine for Willow and Wes, the final dam around my heart burst wide open. He's the most thoughtful man I've ever met and he wants none of the recognition. I know how much it'll mean to both of them to have such a gift.

I grab my book from my bag and draw myself a bath. I run down to the kitchen to pour myself a cup of coffee. By the time I make it back into the bathroom, the soap has bubbled and the water is deliciously warm. I soak for a long time, working my way through my coffee with one hand and finishing off my book with the other. It's a peaceful morning and one I needed. Being able to see so much of Italy is a blessing, but we have a lot of travel in front of us.

Intentionally slowing down is something I've tried to be mindful of over the last few years. Willow is good for that. She reminds me to breathe, look around. I can get swept up easily, caught in the undertow of life and events. These silent moments help recharge my internal battery.

I towel off and get dressed and head back to the kitchen for breakfast. Nonna is waiting for me this time at the dining room table. There's an empty coffee mug by her right elbow and a book in her hands. She glances at me when I stop by the fridge.

"It is lunchtime," she states.

Sheepish, I turn to meet her.

"Yes, I know. I was more tired than I realized."

She nods thoughtfully and sets down her book.

"He is running you ragged," she says, hauling herself from her chair. "Sit. Let me cook for you."

I shake my head. "That's okay, I don't mind doing it."

"Let an old woman take care of you, girl," she says, batting me away. "Someone needs to."

I stare at her. Her eyes are the same shade as my nonna's, a frothy-cappuccino-brown. She smells like linen and lemons and I force myself not to hug her.

"Roman told me about your nonna," she says, as if reading my mind. She pats my cheek. "I am sorry for your loss."

"Oh," I say in surprise. "Thank you."

"What is your family name?"

I lean my hip on the counter as she takes eggs from the fridge and begins whisking them in a bowl.

"My father's last name was Matranga. Nonna was from Sicily originally though she lived all throughout Italy in her twenties and thirties. When dad passed, my mother remarried. I didn't want to change my name, but my stepfather said that would mean we weren't a family if I didn't, so I became a McNeil."

She tuts under her breath. "Men are neanderthals," she complains. "Always wanting to label their property."

I huff out my agreement. "You got that right."

She shocks me by laughing. "Ah, your nonna would be proud, Alexandra. You are a remarkable woman."

My throat burns with unshed tears.

"Thank you."

She finishes making breakfast for me and lays scrambled eggs with fresh tomatoes and olive oil over a toasted piece of focaccia. I don't remember the last time anyone made me breakfast. She hands me the plate and I set it on the counter and hug her.

I don't even realize it until my arms are around her. She stiffens for a moment before she hugs me back. She strokes my hair and soothes me and I shudder against her once. When I go to draw away, her little hands tighten on my back. I burrow against her, breathing her in. She hugs me for a long time, saying nothing. I squeeze my eyes shut.

"I'm sorry," I say, finally letting her go. "I always wished I could hug her one more time."

"You would never let her go if you could," she says quietly. "Anytime you need one, you come to Italy and see me." She taps me gently on the chin and I smile. She nods, satisfied. "Eat outside. Get some sun. Feel her around you. She has never left. It will be okay, Alexandra."

She pats me on the cheek and exits the room, leaving me alone. I take her advice and scoop up my cup of coffee and breakfast and slip out onto the patio.

I settle into my seat and tilt my head back to the sun, letting the heat sear across my face. Goosebumps prickle across my skin. The breeze ruffles my hair, curling against my face like a hand. I know she hasn't gone far. I know she lives on in me.

"Hey, Nonna," I whisper to the sky.

I'm rewarded with a second warm gust of air. It teases my hair from my ponytail and whips around my face. I chuckle.

"I know," I murmur, picking at my toast. "Look at me, right? What a mess. Although," I add thoughtfully, "you'd probably tell me I'm exactly where I'm supposed to be."

A strong gust of wind rolls through the vineyards. I stifle my laughter as Dom's hat flies from his head and tumbles down the hill, and I know I have my answer.

I sit on the patio table for a long time watching the vineyards below me like they're my kingdom. I watch the grapes transfer from hand to bin to wagon before they're tugged over to the winery on the adjacent hill.

"You're up."

His voice knocks me from my trance. I spin in my chair to face him. Roman hovers to my right, skin dappled with sweat. His damp hair is pushed back from his face and curling at his nape.

"Hi." I offer him a smile.

His exhale is rough as he crosses toward me. He takes a knee next to my chair and tips my chin up with his fingers.

"Better?" he asks, eyes searching mine.

"Better," I confirm.

His lips twitch. "Good."

He shocks me by leaning forward and kissing me. His hand moves to cup my jaw as his mouth moves over mine. It's a lazy kiss, something that tells me he has all the time in the world to do this. I'm dizzy by the time he pulls away.

"Good morning," he says, kissing the tip of my nose.

"Morning," I say, stunned.

Casual intimacy with Roman Bendetti was something I always dreamt of, but never expected.

"Want to come and take a walk with me?"

I nod, abandoning my empty plate. He waits for me to get my shoes on and then he takes my hand and leads me down the steps and into the vines.

"It's beautiful," I say.

"It is. I like working outside," he offers. He swings our joined hands between us. "Feels good. It's honest work."

"Working in an office isn't?" I ask.

"It's fine." He shrugs. "I like this. It's tough work, a labor of love. It's a passion project— an art form, really. All I do is answer emails and make decisions. It feels hollow sometimes. I can't see the difference I'm making— if I'm making one at all. Here, I can see it."

"Is that what you think?"

"Maybe," he says. "But we didn't come here to talk about me," he reminds me.

When we reach the top of the hill, another belvedere greets us. The domed roof is made of iron and cut into star-shaped patterns. Roman takes a seat on the curved bench. He downs half his water bottle and offers the rest to me. I take a few sips before handing it back to him.

"Talk to me," he says simply.

I twist my ring around my finger.

"About what?"

"About whatever it is that you're thinking about. Whatever makes this little line appear right here." He gestures to the space between his eyes.

I frown, tracing the movement. I feel the little ridge form beneath my finger.

"My stepfather sent an email yesterday when we were in the car. I guess it just put me in my head."

He leans forward, bracing his elbows on his knees.

"Why's that?"

I sigh, and lean against the pillar.

"We were never particularly close. I guess not in the way I was with my dad. When I left for college, things sort of splintered apart. It's been strained since then."

He waits patiently. I work through what I want to share. I have fond, powerful memories of my dad from when I was a little girl. My mother used to spend hours with me at night after he passed telling me dozens of stories and showing me pictures. At eight, you don't understand the permanence of death. I didn't understand why he wasn't coming home.

I squeeze my eyes shut.

"You don't have to say anything," he says, seeing the tension on my face. "Not anything you're not comfortable sharing."

"No, it's not that," I say. "I... I guess there's two parts to my life. The part before George, and the part after. They're very different lives."

He jerks his chin up. "Tell me about him."

"He met my mom two years after my dad died. She was working two jobs trying to make ends meet while I went through school. She waitressed at night at a little dive bar in our neighborhood and during the day she cleaned houses and schools in the area. She was always exhausted. I'll never forget it." I trace the wooden plank under my foot with the tip of my sneaker. Anything so I don't have to look at him. "She always smelled like alcohol and cleaner. No matter how hard she scrubbed her hands at night, it was always on her. I think she hated it," I confess unevenly.

"I don't know if I necessarily made it any easier on her. I was ten. My friends were joining dance groups and playing sports and I wasn't allowed to. We didn't have the money for uniforms and there was no way to get me to and from practices. We had one car and it barely worked. She walked most places or took city transit. I'd take the bus home from school and the house would be empty. I figured out how to fend for myself at a pretty early age. She didn't have the energy most nights to make dinner. She was killing herself, trying to make sure we survived." I exhale harshly, sending the hair by my eyes fluttering.

"She loved you," he says softly. "She wanted to make sure you were okay."

"I'm sure," I agree. "It didn't lessen the guilt. I couldn't stop thinking that if I wasn't around, it would make it easier on her. She wouldn't need to work two jobs and do so much all the time. I felt like a burden. Another mouth to feed. She never would have said it out loud, but I know she thought it."

"Alexandra," he sighs.

"It's okay, really," I offer lamely. "I asked her if I could move to Italy and live with Nonna. She cried so hard that night." I blink away the moisture in my eyes. "I wasn't trying to hurt her. I just thought… if I was gone, she'd be able to live her life. Those trips were the only thing that kept me alive. Nonna paid for almost all of them after dad died before George came along."

"How did they meet?"

I fold my arms across my chest and roll my lip between my teeth.

"He was out with a few buddies and my mom was working behind the bar. Slumming it, they said." My laugh is dry when it comes. "The McNeil's have more money than God. George didn't need to 'slum it'. I think it made him feel good to go into a place like that and run up an outrageous tab and pay it off in front of people who were desperate for that sort of freedom. For my mom, it looked like a lifeline. He thought she was beautiful. She was. She is," I correct myself. "He came back a few times and left her large tips and then he started taking her out. He was only in our house once. When dad died, she couldn't afford the house so we moved to the projects. George took one look around and told her to pack her things."

"What about you?"

"He knew about me. It was one of the first things she told him. I think he was fine with the idea at the time, but at ten, I needed help with math homework and history and I don't think George was overly interested in being a parent. He wanted to show my mother the world. You can say what you want about him, but in his way, I think he really loved my mom."

"But not you." His eyes move over my face, like he's peeling layer after layer away.

"No, I don't think so," I admit. "For me, it didn't matter. I had Nonna. She loved me. My dad in heaven loved me. My mom loved me. I didn't need George to love me."

"He should have, though," he says sharply. "Why did your mother stay with him if she knew he didn't want to be a parent?"

"Security," I say simply. "I had back-to-school clothes for the first time in years. I was able to play sports with my friends, go to dances and parties. For a while, that was enough. I think she saw how happy I was to be able to play softball with my friends."

"Do you think she ever loved him?"

"I ask myself that all the time," I confess. "It's another thing I feel guilty for. If she married him for me and not because she loved him. If she left him now, she'd have nothing to go back to. I wonder all the time if she's trapped." My throat feels tight. I take a deep breath.

"George's family comes from a long line of money. Mining," I explain. "Oil and precious stones. They make a fortune every year. My grandparents have a lot of opinions on how things are to be done, how we need to dress and act in public. I was ten, you know? Always bleeding somewhere and with dirty hands and feet. I was homeschooled the following year. I had a nanny, which was just a plain word for a governess. My clothes changed. My after school events were no longer softball, but social clubs for young girls in a like-minded setting. They put me through finishing school so I could really learn what would be required of me in this family." I pause. "And then mom and George left."

"They left?" he asks slowly. There's a storm cloud gathering in his eyes and I shiver at the rage etching across his face.

"My mom wanted to see the world, so that's what they did. My mom never had a lot growing up and I think she was hypnotized by the money. I can't blame her. For a while, so was I. The woman that left me that day was not the woman who came back. Her clothes and hair changed, how she spoke, the things she cared about. My mom was gone. She wasn't there to stop my grandparents from doing whatever. The finishing school, the singing lessons. I was always singing as a kid. A gift I inherited from my dad. But they made it a horse and pony show. I sang at events and at galas and balls. It was like I was a little bird they'd pull from its cage when the moment was right. When they were done with me, I went right back."

He clears his throat and scrubs his hand over his mouth.

"What about your family here?"

"They let me come back. It was something my mom begged them for. George agreed. I think he liked it when I was gone. He sent me twice a year for weeks at a time. I didn't complain. I liked running barefoot through the streets with my cousins. I got some of my wildness back. It was my rebellious streak as I got older. Being in Italy. The drinking, the partying." I stare at him for a long moment, doing the math in my head. "Do you think we ever passed each other on the street?"

His lips twitch. "It's possible. Nicco and I were always out when we were younger. We could have been in the same room a dozen times and never known. Although," he says quietly, "I would have noticed if you were."

The blush that covers my cheeks burns under his gaze. His eyes are soft on my face, contemplative. How many almosts and maybes circle around me? It feels infinite.

I don't know what to say, so I say nothing.

"Keep going," he urges.

"I was eighteen and furious at the world for boxing me into this little gilded cage. I didn't want any of it. I wanted to be in Italy with my dad and my nonna and not feel so bad all the time. The McNeils... They didn't want me to go to college," I say.

"They what?"

"They wanted me to get into the family business, meet a nice rich man and settle down." I smirk at him. "A dutiful little housewife who'd pop out a few well-mannered children and continue the family line. I didn't want to do it."

"Andy, I swear to God." He pushes from the bench and paces the small space.

"I spent a lot of time with the chef," I say. "My nanny was a kind woman and I think she felt bad for me. When I was supposed to be working on my artwork— which I was awful at, by the way— she'd take me down to the kitchens and the chef would talk to me for hours about food and different recipes he liked. I wanted to do that. I wanted to understand how it worked. I told my mom first. I wanted to study food science and do something that mattered to me. The fight that followed was..." I shudder.

"Did they touch you?" he asks quietly.

His eyes move up my bare arms, looking for prints that have long since faded.

"My grandmother slapped me clear across the face," I say matter-of-factly, tapping my left cheek. "She said I was ungrateful and wasted all the potential I had."

He crosses the space and cups my cheek. He ghosts his lips over my skin from my jaw to my ear and back again.

"Are they still in New York?" he asks, and I hear the violence in his words.

"Yes."

"Do I know them?"

"Probably."

He exhales with calculated control.

"Keep going, Andy, before I lose my mind."

"I told them I didn't want to pretend anymore. It wasn't who I was. I didn't want to go by Alexandra, I wanted to go by Andy. I had researched the food science program at Cornell and applied without telling them. I got in with a scholarship. It was the first time I saw a glimpse of my mom in years that night. She begged them to let me go, to let me be happy. George agreed, but I wouldn't be welcome back in his home if I went. That was fine with me. I didn't want to go back. We did, however, agree to a term. I would attend one event per quarter without rolling my eyes or complaining. After that, we didn't need to see each other."

"Asshole," he mutters.

"Yes, but I had my freedom back in a small way." I trail off, eyes hanging on the skyline above his shoulder.

The stone around my heart sinks to my toes.

"And then Nonna died," he says softly.

"And then Nonna died," I echo. I wrap my arms around myself. "Willow and I were fresh roommates. She was the only lifeline I had. I clung to her for all I had. My grief was..." I close my eyes. "There weren't words. I felt like my home had been ripped from me. Nowhere else felt safe. I didn't know who I was without her. I had already lost my dad. I didn't feel like I had anywhere to go. I didn't know where I belonged. Some days, I still don't."

He wraps me in a hug, tucking my head beneath his chin. His hands rub up and down against my back. I feel like I'm having an out of body experience as he hugs me like I'm the most precious thing in the world.

"I begged Willow to study abroad that year," I say against his chest. "I knew how badly she wanted to go to Scotland. When Nonna passed, she shoved her dreams to the side and agreed to go with me back to Italy. I think I was drunk for the entire trip. I was there, but I wasn't. She let me take my space. She loved me silently through the long nights. She held me and slept in my little twin bed with me." He steps away and I brush away a tear. "She's the closest thing I have to a home now. She helped me reshape myself over the last few years. I feel like I owe her everything."

"She's an exceptional human," he says softly.

Our Hot or Not list has a lot of items on it. On the top of the 'not' list, I had added how much I hate when a man wipes away your tears but as Roman's hand cups my face again and his thumb brushes against my skin, I realize I had the wrong men doing it before.

"She is. I missed her when she was gone. Having her back in New York has been amazing. I feel a little selfish being so happy she's back."

"It's not selfish. She's your person. I understand."

There's no judgment in his jade-green eyes. Roman is a fortress. Anything and everything I tell him will be safely locked away.

I scrub my hands over my face. "I guess all of that was to say that my presence has been requested next month for the mayor's charity ball for the children's hospital fundraiser."

He blinks in surprise. "I've been invited to that, too."

I grimace. "You've probably already met my stepfamily a half-dozen times and didn't even realize."

"That's possible. I've become the poster child for Cin Cin at these types of events. I'm sure I have."

"Not Nicco?" I ask in surprise. "He's the social butterfly of the two of you," I tell him teasingly.

His eyes dance in the sunlight.

"He usually attends, yes, but... Nic will get the COO position eventually. I don't know what my father is waiting for, but Nic's been skating by for the last few years. The burden has fallen to me for the time being."

It's unfair that it has, but I don't need to tell him that. He already knows.

He hesitates, which is so unlike him. He works his jaw back and forth before saying,

"I'll be there with you, Andy. You won't need to face them alone."

The chunk of my heart that he owns expands into new territory. Who am I kidding? There isn't an inch of me that Roman Bendetti doesn't have wrapped around his finger.

"We'll be back in New York by then," I remind him somberly. "Back to real life, remember?"

"It won't stop me from being there for you." He grasps me by my shoulders. His thumbs rub soothing circles over my skin. "I will always be in your corner," he says, eyes locked on mine. "No matter where we are. Call me, and I will come to you wherever you are."

My throat locks up, but I offer him a weak nod. He presses his lips to my forehead. We stay locked together like that for a long time, just breathing each other in.

I knew this was a bad idea. I won't be able to let him go in two weeks. I won't be able to pry him out of my heart, out of my skin. I'll have to figure out a way to exist without having Roman like this.

The thought is more than I can bear.

Chapter 14
Roman

I can't stop thinking about Andy.

But then again, what else is new? The ghosts in her eyes will haunt me for the rest of my life. I ache for her childhood and all the things she lost.

I can't stop picturing her as a child alone in a house wrapped in silence. Fending for herself, filling all the emptiness around her... The thought breaks something in my chest.

I hate that she ever felt like a burden. I *loathe* that she even thought for a second that the world would be better without her in it.

It'd kill me to see a world without her smile, hear that cackling laugh of hers I love so much. Andy is a bright spot in the heaviness that surrounds me. Knowing she's felt less than that for most of her life...

I want to show her what she means. Just how important she is.

When I walk her back to the main house, I tug her into the cypress trees on the side of the house and press her up against the wall. I kiss her until we're both breathless and dizzy. She has stars in her eyes when she looks at me and I preen in satisfaction that I can make her look like that.

I stare into those gorgeous eyes for a long moment.

"Dinner at the villa. Eight sharp," I say, pressing another lingering kiss to her lips. "It's a date, Alexandra. Let's not get anything confused here."

She nods, fingers pressed against her swollen mouth. I capture her hand in mine.

"Don't make me wait," I warn, nipping at her fingers.

"Yes, sir," she snips, eyes dancing.

I reach for her but she dances out of my grasp, laughing her way up the stairs. I watch her go, a knot forming under my breastbone. Her laughter is precious to me. I hoard it like gemstones.

I meet Dom back in the vineyard and help him with the rest of the harvest. The sun is just sinking behind the hills around us when we call it quits. Half the field is done and the rest will be picked tomorrow.

"We'll have a fresh crew tomorrow," he says. "I don't like to work them back to back like this. It's rough on the joints." He winces, stretching. "Let me show you the cellar while we're this far out."

I nod, falling into step beside him. He leads me through the production facility and down the stone stairs behind the fermentation tanks. I eye the concrete eggs he uses for some of his white wines with curiosity. When I ask him what it does, he explains.

"Helps the wine circulate with the lees," he calls over his shoulder. "Creates this vortex inside and lets the wine move freely on its own. Pretty cool. Watch your head," he says.

I duck, narrowly missing the heavy wooden beam at the base of the steps. Dom's cellar is a fever dream of wine bottles and barrels.

"Some of this is my own personal collection," he offers, running his hands over a few bottles. "But this is what I've been aging."

The champagne bottles I'm after slumber like ghosts in the riddling racks in the back of the room. I brush my finger over the dark glass, peering inside.

"How long has it been sitting?"

"Three years. Could go for longer, but it can be ready for you in a few weeks."

I gently lift a bottle from the rack, eyeing it in the light. The lees and sediment swirl together at the disruption. Gently, I slide it back into the rack.

Willow is going to lose her shit over this, and I tell him as much.

"I'm glad it's going to a good home then," he says.

I tell him about my label idea and he sketches it out, a cluster of grapes with their names wrapped through the vine. It's a simple label, but beautiful. He tells me he'll send it to his marketing firm and get it mocked up. It's only when we're walking back through the vineyards does he ask,

"How's Andy?"

"Better, I think," I say. "She has some ghosts creeping up on her."

"She's a special woman," Dom says, eyeing the window that belongs to her bedroom. "Nonna likes her."

I scoff. "Does Nonna like anyone?"

He grins. "Yes. She likes Andy a lot. She says she has *cuore*."

I laugh. She certainly does have heart.

"I like what you're doing, Roman," he says, catching me off-guard. "I think it's a cool project. I didn't need to meet with you to make my decision, but it was nice to have you here and work the harvest with us. Shows me that you mean it, that you're taking it seriously."

"I am," I say quickly. "I want this to be successful for everyone involved."

He squints against the fading sun. The tip of his nose is pink from the day.

"Tell me one thing," he says, turning to face me. "Why are you doing this? Andy is your client relations manager. I know why she's here. I know what she's getting out of this but tell me why *you're* here, Roman. Why is this important to you?"

I blink at him. Honestly, I don't know why it's important to me other than having it be the justification I need for walking away from my prior life. I know it's not the right answer. There's no heart in it.

"I think I'm learning that still," I say slowly. "I want my father to be happy. I want the tasting room to be full of people enjoying your amazing wines. I want the employees to be happy and feel fulfilled in their duties. I want this company to be successful."

"That's a lot of stress for one man to carry," Dom says, searching my gaze. "Your answer doesn't impact my decision to sell you my grapes, Roman. I was going to do that regardless."

"I appreciate that," I say sincerely. "The world deserves to know your wines."

His smile is a touch arrogant. "I think so, too." He pauses for a moment and drops a heavy hand on my shoulder. "All I ask is that you think about what will make you happy, too. A management role like this is often a thankless one. You need to find some joy in what you're doing before you get yourself into a place you can't come back from. That's all I'll say about that."

"Thank you," I say hoarsely. "I'll try."

"Good. Will you see Andy tonight?"

"I was planning on making her dinner."

He grins, white teeth flashing. "Good. Enjoy it. Send Sergei up to the main house. Nonna wants to ask him about Perry Como some more."

I laugh. "I will."

I take the little go-kart back to the guest villa over the hill. My body is sore from the day, but there's a sense of joy and peace in my chest that I haven't felt in a long time. I'm excited for tonight.

"Sergei!" I call when I get into the house. I toe off my dirty boots and cross to the living room. I find him reading on the couch, an espresso in hand.

"Ah, how was the harvest?" he asks, noting the dirt stains across my chest.

"Good," I say, and I mean it. "I was wondering if you wouldn't mind heading up to the main house for a few hours tonight. I wanted to make Andy dinner."

His eyes sparkle. "Ah, *si!*" He leaps from the couch. "A romantic dinner on the terrace?"

"That's my hope."

"Very good, Roman. Very good." He clasps me on the shoulder. "You are good for each other."

"You think so?"

"Just Andy only seems to smile when she's with you." The thought floors me. "Be good to each other." He offers me a cheeky grin and slips from the house. I hear the go-kart turn over and then he's gone.

***

I have a lot to do and not a lot of time to do it in. I race upstairs and turn on the shower. I strip my dirty clothes and scrub myself clean until my skin is baby-pink. I finger comb my hair, letting it dry in waves over my forehead. I slip on jeans and a white linen button up, leaving the first few buttons undone.

As I jog back down the steps, I slide my signet ring back into place. I pull the chicken breast from the fridge and turn the oven on. I pull out the rest of my ingredients and set them on the large kitchen island in the order I'll need them.

I open the sliding door, letting the warm evening air brush against me. It only takes a few moments to rearrange the furniture on the terrace. I light candles on the table and turn on the bistro lights Dom wrapped around the railing.

I set the table with Nonna's beautiful white china and a few wine glasses. I eye the garden at the foot of the steps and run down before I can think too much about it. I cut a few flowers and bunch them together before heading back into the kitchen and sliding them into a vase. The calla lilies are sweet and fragrant when I set them down in the middle of the table.

I pop a bottle of sparkling and a bottle of white and get to work. My mother's fettuccine recipe is one of my favorites and I want to share it with her. I want to share everything with her. Halfway through my preparations, I turn on the ancient radio in the corner. I scan the stations until I find one that tunes in all the way. It's an oldies love song station and I grin, thinking of the music my dad used to sing to us when we were kids.

Sweet piano music fills the room and I hum along to 'Forever' by the Little Dippers as I chop up fresh garlic.

"Roman?" I hear Andy's voice echo down the hallway.

I straighten up and run my hands down my shirt, checking for last-minute sauce stains or spills.

"In the kitchen!" I call.

Andy walks into the kitchen and I still my chopping, drinking her in. She has on one of those long dresses again, the hem brushing against her calves. The color is a deep, blushing rose. It adds color to her cheeks in the most distracting way. She's barefoot and her hair is loose and full of thick curls.

"You're beautiful," I say hoarsely. "So beautiful."

I can't believe she's real. I can't believe she's here after all this time, letting me make her dinner. I can't believe, after everything, she's looking at me like *that*.

She blushes crimson.

"Thank you." She tucks her hair behind her ear. "Can I help?"

"You can come over here and kiss me first."

She grins at me and skirts the island. She presses up to her tiptoes and sinks her hands into my hair. I groan at the feel of it and drop my mouth to hers. I kiss her leisurely, exploring her mouth with mine. My hands rove up and down her back, skimming up her bare arms, the column of her neck. She's soft everywhere I touch her. She shivers in my arms.

I don't regret what happened the other night, but now I want to take my time. I don't want to rush again. My desperation runs deep, but I'll rein it in for her. When I do take her to bed again, I don't want it to be in a frenzy. I want it to be slow, thorough, life-shattering.

I kiss her softly once more before pulling away. I wrap my arms around her back and sway us back and forth to the Elvis song that's now filtering through the kitchen. Her eyes widen in surprise but she melts against me, letting me lead her in a little circle over the floor.

It's a side of me I haven't let her see before. I want to woo her, romance her. I never want her to forget these two weeks.

"My dad used to do this with my mom," she says softly. "I would sit at the kitchen table and watch them dance."

I take her hand and spin her under my arm before bringing her back into my chest.

"Yeah?"

She nods. "He'd sing to her and spin her until she was laughing. I used to sit at the table and cheer for them. I always wondered..." She trails off, her hand idly drawing circles on the back of my neck.

"Wondered what?" I ask, still moving us across the floor.

"If I'd ever find a man to dance in the kitchen with."

My heart lurches to the back of my throat. I want to be the only man she dances in the kitchen with, but I can't bring myself to say it. I kiss her instead. She whimpers in the back of her throat as my tongue brushes hers. The sound goes straight to my cock.

"If you keep making noises like that, sweetheart, we'll never get to dinner."

She hums. "Would that be so bad?" she asks, voice husky.

I kiss her on the tip of the nose and step away from her.

"I want to do this right, Andy," I murmur. "I've waited a long time to do this with you."

"Okay," she says, surprised. She inhales deeply and glances around the kitchen before her eyes snag on the set up outside. She crosses to the patio doors and opens them, taking in the flowers and candles. "Roman," she whispers, impressed. "This is beautiful."

I can't stop the pleased smirk that passes across my lips.

"For you," I say honestly. "You deserve everything in the world, Alexandra."

Her eyes are misty when they meet mine.

"Thank you," she says, and the sincerity in her voice is so heavy I can practically taste it.

I pour her a glass of sparkling wine and slide it her way.

"Come and help?" I ask, hoping to clear the sadness in her eyes.

We move together in the kitchen as I show her how to roll out fresh pasta. It takes her a few tries to get it right, but the triumph in her eyes practically steals the breath from my lungs.

We make the cream sauce together and bake the chicken. We talk and laugh and steal kisses as we go. It's the second most memorable night of my life. She's easy to be with. Talking to her feels natural, like I've been doing it for far longer than I have.

"Oh," she says, cranking up the radio. "My nonna loved Patsy Cline." As she stirs the pasta into the sauce, Andy opens her mouth and sings.

She *sings*. She doesn't mumble or hum. She sings loudly, just for me. I stop cutting the loaf of bread before me and listen, eyes on the smooth column of her throat and mouth as the words pour out of her. Her voice is rich, husky, as she sings and sways to the song in front of the stove.

For all my life, I'll remember her like this: singing barefoot in the kitchen and me, half in love with her already. Her cheeks are flushed when she turns toward me and I nod, encouraging her to continue. Her smile is soft, pleased when it comes. I grin at her, folding my arms across my chest.

I could listen to her forever. In the morning when I first wake, before bed in the evening. In the car, in our house, bumping around in the next room. I want Andy's voice to mark every inch of my life.

"Beautiful," I murmur, when the song ends. "Can I get you to sing everything to me from now on?"

She smacks my arm playfully. "Shush," she chastises, blushing deeper. "It's just okay."

I scoff. "Baby, that was more than okay. Your voice is gorgeous."

She grins at me shyly and I'm ready to throw it all away for her if she keeps smiling at me like that.

We take our dinner outside to the terrace and pull our chairs close together. The stars twinkle above us and the music floats out from inside. She looks stunning in candlelight, the warm golden glow flickering over her skin. Her eyes are depthless; her mouth is curved into that little smirk I adore.

"This is so good," she compliments, twirling another bite of pasta around her fork. "Family recipe?"

I nod. "It belongs to my mom. She used to make it for Nicco and I every Friday. Felt like a reward for getting through another school week."

"Ah, like the classic Friday night pizza night."

"Exactly," I say. "When the business took off, it became scarcer and scarcer, but I loved those Fridays after school. The whole house smelled like baked bread and pasta and her perfume. They're some of my favorite memories."

"Where is your mom?" she asks gently. "You never mention her."

I sigh, dropping my fork to my plate. "Things have become more complicated in the last few years. Her and my father separated a few years back. The business is his life, and their relationship suffered for it. They don't want to divorce. They still love each other too much for that. She moved back here, to Italy, five years ago. She bought them a house. When my dad retires next year, he's coming back here to try and make it work again."

"So they've just been living separate lives for the last five years?"

"Yeah, they have. It's worked really well for them, actually. We all get together around the holidays, but then she comes back to Italy. They talk all the time and visit each other more frequently, but my father wanted to give her some of her independence back. She sacrificed years of her life taking care of Nicco and I when he worked late." I shrug. "They'll figure it out. They love each other too much to give up."

"Oh," she says, voice small. "I hope they do. Your father is a good man."

"He is," I say slowly. "He means well with everything he does. Cin Cin grew past what he ever imagined. Things changed. The family adapted. We figure it out. We're Bendetti's. It's what we're known for."

She chuckles. "Put that in a signet ring," she teases.

I huff. "We should." I eye the ring on my left pinky finger. The white rose and B stare up at me accusingly.

"All done?" she asks, nodding to my empty plate.

We clean up and pack the rest of the food away and then we're left staring at each other in a dimly lit kitchen. She licks her lips nervously. I could take her to bed tonight. I could crowd her up those stairs and peel the dress from her body and get on my knees. I want to.

"Roman," she begins, wringing her hands together.

"We don't need to do anything, Alexandra. It's been a big day and we've covered a lot of bases." I hold out my hand. "Maybe for tonight, we just look at the stars. Okay?"

She nods, and slides her hand into mine. I grab a blanket from the back of the couch and the wine from the table and slip onto a chaise lounge. I spread my legs and let her lean her back to my chest. I top off our wine glasses and pull her back against me, setting the wine bottle down by our feet. She burrows against me and we gaze skyward, watching the sky move above us.

I wrap my arms around her waist, fingers making idle patterns against her hip bone.

A shooting star whizzes past and she gasps in excitement.

"Make a wish," she whispers.

I already have it, I think.

I couldn't wish for anything more than this.

***

Around midnight, I walk her to her room. Her eyes are cloudy with sleep and wine and her skin is warm from mine. She turns to face me at the door and rests her hands on my chest.

"Thank you," she says softly. "This was the best date I think I've ever been on."

"It won't be the last," I promise her. "We still have two weeks. I plan on making the most of them."

She grins up at me. "You don't need to do that, Roman. Just this," she says, moving her hands to my shoulders, "is enough."

"Hardly," I mutter, tugging her closer. "You deserve everything I can give you, Alexandra. Let me," I insist.

"You're going to spoil me," she warns.

I grin, dipping my head and pressing my forehead against hers.

"Good. You deserve to be spoiled rotten," I murmur.

I kiss her softly. I don't let myself linger too long. I know what will happen if I do.

"Good night, baby," I say against her mouth. I kiss her one last time.

When I go to step away, she grabs me by the collar of my shirt and hauls me back. Her mouth is urgent, insistent, under mine. I give in to her and mold my hands to her waist. She wraps her arms around my neck and kisses me senseless, her breasts crushed against my chest.

I'm ready to beg her to let me inside when she slides down my body, pecking me once more on the lips.

"Good night, Roman."

She shoots me that coy little smile and I laugh incredulously.

"Minx," I call.

She winks at me. "You were the one who said they wanted to go slow, not me."

I nod, laughing. "And so I did."

She wiggles her fingers at me and shuts the door right in my face.

I lean against the wall, laughing.
It's going to be a long night.

Chapter 15

ANDY

"You have everything?" Nonna asks for the millionth time as I roll my suitcase into the living room.

"I think so," I say, scanning the room for anything I may have left behind.

"If you don't, you can always come back."

I quirk my brow at her.

"Are you going to miss me, Nonna?" I ask wryly.

We had breakfast on the terrace this morning, just the two of us. She asked me about my nonna, my dad, and my life in New York. I asked her about her life, her children, and grandkids. Her entire face transforms when she speaks about them. I propped my head into my hand, a bittersweet ache rocking through my chest. They're so lucky they still have her and they don't even know.

She harrumphs, throwing her hands up in the air.

"You kids are so vain these days," she grumbles.

I grin, pressing a kiss to her soft cheek.

"I'm going to miss you, too," I say. "Thank you for everything."

Her eyes soften just a fraction. She surprises me by placing a weathered hand on my cheek.

"I'd be proud to call you one of my grandchildren," she says.

"Damnit, Nonna," I bark, tears pricking at my eyes. "You're killing me."

She laughs, patting my face. "Take care of Roman, will you? He's a good boy, but I think he's a little lost, too." I stare at her. "Perhaps you can find your way together."

"Maybe," I say softly. "I hope so."

Roman and Sergei pick me up from the main house shortly after. Roman hugs Dom and Nonna goodbye. Nonna whispers something furiously to him, wagging her finger in his face. Dutiful and slightly chastised, Roman nods.

Dom hugs me hard, pressing a kiss to my cheek.

"You're welcome back anytime," he says to me. "Thank you for everything."

"Thanks for signing on," I counter. "It means a lot to him." I nod my head toward Roman.

Dom shoves his hands into his pockets and rocks back on his heels. He looks like he wants to say something else to me, but Roman drops his hand to my arm.

"Ready?"

I nod, offering Dom and Nonna a final wave before sliding into the back seat.

Veneto passes in the same fashion as Umbria and Tuscany.

We make the long drive through the countryside and Roman makes his pitch to Lorenzo Borelli at his estate. The Venetian Prealps spread around the vineyards, rising like spikes of a crown from the earth. It's the most beautiful place I've ever seen.

I have half a mind to twirl in the field of wildflowers like in *The Sound of Music*.

Lorenzo is a behemoth of a man with a neck the size of a tree trunk. His Garganega is world-renowned for its melon and tangerine notes.

Lorenzo counter offers Roman for three tons instead of four but he'll add in a ton of Glera that we can use to make Prosecco. Roman reruns the numbers but agrees. He sends Dom and Lorenzo's contracts to his father when we get back on the road.

The next time we stop to stretch our legs, he lifts me around the waist and kisses me until I'm out of breath. Sergei whoops and cheers as a wine-red blush stains my cheeks.

Roman is grinning too broadly to be embarrassed. He kisses my knuckles and winks at me and I feel like everything around me is some sort of cotton candy-colored dream. The emotion rolling through my chest has sweat prickling along the back of my neck, but I choke it down.

We're on the road to Piedmont when Sergei makes an abrupt exit switch, ditching the highway to get off for Milan.

"Where are we going?" I ask, leaning forward in my seat.

Roman smiles at me in the rearview mirror. "Thought we could go shopping," he says casually. "We were driving right past it anyway. I thought you'd enjoy it if we stopped."

The excited screech I let out makes them both laugh. We navigate our way through the city and I soak in as much as possible at the churches and historic buildings we pass by. Sergei fights off traffic and finally gets us to the Galleria Vittorio Emanuel II.

The building before me is massive, stretching far enough to cover three city blocks. My eyes sweep over the arches and columns and even from the street, I can see the rise of the dome in the center of the plaza.

When we step inside, the glass dome ceiling has my neck breaking to take it all in. Sunlight filters through the windows and I marvel at the artwork around me. Each storefront is built into marble arches and columns with street lights hanging overhead.

The names make me dizzy. I wince, patting my wallet apologetically as I eye Prada with naked lust.

Roman says we can grab lunch while we're here since the Galleria has a few restaurants tucked inside it. Sergei excuses himself and says he'll meet us for lunch. Roman takes my hand and leads me to the middle of the central dome.

He points to the mosaic at our feet.

"That's the Savoy coat of arms. Legend has it, if you spin on the bull with your right foot, it'll bring you good luck. It needs to be a full circle though," he warns.

I use his hand for balance and step on the bull, offering up a silent apology. I spin in a circle, laughing as I fight for balance. His eyes are tender on my face when I step off.

"Don't you want some luck?" I ask as he leads me away.

"What do I need luck for?" he says over his shoulder. His smile is devastating. "I already have you."

I float on a cloud behind him, my heart lighter than air. We walk for a while and I feel overwhelmed and intimidated by the designer stores we pass.

"Where do you want to go first?" he asks.

"Honestly, Roman, I don't think I can afford most of this," I admit. "Maybe a bag at Prada, but not much more."

He furrows his brow. "Was I not clear?" he says. "I wanted to take you shopping, Alexandra. We'll be spending *my* money, not yours."

My jaw drops. "What?"

He grins, kissing me on the nose. "I told you I was going to spoil you."

He tugs me along before I yank him to a stop outside of Dior. I gape at the dresses on the mannequins and he takes that as a sign to lead me into the store. I nearly stuff my hands in my pockets. I don't want to touch, look, or breathe on *anything* in here.

"Can I help you?" The woman working the floor stops us.

Her silk black suit hugs her like a second skin. I'm very aware I'm in old blue jeans and a sweatshirt and sneakers. I glance at the name tag pinned to her blazer. Maria.

"What do you want to look for?" Roman asks. "Maybe a dress for the gala next month?"

Maria's eyes widen in surprise. I feel a touch smug and hide my laughter behind my hand. Roman grins at me. This must be how Vivian Ward felt in *Pretty Woman*.

Big mistake. Huge.

"This way."

She leads us to the back of the store where the dresses are. I eye each one with trepidation. The prices on the tags are enough to make me feel nauseous.

"Roman," I whisper. "Roman, this is way too much. I can't let you do this."

He smirks, dropping his hands to my hips.

"*Let* me?" he repeats. "I want to. Pick what you like. Money isn't a problem, Alexandra."

I move to the right, nearly dizzy, and eye a sparkling dress in the color of spilled champagne. The neckline plunges to the navel. There's a thin layer of mesh covered in crystals to close the dress together. The train is long, longer than I would need. Out of everything in here, this one feels the most like me.

Roman gestures to Maria.

"Can she try this on?"

Maria takes my measurements. Someone comes by and offers Roman a flute of champagne. He follows me back to the dressing room, taking a seat on the blush-pink velvet couch. I step inside the fitting room, heart racing.

I eye the price on the dress and wince. It's too much money. I tell myself no matter how much I like it, I won't let him buy it. It'll be enough of an experience to just try it on. I shimmy out of my jeans and sneakers and yank my sweatshirt over my head.

The silk on the inside of the dress whispers over my skin as I step into it. The color is beautiful, more dusty-rose up close than I was anticipating. I slide the off-the-shoulder sleeves into place and call for Maria to zip me up.

She slides into the room behind me and fastens the clasp and works the zipper up and secures the buttons that fold over it. I twist my hair off my shoulder and stare in the mirror.

"It suits you," she says almost begrudgingly. "The color is lovely for your skin tone."

"Thank you," I mumble.

She opens the door and leads me out into the main fitting room area. Roman pauses with his champagne flute halfway to his mouth. I step up onto the pedestal, blushing furiously as his eyes rake over me.

Maria helps me fix the train, letting it fall to the ground behind me. The straps hug my upper arms like a second skin and the sweetheart cut of the décolletage puts my breasts on proud display.

The plunge to my navel sparkles in the light and I run my hands against the glittering fabric.

"It'll need to be hemmed, of course," she says, waving her hand toward the train. "Otherwise, it will need no other alteration."

Roman runs his tongue over his upper lip. His normally light eyes are nearly black as they meet mine in the mirror. He discards his champagne flute and moves beside me to stare at my reflection.

"I know you, Alexandra," he mutters, twisting a lock of my hair around his finger. "I know you're working out a way to convince me not to buy this for you."

"I'm not," I lie.

His laugh is dark as midnight.

"Liar," he purrs. "Tell me how much you love it," he commands softly. "And don't even think about lying to me again."

I shiver at his voice. I love when he gets demanding. When he looks at me like this.

"I love it," I confess. I twist in the mirror, admiring the back and the silk buttons that cover the zipper. "I think it's beautiful."

"Then you're going to let me buy it for you," he says. "So that way when you put it on, you remember who you're wearing it for."

I nod, unable to speak.

"We'll take it," Roman says, addressing Maria for the first time.

Maria notes my measurements and where the dress needs to be hemmed before gesturing me back into the fitting room. I change, watching her sweep the dress from the room. By the time I re-lace my sneakers, Roman is sliding his credit card back into his wallet.

"I had them ship it to my place since we won't be home for a while. It'll be waiting for us when we get back."

Us. We. Our.

I latch onto each of those words, clutching them tightly against me.

I take his hand.

"Thank you."

His smile is all teeth and sharp edges.

"You're welcome."

The way he's looking at me... I'm ready to tug him into a fitting room and get on my knees for him. His brow quirks.

"Careful, sweetheart," he murmurs, running a thumb beneath my lower lip. "I just might let you do it."

He practically drags me from Dior and back into the main hall of the Galleria. We wander for a while, popping in and out of stores. I wander around Prada but can't settle on anything. I find shoes to match my dress in Louboutin. I cringe at the price, but they're perfect and beautiful and I rarely splurge on myself like this.

When I move the counter, Roman beats me to it and slaps his card down on the counter.

"Roman," I begin.

He hushes me. "Let me."

I press my lips together and watch him tap his card against the terminal like he's buying a casual cup of coffee.

"Why?" I ask when we step back out of the store. "You don't need to do this."

He stops walking and drags me to the side and out of the way.

"Alexandra," he begins, his patience thinning. "You don't ask for *anything*. You ask for *nothing* for yourself. I know you love this." He jerks his head toward the storefront. "It makes you happy and believe it or not, I *love* making you happy. So let me, okay?"

I nod unconvincingly. "It's a lot of money, Roman. It's too much."

"If I didn't want to do it, I wouldn't have offered. I can promise you that, Andy. Everything I say to you, I mean."

"Okay," I finally say. "All right. Thank you." I loose a long breath and grin up at him. "That dress was pretty fantastic, wasn't it?"

His smile is blinding when it comes. "It was."

He takes my hand and we meet up with Sergei. We grab lunch at a little bistro and head back to the car. My heart and stomach are full as we head back toward the highway and to Piedmont.

***

It's late Wednesday night when we finally reach the winery we're staying at. We drive up a long narrow driveway that's flanked by olive and cypress trees. Little lanterns guide us toward the main house. White stucco and green ivy greet us when Sergei throws the car in park. The house is huge, and looks more English than Italian in its architecture. I can't wait to see it in the daylight.

We'll spend five days here and visit two different places.

Roman helps me from the car, dropping a sweet kiss to the top of my head as I brush past him. The little dance we've been doing around each other feels like it's coming to a close. I feel his eyes linger everywhere as I roll my bag inside.

There are three skeleton keys left for us on the entryway table. My name is elegantly scrawled on a little piece of parchment and I grin, thinking of the potion bottles in *Alice in Wonderland*. There's a note from our host, saying she'll meet us at the breakfast table at nine.

Our host, Roman says as we find our room, is Lena Alto. She's one of the top female winemakers in all of Italy.

"We go way back," he says, walking me to my room. "She has two daughters of her own. Nicco was half in love with Aurora when he was younger. He ran her ragged, but I think he broke her heart a time or two. They don't speak anymore."

It's hard to imagine Nicco serious enough to ever be in love.

"And you?" I hear myself ask. "Were you in love with the other one?"

That cocky little smirk spreads across his face.

"Jealous, sweetheart?"

I shrug. "Not at all."

I slip the skeleton key into the lock of my room and let myself in. He hovers in the doorway as I wheel my suitcase to the bench at the foot of the dreamiest bed I've ever seen.

White gossamer curtains hang from the four-poster frame, draping to the floor in an elegant sweep. The pillows are pink and white satin. The thick white duvet is turned down for me and I'm itching to crawl right into it and sleep fully clothed if it gets me there sooner.

"No," he finally says, answering my question. "Mira never gave me the time of day. She was pretty, but there was never anything there between us."

Pacified, I nod. I dig my pajamas from my bag and find my toiletry bag in the mess. I love traveling, but I'm getting tired of packing and unpacking my suitcase

I feel him move behind me. He turns me gently and tilts my head up, searching my eyes.

"No one else exists for me but you," he murmurs, eyes flicking to my lips and back again. "No one."

"Roman."

"I mean it," he says, brushing the hair from my eyes. "There is no one else."

I pause, staring at him. "You haven't dated since that night?"

He shakes his head. "No."

My heart drops to my feet. All this time, I wondered. I wondered how many other women saw him the way I did. Touched him, kissed him, learned his body the way I know it. The thought was agonizing, torturous, as I watched him leave night after night, not knowing if there was someone waiting for him at home.

"Did you?"

"I tried," I whisper, unable to take my eyes off him. "They weren't you."

He nods, like he understands.

"It was one night," I hear myself say. "I don't understand how it feels like this."

"It wasn't," he disagrees. "It wasn't just one night." His smile is sad when it comes. "It was three years of staring at you in meetings and savoring every glare and smart ass comment you threw my way. It was sending you coffee when you were late and watering your stupid ficus that you should have just let die. It was taking any chance I could to be near you, see you. I know you think I ruined your nights, Alexandra," he says, voice breaking, "but I didn't have any other choice. I was tired of staying away. Tired of fighting all the damn time to be indifferent." He slides his hands into his pockets and hesitates before he asks his next question. "That morning on the beach," he says, "do you know what I was running from?"

I nod, but I don't say it. I can't say it.

"I feel like I've been running to you and away from you for far too long. I watched Willow leap into Wes' arms after the football game and I was desperate for you to do the same. When you said the loser got to take care of you later on I..." He huffs, shaking his head. "It's a privilege to take care of you, not a burden. That Harper boy raised his hand and I wanted to break his arm. I wanted to tell you that the only person who was going to take care of you was me."

I gape at him.

"You consume me," he murmurs. His hands are shaking as he cups my jaw. "Own me. Rule me. Whatever it is, Andy. You've got me on my knees."

"I—"

"Don't. You don't need to say anything. I just needed you to know. Just once." He presses a kiss to my forehead. "Go get ready for bed."

My body feels stiff, unsure, as I walk into the bathroom and close the door behind me. I stare at my pale skin and wide eyes in the mirror. My hands shake as I grip the edge of the sink and lean against it. There are so many things I want to say. So many things I should have said. He has the power to break me like no one else. He undoes me, unravels me. I stare in the mirror and work up my courage.

The eyes that stare back at me are hard, determined. I'm going to be brave, for once in my damn life.

I throw open the door. He jumps in surprise. He managed to change while I was in there. His feet are bare and there are gray sweatpants hanging low on his hips. His black sweatshirt is warm and thick against him and his hair is ruffled.

"I need you to know," I begin, heart racing against my ribs, "that if I own you, you've undone me." I lick my lips nervously. "Every wall, every parapet, every brick I laid around my heart never stood a chance. It was yours from the second you looked at me in the club. It was yours when you broke it three years ago. It's still yours now."

"Andy," he breathes.

"I told myself when we got to Italy I would keep my guard up. I wouldn't let you get close to me and I did it anyway. I told myself that I would stay away from you and find every reason in the book to keep my distance. But you offered friendship and I... I couldn't say no. I was desperate for any piece of you that I could get. And then after Verona, you offered me something more. I agreed to this stupid arrangement because I needed to know," I whisper.

"Needed to know what?" He's immobile, frozen in place.

"What it was like to really be yours."

Chapter 16
Roman

The clock on the bedside table strikes ten, but I'm suddenly wide awake. The exhaustion that clung to me like cobwebs in the car evaporates as Andy stands in the door of the bathroom, breathing rapidly.

I know I couldn't have heard her right. I know she didn't just tell me that every ounce of that beautiful, precious heart belongs to *me*.

"What?" I say, staring at her.

She lets go of the doorframe and crosses the bedroom toward me.

"I've been yours since the first day," she says.

She presses up to her tiptoes and drags her fingers over the scruff on my jaw. Her smile is a little wobbly when it comes.

This beautiful, stunning, outrageous woman…

I'm nearly vibrating as I reach for her. Tonight, there won't be any games. No teasing touches or promises of later. I can see it in her eyes.

"Kiss me," she says, lips hovering below mine. "Kiss me like all of this is real."

I search her eyes.

"It *is* real, Andy. Every bit of it."

She gasps when I drop my mouth to hers. I back her against the wall, grabbing her hands and pinning them above her head as I devour her mouth. My heart thunders against my ribcage, a riot of nerves and lust roiling together.

I want this to be right. I want this to be everything she needs. Everything she's ever dreamt of.

I lick into her mouth and she whimpers, rubbing her hips against mine. I could kiss her every day for the rest of my life. She's so responsive, so eager. She meets each bruising kiss with one of her own, pressing those perfect breasts right into my chest.

I cage her wrists with one hand and use my other hand to slowly slide it down the curve of her neck, her collarbones before palming her breast. She groans into my mouth as I rub my thumb over her nipple.

"I was supposed to just let you get ready for bed and catch up on some sleep," I rasp, thumb still moving over her. She twitches beneath me. "You make it so difficult, Alexandra, when you say things like that."

She shudders against the wall.

"Then don't fight it," she pleads.

"I don't want to rush this," I murmur. "I want to unravel you. Tease you. Make you as crazy as I've felt over these last three years."

Her laugh is incredulous. When she pulls against my hold, I release her hands.

"Roman," she says in disbelief, "did you not hear what I said? Do you think I haven't been out of my mind for you every day since then?" Her eyes search mine. "That I haven't been *aching* for you?"

Her nimble fingers move to the hem of my sweatshirt. She tugs the fabric up, exposing the lower half of my stomach. Her fingers brush against my skin. I groan, dropping my forehead against hers.

"Fuck."

"Don't make us wait any longer. Please," she says against my mouth. "We've waited long enough."

That little word undoes me.

I can't deny her anything.

When she reaches for my sweatshirt again, I let her lift the fabric. I grip the back of the collar and tug, pulling it over my head. She stares at me, eyes roving over my chest and stomach. A hungry little sigh escapes her as she moves her mouth over the skin of my heart.

I sink my fingers into those honey-blonde curls I love so much and tug at the roots. Her gasp is sweet across my skin.

"Are you sure?" I ask, searching her eyes.

"Yes," she says immediately.

She gently shoves me away and I take a step back. She unzips her jeans, her eyes never leaving mine. I should be doing this, undressing her, kissing each new inch of skin that's revealed, but I can't move.

I can't move as she kicks off her sneakers and steps out of her jeans, dropping them into a heap by her feet. I'm rooted to the floor when she removes her shirt, flicking her hair from the collar and letting it cascade down her back.

Moonlight coasts over her skin, highlighting the goosebumps on her arms and legs. Her little black bra barely holds her breasts in place. My eyes fall to the black triangle of lace between her legs and I don't know what I've done to deserve this— deserve *her*.

She walks to me, head held high. I'd die for her, live for her, whatever it is that she asks of me. I'd do it.

I run my thumb over the curve of her bra, tugging the material down. Her breast spills into my palm and I test the weight of it, rolling her nipple between my forefinger and thumb. She gasps, eyes rolling back in her head as I give it a sharp tug. I'm starving for her. I remind myself to be gentle, to take this slow.

I reach around her and unclasp her bra, letting it fall away. She pants as I drink her in, ready to drop to my knees at her feet.

She moves into my arms and presses against me, skin to skin for the first time in three years. It feels miraculous to hold her like this, to feel her against me. I gasp at the contact of her skin against mine, at her nipples brushing against the hair on my chest.

Her eyes are bottomless and I dive in head first. She stretches up to her tiptoes and kisses me, arms twining around my neck.

My hands skim up her back, across her ribs, down to the curve of her ass. I grip her and drag her against me. She groans into my mouth, tongue swiping along my bottom lip. Andy is as hungry as I am and as much as I want to go slow, I know she has different plans. Her hands skim down my chest and across my stomach.

She fiddles with the tie on my sweats before slowly untying it and working them down lower on my hips.

"Alexandra," I bark when her hand slips inside.

"Roman," she breathes, gripping me through my briefs.

She squeezes and I thrust up into her hand.

"God," I choke out, watching her hand move over me. "All I do is dream about you," I murmur, brushing the hair back from her shoulder. I drop my mouth to her neck and suck the skin into my mouth. She bends against me, her hand still working me up and down. "I want to go slow. I want to savor this," I say, barely recognizing my own voice.

She slips her hands from my sweatpants and slowly works them over my hips. She glances up at me, that pretty little mouth parted in an unsteady breath.

"I think I might die if you go slow," she confesses. "I can't wait any longer."

I help her work my pants down my legs. I step out of them and it's her turn to drink me in. Her eyes are nearly black in the light as she hooks her shaking fingers into the waistband of her underwear and shimmies it down her legs.

We stand there, naked before each other. God, I'm dreaming. I know I am. I can't believe I'm here.

We reach for each other at the same time.

I hoist her into my arms and wrap her legs around my waist. She grinds herself against me, kissing me with a ferocity that has my knees weakening. I barely manage to navigate us to the mattress before I feel her reaching down for my cock, getting ready to notch it against her.

"Easy, baby," I murmur, stretching out on top of her.

She groans in protest, lifting her hips for mine.

"Let me touch you," I say, dipping my head.

She twists her fingers into my hair as I flick my tongue across her nipple, sucking it into my mouth. Her legs move against mine, spreading wider and wider until the tip of my cock is notched against her.

The heat of her, the dampness spreading up my shaft, is making it hard to think straight.

"You feel so good, sweetheart," I praise, moving my head down her sternum.

She pants out my name and I leave open mouth kisses across her stomach. I grip her thighs and spread them wide.

"Roman," she begs. "Please."

I sit back on my heels and stare down at her. She's so pink and perfect and glistening for me already. Eating Andy out is my favorite meal, my favorite pastime. I dip my head between her legs and run my tongue up her slit. Her back arches clear off the bedspread and I grin, watching her squirm over my tongue.

"Good girl," I say, kissing her clit over and over again. "So good for me, aren't you?" I slide a finger inside and she clenches around me. "Oh, yes, Alexandra. Look at you." She rides my finger and I watch her hips move in little circles. She's the hottest thing I've ever seen in my life. Her fingers twist tighter into my hair and I moan against her.

"You going to come before I even get inside you, sweetheart?" I ask, sucking and licking as my finger keeps up a steady pace. "Right on my face?"

She whimpers. "If you don't stop, yes," she grinds out, working her hips against me.

I slide my finger out from between her legs and lean back. Her fingers fall from my hair and she shudders against the mattress.

"So mean," she pouts, hands sliding between her legs.

I smack it away.

"Your orgasms are mine, Alexandra. Touch yourself again without my permission and see what happens."

She bites down hard on her lower lip. She makes a show of spreading her legs for me and drawing her knees to her chest.

I reach for my bag and grab the box of condoms and tear one out of the pack. I rip the foil with my teeth and roll it on. I give myself a few hard pumps, staring down at her. Her eyes are hungry as they watch my hand move up and down.

Her hands slide to her breasts, twirling and pinching her nipples. I grin down at her.

"I never forgot, Alexandra, how much you liked those beautiful tits sucked and pulled on."

She hums deep in her throat and I slide back between her legs. Her arms open, gliding up my back and hooking around my neck.

"Tell me I'm not dreaming, baby," I say, notching myself against her. I give the slightest push in. "Tell me I'm about to get between these legs for real."

"You are," she pants. "Yes, Roman."

I push in another inch and the moan that spills from her mouth is down right erotic. I grit my teeth together and inhale deeply, trying not to blow before I even get inside her.

"Keep your eyes on mine," I command. "I want to watch it. I want to see what I do to you."

She nods, nearly incoherent as I slide home deep inside her. She gasps, back arching, but her eyes never stray from mine.

She's so fucking tight. I feel her walls flutter and pulse around me as I rock back and forth, letting her adjust to the size of me. I hike her legs higher around my hips and sink in another inch.

Home, I think. I'm home. This, with her. This is home. Being together like this. The way we fit, the way we move. The rawness between us.

"Oh, fuck," I moan. "God, better than I imagined. I thought I convinced myself it couldn't have been this good. That you didn't feel like fucking heaven wrapped around me but you do, don't you? My dream girl." I slide out and thrust back in with a sharp snap of my hips. "*Mine*, Alexandra. Tell me."

"I'm yours." Her nails rake up my back. "I've only ever been yours."

Her words set me off. I drive my hips up and into hers with more violence than I mean to, but I can't stop myself now. I fuck her with everything I have, my eyes glued to hers. This is what I remember, the way we seem to speak without words, the way we know what the other needs just by the smallest touch or gasp.

"Ask me who I belong to. Who has me this fucking whipped," I grit, my skin slapping against hers.

"Wh–Who?" she mumbles, clinging to me.

"You," I say. "Only you. Forever owned by you," I grunt.

She cries out my name when I lean back and hike her legs over my shoulders. She's nearly bent in half underneath of me, sobbing as I slide back into her. Like this, I can slip my hand between her legs and thumb her clit until she's shaking beneath me. Every time she's close, I remove my thumb.

Her grin is terrifying, electrifying when it comes. She likes how I play. She likes being denied, likes the build up and the explosive release she knows she'll get.

"You like it," I pant. "You want to come, Alexandra? Beg me for it."

She twists her hands over her head and wraps them around the iron poles holding the headboard together. I ease my pace, thrusting into her with exquisite slowness. I love it like this. Love watching her move, the haze in her eyes. Love watching her suck her lower lip into her mouth, love the desperation in the lines of her body. I can feel every inch of her like this. I watch myself slide in and out of her, nearly insane at the sight of it.

"Oh, yes," I breathe. "Andy."

She doesn't take her eyes off me as I move, rolling my hips against hers.

I can feel her tightening around me and I know she's close.

"I want to come," she breathes. "Please, Roman. Let me."

I shake my head. "Not yet."

"Please, please. Let me." She's almost out of her mind now. "Let me come. Let me squeeze you. Let me give it up for you."

Fuck.

"Look at you," I murmur. "Taking it so good for me." I drop my thumb back to her clit. Her fingers are white-knuckled on the headboard. I make a few quick fast circles and bottom out inside her, picking up the pace. I watch it build inside her, the blush that spreads from her cheeks down to her neck. "Come, Alexandra. Let me feel it."

She cries out my name and comes, squeezing me so tightly my vision blacks out. I drop on top of her, thrusting as fast as I can. Her orgasm goes on forever as she quakes around me. I come, jerking against her as I spill myself inside her over and over again. Her hands are in my hair, on my face, her mouth is everywhere as our tongues tangle.

I roll her to her side, cupping her face. I kiss her with everything I've got, locking her leg over my hip. I can't bring myself to pull out of her. She rocks against me, still whimpering against my mouth. She's going to come again if she keeps squirming like that.

I grip her ass and grind her against me. Her clit hits my pubic bone and she gasps.

"Another one, Alexandra?" I ask, nipping her lip.

She nods, kissing me again.

God knows I'll never deny her anything she asks for. She grinds against me, fucking me with a desperation I've never felt before. I slip my hand between her legs and pinch her clit. She comes on a near-scream, squeezing me almost painfully as she does.

I watch, with wide eyes, as she shudders beside me, her eyes screwed shut tightly, her mouth parted.

"You're exquisite," I breathe, licking up the column of her throat.

I suck and kiss her skin, listening to her heart race against mine. She shivers against me, fingers scratching against my back.

I slip from between her legs, wincing at the loss of pressure as I remove the condom.

She stares up at me like she's never seen me before. I brush the hair from her eyes and press a soft kiss to the space above her heart.

"Okay?" I ask.

She nods, and her smile is blinding when it comes.

"Again?" she asks, pulling me closer.

I grin at her.

"Again."

***

The plans I had to rest never came.

But Andy did. Over and over and over again.

She woke me in the middle of the night, her hand slipping below the sheet to tease me. I repaid the favor ten fold and had her sit on my face until she had to slap her hand over her mouth to keep from screaming while I tongue fucked her.

She was still pulsing from her orgasm when I slid back inside her and drilled my hips into hers. Now that I've gotten a taste again, I'm never going to be able to give it up.

She stirs beside me on the mattress, her hand blindly searching for me.

"Morning," I say, rolling over to face her.

I wrap an arm around her waist and tug, cocooning her against my chest. She snuggles against me, tangling our legs together. I kiss a lazy path up and down her neck and she sighs, content.

"Sleep okay?" I ask.

She snorts. "Not at all, but thanks for asking."

I grin, nipping her earlobe.

"I wonder whose fault that was."

She scoffs, indignant. She wiggles out from under my arms and then she's rising above me, gloriously naked as she plants a hand on my chest.

"Um, I seem to remember that you instigated, too," she sasses. "Don't blame me."

I stack my arms behind my head and smile up at her.

"There's no blame, baby. I'm exhaustedly thrilled."

Her mouth lifts into a half smile.

"Too tired to go again?"

I heat under her gaze.

"Never."

Her grin is sly when it comes.

"Do we have to go to the meeting? Can't Sergei do it by now? Can I keep you here all day?"

I grin and sit up, bringing us nose to nose. I brush mine against hers playfully before kissing the tip of it.

"The sooner we get this day started, the sooner it ends and I can get you to make that little whimpering noise that drives me fucking crazy."

She sighs, allowing me to rise from bed.

"I don't think that's how it works."

Even with the time constraint, it doesn't stop her from jumping in the shower with me. We're both breathless and flushed by the time we turn the water off. Scrubbing her clean is just as much a turn on as everything else she does.

Sergei passes us on the stairs, offering me a little salute.

"Where are you headed?" I ask as he nearly skips down the steps.

"My brother is in Piedmont on business. I thought I'd spend a day or two with him. Catch a game."

I wave him on. "Tell Alessandro hello from me."

"Will do," he says, heading toward the door. "See you soon, Just Andy!"

Andy waves, watching him go.

As requested, we meet Lena in the kitchen at nine sharp. Andy's face is still the color of rosé. Her eyes are dancing and full of life. We find Lena hunched over the stove, muttering under her breath.

"Hey, Leen," I say, smiling.

"Roman!" She nearly drops the tray of quiche when she sees me.

Lena is exactly as I remember her. Her long brown hair is braided back from her face and her hazel eyes are warm and welcoming. There are wisps of gray hair at her temples, but she doesn't look a day older than when I saw her last. She rushes across the kitchen to hug me, peppering my cheeks with kisses.

"Look at you!" she says, pulling back and cupping both of my cheeks. "What did you do with my best boy? Who is this man?"

I chuckle, gripping her wrists and giving them a comforting squeeze.

"I'll be thirty-four, Lena," I remind her. "I haven't been twelve in a long time."

She waves me off. "Kids always grow up too quickly. Time seems to pass even faster for us parents."

"Let me introduce you to Andy," I say, and I can hear how absolutely infatuated I am.

Lena's hazel eyes sparkle with mischief and joy.

"Andy." Lena grips Andy by the shoulders and looks her over. Andy's chuckle is nervous when it comes. Her eyes widen in alarm when Lena crushes her to her chest. "It's so good to meet you."

Andy hesitates for only a moment before hugging her back.

"Thank you for having us. Your home is beautiful."

Lena flushes under the praise. "Roman is as dear to me as my own children. Both the Bendetti boys are," she amends. "It's a true joy to have you back here again. Sit. I made breakfast. Tell me all about your adventures."

We follow Lena to the breakfast nook. The coffee is strong and delicious and I guzzle down half a pot. Lena asks about the last few years and peppers Andy with friendly if not probing questions, but Lena is the type of person who doesn't beat around the bush with small talk. She wants to know the intimate details. Heart-to-hearts, she calls them.

Andy warms up through breakfast, but I can see the curiosity on her face. Lena is a walking embodiment of home and comfort. She's always aimed to make Nicco and I feel welcome when we could come to visit. She's a born hostess, and it shows.

"Rora is in the vineyards," Lena says, gesturing to the bay windows that overlook her land. "Mira and her husband will join us later on tonight."

"Mira is married?" I ask, surprised. "I didn't know that."

"Two years this fall. He's a good man. He can handle her," she adds wryly. Here, she turns to look at Andy. "My eldest is... stubborn. She needs someone who will challenge her and help her see sense when the time comes."

"Sounds like a good balance," Andy offers. Her eyes flick to mine.

"Yes, the perfect blend," Lena agrees. "Just like wine. Some grapes work better together than others. They complete each other, balance the other out. Two halves of a whole, singing together in the glass."

Andy blinks rapidly. "That's a beautiful way to put it."

Lena pats her hand in a very motherly gesture.

"What is wine if not romance, huh?" She shimmies her shoulders and Andy's mouth pops open.

"I think you're my soul mate," she whispers in shock.

Lena erupts with laughter and wraps an arm around Andy on the bench they share.

"My ex-husband will be disappointed to hear that, but I think we'll be able to work it out."

I can't stop the smile spreading across my face. Sharing my family with Andy is... everything.

"Let's go explore outside, shall we?"

We clear the table and Andy hovers behind, still a little shell shocked.

"You okay, baby?" I ask as Lena tugs on her boots.

"She's... wonderful," Andy whispers reverently. "If Nicco doesn't marry into this family, I'll do it."

I snort. "Considering the only single male relative is fifty years old, I doubt it."

She shrugs. "If it makes Lena my mother-in-law, I'll do it."

"You're going to make me jealous," I caution.

She presses a smacking kiss to my cheek and follows Lena out to the vineyards. I stare after her, a little awestruck.

Lena's property is gorgeous. Lush green hills roll for miles, the lines of vineyards waving to us from a distance. From this spot in her vineyards, Mount Monviso rises before us. The sky is blue, the air is crisp with the first signs of fall. Andy hugs her arms around herself as we walk the rows of grapes. Lena talks about her growing season and all the things she's excited about.

The Barbera and Dolcetto are perfectly ripe and ready for picking in the next few days. I'm anxious to get my hands on some of the Dolcetto. It's the main indigenous grape in this region of Italy, and most of the world barely knows about it.

"ROMAN!" My name is bellowed from somewhere to my right. Lena grins, crossing her arms across her chest.

"That'll be Rora," she says to Andy. "Roman was the big brother she never had growing up. They were quite close."

Andy's expression closes off as Aurora sprints down the hill toward me. I always remembered her laughing smile, and it hasn't changed one bit. Her black hair swishes behind her in a long ponytail and her green-gold eyes are lit with happiness as she launches herself into my arms.

I barely catch her, staggering a step back as she throws her arms around my neck. The buckle from her overalls digs into the curve of my cheek and I laugh, squeezing her back.

"Hey, Rora," I chuckle, patting her awkwardly. "It's good to see you, too."

She squeezes me hard, body trembling with the boundless energy she always seems to have.

She hops from my arms and grips my face the same way Lena did earlier.

"Look at you!" Her entire face is flushed. "Who knew you'd grow up to be so handsome? I was worried you'd never get your braces off." She grips me by either side of my jaw and gives it a little shake.

I flick her nose. "Why do I need to remind *both* of you I was twelve at the time. I wasn't going to be a metal mouth forever. Plus," I add, "you've seen me since then. I know it's been a while, but I had my braces off the last time I was here."

Rora laughs. "Thank God for that." She pops her hands on her hips. "What took you so long to come back this time?"

"Life is a little busy," Lena reminds her daughter. "He can't jet off like he used to do, Rora. We're just glad you're here now, right?"

Rora nods, looping her arm through mine.

Andy stands stiffly beside Lena, eyes locked on the place where Rora's hand rests on my forearm.

"Aurora, this is Andy," I say, gesturing between them. "Andy, this is Rora."

"Nice to meet you," Andy says tightly.

Rora's hazel eyes swing to Andy and widen.

"And you brought a girl home?" she asks incredulously. She whacks me hard in the chest. "Things certainly do change, don't they? It's nice to meet you, Andy."

Andy nods, but says nothing.

"Are you still painting?" I ask her. "It's been a while since I've gotten an Aurora original sent my way."

She snickers. "Yes, but not as much as I'd like. I do okay at the markets in town, but still waiting to break out. I'll show you my studio later on."

Lena takes us on a tour of the winery, leading us down into the barrel room where she does some of her higher end wine tastings and barrel samples. Rora keeps her arm locked through mine, like she's afraid I may disappear if she lets me go.

Andy inspects the winery equipment and the foot stomping trough in the corner.

"Have you stomped before?" Rora asks, gesturing toward the trench.

"Yes, but it's been a long time."

"Gross, isn't it?" She crinkles her nose, sending her freckles dancing. "My feet are almost always purple." She lifts a booted foot, wiggling it back and forth.

"It's an experience," is all Andy says.

Lena comes over with a few glasses of red wine. She passes them out and raises hers in a toast.

"To old and new friends," she says, catching Andy's eye. "*Cin cin!*"

Chapter 17

Andy

I'VE NEVER CONSIDERED MYSELF to be an overly jealous person, but I'm sick with it watching Aurora cling to Roman's forearm while she talks his ear off. I have no reason to be, considering what we did last night and whose bed he slept in. I swallow down the lump in my throat when she makes him laugh for the fifth time in as many minutes.

He bends his dark head toward her and she mutters something else that makes him smile. I worked hard for his smiles over the years, not that I got many. Watching him toss them out right now so carelessly makes my blood boil. He's just now beginning to look at me like that.

I hate knowing someone else has seen it, too.

Lena is charming and lovely and the perfect host. Seeing the level of openness she shares with those around her is new to me, but I find I don't mind it. The house is just as stunning as I thought it'd be. A large glass sunroom sits to the right of the kitchen on the first floor. I eye the hanging plants and vines that dance across the windows from inside and already know I'll find myself there later tonight with a cup of tea.

Aurora leads us to her studio downstairs. Afternoon sunlight streaks across the warm wooden floors. I gingerly step over the tarp that's been spread haphazardly over the floor and eye the paintings on the wall. There are postcards from all over the world thumbtacked to the wall behind her easel, creating a collage of images.

I study each picture, a little awe-struck at the images she's managed to capture. The golden hour of the sun as it sets behind the vineyard, lush green canopies, crystalline waters from the beaches on the coast.

"Watercolor is unfortunately my chosen medium," she says, breaking my eyes away from a picture of a pond coated in lilly pads and lotus flowers.

"Why unfortunate?" I hear myself ask.

She shrugs, looping her arms into her overalls.

"It's a challenge, but it's rewarding when you get it right. Messy, too." She wiggles paint-coated fingers in my direction.

I fold my arms across my chest and turn to the wall to my right. There are a handful of taped up pictures on the walls, but I pause when I see a watercolor portrait of Nicco. He can't be more than twenty. He's laying in the grass, grinning up at the sky.

Roman bends his head, running his thumb around the edge of the photo.

"These are beautiful, Aurora," he says. "Does he know?"

Her snort is the only reply she offers.

We spend the rest of afternoon talking and getting to know each other on the terrace while tasting Lena's extraordinary wines. When the sun begins to slip behind the horizon and Aurora's stomach growls loudly, we head inside the house to begin dinner.

Lena has a pretty impressive garden along the far side of the house, so she sends me out to forage for a few ingredients for dinner. She sends Aurora with me.

"How do you know Roman?" she asks, squatting to admire a head of lettuce.

I adjust the wicker basket on my arm.

"We work together."

She squints up at me. "He looks at you like he loves you."

I choke on my next breath.

"Does he?" I rasp.

She nods solemnly. "Yes. I've never seen him look at anyone the way he looks at you."

I rip a carrot from the ground with near violence.

"You were that close then?" I ask, trying to keep the irritation from my voice.

"Oh, yes!" She nods enthusiastically. "Roman was the secret dreamer of the group. Mira was always too bossy to play with and Nic was…" She trails off, eyes falling into shadows. "Well, he was Nic. I probably don't need to explain him to you."

"No," I say, "you don't."

"Roman was always the romantic of the four of us. We're kindred spirits that way, but he was like a big brother to me. I've seen him have crushes before in the past, but I haven't seen him like this."

I yank another carrot from the ground, hands shaking.

"Things are complicated," I mutter.

"I don't think love should be," she says simply.

My laugh is a little harsh. "You're probably right."

She studies me for a long time as I fill my basket with carrots and fresh garlic.

She stops me with a hand to the arm.

"It's good to see someone care about him so much. He's a good man."

I nod, but can't bring myself to say anything else. I follow her back into the house when our baskets are full. Lena takes our baskets from us when we step back inside the kitchen.

Roman has his sleeves rolled up at the butcher block kitchen island as he rolls out dough for the ravioli. He catches my eye when I come in.

He gestures to me to come around to where he stands and I do, leaning against the counter.

"Want to learn?" he asks, nodding down to the little squares of dough.

I shrug. "Sure."

He moves me in front of him before the counter and cages me in on both sides. I can see Lena's smile out of my periphery as Roman walks me through the steps.

"There's no need to be jealous, Alexandra," he says against my ear. "Considering where my mouth was a few hours ago."

I shiver against him, but don't stop kneading the dough.

"I can't help it," I admit in a small voice.

He brushes a kiss to my temple.

"Can't say I'm not a little bit flattered."

I elbow him in the ribs. "I can't believe you're getting off to the fact that I'm jealous of someone you've known for half your life."

He rumbles deep in his chest. "I like you possessive, sweetheart. What can I say?"

I sigh, exasperated. A silent chuckle moves through him.

We work the pasta out into sheets and spoon in the mixture that Lena just whipped up. Roman helps me lay the second sheet on top before taking the little pasta cutter and making squares. My few attempts are messy but by the end, I've got the hang of it.

Aurora runs up to change and wash the dirt from her face and we help Lena set the table. The front door bangs open and a little yellow golden retriever darts through the living room. He zooms between my legs and under the table before rushing back to the front door.

"Oh, my God. Harold. *Stop.* You were just here!"

My lips quirk at the exasperation in what must be Mira's voice. Harold knocks into my knees, licking my hand before jetting off again.

Mira rounds the corner and grins at Roman.

"Hey, stranger."

He opens his arms and hugs her hard.

"Hey, Mi Mi. Good to see you."

She pats him on the cheek. "You, too. Hey, you got your braces off."

He sighs in exasperation. "What is it with you Alto women and my braces? It's been *years*, Mira."

She snickers and clicks her tongue. "It was a rough time for you."

"Christ," he grumbles, rubbing his jaw.

Her laughter is amused, joyful when it comes.

"Roman, meet my husband."

A man rounds the corner, his dark head bent to scratch behind Harold's ears. I can barely make out his profile, but there's something familiar about him. When he straightens up, I drop the pasta cutter.

I'd know that face anywhere; the shooting star shaped scar by his left eye that he got when his brother, Gio, knocked him into a dining room chair. I'd know his crooked smile, the deep brown of his eyes in the most crowded of rooms.

At the same time, Mira and I say,

"Luca."

Every head in the kitchen turns my way. Luca stares at me, bewildered. His eyes widen in surprise.

"Alexandra?" he whispers, walking toward me. He squints, taking a good look at my face. He lets out a shout of joy. "Holy shit, Andy!"

He rips me out from behind the counter and hugs me so hard my back cracks. I laugh against his chest, banding my arms around him.

"What is happening?" Roman growls, watching as Luca rocks me side to side.

"What are you doing here?" Luca asks, stepping away. "Jesus, look at you! Where are all the mud stains and battle scars?"

"I'm here for work," I say, swiping at my tears. "Luca." I grip him hard by the shoulders and give him a little shake. "I can't believe it."

Mira looks ready to kill me when she comes to stand beside her husband. She looks between us, dark eyes stormy.

"Luc?" she asks, glancing up at him.

"Mira," he says, still laughing in disbelief, "this is my cousin, Andy Matranga. Well, McNeil now. Right?"

"Cousin?" Roman blurts, looking between us.

Luca nods, still staring at me.

"Our fathers were brothers." He drops an arm around my shoulders and tucks me into his side. "This girl right here was my best friend in the entire world when we were kids."

I blush, ducking my head.

Mira visibly relaxes. "Wait, this is *the* Andy? The one you raced mopeds with?"

Roman stares right at me.

"Guilty," I offer weakly, raising my hand.

Lena watches the exchange with a deep level of amusement.

"The very same," Luca states proudly.

"I have," Mira says slowly, "so many questions."

Aurora joins us and Lena catches her up. Her eyes dart back and forth between me and Luca.

"You have the same eyes," she says, gesturing between us. "Wow, this is so crazy. Mira, what are the chances?"

Mira's lips twitch. "Non-existent, really."

Lena announces dinner is ready and we gather around the old oak table in the dining room. Roman drops a possessive arm around the back of my chair and drags me closer to his side. Luca takes the seat across from me and presses his lips together to keep from laughing.

"Andy, tell me everything. Why didn't you come back to Italy after Nonna passed? We would have loved to have seen you. It was like we lost you and her at the same time."

I nearly drop the bowl of ravioli. The thought makes me sick.

I stare at him for a long time.

"I came back once. It was... too painful to be here. Without her tying me to the family... I just thought..."

"You thought what?" he asks, dark brows drawing together. "That we wouldn't want you around anymore?"

Every conversation has stopped. Roman's hand drops to my knee under the table.

"Maybe," I whisper. "Mom remarried and Nonna died and I guess I didn't know if I could come back."

"Andy," Luca says, bewildered. "You are our *famiglia*. Our sunshine girl. There is always space for you. My mother asks about you every chance she gets."

I suck in a sharp breath at the pain that shoots through me.

"Your mom was always my favorite," I say.

He grins. "I'll be sure to tell her."

Mira watches with the strangest expression on her face. Lena's eyes are sad when they meet mine.

"To second chances," Rora says, lifting her glass. "To the family that lasts forever."

***

After our heavy conversation, dinner passes in a blur. Luca shares every embarrassing story he knows about me. Roman is utterly delighted, leaning his weight on his forearm and staring a hole into the side of my head as Luca tells story after story. His eyes glitter in delight, his index finger running absentmindedly over his mouth.

I squirm under his gaze, trying and failing as I defend myself.

"Okay, okay," I finally say, holding up my hands. "Maybe Mira would like to know every deep dark secret I know about *you*."

"Oh, yes. Please," she says, straightening up in her chair.

"Do *not*," Luca bites out, staring at me. "Andy."

"Why not? You've just dragged me through the mud for the last two hours. It's only fair that I do the same."

Luca gulps. "Okay, but—"

"When Luca was twelve, we dared him to drink two gallons of lemonade. He did, but he peed the bed everywhere."

Mira gasps before dissolving into laughter.

"—anything but that," he says in defeat.

Aurora claps in delight. Lena hasn't stopped laughing once. She's still chuckling as she brings dessert out along with a fortified wine from her cellar.

"Gio dared him to drink all the unfermented grape juice one summer. He threw up purple everywhere."

Luca's cheeks flush scarlet.

"Should I go on?"

"Please, God, no," he begs, even as Mira and Aurora cheer me on.

Roman's chuckle moves through me.

"Why are all of your stories food related?" Aurora asks, biting into a cannoli.

"Because I was a stupid boy who thought he had an iron constitution," Luca says, patting his stomach.

"Which we now know isn't true," I snicker, licking cream from my finger.

He grins at me. "Still the same pain in my ass."

I shrug, smirking. "Still annoying."

"I feel like I'm learning so much," Mira stage whispers. "Andy, give me your number. I'm sure I'm going to have follow up questions."

I blink in surprise, but do my best to cover my shock. Mira does in fact slide her phone across the table toward me.

"I think it would be nice to have you come and visit, too," she offers. "Gio and his wife live up the street from us. We could have a reunion."

My throat is thick with unshed tears.

"I'd like that," I murmur, and I mean it.

"I'm happy for you," Roman says low enough for only me to hear.

I glance at him, cheeks flushed from wine and laughter.

"Yeah?"

He nods, fighting his smile.

"You deserve it," he says. "A chance to reconnect again."

"Italy seems to be giving me everything," I say. I wrap my arms around myself. "I never want to go back."

His smile falls just a bit.

Lena announces that it's time for joint clean up and we all head to the kitchen like dutiful soldiers to clean up the mess from dinner. Luca asks how long we'll be staying and he promises to come back and see me and spend a few days so we can catch up. Lena seems thrilled to have all of her children back under one roof again.

When the kitchen is clean, Mira and Luca head out for the night. Luca hugs me hard, kissing me on the forehead.

"I won't be able to make it tomorrow, but I should be able to get back up here on Friday. Maybe we can grab lunch, just the two of us? I would really love to catch up."

"I'd like that," I say.

He grins and tweaks my cheek. Mira surprises me by hugging me hard around the neck.

"He talks about you all the time," she whispers against my ear. "He misses you."

"I miss him, too," I assure her.

She tosses me a little smile and a wave before marching a sleepy Harold to the car. Lena and Rora say their goodnights and head up to their room, leaving Roman and I alone in the kitchen.

I blow out a breath. "What a day, huh?"

"A day, indeed," he says, holding his hand out for mine.

The playfulness around his eyes is gone and I shiver because I know what happens next. I'm practically vibrating in anticipation as he leads me up the steps and into our room.

As soon as the door is shut, he's on me.

"I can't believe," he murmurs, voice husky, "that you were jealous." He bites down on my neck and I jolt in his arms. "When you know there's no one else I want in this world."

I arch my head back, giving him better access. His mouth is wicked as it teases the spot below my ear.

"You never smiled at me like that," I pant, as his hands cup my ass. "For so long. I guess I was jealous because it seemed so easy with other people who weren't me."

His dark head lifts. "Is that what you think?"

I shrug. "Well, yeah. Roman, you never really smiled at me before this. Here, you can't stop. You're hugging and kissing and smiling at everyone we meet. I wished I could have had that, just once, back in New York."

He stares at me for a long time, jaw working back and forth.

"I'm sorry, Alexandra," he says quietly. "I didn't realize how much I was hurting you."

I cup his face, brushing my thumb over his cheekbone.

"How could you? I had all my walls up, remember?" I ask teasingly. "I didn't want you to know."

He sighs, leaning into my palm. He shuts his eyes, soaking me in.

"I know now," I whisper. "I know which smiles are meant for just me and me alone."

His eyes snap open, flaring with heat.

"Everything is yours," he murmurs, tugging me with him into the bathroom.

He reaches into the shower and turns the water on. The ache that's been building between my legs all day intensifies. My nipples pebble against my shirt, heavy and full.

He turns me to look at our reflection in the mirror. There's a blush rising to my cheeks as he moves behind me and meets my eyes. Steam curls up from the shower stall.

"I want you to watch," he says, voice like velvet. He brushes the hair from my shoulders and runs his mouth up my neck. His big hand splays across my stomach. "I want you to see just how much you own me. That you never, ever, need to be jealous."

I nod, watching his hands move up my body and down my arms. He guides my hands to the edge of the sink and he presses down, a silent command to keep still. I gulp, watching him watch me.

He slides his hands around to the button on my jeans. With a flick of his fingers, he undoes it and works my zipper down. I'm practically panting, already so uncomfortably wet for him. His mouth doesn't leave my neck as his hand slips below my waistband. I widen my legs for him, giving him better access.

He rewards me with a nip to my earlobe and sinks a finger inside me. I can't stop the moan that rips from my throat as the tip of his index finger circles my clit before pushing back inside me.

To see the smile split his face, to feel it against my skin, is like a drug hit. I can't stop the thrill that races through me as he meets my eyes in the mirror again. His finger works in slow strokes and we watch his hand together. My nails dig into the marble as he adds another finger.

"Enough yet?" he asks, watching me.

I shake my head, biting my bottom lip.

"No?" he asks. His other hand skims up and slides under my shirt, palming my breast over my bra. "You need more?"

I nod, lightheaded.

"That's my girl," he murmurs.

He slides his hand out from between my legs and I whimper in protest. He yanks my jeans down my legs and I step out of them when he taps my knee. He kneels at my feet, kissing up my calves before planting a kiss to the apex of my thighs. Watching his mouth move over me makes me want to collapse.

"Take off your shirt and put your hands back on the sink."

I'm shaking as I do what he asks. He shucks his own shirt, baring all that glorious muscle to my eyes. The warmth of the steam pebbles against my skin and I remove my bra, watching my breasts fall free in the mirror.

I place my hands back on the sink and wait for his next move. He drinks me in, rubbing his cock through his jeans.

"So fucking beautiful, Alexandra," he murmurs, running a hand down my hip. "Watch me."

His hands slide up my ribs, the deep tan of his skin a stark contrast to mine. He cups my breasts, palming and tweaking my nipples until my eyes flutter shut. Watching him touch me feels like too much to take in. The flush on my cheeks, the drugged haze over my eyes. My mouth parts as he tugs. I feel it between my thighs like a lightning strike.

"Look at you," he murmurs against my skin. "Look how beautiful you are right now."

He slips his hand back down between my legs and I watch as he parts me and runs his finger around my clit again. I watch him gather the moisture at the tip of his finger before bringing it to his mouth and licking it clean.

"So good," he praises, dipping his fingers back down.

He pumps slowly, working me up until my legs are almost boneless.

"Roman," I murmur, pushing back against him.

I need more. I need *everything* he can give me.

He grips my hip with his free hand, giving me a thrust through his jeans.

"I don't have a condom," he says, rubbing against me.

The rough brush of his jeans over my bare skin has my fingers flexing on the marble counter.

I shake my head.

"I don't care. I'm clean. Birth control." I'm panting, watching his eyes glaze over.

"You want it raw, Alexandra?" he asks slowly, almost in disbelief.

"Yes," I practically shout. "Yes, I want to feel you."

"Oh, my God. *Andy*."

He pauses for only a moment before sliding off his jeans and knocking my legs wider. I watch him grip himself and slip between my legs. He runs his crown over my folds, soaking himself in me. I watch his eyes flare, the hunger and desperation in his gaze as he glances up at me.

He's starving, I realize. For *me*.

He notches himself against me and pumps his hips, working the long thick length of him inside me. My head drops to the marble as he stretches me. It's so deep at this angle, I can feel him everywhere.

"Eyes up," he says, voice tight. "Don't look away."

I manage to lift my head as he sinks the rest of the way in.

"God," I moan. "Roman."

"That's my girl," he murmurs. "Only mine."

The feel of him is incredible. He shudders when he's fully seated inside me. I clench around him and feel him twitch inside me.

"God," he chokes out. "You feel..."

"Unbelievable," I finish for him.

He winds a fist through my hair while the other finds a home on my hip bone. He works himself slowly inside me, rolling his hips and hitting me in that perfect little spot each time. My eyes are glued to him as he moves. His abs flex and contract with each thrust. His chest is heaving, his mouth hangs open as he watches himself move in and out of me.

I've never seen anything like it. The way he looks at me...

I push back against him, desperate for more friction. More everything.

He groans, dropping his head back as he thrusts to meet me. The long column of his neck shines with a thin layer of sweat from the steam and I've never seen someone with so much abandon before.

Every thrust, every look, every touch, burns into me.

My hands slide further and further up the marble until I'm nearly flat on the counter. Roman is content to take his time, winding me up till I'm ready to snap. His thrusts are deep, slow, methodical.

"More," I murmur. "I want more."

"You should know by now I'll give you whatever you want," he grunts, thrusting faster.

I'm almost incoherent as his hips slam into mine. I watch him move in a daze. I hardly recognize my own face in the mirror.

"I can't stop," he says, working himself faster and faster. "Touch yourself for me, sweetheart."

I'm too eager to do what he asks. I'm shocked at how wet I am and I circle my clit, watching it all in the mirror.

His grin is lazy when it comes. He rolls his lip between his teeth.

"Do you see it now, Alexandra?" he asks. His hand squeezes in my hair. The bite of pain makes me gasp. "Do you see how you fucking own me?"

I nod, biting down so hard on my lower lip I nearly draw blood.

"Roman," I breathe.

"That's it," he encourages with a jerk of his head. "Watch yourself come, Andy."

I pulse around him and my orgasm rips through me in waves. My mouth parts on a silent scream.

He moans my name and comes, jerking inside me. His hips ram into mine again and again and again. I can only hold onto the sink as I watch him unravel. The shock on his face, the pleasure, sears into my mind.

He drops his head to my shoulder, breath rough against my fevered skin.

"Oh, God," I pant, legs giving out.

He catches me around the waist and drags me against him. We slide, limp, to the tile floor. He holds me against him, both our hearts racing.

"Now you know," he rasps. "There could never be anyone for me but you."

Chapter 18

ROMAN

I AM THOROUGHLY AND utterly wrecked.

My legs are still trembling under the warm spray of the shower. I scrub my hands over my face, my chest hollow and full all at the same time.

I pull Andy's naked body against mine and rinse her off. She clings to me, kissing my neck and chest like she can't let me get any further than this.

"Are you okay?" I ask, searching her face.

There are unshed tears in her eyes. My own heart has been eviscerated. Whatever shreds of it are left after that, she owns them.

"Yes," she murmurs, voice thick. "It's never—"

"It was intense," I say, brushing a wet strand of hair from her face. "I know."

"*I've* never..." She shakes her head, swallowing thickly.

I've never felt like that before. The unspoken words hang between us.

"Me, neither," I confess.

I brush my thumb over her full lower lip, watching the way she rises to my touch.

She nods, speechless.

We dry off and crawl into bed. I tug her against me, her cheek finding its rightful place on my bare chest, right over my heart. I drag my fingers through her hair and she purrs against me.

"Roman," she murmurs.

God, I love that sleepy and satisfied voice. I love how my name sounds in her mouth. I love the way she knows me, touches me, moves me.

"Sleep," I whisper, tracing her arm with my free hand. "I'm right here."

She throws her leg over mine and presses as close to me as she possibly can. She's asleep in minutes, sweet breath tickling my chin.

What we just did… It changes things.

I lay awake for a long while, just listening to her breathe. I don't know how I'm supposed to walk away in a week. How I'll get on that plane and go home and leave all this here. How I'm supposed to go back to my brave and indifferent face.

I tug her against me as close as I can. I memorize the feel of her, the smell of her skin, the way she fits against me.

I don't think I sleep at all.

***

Lena marches us through the vineyard the next morning, shouting instructions as she goes. Andy slides on her gloves and grabs her pruning shears. Rora bounds behind us, practically skipping to her rows of grapes.

After last night, I'm all too thrilled to work off some of this anxious energy. Andy shoots me a shy smile and I'm ready to lay the world at her feet. She blows me a kiss before following after Rora, her cheeks rosy in the sunshine.

Our sunshine girl, Luca had called her.

It fits her, I think. Bright, bubbly, fiery.

My sunshine girl.

Halfway through the afternoon, my phone buzzes with a text.

I fish it from my pocket and sigh, swiping on the text from Brooks in our group chat.

> BROOKS: I've been elected by the group to send a wellness text. No one has heard from you in days. Your brother is concerned that Andy has hogtied and gagged you and left you for the coyotes in the back of a vineyard somewhere no one will ever find you.

I snort and tap out my reply.

> ROMAN: I appreciate the concern but no, I'm fine. And Italy doesn't have coyotes, jackass. They have jackals.

> WES: Aren't they pretty much the same thing?

> BROOKS: Call your brother. He's worried about you.

> ROMAN: Since when does Nic worry about me? Why are you hanging out with my brother?

> WES: He's our stand-in until you get home. When is that again?

> ROMAN: You both have my itinerary.

> BROOKS: Wait… wait.. Listen. If you concentrate hard enough, you can hear Roman's ass clenching in a vineyard somewhere.

> ROMAN: You're both dead to me.

> WES: How are things with Andy?

> ROMAN: We've called a truce. We're… friends.

> BROOKS: Is that what they're calling it these days?

My lips twitch, but I pocket my phone without a response. My relationship with Andy is my business and no one else's.

We prune and harvest for hours, pausing for lunch. Lena makes pesto and tomato sandwiches and we scarf them down before wrapping up the Dolcetto. It's the coolest day on our trip so far and as the sun sets, the temperatures plummet to the low-forties. Andy shivers in my sweatshirt in the sunroom, her legs propped up in my lap.

Lena and Aurora both turn in early. They have another early start tomorrow, but Andy and I have separate plans. After dinner, Lena pulls me aside and tells me about the farmers market in town nearby. It draws hundreds of vendors from all over Italy.

"When you get back," she said, "we'll talk numbers, okay?"

She gives us a free pass and tells me to make the most of the day. I jump at the chance to spend the day with Andy.

I make idle strokes over Andy's skin as she reads. I watch the Gladiators game on my phone.

"How are they doing?" she asks, nodding toward my phone.

I flip the screen her way so she can watch the game with me. Her eyes dart over the screen just as the ref blows the whistle, signaling a time out.

"Christian's scored two goals so far. He's on fire tonight."

She smirks. "Matteo must hate that."

"Nah, Matteo will be happy for him. Plus, it's better for his ego if he gets a humility check every once in a while," I tease.

She laughs, reaching for her mug of tea. She blows against the surface, sending sweet smelling steam into my face.

"Mmm," she hums, passing me the mug. "Taste that."

I take her mug and sip, letting the hibiscus and berries burst over my tongue.

"It's good," I say, taking another sip— larger this time.

"Hey!" she protests, reaching for her mug. "You're drinking all of it."

I tickle her feet. Domestication with Andy is everything I've ever dreamt of. I love these quiet moments with her. I love having her feet in my lap with my sweatshirt hanging off her. I love seeing her like this. Mine, at long last.

"I'll make you more." I nod my head to the book in her hands. "How's your book?"

She folds the paperback cover down and eyes me suspiciously.

"It's good," she says slowly.

I set my phone down against my leg.

My eyes narrow. "Are you reading a sex scene right now?"

She shrugs. "Maybe."

"Give me that." I pluck the book from her hand and dodge her grabby fingers and hold it away from her. My eyes skim the page. "Holy shit, Alexandra."

"Roman, knock it off!"

I chuckle, reading.

"Is this really what you read?" I ask, glancing over at her. "'His thick, huge member slipped past her folds, stretching her until she couldn't take anymore.'"

She blushes scarlet and snatches her book away from me.

"Leave me alone," she grumbles, holding the book protectively to her chest.

"I'm all too happy to give you a real life show," I say, walking my fingers up her thigh. "All you need to do is ask."

"I'll keep that in mind," she says primly, knocking my searching fingers away.

I chuckle, bending to kiss her.

"You know I can do it better," I murmur against her mouth. "And I know you can take it."

She shivers against me.

"Maybe," she mutters, seemingly unconvinced.

I flick her nose.

"Smart ass."

She grins at me and cracks the spine of her book and picks back up where she left off. She reads for a few more minutes before she glances up at me. She twists the ring I gave her around her finger.

"Roman?"

"Hmmm?"

"I... I'm happy," she says quietly. "I just wanted you to know."

I turn to look at her. My heart stutters and stops in my chest at her words. There was a time I thought I'd never hear anything like that coming from her mouth. God knows I hardly deserve to hear it after everything over the last three years.

"You are?"

She nods, looking pleased. Her golden eyes are lit from within.

"I'm happy with you. *You* make me happy," she clarifies. A balloon fills within my chest. "Are you?" she asks, looking at me with so much hope it nearly kills me.

"Am I what?"

"Happy," she says, nudging me with her foot.

I snatch her hand and kiss her knuckles over and over again. I press her hand to my cheek, nuzzling against it. The tenderness in her eyes makes my tongue feel thick in my mouth.

"Happy doesn't begin to cover it."

Her smile is radiant when it comes. It settles deep in my bones.

No matter where I go, what I do, I'll never forget that smile as long as I live.

Chapter 19

ANDY

I FALL IN LOVE with Roman Bendetti between the mountains and valleys of Piedmont.

Falling doesn't seem quite right. I step into it wholeheartedly. I think I've been half in love with him for years, but there's no denying the line I've crossed to get here.

I love him.

I love him more than I've ever loved another person in my life. He's everything all at once. He's romantic, caring, and sweet. He's intense and thoughtful, strong and confident. I drink in every bit of him that I can.

We wander the farmer's market ten minutes from Lena's house, his arm wrapped snug around my waist.

The wind is cool again today and I pull the sleeves of my flannel down over my hands. I wanted to check out the glass blowing tent and Roman left to grab us coffees while I explored.

I lean against the pole of the tent behind me, watching Roman stop in front of a flower booth on his way back over to me.

Lilies and Dahlias brush against his knees in riots of colors. The black bins before him house flowers of every shape, size, and color. He bends his head, listening to the older man who runs the cart explain each of the flowers to him. Roman nods along, skimming his choices.

I could go to him, wrap my hands around his arm and listen to his beautiful voice, but I stay where I am. I fish my phone from my back pocket and train the camera on him. The white cable knit sweater he has on hugs his arms in the most distracting way. His dark jeans and boots are perfect for the cool weather and I sigh dreamily, soaking him in.

I wait for his smile to come before I snap a picture. I inspect my work, zooming in on the color in his cheeks and the wind swept curls in his hair. He's beautiful.

I send the picture of Roman and a few others of the stalls around me to Willow.

Her answer comes in a few minutes later.

WILLOW: Omg. Andy.

WILLOW: Look at his face.

WILLOW: That man is in love.

I blush, shaking my head even though she can't see it.

ANDY: You think so?

WILLOW: I know so.

I tuck my phone against my chest and watch him pick a few flowers out.

Is he? Could he be in love with me? The way he looks at me, holds me, touches me, makes me think that maybe he is. The things he says, the things he does, all point to those three little words. My hands are slick with nerves at the thought.

The man behind the flower cart grins, gesturing to a few other flowers. Roman selects each one with care. The man asks him a question and Roman gestures to where I stand.

I grin, waving my fingers at him.

Roman's arms are full of flowers when he finally makes his way toward me. He juggles our coffees between one hand as he extends the flowers to me, grinning like a schoolboy. I press my face against them and inhale.

"They're beautiful. Thank you."

"I picked only the best ones," he says. "Just for you."

He lets me adjust the flowers in my arms before passing me my coffee.

"What do they mean?" I ask. "I know you didn't stand there all that time without him telling you."

"Ah," he hedges, scratching the back of his head. "They mean all sorts of different things."

"Like what?" I press, grinning up at him.

Roman on edge is my new favorite side of him. He's usually so calm and collected. Seeing him flustered makes my heart summersault in my chest.

"Well," he begins, running an index finger over the blooms, "wild roses are for passion and bravery. Sunflowers are for adoration." He licks his lips, eyes flicking to my face. "Yellow lilies are for happiness. Heliotropes are for devotion."

I don't let him get any further before I stretch to my toes and brush my mouth against his.

"Thank you," I murmur against his lips.

He grins, tucking a strand of hair behind my ear. I love that he does that. It makes me feel cared for. Loved.

"I'm glad you love them," he says softly. His eyes sparkle in the afternoon sun.

"Should we keep walking?"

"Willow asked us to send her pictures," I blurt. I wave my phone at him. "She wants to see more of the market. Will you...?"

His eyes narrow. "She did?"

"Yup," I lie. "I told her where we were. She said she wanted to see it."

He purses his lips like he doesn't believe me.

"Fine." He gestures for me to open my phone camera.

I want something to remember this by. I want something to look back on. I want to see myself in love and happy for the first time in my life.

I press my flowers to my chest and Roman bands a strong arm around my shoulders from behind. I beam at the camera when he presses his lips to my cheek. I take the picture. He kisses me a few more times, making me laugh. I click the shutter button over and over and over again.

I get a brief second to stare at the pure joy on my face before I send it Willow's way.

> WILLOW: You're in love, too.

I am, I think. I really, really am.

We spend most of the afternoon exploring the farmer's market. There are a million tents to explore. We eat fresh honeycomb from a woman who runs a nearby apiary. I buy fresh fruit for after dinner and a blueberry jam for breakfast in the morning. Roman stops to inspect a tent of wood carvings.

"Wes would love this," he says.

He pulls out his phone, opens a group chat, and sends a few pictures.

I peek over his shoulder.

"Do you have a group chat with Brooks and Wes?" I ask in disbelief.

He shrugs, eyes sparkling with amusement.

"Do you and Willow have a Hot or Not list you still won't let me see?"

I scoff, gaping at him. "That's... That's not the same."

He winks at me. He actually winks. I feel it down to the soles of my feet.

"Isn't it?"

He threads his fingers through mine and leads me into the fray. I stop at a tent selling dresses and run my fingers down a sheath dress in burgundy silk. The back is practically non-existent and there's a slit that runs high up on the thigh on the mannequin.

"Now you're just being mean," Roman mutters.

I smirk at him before turning my back on him and addressing the woman who owns the tent. She takes my measurements and we find the best size for me. The dress is beautiful and a little expensive, but I don't care. Roman is practically salivating at the sight of it, and that's enough for me.

We buy fresh bread and cheese for lunch and find a sunny spot in the grass to eat. We taste test a few wines from local wineries and Roman convinces me to try mead. It's not overly sweet, but it's not to my taste.

We get another round of coffees at a little espresso tent. Just when I think I've found my favorite, I find another one that I like better.

"I don't think we even covered half of it," he says in the middle of the afternoon. He gestures to the white tents in the distance. "At this rate, we'll be here all night."

I set the dozen bags down by my feet. Roman shifts the massive bouquet of flowers he bought me to his other arm.

"Should we head home then?"

Home.

I can't take it back and I don't want to. His eyes soften on my face. Roman Bendetti becoming the person I thought of as my home was not on my Bingo card this year, but here we are.

"I'm not ready to go back yet. Maybe we head into town for dinner? Just you and me?"

"I'd like that."

We walk back to the car and stow our bags in the trunk. Without Sergei in the car, I slip into the front seat. Roman throws the car into drive and drops his hand on my thigh. He navigates us toward Turin. Boutique shops and restaurants line the streets while the spires of Mole Antonelliana shoot into the sky. The Alps rise to my left, their tips covered in snowy caps against the darkening sky.

Roman huddles me into his side once we find a place to park. I shiver against him as the wind picks up. He leads me toward a little cafe, warm yellow lighting spilling out onto the street.

Loud music greets us as a young Italian woman hammers out a song on the Baby Grand Piano on the riser in the back of the room.

Roman leads us further inside in search of a table, taking my hand and navigating the packed room. We find a booth tucked back into the corner. The music is loud, the air is warm, and they've got a cocktail list a half-mile long.

He shucks his jacket and rolls up the sleeves of his sweater. His cheeks are ruddy from the cool air and it takes everything in me not to tell him how much I love him.

The woman playing the piano concludes her song with a few drawn out notes and the cafe explodes in applause. A waitress comes to take our order.

"Wine and pizza okay?" he asks before he orders.

"Order away," I say with a wave of my hand.

I could listen to him speak Italian all day. His voice is rich, deep, smooth as melted chocolate. He orders for us and pulls me against his side as another song starts up. Our wine is delivered and he pours us each a glass.

We talk and laugh until our ribs ache. He tells me stories about Aurora and Mira and the summers they spent together. He tells me how Nicco broke her heart and she's never forgiven him for it.

We decimate our pizza and polish off the bottle of wine. We sing loudly and off-key with the rest of the cafe when the pianist plays 'Piano Man'. I'm half-drunk on him and the wine when we stumble back out onto the street.

The lights around the shops and above the street have kicked on, painting the world in a hazy glow. Roman's still laughing and his face flushed by the time we reach the car.

"That guy behind us was in rough shape," he says, sliding into the driver's seat. "Our poor waitress."

I laugh. "You tipped her well enough for her to still call it a good night," I remind him.

"Even still. He's going to need all the pizza in the world to fight off that hangover."

We pull back onto the road and this time, I reach over for his hand.

When we get back to Lena's, the house is dark. We tiptoe through the kitchen and put away the things we bought at the market. I find a vase and set my flowers inside before filling it up with water. Neither of us are ready to go to bed, so he gestures to me to follow him toward the sunroom.

He closes the door behind us and leads me to the table in the corner. He pulls a deck of cards from the drawer by the couch and waves it my way.

"Up for a game?"

"What did you have in mind?"

"500 Rummy alright with you?"

I shrug off my flannel and drape it over a chair.

"Sure. Want some tea?" When he nods, I head back toward the kitchen. "Deal away. And don't cheat," I call over my shoulder. "I'll know."

He offers me a little salute while I fix each of us a cup of tea. I lean against the counter, smiling in the shadows. I allow myself to freak out where no one can see, dropping my face into my hands and letting out a silent scream. When the water boils, I fix our cups and head back toward the sunroom.

I drop back into my chair and slide him his mug.

He takes the seat across from me and picks up his hand. He studies his cards for a moment before picking up a new card and discarding an old one into the discard pile.

"The pictures you took earlier," he says, jarring me from the mental organization of my cards. "Can you send them to me?"

I flick my eyes to his. "Sure."

I send the pictures to him. He opens my text and stares down at our smiling faces. His eyes are unreadable as he takes us in, the light and joy in my eyes, the smile on his face even as he kisses me. He makes a few quick taps, saving the photo to his own camera roll before setting it as his lock screen and home background.

I don't say anything, because I can't.

He offers me a soft smile before gesturing to my hand.

"Your turn, sweetheart."

I make my move, drawing one card and setting down another.

Halfway through the game, Roman gets up to turn on the radio beside us. He tunes the dial in and picks up a fuzzy station playing oldies classics. He wins the first hand but I win the second.

'Moon River' floats through the room and he spins to face the radio.

"That song has played too many times," he says. "In the car on the way here, again in the kitchen the other night and now this." He shakes his head. "Do you believe in fate?" he asks me suddenly. "Because it feels like this is it."

I lay my hand down and he groans. He shows me the aces in his hand and I smirk. His point total is in the negatives now.

"In what way?"

"It feels like it's our song," he says, and I can tell he's surprised himself. "Every time we're together, it plays."

Perry Como's soft voice floats between us.

"It's not a bad song to have," I whisper.

He stands from the table and offers me his hand. I don't think twice before I take it. He pulls me into his arms, our hands against his chest, our cheeks pressed together. I squeeze my eyes shut, committing the feel of him to memory. His heart is steady against mine as he spins us in a small circle.

When the song ends, he kisses me.

He kisses me up the stairs, our game forgotten. He kisses me until I'm on the mattress and he's moving above me. There's no commands tonight as he slides between my legs. His eyes stay on mine, our fingers twine together.

He takes his time, drawing it out until we're both a little bit desperate and breathless. This is more, I think to myself as he pulls me against him.

This is everything.

Chapter 20

ROMAN

True to his word, Luca pulls up the long driveway Friday evening. I'm licking my wounds and stretching my sore back from another day hunched over rows of grapes. Andy rubs unconscious circles over my back as she watches her cousin pull into the driveway.

I was up at dawn, meeting Rora and Lena in the vineyard. While Andy slept, I made my pitch. I ran the numbers and delivered my projections. Lena's answering smile lit up the dark.

"Of course, Roman," she said. "Of course."

I hugged her hard, thanking her for trusting us with her fruit and her wine.

"You are a good man," she said, cupping my cheek. "There's no one I trust more."

Her compliments humbled me and I squeezed her a little tighter in thanks.

"Let's harvest your grapes, shall we?"

I spent the next several hours handling my Dolcetto with kid gloves. I'm excited to see what it becomes, how it will age and change in the bottle. I think of the dinners I want to have with Andy where we can talk and laugh and drink our wine together.

"What's that?" Andy asks, gesturing to the plume of dust kicking up between the trees lining the driveway.

I squint. "It's... cars. Lots and lots of cars."

Andy takes one dizzying step down the front porch when a fleet of minivans and sedans squeal to a stop at the top of the drive.

Luca and Mira amble up the steps, hand in hand. He brushes a kiss over Andy's cheek.

"Thought you might like this a little bit better than lunch," he says, squeezing her shoulder.

A man who looks remarkably like Luca slides from a silver minivan.

He lets out a loud expletive when he spots Andy.

"Gio?" she asks, taking another dazed step toward him.

"Hey, sunshine," he calls, waving above his head. "I thought you'd like to see the family."

His twins, by the look of them, explode out of the back seat. His wife exits the passenger side and yells at the boys to slow down. They blow past Andy and I, darting inside the house.

Gio meets Andy on the steps and wraps her in a hug. His eyes are smiling as they meet mine.

"I can't believe you're here," she says to him.

"Luca called me on the drive home and told me what happened. I called my mom and she called her sisters, and then uncle Milo, and well, here we are."

Andy laughs. "I'd expect nothing else."

"Andy." The tremulous voice comes from somewhere over Gio's left shoulder. He grins, stepping aside.

A woman hovers behind him, worrying a diamond pendant around its chain. Her hazel eyes are rimmed with tears.

"Lottie," Andy breathes, voice uneven.

Andy breaks from Gio's hold and rushes to her aunt, throwing her arms around her neck. Tears prick my eyes as two other aunts and one uncle unfold from their cars and corral her into a massive group hug.

I can hear her choked laughter, her sniffles, as she's passed around her family and squeezed until she's blue in the face. They speak all at once, their Italian loud and happy.

"Come inside," Lena calls, wiping her hands with a dishtowel. "Dinner is almost ready."

Luca shakes my hand in passing and leads the rest of the pack inside. I wait behind for Andy. She stands at the bottom step, blinking in astonishment.

"They all came," she says softly. "I can't believe it."

"I can. You're worth traveling for, Andy. They love you. They've missed you."

"I feel awful," she confesses. "I couldn't come back after Nonna died. I keep thinking of what Luca said. That they lost me, too."

"Hey," I soothe, taking her hand in mine. "They knew how close you were. No one blames you, Andy, for grieving. They didn't go anywhere."

She gives me a short nod and climbs the steps.

"You're going to meet my family," she says in realization. "Oh, shit."

I laugh, kissing her forehead.

"I can't wait."

***

Dinner is loud, full of shouting, wine, and laughter. Lena takes it all in, calm and delighted. Aurora watches it all like a ping-pong match, her eyes volleying back and forth between every conversation.

Andy introduces me to her family, and I'm kissed and hugged and poked and prodded more than anyone should ever be in their lifetime. Her aunts grill me, but that's to be expected.

Andy is passed around like a prized trophy. Her aunt Lottie wraps an arm around her and draws her to her side. I lean against the counter sipping my wine while the twins, Micah and Peter, destroy Lena's living room with help from Harold the dog.

Andy's uncle doesn't say much, but I notice him wiping his eyes every few minutes.

Her aunts fuss and squawk over her.

"So like your father," Lottie says, brushing her finger along Andy's cheek. "You have his eyes. You have his spirit."

"She does," her aunt Anna chimes in. "That stubborn tilt of the chin." She taps Andy's chin fondly.

"You're smothering her," Lucinda chimes in. "Christ, she's not the Pope."

Lottie and Anna glare at their sister.

"We brought you pictures," Lottie says, gesturing to the overflowing tote bag full of photo albums. "We thought you might like to have them."

"Oh."

"Have a seat, have a seat." Anna practically kicks Andy's legs out from under her to take a seat at the table.

I move to the seat next to her, capturing her hand in mine as the first photo album is laid out before her. Her breath is unsteady as she opens the first book and turns to the first page. I feel it, the moment she freezes.

A man grins up at the camera. He has Andy's deep brown eyes, her laughing smile, and—Anna was right— the proud jut of her chin. She traces the corner of the photo almost reverently.

His hair is dark, which means Andy gets her honey-blonde hair from her mother.

"He was the very best," Anna says, sniffling into a tissue. "He was so funny. Always making everyone laugh."

Andy nods, swallowing thickly. "He was," she rasps, voice laden with tears. "I remember laughing all the time."

"He adored you," Lottie says, turning the page for her. "He was so proud, Alexandra. He told us every chance he got."

I stare down at baby Andy, her chubby cheeks covered in chocolate. I can see the fire in her eyes even then. Her dad sits across from her, feeding her ice cream. He's wearing most of it, but damn if the joy in his eyes doesn't take my breath away.

We move through her childhood and the years of her running wild with Luca and Gio. I laugh at the picture of the three of them standing in front of their mopeds, grinning in defiance at the camera with bloody knees and skinned palms. A helmet dangles from Andy's hand, a fierce sort of triumph in her eyes.

My phone vibrates with an email from my father, asking if I secured the Alto contract and if I have, why haven't I sent it to him yet? For the first time in three years, I clear the notification and ignore him. This is too important for me to miss. He can wait a few hours.

When we land on a picture of Nonna, I still. I understand why Dom's nonna had such an effect on her. They look nearly identical with their short and slender build and trademark braid hanging over their shoulders.

"What was her name?" I ask, tracing the curve of Andy's cheek in the photo.

"Elena," she says softly.

Elena has kinder eyes and I can practically feel the love radiating out of the photo as she clutches Andy to her chest. I spy the silver and emerald ring Andy wears in the picture. I bring it to my mouth and brush my lips across it.

Her tears are silent when they stream down her face. I hook my hand around the leg of her chair and draw her closer, practically pulling her into my lap as Lottie flips to another page.

It's the first glimpse I have of Andy's mother. Her hair is a shade lighter than Andy's but I was right in my first guess. It's a picture of the three of them huddled outside their apartment in New York. There's photos of Christmases and birthdays, school trips, and Andy in her playroom at home.

"How... How did he die?" I finally ask.

Lottie dabs her eyes. She glances at Andy.

"He was hit by a drunk driver." It's the first time her uncle has spoken all night. Milo blows his nose. "Leaving a work function, I think. The truck blew through the intersection. Killed him instantly."

"Alexandra." Her name is a long sigh from my lips.

She glances up at me, eyes red and brimming with tears.

"Mom hated his motorcycle," she murmurs. "Begged him to get rid of it, but he loved it."

I close my eyes. The terror on her face on the four-wheeler at Gilbert's springs to the forefront of my mind.

"I never would have made you get on that thing if I'd known," I begin.

I'll never forgive myself for putting her through it.

"I know, Roman," she says softly, linking her fingers with mine. "I know."

"I'm so sorry," I murmur.

"It's okay. You drove me back, remember? You took care of me."

Her words do nothing to ease the knot in my chest.

It's a somber sort of evening as Andy moves through her childhood. At around age eighteen, the photos abruptly stop.

"You were her favorite girl," Lucinda says, eyeing Andy's ring. "She worried about leaving you most of all."

Andy wipes at her eyes. "I'm sorry I didn't come home."

Anna clucks her tongue. "You two had a special bond. I can't imagine how painful it would be coming back here without her waiting for you. No one holds it against you, Alexandra. We're just glad you're back now."

Andy offers her a watery smile.

"I'd like it if you'd come for Christmas," Luca says, drawing everyone's attention. "Get the whole family back together. I know it's a quick turn around and you don't need to give me an answer right now. Just think about it, okay?"

"I will," Andy promises. She spins in her chair to face me. "What do you think?" she asks, as her family dissolves into their own conversations. "Christmas in Italy?"

I drag my fingers down the curve of her face.

"I think that sounds wonderful."

She brushes her lips against mine, nearly melting into my arms.

"I'm glad you got to meet them," she says against my chest. "I'm glad you got to hear about my dad."

I close my eyes. She's wrecking me from the inside out.

"Me, too."

"I think they both would have loved you," she says so quietly I almost don't hear it. "Nonna would have fussed over you to no end. She would have whispered about you as soon as you left the room."

"What would she have said?"

"That you're too handsome for your own good."

I chuckle. "I doubt it. What about your dad?"

She sits up straight in her chair.

Her eyes grow soft when she thinks about him.

"He would have been tough at first, but he would have come around when he saw..." She stops talking abruptly, worrying her lip between her teeth.

When he saw how much I loved his daughter.

"Saw what?" I ask, encouraging her to continue.

"Nothing," she says, glancing down at the floor.

"Alexandra."

"Just... When he saw how much I liked you," she finishes, unable to meet my eyes. "That's all."

I let her slide with that one.

Her family packs up around eleven. Lena hands out packed boxes of food and wine and hugs each of them goodbye. I think I overheard her invite Lucinda for brunch on Sunday and Lottie to dinner on Monday and Anna to drinks on Wednesday.

Luca squeezes Andy hard when his turn to say goodbye comes.

"Please come for Christmas," he mutters beneath his breath. "It would mean the world to me."

"I'll do my best," she promises.

Gio hugs her, his dark head bent to hers.

"If you can't come here, we could always go there."

Andy's cackling laugh stirs my chest.

"Like half of you would even be able to fit in my tiny little apartment," she says. "No, I'll try to come back out." She glances back at me. "I'll let you know when I get back to New York."

Mira hugs Andy and I goodbye, slipping her hand into Luca's before they head to the car.

"I'll text you," she calls to Andy before sliding into her seat.

Andy and I lean in the doorway and watch them go, disappearing within the same cloud of smoke and dust they arrived in.

***

When we're wrapped around each other in bed that night, my hand twisting in her hair, I ask her,

"How did your parents meet?"

She props herself up on an elbow and drops her chin into her hand.

"Dad moved from Italy when he was in his mid-twenties. He wanted to see if he could sell the olive oil Nonna made at the markets. Maybe start a brand. He had good sales at the markets, but not enough to make a living on. He worked in construction on the side to make ends meet. He was at the Italian market in the fall on a Sunday. My mom walked by with friends. They'd tell you two different stories at this point," she says, laughing a little.

I adjust myself on the pillow, tucking one hand behind my head.

"What would those be?"

"Mom would tell you that he stopped blinking entirely. He just stared at her. He forgot how to talk. He just gaped. She thought he was a little crazy and was definitely a little put off by him. Dad would tell you his world stopped spinning when he saw her, that the earth's axis tilted a few extra degrees to the right. He said he loved her from the moment they locked eyes." She grins a little.

"So that's where you get all those romantic bones in your body," I tease lightly. "Your dad."

Her smile is pleased, almost proud when it comes.

"Yeah, I guess so. Well, anyway, it took three separate trips back to the market for my dad to finally get the courage to ask her out. Even if mom tells a different story, I think she felt it, too. Why else would she have gone back so many times? They started dating and by Christmas of that year, he took her to Italy to meet the family. Mom and Nonna hit it off and my dad got her blessing. They got married on New Year's

Eve in a courthouse in the city with only a handful of witnesses." Her eyes grow wistful. "Mom wore a tea-length white satin dress and dad wore a tux." She reaches over and grabs her phone. "I digitized their wedding photos years ago. I was worried George would get rid of them or let them rot in an attic somewhere."

"I don't think I like him," I mutter.

"Get in line," is all she says.

She navigates to a saved folder and then a hundred black and white photos erupt on screen. So young, so in love. I've only seen joy like that once in photos, and it's in the photo we took earlier today.

"The rings they bought had engraved hearts in the band. See?" She zooms in on a picture of their joined hands. The smallest little heart sits on the top of their matching rings.

"Beautiful," I murmur.

"I still have his."

"You do? Your mom doesn't have it?" I ask in surprise.

She nods, running her finger over her lip.

"When we had to go to the morgue to identify him, they gave us a plastic bag of his things. All that was in there was his wallet, wedding ring, and the key to his bike. Mom couldn't touch it. She told me to get it away from her; she never wanted to see it again. I was worried she'd throw it out, so I hid it in my room."

She slides from bed and crosses to her suitcase. I sit up and watch her dig through her makeup bag. She plucks a little velvet pouch and crosses back to the bed. She opens the drawstring and dumps the ring into her palm.

"I carry it with me when I travel," she says, sliding the gold band down her thumb. The movement is hypnotizing. "I'm terrified I'm going to lose it, but it feels like he's with me. When he tucked me in at night, he used to tell me about all the trips he took when he was a boy and how much he wanted to show me the world." She spins the ring around her finger. "I guess this is my way of doing it with him."

When I reach for her hand, she lets me take it.

I brush my thumb over the little heart engraving.

"Can you get it resized?" I ask. "That way you can wear it yourself."

She hesitates, looking up at me sheepishly.

"I... I didn't want to change the size. I didn't think it was going to be Cinderella's slipper or anything but... I used to dream about the man I'd marry. That the ring would fit him and it would be like my dad sent him just for me." She doesn't look at me when she says it.

The urge to slip that little gold band down my left ring finger is all consuming. I want to try it on. I want to watch it slide against my skin. I want to know if it's me that he's sent her.

She clears her throat and slides the ring from her thumb, dropping it back into the pouch for safe keeping.

"Does your mom still have her ring?" I hear myself ask.

She sets the pouch down on the bedside table and curls back against me.

"I don't know," she mumbles. "I'm afraid to ask her. It would kill me if she got rid of it but... She was inconsolable when he died. She stayed in bed for weeks. The only reason she got up to go back to work was because the waitress covering for her refused to keep doing it. I don't know if she would have ever gotten up again."

My arms tighten around her. To love someone like that...

Andy snuggles against me, and I know that I understand.

Chapter 21
Andy

Roman heads to the second winery location Saturday morning without me. He and Sergei hit the road a little after nine, and he kisses me senseless while I'm still half asleep in bed.

"Have a good day," he says against my lips. "I'll be back as soon as I can."

He nuzzles his face against my neck, his scruff tickling me until I dissolve into a fit of laughter. His answering smile is my favorite thing in the world.

I love the way his face transforms, the little dimples that appear on each cheek. There's such light in his eyes. It makes me weak in the knees. Happy Roman is devastating. He's relaxed and easygoing and playful. He's romantic and affectionate and I am so insanely swept up in him, my feet will never touch the ground again.

I lay in bed for a long while, imagining what our life could be in New York. Coming home to him at the end of the day, kissing him good morning and laughing our way through our days. Going up to his brownstone on the weekends, inviting our friends and family for football Sundays and holidays. The explosive nights, the tender moments. I can see a life stretch out before me, one where we're both blissfully in love and out of our minds for each other.

I can't stop the daydreams, the incurable longing in my chest. I want an entire lifetime with Roman Bendetti.

I'm still dreaming when I help Lena in the garden and in the vineyard. Aurora makes us iced coffees and we talk about life when we stop for lunch. I want to ask her about Nicco. I want to know what happened between them. It's like she has a wiretap to my brain, because she grimaces.

"You can ask, you know," she says, scuffing a dirty boot against the grass. "Everyone does."

"I don't want to make you talk about it," I say, feeling guilty.

She shrugs. "We were kids. He broke my heart but what was I expecting at nineteen, you know? Nic was wild and wonderful and hilarious and I just felt lucky he was looking at me half the time. We dated that summer. It was the best three months of my life. He was my first everything." Here, she blushes. "I saved up my first kiss just for him. I had it in my head I'd die never having been kissed if he didn't take my first one."

"Rora," I murmur sadly.

"It was a childhood crush," she dismisses, waving her hand in the air. "Everything is dramatic when you're young and in love. It wasn't fair of me to think he'd stay."

I take her hand. "It wasn't fair if he led you on, either."

She shrugs. "We both hurt each other in one way or another."

"You haven't seen him since?"

She shakes her head. "When he comes home, I travel. I don't know what I'd say if I ever saw him again." She nibbles her lip. "I'm afraid I'm going to look at him again and fall right back in love. I don't know if I'd survive a second time." Her smile droops at the corners.

"Maybe it takes a second shot to get it right," I say. "You never know. He's not dating anyone. Come to think of it," I say, searching my memories, "I don't remember him dating anyone since he's been in New York."

She holds up her hand. Her eyes plead with mine.

"Don't tell me more. I don't want to know. It's better that I think of him with someone else."

"Is it?" I ask skeptically.

"Shit," she mutters. She rubs a dirt-stained hand across her forehead. "No, I guess not. I don't know. These Bendetti men, you know?" she asks in exasperation.

I nod in commiseration, because I *do* know.

The second harvest crew comes and finishes off most of the vineyard. I help Lena and Rora in the winery, foot stomping grapes until my legs ache and my feet are stained purple. We pump the fresh juice into barrels and tanks and collapse on the dirty concrete floor when the last of it is put away.

"God," I say, laughing. "I'm exhausted."

Lena's hand blindly searches for mine as we stare up at the barn ceiling.

"Feels good though, doesn't it?"

"It does," I agree.

"You can come work for me anytime," she says, still out of breath.

"You kicked ass today, Andy." Rora sighs beside me. "My thighs are killing me," she complains, rolling to her knees. "I need to go soak in my tub for an indeterminable amount of time."

I raise my hand for help and she drags me to my feet.

"That sounds like a great idea."

Lena stays prone on the floor.

"Dinner in an hour," she calls after Rora and I as we hobble our way back toward the house.

The tub in my bathroom practically swallows me whole when I slip down beneath the bubbles. I have to drain and refill the water twice until my feet finally lose their purple stain. My body is sore, but it feels good.

When I come into the kitchen to help with dinner, Lena is just dropping the steaks on the grill. I'm dicing tomatoes for the salad when the front door opens and Roman and Sergei stroll in.

Roman sets his bag down on the counter and levels those gorgeous jade eyes my way.

"Hi," I say, just a little breathless when he grins at me. "Did you get the contract?"

"Nope," he says, still smiling. "Drug me all over that property, strung me along like a bad date, and then he rejected me."

"Then why are you smiling like that?"

"Because I can do this."

He crosses the island, cups my face, and kisses the daylights out of me. I grip his wrist, locking him into place as Lena catcalls us from outside. His hands sink into my hair, tilting my head up exactly where he wants me. His tongue brushes against mine and my hip meets the counter. He cages me in, kissing me like we don't have an audience watching us. Sergei laughs.

"Roman, let her breathe."

When he finally pulls away, I'm dizzy.

"I missed you," he says, kissing me again. "I couldn't wait to get back."

"This is true," Sergei says, sliding onto the barstool. "He keeps asking me to go faster and faster."

I smirk up at him. "I missed you, too."

He flicks my nose playfully.

"How was your day, baby?"

I practically ooze like melted ice cream at his feet.

"They worked me hard, but it was good. We finished the crushing today."

"Not too hard, I hope," he murmurs, fingers teasing the sensitive skin on my inner wrist.

"No," I blurt, already feeling the ache between my legs. "No."

His grin is wolfish when it comes.

"Good." He loosens the tie around his neck. "How can I help?"

We take advantage of the cool weather and eat out on the patio beneath Lena's artfully arranged fairy lights. Wine flows freely, and we laugh and play games until the clock inches toward eleven.

I love this. I love the deep knit bond between them. I love that they make dinner together every night and play games. I love that they're open and honest with each other, that they accept each other as they are. I think of the cold dining rooms I ate in where there was no noise other than silverware scraping plates. There was no conversation, no laughter, no jokes. I look around the patio and see the love flowing between everyone around me. It feels good to be a part of it, even if it makes my chest ache.

Roman's hands are everywhere under the table. On my thighs, my knees, my hips. His mouth brushes against my shoulder and my neck and nose and forehead until I'm practically vibrating beside him.

"Let's go to bed," he says, and tugs me from the table.

He herds me up the stairs and as soon as the door closes, he's on me. He lifts the hem of my shirt up and over my head and drops his mouth to my neck.

"I couldn't stop thinking about you today," he says, tugging my bra down my arms. "All I wanted to do is kiss you, hold you. Gerard was talking to me about his harvest and all I could think of was that little noise you make right before you come."

He boosts me up into his arms and walks me toward the mattress. I loosen his tie and skip my fingers down the buttons on his shirt. He twists so I straddle him as he lays back against the pillows.

"You want to watch?" I ask, unzipping his slacks.

His tongue darts out to touch his lip.

"God, yes."

He strips me quickly, hands shaking as he wrestles his pants down his hips. We're barely undressed before I throw my knees over his hips and sink down on him. My head falls back on a moan as I work him inside me, swiveling my hips in little circles. His hands are everywhere as I sink all the way down on him.

"Damn," he breathes, watching me with wide eyes. "Take it, Andy. Make yourself feel good."

I do. I set my own pace, slowly working myself up and down against him. His eyes are wide, pupils dilated. His breathing is ragged as he fights for control, letting me take my time as I drop down on his lap.

I slide my fingers up my stomach and play with my nipples, pinching and twisting them. I feel how wet I am as he slides deep inside me on a hard thrust. It only spurs me on, my hips circling faster and faster over his.

"I'll never get tired of this," he says, thrusting up to meet me. "Seeing you like this. So wild for me. So beautiful."

His hand trails up my sternum and lightly grips my throat. His thumb brushes over the pulse point in my neck. I know it's wild against his finger. His smile tells me as much. His thumb coasts to my jaw and over my lips where I suck it into my mouth, twirling my tongue around the pad of his finger. His eyes flare and he thrusts up hard inside me.

"That fucking mouth," he grits out.

I suck hard, drawing another moan from deep within his chest. The time for play has ended, I can see it in the taunt lines of his arms. He pops his finger from my mouth, lifts my hips, and slams himself inside me.

"So good," he pants, watching me bounce on top of him.

Every time he bottoms out inside me, stars bloom behind my eyes. He doesn't even need to touch me before I start to pulse around him. His eyes widen.

"Milk it, sweetheart. Take me for all I'm worth."

His words set me off like a firecracker. I come for the first time without needing to touch myself. It's intense, earth-shattering, as my orgasm rockets through me. He grunts, coming on a gasp. I feel him twitch and jerk inside me, his neck and eyes tight with strain as he spills himself over and over again.

I collapse on his chest, my ear pressed to his racing heart.

"God damn," he mutters, banding his arms around me. "Andy."

There's nothing else to say.

I feel it, too.

Chapter 22
Roman

Taking Andy from Piedmont feels like a cardinal sin.

She was able to find something over these last few days. Her family, a piece of herself that's long since been missing.

She sobs into Lena's shoulder when we leave Monday morning. I hate myself for making her leave. Even Aurora's hazel eyes are misty when Andy hugs her goodbye.

"If I come for Christmas, can I come and see you?" Andy asks Lena before she slips into the back seat.

Lena's eyes fill with tears.

"Anytime, my girl. You'll always have a space here."

Lena kisses her on the cheek before stepping back, fingers pressed to her mouth.

She hugs me hard when it's my turn to say goodbye.

"You take care of that girl, Roman," she says into my ear. "They don't make them like that anymore."

"I know, Leen. I will."

She cups my face, eyes tender.

"It's good to see you in love," she murmurs. My body stills at her words. "To see you so happy. It means the world to me." She kisses my cheek before stepping back.

"Don't wait so long next time, okay?" Rora says, squeezing me around the hips. "Maybe I could come visit you in New York? I've never been."

I stare down at the freckles on the bridge of her nose.

"Nic is in New York," I remind her.

She fortifies herself, drawing her slender frame to its full height.

"Nicco Bendetti doesn't run my life," she says with more bravado than I think she actually feels.

"Then my door is open for you anytime."

"Maybe in the New Year, when the harvest dies down."

"Just let me know," I say, brushing a kiss across her forehead.

She grins up at me and steps back, wrapping her arm around Lena's waist. They watch us go, standing at the top of the driveway until we're out of sight.

Andy sniffles in the backseat.

"God damnit," she sighs, mopping her face. "I blame you for all of this," she accuses. "I never cried before I came to Italy."

I twist in the passenger seat as we hit the highway.

"It's a good thing, baby. Trust me."

She glares at me. "Not when my heart hurts this bad, it isn't."

She's thoughtful for the rest of the drive to Cinque Terre. I send the Alto contract over to my father a full three days late. I've ignored every follow up email he sent me and even sent one of his phone calls to voicemail. It's a small act of rebellion, but one I'm proud of.

I click through my spreadsheets and eye the tonnage we'd estimated on getting. We're right on the mark for where we wanted to be, which is great. I have a feeling he'll want more, but it's a start.

If he asks me to go again, I'll pass that burden off to Nicco. As enjoyable as this trip has been, this nomadic lifestyle is exhausting. I'm glad we'll have a few days in one place to rest before we head back home.

As sad as Andy is to leave Piedmont, I can't wait to show her Cinque Terre. I booked us an incredible villa that's only a quick seven-minute walk to the beach. I scan for restaurants as we drive. I want to make these last four days as memorable as possible. New York looms in the distance and I turn my face away from it.

I'm not ready to go back yet. I'm not ready to give this up.

I find a stunning little restaurant right on the coast. The pictures on the website show the panoramic view of the Gulf from their rooftop, but there are no seating options. I tap on their contact link and send them a message. Regardless of what they say, it'll be a romantic way to end the trip.

I'm buzzing in anticipation as we swing toward the coast, the cliff face falling away down into the ocean.

Andy scoots to the other side of the car and rolls down her window. Cool air sweeps in and she rests her chin on the ledge, eyes closed. The Gulf of Genoa glistens a perfect cerulean blue, the sun bouncing off the surface like hand cut diamonds. Sailboats dot the horizon and all the beautifully colored homes of Cinque Terre come into view.

Monterrosso's Fegina Beach sits like a pearl below us, the water so clear and opaque the reefs and rocks below are visible. Andy sighs dreamily at the sight.

"This is heaven," she murmurs from the back seat. "Look at this. God, do you ever look at something and wonder how it's real? That's what this place feels like."

I smile to myself as we pull into the village, Sergei's car too large for the small streets we navigate. He comes to a stop outside a building practically built into the rock face, the stone painted a rich umber.

We lug our suitcases up a crumbling flight of stone steps to reach the front door. I pop in the pin code on the padlock by the door and step inside. Nothing but sea greets me as I step into the living room.

"I think I'm going to faint," Andy whispers, staring over my shoulder.

She abandons her bag and crosses the room, sneakers squeaking over the mosaic floors. She heads right to the double set of patio doors and throws them open, letting in warm sunshine and fresh air. The curtains by her legs flutter happily in the breeze.

The terrace that greets us when we step outside is large, complete with its own private pool and hot tub. The jets in the tub gurgle softly, water trilling in the silence around us. Andy drops a hand to the sun lounger that's been built into the shallow end of the water, head shaking in disbelief.

A cheery red and yellow umbrella casts a long shadow of shade across the deck. I run my fingers over the marble table outside and eye the chilled bottle of champagne and flowers our host left for us.

"Unreal," she murmurs, staring down at the beach.

It's still warm enough to swim in the ocean this time of year, but those days will fade quickly once September wraps up.

We explore the house together. The living room is open and spacious with a long L-shaped couch in the middle. The built-in shelves on either side of the TV are riddled with games and books for our use.

The kitchen is large with its light-blue cabinets and white countertops. Pots and pans hang from the ceiling above the island, whispering together in the wind.

Our bedroom has its own private balcony, set with a set of iron tables and chairs. The bathroom is huge, complete with a rainfall shower and a soaking tub with jets. My mind is racing at all the opportunities in this room.

When I walk back into the bedroom, Andy trails her fingers over the pristine white duvet. There's another bottle of wine waiting for us in a chiller with two flute glasses.

"Roman," she mutters, still in shock. "This is incredible."

I come behind her, watching the waves lap against the shore. I wrap my arms around her hips and drag her against me, kissing up the column of her neck.

"You like it?" I ask.

Her laugh is a little unstable when it comes.

"It's beautiful." She spins in my arms and links her hands behind my neck. I grin down at her. "Was this what you originally booked?"

Damn. Caught.

I shake my head, chagrined.

"No. I changed it when we were in Verona and things shifted between us."

"You didn't need to do that," she admonishes. "I would have been happy with anything."

"Yes, but you're happier here. That's all I care about."

Her kiss is sweet when it comes. I'm ready to toss her on the bed when she slips from my grasp.

"Can we go explore? Maybe go to the beach?"

"You're not tired?" I ask skeptically.

"Not anymore," she says. She holds out her hand for mine. "Come on, Roman. Walk with me."

How can I say no?

***

We change into our bathing suits. I'm gaping at the little black bikini that rides high up on her hip bones. The top is tied together with one measly string in the back. My fingers twitch down by my side. She notices my stare and points a finger at me.

"Do not," she chides, trying and failing to be stern. "Adventure first, sex later."

"That's backward," I argue. "You should let me get my head between your legs. *Then* we go explore."

She shoves me away playfully.

"Exploration first. I'll make it worth your while," she promises, nipping my lower lip.

I scrub my hand down my face but relent.

Triumphant, Andy wiggles into a sundress and slides on a pair of sandals and ducks out of our room, letting me change. Sergei makes use of the guest room down in the basement and shuts himself away for a nap. I button my shirt, tucking my phone and wallet in my pocket.

Andy waits on the terrace, dress fluttering against her knees.

"Where should we go first?" she asks when I join her.

"We could grab lunch. Explore the village."

"That sounds nice."

I lead her down the stone steps, her hand in mine. It's a quick walk down to the heart of Cinque Terre. Loud music plays from a few of the cafes. The smell of fresh bread and seafood wafts by us in the most enticing way.

We stop everywhere she wants to. These days are for her and her alone. Anything she wants, I'll do. She weaves in and out of different stores. She buys herself a new pair of sunglasses and a beach cover up splattered with wild roses. She finds a long gold chain with two little hearts dangling on the end.

That I buy for her myself.

I take great care fastening it around her neck, kissing the skin under her ear as I do it. Her face is flushed when she turns to meet me. We grab lunch overlooking the ocean. We eat oysters on the half-shell and split a bottle of champagne.

Andy props her fist into her hand and lets out a dreamy little sigh.

"I'm going to get used to this, you know," she says conversationally. "Nothing else will ever be good enough for me again."

I wink. "That's the point, sweetheart."

She grins at me, eyes twinkling.

"I didn't peg you for such a romantic," she says.

"No?" I ask, leaning back in my chair. "What did you expect?"

Her eyes dip to the skin of my chest and I grin lazily at her.

"I don't know," she finally says, sipping her champagne. "You're a man who gets what he wants," she says, tossing my words back at me from three years ago. "I didn't think you'd need to do all of this."

"You're telling me you'd be mine without it?"

She grins fiendishly. "I guess we'll never know."

"Alexandra." I pin her to the seat with my stare.

Her mouth lifts into that infuriating smirk and I want to kiss it right off her face.

"Of course I would," she murmurs. "It's not why I want you, Roman. It's nice, but I'd be happy with Chinese takeout on the couch and sitcom reruns."

"This," I say, twirling my finger around the cafe, "is part of it for me. I like making you happy. Like seeing that blush on your face and knowing I put it there. I *want* to do this. I'm fine with takeout on the couch too, but I like giving you everything I possibly can."

Her fingers touch the gold chain around her neck. She's thoughtful for a long moment.

"It's more than enough," she says lowly. "More than."

We stare at each other for a moment. The tip of her nose is burnt from the sun and the freckles on her shoulders are hypnotizing in the most distracting way.

Our waiter drops off the bill, breaking the spell between us. I pay and lead Andy back down toward the beach. We didn't bring towels with us, but Andy drops her shoes on the only remaining lounger on the beach.

"You coming with me?" she asks, glancing over her shoulder.

She lifts her dress over her head and discards it on the blue padded chair. Those two little hearts dangle right between her breasts and I think it's just about the sexiest thing I've ever seen, the way the gold glints against her skin.

I smother my groan with the back of my hand. Her ass looks phenomenal in those little black bottoms. I'm ready to drop to my knees and sink my teeth into it when she saunters away, hips swishing.

I watch her go, mouth hanging open. Several heads turn on the beach as she walks by, steps lazy and unhurried.

I undo the buttons on my shirt and stow my wallet and phone beneath. I jog down the beach after her, catching her around the waist. She squeals as I lift her up, legs flailing as I toss her over my shoulder. I swat her ass for good measure and march us straight into the ocean.

"Roman!" she shouts, laughing. "Put me down!"

"Nope."

When we're deep enough, I sink below the surface. I hear her shout of protest, the laugh on her lips, before I take her down with me.

She comes up spluttering, brushing her wet hair from her eyes. She splashes me, grinning.

"Rude," she calls, sending another wave of water in my face.

I shake the hair from my eyes and swim toward her. I grip her around the waist and drag her against me. She locks her legs around my hips, her arms resting over my shoulders.

"Rude?" I ask, watching a water droplet roll from her jaw to her neck. "Rude is this bathing suit, Alexandra." My hands slide up the little straps on her hips. I slide my fingers underneath, running my nails against her skin. I lean forward, nuzzling my nose against hers. "Rude is not letting me get my head between your legs earlier."

She rubs against me, her skin slick against mine. My cock stirs painfully, despite the cool temperature of the water. I'm ready to sink into her right now.

Her eyes dance with mischief as her hands thread into my hair.

"I thought you might like a taste of your own medicine," she says haughtily, tugging at the roots. Her tongue licks up my neck. "A little delayed gratification."

I'm practically growling when I drop my hands to her ass and squeeze.

She laughs, pushing away from me. We swim for hours, floating in the cool water. We talk, we laugh, she lets me kiss her behind the sea stacks emerging from the water. When the sun begins to set, we trudge from the water. I move our things to the side and pull her to sit between my legs on the beach lounger.

The world explodes before us in a riot of varnished golds and pinks. The water turns a beautiful mirrored silver, the waves softly kissing the shore before falling away again.

The sailboats on the horizon make their return to the docks, their brightly colored sails and hulls adding to the rainbow that is Cinque Terre. The air feels good against the sunburn on my shoulders. There's laughter and music echoing behind me and I think, for the first time in my life, I've discovered a true level of peace.

She sighs, content, linking her fingers with mine where they rest on her navel. She reaches for her phone, snapping a few pictures of the sunset. When she turns the camera to face us, I don't hide my face this time. I smile, putting every inch of happiness into it.

"This is nice," she exhales. "No schedule, no vineyards to maintain. We don't need to be up at the crack of dawn. Nowhere to be but right here."

She snuggles back against me, her head tucked into the curve of my shoulder.

I brush my lips across her temple.

"Here is my favorite place to be."

Chapter 23

Andy

With nowhere to be and nothing to do but relax, Roman and I sleep in.

The clock on the bedside table reads eight when I finally crack my eyelids open. My body is warm from the sunburn on my cheeks and nose and the air from the ceiling fan is cool, sending me back under the covers. From my spot in bed, I watch the ocean sparkle in the distance.

Roman sleeps soundly beside me, his long lashes resting on his cheeks. His dark hair falls in a mess of curls over his forehead and I study him quietly. The black tattoo snaking over his shoulder looks stark in contrast to the white bedding on his hips. I trace the mark with my eyes, following the swirling whorls of ink that make up the shield, roses, clusters of grapes, and vines that hook into his skin.

I grin a little, thinking of that night three years ago when I sank my teeth into it to keep from screaming while I rode him. I press a kiss to his forehead, careful not to wake him. I slip from bed, tossing on a pair of shorts and pulling up my hair.

I shiver as I cross through the kitchen, the tile cool on my bare feet. I head to the door and step into my slides and let myself out. I make the walk down the hill to the beach, the world still quiet around me. I pick a spot on the sand and settle into it, looping my arms around my knees.

The last three weeks have been a whirlwind. My family, Roman, revisiting my past and dreading the future that awaits me. Every time I think of George's email and the gala, my gut twists. Anxiety prickles against my scalp like an omen.

I sit for a long time watching the ocean, warring with myself.

I'm going to tell Roman I love him.

I'm not sure where or when, but I know I'll tell him before we leave Italy. I'm going to ask him if we can make it work. I decide that if it means that I have to leave Cin Cin, transfer to another department, I'll do it. Whatever it takes.

I want a life with him. I want forever. I don't want to say goodbye when we fly back in three days.

Resolved, I brush the sand from my legs and make the climb back up the hill to the villa. When I step inside, I head right to the kitchen.

I struggle for a long time to figure out the coffee machine but finally, I get it to work. The smell of brewing coffee fills the villa and I make breakfast. I whisk eggs, cut up fresh fruit, and pour us each a glass of orange juice. I carry a serving tray outside and set our places, gazing out over the sea. I pop a piece of pineapple in my mouth, the tart and sweet juice bursting over my tongue.

Sergei joins me a few minutes later, a book in his hands.

"This is lovely, Just Andy. Thank you."

"You're welcome."

He pours himself a cup of coffee and takes a seat by the railing. His eyes squint out over the horizon.

"It is nice to relax," he says, raising his cup to me. "We have been busy, haven't we?"

I take the seat across from him and help myself to a cup.

"Yes. It's been a quick three weeks."

He eyes me, a question in his gaze.

"Are you ready to return home?"

I pause, running my lip between my teeth. I can barely think about it.

"No," I confess. "I never want to leave."

He nods in sympathy. "You will work it out, I am sure."

"You think so?"

"I know so."

I offer him a little smile.

"I hope you're right."

Sergei and I fall into easier conversation as we eat breakfast together. We clean up and put the extra food away for Roman to enjoy later. I tiptoe back into our room and grab another bathing suit and my new cover up and change in the bathroom downstairs. I grab my book and my sunscreen and sink into one of the semi-covered loungers in the pool, the water gently lapping against my thighs.

I can see the entire coastline from this seat. The plants on the cliff's edge sway in the breeze and I spy a few kites hovering between the clouds. I slip my AirPods in and shuffle a playlist someone made for the coast of Italy and close my eyes.

I doze for a little, lulled into the deepest sense of relaxation.

Roman doesn't show his face until nearly noon. When he finally emerges, his hair sticks up in tufts and his eyes are clouded with sleep. He's adorably ruffled and my heart bursts at the sight of him. His swim trunks hang low on his hips, offering me a perfect view of his chest and stomach.

I could stare at him for hours. I trace each dip of muscle, the hard planes of his chest.

He steps into the pool and comes over to my lounger.

I glance up at him, shielding my eyes from the sun.

"Hi, sleepy head."

He grunts. "Slide over," is all he says.

I look around me.

"Roman," I huff, "there's nowhere to go.'

He waves his hands at me and I stand from the chair. He collapses against it and pulls me into his laps, banding his arms around my waist. He tucks my head under his chin and pulls me tight against him.

"Don't like waking up without you," he mutters, big hands splayed on my hips. "Where'd you go?"

"I came out here and made Sergei and I a very glorious breakfast—which you missed, by the way." I trace the tattoo on his shoulder. "I wanted to let you sleep. You've been burning it at both ends for a long time."

He drops a kiss to my shoulder.

"What do you want to do today?"

"This," I say simply. "Be with you. Relax. Swim. Just soak it in. Is that okay?"

"Perfect."

Sergei joins us at the pool and Roman lifts me off his lap and heads in for his leftover breakfast and a fresh pot of coffee. Sergei grabs a flamingo float and settles in, folding his hands over his stomach and shutting his eyes. Roman slips into the pool beside him when he's done eating, folding his arms on the edge.

He stares up at me from where I read above him. Water droplets race down his jaw and to his neck before disappearing back down into the pool. His light eyes are dark, hungry, and I wonder if he'll ever be satiated. His lips twitch.

He won't.

It's miraculous the way he knows me, reads me. Just a raise of my brow and he's answering my unspoken question.

We lounge all day, talking and hovering in contented silence.

I can feel my back begin to burn, so I ask Roman to put sunscreen on me. He hoists himself from the pool, water droplets racing down his chest. I feel my mouth go dry at the sight of him. It's his turn to smirk now as I blatantly check him out.

He rubs lotion into my skin, thumbs working the kinks in my shoulder blades.

I groan when his thumb rolls over a knot. He works his thumb against my skin in slow circles.

He huffs, breath skittering over my skin.

"I can do this for real tonight for you," he says, rubbing the last of the lotion in. "If you'd like."

My answering moan is all he needs to know.

Around dinner, Roman announces that the piazza in town is having live music tonight under the stars. The three of us decide to go as a unit. I shower and blow out my hair, letting it fall in loose waves around my shoulders. I shimmy into a navy blue and white romper and pull on a pair of nude heeled sandals. I'm just straightening my necklace when Roman steps into the room.

His eyes rake down my legs and up again. He folds his arms across his chest and leans on the doorway, drinking me in.

"Don't look at me like that," I chastise at his reflection. "Sergei is waiting for us."

"He'd understand," he says amicably.

I roll my eyes. He looks good. Light jeans, a white linen shirt unbuttoned to mid-chest and a pair of pristine white Nike's. His hair is brushed back in its usual fashion and I'm dying to sink my fingers into it.

"Don't *you* look at me like that," he says, jerking his chin at me.

"I can't help it," I complain, snatching my clutch from the bed and tucking my phone inside. "You're too good-looking for your own good."

His laughter chases me down the hall.

It's a perfect night, warm and breezy. It's a night where anything feels possible, like the stars and the heavens are listening in.

We walk into town and into the village. The piazza sits back from the beach and when we reach it, I stop.

The cobblestone square is nestled between store fronts and restaurants. A zigzag pattern of bistro lights and white and green flags hang overhead, fluttering in the breeze. There's a live band on a riser in the corner, singing away into their microphones. The middle of the piazza has turned into a dance floor.

A group of children race by us and Roman leads us to a free table in the front of the crowd. Sergei slides a chair over and we watch the night unfold around us.

When our waitress comes, we all order an Aperol Spritz and a handful of appetizers.

"This is incredible," I say, settling into my seat. "I know there are places like this in New York, but it's different here."

"I know what you mean." Roman's eyes drink it all in. "It feels… special."

I nod, watching a group of young girls dance together, shrieking and laughing. There's a group of young men in the corner, watching them. I grin, thinking about Willow and the nights we shared in bars and clubs, giggling and laughing, oblivious to the rest of the world.

I slide my phone from my bag and shoot her a text.

> ANDY: Permission to share the Hot or Not list with Roman?

> WILLOW: Daaaaaamn. It's really serious then. Fine, but only if you get it in writing that he won't think of me any differently after tonight.

> ANDY: Deal.

A little thrill races up my back. I'm excited to share it with him. My final secrets exposed, all out in the open for him.

Our drinks and appetizers are set down. We eat and drink and sing along to the band. Roman pulls me to my feet when the first slow song comes on. He spins me across the piazza, listening to my laugh. His cheek is warm against mine from the hours in the sun. I play with the curls on the nape of his neck and sway my body against his. His fingers link through mine. He kisses me in the middle of the crowded piazza, his lips moving over mine lazily like there's no one else in the world but us.

We dance through three songs, even as the tempo changes. He doesn't want to let go, and neither do I.

The moon rises above the piazza, full and pregnant. It's the perfect night to fall in love, I think.

Roman takes my hand and we leave the crowds and music behind. My feet are aching, but I'm too happy to care.

"I thought we could make one more stop," he says, leading us further into town and away from the piazza.

"Where's that?"

His only answer is a secret little smile. We walk for a few more minutes until loud bass music reaches my ears. I eye the neon sign and stop dead.

"Roman. No. Absolutely not."

"Roman, yes," he calls over his shoulder. "I want to hear it, Andy. For real."

Sergei rubs his hands together gleefully. "*Si, si!* Let's go!"

He practically barrels his way into the karaoke bar. I groan, letting Roman drag me along.

"I specifically researched this," he shouts over the music. "I need to see it."

There's a guy in his mid-twenties on stage absolutely massacring a Creed song, but his friends cheer him on anyway. Sergei grabs the sign-up sheet and shoves it into my hands.

"I hate you for this," I grumble, signing my name on the next available line.

"No," he says, pressing a kiss to my cheek, "you don't."

When it asks for my song choice, I debate for a minute. Willow and I always sang 'Islands in the Stream' or 'Where Does My Heart Beat Now', but without her, they feel wrong to belt out. I tap my lip and scribble my song choice on the paper and hand it back to the DJ.

"Ten minutes," he shouts, and waves me off.

Sergei and Roman grab a booth. They order us a round of drinks and I bounce my knee under the table. I spin my ring around my finger. I'm nervous and not sure why. I've done this a dozen times—well, after having a few tequila shots, that is.

It feels like the final reclamation of my life if I get up there and grab that microphone and sing publicly for the first time in years.

I manage to chug half of my drink before the DJ calls my name.

The Creed guy exits the stage, arms thrust above his head in victory. The club roars for him and he high fives his friends as he melds back into the crowd.

I freeze in my seat.

"Go, Andy," Roman says.

"Roman," I protest. "I really don't want to do this."

"Yes, you do." He nudges me forward. He leans close, staring deep in my eyes. "Do it for me."

"Damnit," I mutter, glaring at him.

His grin is serpentine when it comes.

My legs stand on their own accord.

"Knock 'em dead, baby!" Roman calls.

I push through the crowd and take the two small steps on the side of the stage. The lights are blinding and I squint, focusing in on the screen where the lyrics will populate. The DJ gives me a nod and spins his record around, the music queuing up. I shake out my hands and inhale deeply. I can do this. I can do this.

I grip the microphone in my sweaty palms and count myself in.

Whitney Houston pumps through the speakers and I toss a quick prayer up to whoever is listening right now. The words come up on the screen and I brace myself.

I open my mouth, and I sing.

It takes me only a few words into 'How Will I Know' to relax. Someone whistles sharply from the back of the room and I feel the grin split my face. A few more lines and my confidence rises. Suddenly, I'm not afraid to belt it out, make a fool of myself, and I give it all I've got.

The girls in the club rush to the stage, scream singing it right back in my face—as only girls in love can do. It gives me the confidence I need. I laugh, dancing with them. The disco ball in the middle of the ceiling spins, casting fractals of light around me. It's an out of body experience, and I barely know the woman I'm seeing, flushed and happy and in love, confident and bold in who she is.

It's an extraordinary moment. The stage lights move and I see him, smiling so broadly it's about to stretch clear across his face. Sergei is gaping at me, singing and laughing all at once.

I glance down to the phone screen in Roman's hand and Willow's face jumps in and out of the screen. She's singing through the phone at me and I could cry. I miss her face more than I can say.

I blink away my tears, singing the final notes with abandon. I close my eyes and let it go, belting into the microphone with all I've got. The whoops and cheers reach me when the song ends and I bow, grinning from ear to ear.

I barely get two steps off the stage before Roman is on me, kissing me senseless and smiling against my mouth.

"That was," he says, hands everywhere, "the hottest fucking thing I've ever seen. You're not seeing anyone, are you? Can I take you home?"

I laugh, smacking his roving hands away.

"Sadly for you, I am. He's not the type to share, either."

"Fucking right about that," he says, kissing me hotly.

Someone catcalls us across the room and we pull apart from each other. He runs his thumb over my lip and groans. The promise in his eyes makes me shiver.

He walks me back to the booth and Sergei bows to me.

"You were holding back on us, Just Andy," he scolds.

I grin, finishing my drink.

"You're up, Sergei. You're not getting out of this unscathed. I'd tell Roman to do it, but that's a lost cause."

Sergei puffs up his chest.

"I will do this."

He signs himself up on the sign-up sheet and gets called to the stage a few minutes later. Roman drapes his arm around me and tucks me against his side. To no one's shock, Sergei chooses a Perry Como song. The opening lines to 'Papa loves Mambo' pump through the speakers and he shimmies across the stage.

Roman and I laugh so hard we're in tears as he sings loudly and off-cue, but the bar loves him. He sings three more songs before finally rushing off the stage. Groans of protest reach our ears and Sergei grins like a lunatic sliding back into the booth.

He wiggles his eyebrows at me.

"Next?"

I hold my aching ribs. I don't think I've ever smiled so much in my life. We stay until the club shuts down. Sergei sings two more songs, but I'm content to stay snuggled into Roman's side.

It's nearly two a.m. when we stumble back into the villa. Sergei heads to bed with a simple wave of his hand. Roman leads me up the stairs, hands on my waist. My heart is racing when he shuts our bedroom door.

He cups my face, threading his fingers through my hair as he slants his mouth over mine.

"You are," he says between kisses, "extraordinary."

I blush under his praise. "So are you."

He shakes his head. "I mean it, Alexandra. You're the most exquisite thing I've ever seen. I don't have enough words for all the things you are. They haven't been invented yet."

He takes my hand and presses it to his racing heart. I can only stare at him, dumbfounded.

Tears prick behind my eyes. He's gentle when he undresses me, touching me reverently and softly. He takes his time. Each touch is intentional, soft, when it comes. His mouth cruises over my skin lazily, content to take its time. It's a different side to Roman than I'm used to. I've seen him crazed and undone and filthy, but not like this.

He kisses the ring he bought me on my left hand and the space above my heart. He kisses each eyelid, the tip of my nose, the freckle on the corner of my chin.

When he lays me down on the mattress, his palm cups my head. His hand hooks under my knee and lifts it high on his waist. His lips stay against mine when he slides inside me. He says only my name, over and over again. He speaks to me in Italian, low and soft. Tears slide down my temples at his sweet words.

"With me," he murmurs, hips moving slowly against mine. "Only with me."

When we come, we do it together.

He links his fingers between mine and never looks away. He sees what he does to me, and I don't turn away.

It's one of the most tender and raw moments of my life.

After, he curls against me and presses our foreheads together. When his breaths turn deep and even with sleep, I lay awake for a long while, just feeling his heartbeat against mine.

I trace his face, the slope of his nose, the sweep of his eyes and the curve of his lips. I smile in the darkness.

"I love you, Roman," I whisper, pressing a soft kiss to the tip of his nose. "I think I'll love you forever."

Chapter 24

Roman

I JOLT AWAKE A little after seven a.m. Thursday morning, anxiety churning in my gut.

Andy sleeps peacefully beside me, her naked skin bronzed from two days lounging on the beach and by the pool. I grin, thinking about last night after Sergei went to bed, when she let me lift her and set her on the edge of the pool and lick between her legs until she was whimpering into her hand.

There's a constellation of stars skipping down her spine and I brush my fingers against them. I've mapped her body a hundred times, but I'm just as stunned now as I was the first time we were together years ago.

I press a kiss to her shoulder and slip from bed. I throw on my running gear and sneakers and head out the door. Cinque Terre slumbers around me as I run the piazza and the beach, working out the knot in my chest.

We leave to go home tomorrow.

Tonight, we have our romantic dinner on the rooftop.

In two days' time, we'll be back in New York and back to real life. How am I supposed to walk away? How do I say goodbye? How do we move past this?

Sand kicks up behind me. Lightning flashes out of the ocean, the sky the bluish-green of a fading bruise.

I tell myself to make the most of it. To soak her in. Take extra care when I'm with her. To kiss her like it's the first time or the last time. Savor every second of this day. I'll silence my phone. Tuck it away. I have twenty-four hours to drink her in, and I don't want to waste a second of it.

I run for close to an hour, looping through the village three times before heading home. When I step back into the villa, the nausea in my stomach hasn't lessened. The run hasn't burnt off any of my anxiety. My hands are shaking as I fill a glass of water and chug the contents in one go. I rub my forefinger and thumb into my eyes.

I'll make her breakfast. Surprise her with it in bed. Having the next task helps me focus and I get to work. I make her french toast and eggs. I cut up fresh strawberries. I fix her a coffee and fill a little glass with juice and carefully navigate the tray up the steps.

I hate to wake her, but I need every second I can get.

I set the tray down on the bedside table and brush my hand down the back of her head. She stirs, grumbling my name.

"I made you breakfast," I whisper. "Sit up."

"In bed?" She sounds infinitely more awake now than she did a second go.

She sits up and presses the sheet to her bare chest.

"Don't cover up on my account," I tease, staring at the swells of her breasts.

She sticks her tongue out and reaches for my t-shirt that I stripped her out of last night. She slides her arms through the holes and settles back against the headboard.

I stretch out beside her on the bed, popping a berry into my mouth. She cuts into her french toast and feeds me a piece before cutting one for herself. Rain drums on the window.

We don't talk as we eat. We watch the storm roll through Cinque Terre, huddled together in bed. I check the forecast on my phone and it's supposed to clear in an hour or two, but for now it feels like a gift to linger in bed with her a little while longer.

"No one's ever done this for me before," she says curling her hands around her coffee cup. "Thank you."

Her kiss tastes like fresh fruit and syrup and I lean in for another taste.

I drop my head to her lap and she threads her fingers through my hair, humming 'Moon River'. I squeeze my eyes shut. Fuck, my chest is cracking open.

I love her. God, I know I do. I love her more than anything. I love her more than sense, more than logic. I love her for everything she is. I love who we are when we're together. I think of Lena's words. She's my perfect blend— my best friend in the entire world. She is *everything* to me, and I have to let her go.

I control my breathing, choking down the knot building in the back of my throat. She burrows down against me and when I lift my head, there are tears streaming down her cheeks.

"Baby," I breathe, pulling her against me. "Shh, it's okay."

"Roman." My name is nothing but a sob.

"I know," I soothe, my own heart breaking. "I know."

"I don't want to go."

"Neither do I," I murmur.

I wrap her arms around me until there isn't a fissure of space between us.

"Can we stay here all day until dinner?" she asks against my throat. "I don't want to do anything else."

"Okay," I answer. "We can do that."

She nods against me, fingers clutching me so hard I know I'll crescent moon marks from her fingernails.

I rub my hands up and down her back until her breathing evens out and returns to normal. When she wipes the last of her tears away, she sits up.

"I have something I want to show you," she says, reaching for her phone.

I prop myself up on my elbow as she hands me her phone. I glance down at the screen and feel my eyes widen.

ANDY AND WILLOW'S HOT OR NOT LIST.

"Are you serious?" I sit up in one motion.

She laughs, blushing.

"Yes, but Willow wants you to sign an NDA."

"Done," I say immediately, scrolling through the list.

"She says you're not allowed to judge her, either."

I scoff. "I won't agree to that."

She smirks, hugging her knees to her chest.

"I figured as much."

The list is a gold mine. There are some very, very specific things on there that I know come from Andy.

"This is Willow for sure," I say. "Anything wine related I can immediately rule out. Backward baseball hats?" I ask.

"Don't worry about it," she says. "It's a girl thing."

I shrug and keep reading. I go through the 'nots' and groan. Some of them are brutal. I skim back up the list and pause when a number catches my eye.

I hold up the phone. "Number one hundred and sixty-one."

She hides her face in her hands.

"Say it, Alexandra."

She glares at me from between her fingers.

"He tells you to tell him all the ways you like it."

"I made your list," I state. "That night made your list."

"Roman," she sighs, "you *are* my list."

I toss her phone to the bed and tackle her into the mattress. I pepper kisses over her face. I don't even need to read the rest of it. I know everything I need to. She laughs, squirming beneath me.

"Say it again," I demand, rubbing my stubble against the juncture of her neck.

"You're my list," she pants, chuckling. "You're everything."

I duck my head beneath the covers and show her *exactly* how much I like that.

***

The rain blows inland, leaving the coast dappled in warm and golden sunshine. We have lunch by the pool and get in a few extra hours of relaxing before Andy heads inside to get ready for dinner.

Sergei makes himself scarce for the evening. I ignore the pleading look in his eyes before he goes.

I grab my suit and change downstairs in the extra bedroom, hands shaking as I pop the buttons on my shirt into place. Despite wanting to hide away all day, time slipped right through my fingers. We'll be on a plane this time tomorrow. We'll be back to real life.

My phone is burning a hole in my pocket. I've neglected phone calls and emails for the last four days, choosing Andy and peace over facing my responsibilities. Christian and Matteo leave me messages, telling me to come back and visit soon or they just might invite themselves to New York if I can't get it together.

Aurora asks if she can come to New York for New Year's Eve, and I leave it unanswered.

Brooks and Wes blow up our chat, asking if I'm okay.

I'm not. I'm really, really not.

I head out to the terrace and pour myself a glass of wine. I watch the sun sink closer and closer to the horizon. I timed dinner perfectly. I wanted her to see the world in its best colors. I wanted to see her in it, painted in all that warm light.

I hear the click of her heels over the marble and I brace myself.

"Roman." Her voice is a caress against my skin.

I press my lips together and turn, and the world falls away.

She is *beautiful*.

The burgundy silk of her dress hugs her like a second skin. The slit up her left thigh has me weak in the knees. When she turns, offering me her bare back, I spy the constellation of freckles I love so much. I trail my eyes up her neck and shoulders, her twin hearts resting right above her own.

Her hair is swept back on one side, falling in a riot of messy curls down her back.

I press my hand to my chest, utterly speechless.

The sunset hits her eyes and nothing but melted gold stares back at me.

"Andy..." I trail off, not even sure what I'm trying to say.

Her glossy lips lift at the corners.

"You, too," is all she says, voice uneven.

Her eyes roam all over me and I rise beneath her gaze. I love the way she looks at me. I love seeing how much she wants me, how I affect her.

We cross to each other at the same time. The kiss is achingly sweet, so tender it makes my eyes well up.

"You're so beautiful, Alexandra," I murmur, kissing her nose and forehead. "Look at you."

She tucks her hair behind her ear.

"So are you." She presses her hand to my navy suit and unleashes an unsteady exhale. "I really want to go to dinner," she whispers, "but if you keep looking at me like that, we'll never make it."

I press a lingering kiss to her lips.

"Tonight," I promise against her mouth.

She nods against me. I take her hand and lead her through the villa. Andy grabs her wrap and clutch from the kitchen table and we walk together in the sunset toward the village. She navigates the cobblestones with expert ease in those ridiculous heels, but it doesn't stop me from wanting to scoop her up and carry her the rest of the way.

The restaurant I booked us sits tucked in the mountain side. I give my name at the host stand and we're led through the throng of diners on the first and second floor. We take the stairs in the back of the dining room to the very top.

Our host grins, tossing open the metal door at the top of the stairs.

Andy curses under her breath, and I can see why.

The curve of the coastline and the expanse of the ocean hover before us, glimmering pink and gold and lavender. The breeze ruffles Andy's dress against her ankles as she walks to the little table set up for us. The pristine white linen is laden with glass, flowers, and candles. There's a small standing table propped up by my chair, a bottle of chilled champagne waiting for us.

The curved balcony rail is wrapped in soft, twinkling lights. The stone walls blocking us from the rest of the world are crawling with ivy and roses.

"Roman," she says in disbelief. "Look at this."

"Trust me, I am."

I could give a damn about the view, but watching Andy lean out over the ledge, drenched in late afternoon sunshine, so happy and glowing, takes the breath from my lungs.

"It's to your liking?" our host asks.

"It's beautiful," I reassure. "Thank you."

Our menus drop to the table and then we're left alone. String music floats from the speakers hidden in the stone walls and Andy gives me a maniacal little chuckle.

"This is crazy," she whispers when I join her at the rail. "How did you find this place?"

I shrug. "I searched. And when I couldn't find something, I sent them a message and asked if they could do it."

"Roman." She turns in my arms, staring at me in disbelief.

"They said they could, for the right price."

She drops her forehead to my shirt.

"I don't deserve you."

I laugh, ruffling the top of her head.

"It's the other way around, sweetheart." I tilt her chin up. "*I* don't deserve *you*."

Her kiss is sweet and a little desperate against my mouth. When I squeeze her waist, that little whimper I love so much claws up the back of her throat.

"Dinner," I remind her, gesturing my head toward the beautiful table waiting for us.

She sighs, but lets me lead her over to the table. I pull out her chair for her and pop the bottle of champagne, pouring us each a glass. Her eyes glow in the candlelight in the middle of the table.

"To us," she whispers, holding her flute in the air.

"To us."

***

It's the best meal I've ever eaten in my life.

We're brought course after course after course of fresh seafood, filet so soft it melted in my mouth, fresh cheeses and meats, and the most luxurious chocolate torte for dessert with fresh raspberries.

Every course comes with an expert wine pairing led by the in-house sommelier. By the time the dessert plates are cleared, we're both uncomfortably full.

Darkness pulls up over the sky, the stars twinkling overhead. They seem extra bright tonight, and I thank whoever is listening for giving her a night like this.

Andy rubs her stomach, wincing.

"I need to go for a walk," she groans, standing from her chair.

"We could go to the beach," I offer. "Walk for a little while."

"That sounds nice."

We head back down through the restaurant and into the street. The piazza is raucous with loud music and peals of laughter, but neither of us stop. Andy withdraws on the walk, quiet and thoughtful. We walk to the sand, hand in hand.

Andy slips off her shoes and I do the same, stowing them to the side. She pulls up the skirt of her dress with one hand and reclaims mine with the other. I undo the first two buttons on my shirt and lead her down to the water.

The moon is full over the ocean, hanging low enough and close enough to make out nearly every detail. The surf washes against our feet as we walk, hands lazily swinging between us.

I can feel her thinking. My eyes flick to her profile. Her eyes are far away, lost in thought. She worries her lower lip between her teeth before suddenly stopping. Her hand slips from mine and she wraps her arms around herself.

I pause beside her, waiting.

She wrestles with herself for a long time before opening her mouth.

"Roman," she begins, but stops abruptly.

"What's wrong?"

Her hair is almost silver in the light. She looks like a sliver of a falling star standing before me, waves soaking the bottom of her dress.

"I—" Her voice breaks. She turns to face me, and the devastation on her eyes has my heart stilling inside my chest. "I—I need to tell you something."

"Okay," I say slowly, waiting.

My own hands dampen with nerves against my thighs. I force myself to suck in a controlled breath and calmly let it go.

She nods to herself, working up her courage. I watch her chest move on a deep inhale.

"I'm—I'm in love with you," she whispers, voice broken. I freeze in place. The world tilts on its axis beneath my feet. "I don't want to leave here and be apart again. I want to be together. I want to find a way to make it work."

Every thought eddies from my head. I can only stare at her in shock, wonderment, fear, and a little bit of awe.

"I want to talk to your father. I want to tell him everything. He's a good man," she nearly pleads. "He'll be happy for us, I know he will. So will our friends. This," she says, gesturing between us, "doesn't come every lifetime. I *love* you, Roman. I love you so much I can barely breathe with it. I want a life with you. I want to come home to you and make dinner and wake up beside you. I want all of it."

I can't get my tongue to move. A dozen thoughts crash together in my mind.

I need this project to work. I need the company to be successful when I take it over. I need to take care of my employees— including her. I've clung to making this job transition work, trying to justify giving up the thing that made me happiest in the world. The source of my happiness has changed. It's coming from her now, and that thought is terrifying.

I've been so out of my mind for her over the last two weeks, I've forgotten. Who I am. Who *she* is.

Can I do both? Can I do this right and love her at the same time? I've been killing myself trying to figure out the way I fit into this job, into this space. It's the only thing I've allowed myself to care about for months.

Losing the team, losing part of my identity... Cin Cin has swallowed me whole. My failure is not an option. If I fail, what has all of this been for? I can't be distracted, I can't afford it. I need to be able to take over the CEO position. I need to do it right.

She's probably right. My dad would be thrilled. He'd welcome it, revel in it, but on the off-chance he thinks I've been distracted, shirking my duties... The fear keeps me from saying anything else.

"We— we said two weeks," I blurt.

It's immediately the wrong thing to say.

The light, the hope in her eyes, goes out like a flame being snuffed. She takes a step away from me and it might as well be on the other side of the world.

"I know what we said," she says quietly. "But things changed. *We* changed. You've changed our deal twice since we've been here. I'm just changing it again." Her chin lifts, that stubbornness I love so much on display.

"Andy," I say a little desperately. "We knew what this was."

"Did we?" she asks bitterly. "Because I certainly didn't see this coming. Did you?"

"No," I say, heart racing. "But... Alexandra. I'm your boss." She physically flinches. "You're my employee. I'm taking over the company. This was all it was ever going to be."

I can feel myself losing her. She curls in on herself, fingers digging into her arms so deeply she's going to leave bruises on her skin.

"Then I leave Cin Cin." She says it easily, casually, like she wouldn't be giving up her life for me.

"What?" I ask incredulously. "You love your job. You work with your best friend. How could you even say that?"

Her eyes are so sad when they meet mine.

"BecauseI love you more," she murmurs.

"I can't let you do that," I say, shaking my head.

"So how was this going to go?" she asks acidly. "You were going to take me to the airport and shake my hand, thank me for the good lay and then be on your way?"

I cringe. I would *never*.

"Andy, *no*—"

"So what was it going to be? Some tearful goodbye and then we go back to life like it never happened? What, we're supposed to go to conference meetings and shake hands like we're strangers? We're supposed to work on projects together like we didn't just spend two weeks utterly out of our minds for each other?"

"Alexandra."

"We're supposed to watch each other fall in love with someone else after this?" Her throat is so tight she can barely get the words out. "I'm supposed to listen to you talk about your wife and you're going to watch me go on dates and it'll be agony for the both of us. *Roman,*" she begs, eyes filling with tears. "Please."

The word rips through me. I don't know what to do, what to think. The measly five feet between us feels like the world's largest divide.

"I don't know," I whisper, and it's not enough of an answer.

She looks at me like she's never seen me before.

"I knew I shouldn't have done this," she whispers, eyes falling to the sand. "I knew it was going to be my heart that was broken in the end, but I just needed to know. That's on me, right?" she asks on a humorless laugh. "After all, you told me yourself." I stare at her. "You told me you mean everything you say to me."

It's as if she's slapped me. I stumble back half a step.

Her gaze is full of pity when she meets my eyes.

"You can have both, Roman. You can be happy and in love and run this business and do it well. You can have new dreams. It doesn't need to be singular. I know what it cost you to leave, but I was hoping you coming back and seeing it would give you some closure."

"It did," I breathe.

Oh, God. I've wrecked this beyond repair. Her eyes are distant, haunted. My beautiful girl, so strong and brave and courageous, is slipping through my fingers.

"Then what's the issue?" she asks, frustration bleeding into her tone. "Do you not feel the same? Is that what it is? If you don't love me," she says, voice breaking, "then tell me. I'll drop it but... I think you do. I think you do and you're afraid."

"I'm not afraid," I say immediately, even though it's a bald faced lie.

"Then tell me why," she begs.

Her eyes fill with tears and it's the worst thing I've ever seen. I'm hurting her. I'm watching her heart break right in front of me.

I can't latch on to logic or sense. I can't get the words out correctly.

"It won't work," I hear myself say. "I have too many responsibilities. There's too much pressure on me to do this. I am your boss," I say again.

"Pressure that you're putting on *yourself*," she nearly yells. "No one is forcing you into this pit you've dug yourself, Roman. You did that on your own."

"Alexandra," I grate, "you don't understand."

"Don't I?" she asks. "Trying to fit into a mold, figuring out where you exist in your life. I don't get that, really?"

"Fuck," I mutter, scrubbing my hand over my mouth. "That's not what I meant. Listen, can we just go back to the villa and talk?"

"About what?" she asks, shrugging. "You've made it clear. I won't convince you to love me," she says, blinking away tears. I want to tell her that's not the problem. I love her *too* much. I'll only let her down. "Be sure, Roman. When I leave this beach, I won't come back."

My sigh is heavy, agonizing. I've ruined this beyond reproach.

"I know," I say, and seal my fate to be without her.

Her eyes widen and then fall. When the tears come, she doesn't stop them. She looks me in the eyes as I break her heart.

"Fine," she says, scooping up the hem of her salt-soaked dress. "Then I'll see you in New York."

She turns and walks away from me and being the coward I am, I can only watch her go.

Chapter 25

Andy

My hands are shaking as I push back into the villa. The soles of my feet are cracked and bleeding from my sprint up the cobblestone street. In my haze, I forgot my shoes.

I was half expecting him to chase me, call me back to the beach. I didn't think he'd let me get further than a few steps before pulling me back into his strong chest.

It cuts me to the quick that he didn't.

That he was able to stand there and watch me go.

Sergei lifts his head from the book he's reading on the couch. He takes one look at my tear-stained cheeks and curses.

"Just Andy," he says, leaping off the couch. "What has happened?"

"I'm an idiot," I sob. "That's what happened."

Roman doesn't barge in, he doesn't chase me down.

He lets me go.

"Andy, just wait a second," Sergei says, following me into the bedroom. "Tell me what has happened. We can fix this."

"We can't," I bite out. "We can't fix anything. I can't convince him to love me," I cry, shoulders shaking. "Only he can decide that and I won't sit here for another three years waiting for him to figure it out."

Sergei curses, rushing from the room.

I whirl through our bedroom, barely able to look at the rumpled sheets from this morning. I shove my things into my bag. Everything I own smells like him, feels like him. I have half a mind to leave it all behind.

I stuff my makeup back into the bag, wrapping up charging cables and swiping my book off the bedside table.

I need to call Willow. I need to tell her what happened, but she can't get me home. No, there's only one person I know with the money to get me out of Italy tonight.

My hands are shaking as I press my phone to my ear.

Brooks Harper answers the phone, his breath choppy down the line.

"Andy?" he asks, surprise evident. "Isn't it like midnight in Italy?"

"Yes," I croak, ripping the zipper down my dress. I hear the fabric tear and my throat threatens to close up. "Did I wake you?"

"I'm at the gym," he says slowly. "What's going on?"

"Are your parents still in Europe?"

"Yes, they're in France. Why?"

"What are the odds you have a plane?"

It's a last ditch effort. I can't sit in the car with him for three hours and then endure a nine-hour plane ride home, not speaking.

I can't fight with him.

I can't love him.

I need to get away.

It's the only solution.

"High," he says, tone weary. "Where are you?"

I give him all the details as I change. I stuff my ruined dress into the trashcan and jam my feet into my sneakers. I roll my bag into the living room and throw Sergei his keys.

"Andy," he sighs, "it's late."

"I'll pay you," I blurt. "Whatever it costs. I'll figure it out but please, Brooks. I am begging you."

"God, what did he do? And you don't need to pay me, Andy. Jesus Christ."

I can't bring myself to say it.

"Where can I go?" I ask instead, rubbing my eyes.

"All right. It looks like there's a little airport just about an hour away from you. I can have the jet there in two hours. I just need to wake the pilot."

"Please," I practically beg. "I need to come home. I need to get out of here."

"Andy, just slow down. I'll get the plane to you. Hang on a second." He mutters something to someone on the other side of the phone. There's a two-minute delay before he gets back to me. "Okay, the pilot is up. He's on his way."

"Thank you," I say, the relief so intense my legs go out from underneath me. "Thank you, Brooks. I wouldn't have called if I really didn't need it."

"I know, honey," his deep voice rumbles over the line. "Take a breath. You'll be home soon. I'll call Wes."

I want to tell him I can't. I'm barely functioning. I don't know how I'll ever be able to breathe fully again. Brooks gives me the address to the airport and Sergei takes my bag.

"Thank you."

"It'll be okay," he promises. "Call me when you land."

"I will," I say, and disconnect the call.

"I'm sorry," I whisper, turning to face Sergei. "I need to go. I can't be here."

Sergei nods, defeated.

"What will I tell him? Why isn't he here?"

"I don't know," I mumble, gut twisting.

I *hate* that he's not back yet. I hate thinking of where he is, what he's doing.

"Just tell him I needed to go home."

He nods, forlorn.

"I am sorry, Just Andy. I had hoped he'd be able to move on from this."

"Me, too."

Our yellowing headlights cut through the dark. I sit in the passenger seat and Sergei holds my hand as we navigate the dark streets. He doesn't tell me to stop crying and I couldn't if I wanted to. He doesn't turn the radio on. The car is suffocatingly silent. I feel bad for making him drive me so late.

"I would do this for anyone in my family," he says, reading my mind. "You are part of that now, Andy."

Gratitude knocks my vision out of whack. I squeeze his hand and he offers me a little smile.

When we reach the airport, I hug him hard.

"Thank you," I say, kissing his leathery cheek. "I appreciate everything. If I come back for Christmas, I'd love to see you."

He smiles, but his eyes are infinitely sad.

"I am only a phone call away for you," he says, squeezing my hand. "Do not give up on him," he urges. "He will come around."

My smile is brittle. "I won't be here when he does. I spent three years waiting, I can't do it again."

He nods and lets me go.

"Take care of yourself, Just Andy," he calls after me.

I wave over my shoulder and push into the little airport. I breeze through security and make it to the tarmac. I wait for a long time in the darkness, watching the plane land and refuel.

The pilot is a man in his mid-fifties and I can tell from his body language how annoyed he is when he meets me on the stairs of the plane.

I lift my eyes to his to apologize, and the frown melts off his face at the sight of the tears brimming in my eyes.

"All set?" he asks gently, taking my bag.

I want to tell him no. I'm not set. I'm not even close. I'm leaving without the one person I can't live without, the person that makes me the happiest in my life.

"Yes," I force myself to say, stepping into the plane. "I'm set."

***

I call Willow while we take off.

"Wes just got off the phone with Brooks," she says. I can hear her coffee pot struggling to percolate in the background. "I can't believe he didn't say *anything*."

I spared no detail. Our conversation spilled out of me almost verbatim as soon as she answered the phone.

I'll never forget the look on his face, the shock in his eyes, when I told him I loved him. I spent all day thinking of the different ways I could say it.

When I saw him on the terrace, bathed in that warm sunset glow, I nearly told him then.

Then again when we reached the restaurant and I saw what he did for me.

I had built it up in my head. He was going to say it back, drag me to the sand and peel the dress from my body. He was going to say, of course we'll make it work.

Of course, I love you.

Of course, we'll figure it out.

I had hoped that what had grown between us over the last two weeks was enough to fight for.

I was wrong.

I close my eyes and burrow into the leather seat at my back. The flight attendant took one look at my face and brought me a thick blanket and every alcohol selection the plane had to offer.

"You and me both," I say, knocking back a shot of whiskey. "He just told me he couldn't. He couldn't even tell me he loved me. I know he does, Will. You don't experience what we just did over those last two weeks and not fall in love."

"I know, Andy," she says, sighing heavily. "I know he does. I could see it in the pictures you sent. I wasn't even there and I know it."

"I wish that made me feel better," I grumble, wiping away another tear.

"I'm proud of you though," she says.

"For what?"

I practically feel her shrug against me. I'm itching to hug her, cry into her shoulder and let the comforting scent of her perfume, oranges and vanilla, wash over me.

"For a lot of things. For opening yourself up and telling him how you felt. For walking away. For knowing what you deserve. You're the strongest person I know, Andy."

I huff. "I don't feel it right now."

"I know you don't, but you are."

Wes' deep voice rumbles in the background.

"Wes wants to know when you land."

I check the little inflight screen in front of me.

"I don't even know what time zone I'm in," I confess. "It says six p.m., New York time."

"I can come and pick you up at the airport," she offers, voice soft.

I'm flooded with love and gratitude for her. She's the calm in all my storms, the lighthouse on my tough days. Willow is half the reason I'm still standing.

"You don't need to do that," I say, sniffling. "I'll call a cab. I just want to sleep," I whisper. "I want to get the feel of him off me."

"I know," she echoes. "I know how that feels."

I know she does. She lived it herself last year when she and Wes went through a rough patch. I empathized with her then, but now I realize I didn't do it quite enough.

"I'll call you when I land, okay?"

"Okay," she says. "We'll get you through this."

My laugh is doubtful when it comes.

"Right now it doesn't feel like that."

"I know, but we will. I love you, Andy." The tenderness in her voice threatens to undo me. "I've got you."

I grin, tearing up at our mantra.

"And I've got you."

Chapter 26

Roman

I'M TREATED TO THE hangover of a lifetime and Sergei's glowering gaze when I stumble into the villa Friday morning, reeking of alcohol and sweat.

I avoid his gaze as I head right into the kitchen and pour myself a cold glass of water.

I chug it, beads spilling out over my lips and dripping down my chin.

It's eerily silent. It feels like someone has died.

When I turn to face him, I blink.

I've never seen Sergei so angry in all the years I've known him.

"You promised," is all he says, voice hoarse.

There are dark circles under his eyes, like he hasn't slept. An untouched cup of coffee sits by his elbow. I turn and refill my water, sipping slowly this time. The alcohol in my stomach pivots and twists and I swallow down the bile that's climbing up the back of my throat.

"Don't," I bark, voice like gravel. "I don't want to hear it."

"You need to," he bites out. "Someone needs to say it to you."

"Not now," I say, turning out of the kitchen.

"Yes, *now,* Roman. Right now."

I ignore him and quicken my steps through the living room.

"Andy?" I shout. "Alexandra!"

Anxiety climbs up my spine when there's no response.

I storm up the stairs, expecting to find her in bed. When I throw open our bedroom door, it's empty. A cursory glimpse around the room tells me what I feared most:

She's gone.

"You didn't come home," he accuses. "Where were you?"

"I went to a bar. I had a few drinks," I say, glancing away from him. Shame tinges my cheeks pink.

"All night?" he asks.

I can hear the accusation in his voice. It looks bad. It looks *really* bad.

"You think I hooked up with someone?" I ask, glowering at him. "Like I'd ever be able to do that to her."

"Where did you sleep, Roman?" he grits out.

"Jesus, Sergei. I didn't go home with anyone. I fell asleep on a beach lounger. I stumbled out of the bar and passed out some time around four, okay? A patrolman saw me and woke me up a few minutes ago. It's inexcusable, I know."

"She is sick over it," he says. "You should have seen her. You left her to assume the worst. That you would go and find someone else. Why didn't you come home, Roman? *Why?*"

I wish I had a good answer for him. I wish I had an answer for myself. I watched her storm up the beach, frozen in place.

I should have gone after her. I should have chased her down, apologized, and begged her to forgive me. My fear kept me locked into place. In comparison to her, I feel like a coward.

I should have told her how over-the-moon in love with her I am.

My eyes fall to the wadded up dress in the trash can. The zipper is ripped clean out of the liner. My hands shake as I curl them into fists. I can almost feel the desperation hanging in the air.

"You didn't chase her down. Ask her to stay. Ask her to talk."

"I did," I defend, ripping my suit jacket from my arms. "She walked off the beach."

"Can you blame her?" he shouts, making me freeze.

I've never heard Sergei's voice rise in anger. At a Guardian's game, yes, but never directly at me. Not like this.

"You practically shoved her away," he says, switching to Italian. "You fucked up, Roman. Big time."

I strip out of my shirt and tug on a clean t-shirt.

"Where did she go? Did she get a hotel?" I ask. "I can fix this. I just need to talk to her, get her to understand."

"She is gone," he says succinctly.

"What do you mean?" I glance at him.

"Brooks Harper sent his plane for her last night. She is probably home in New York by now."

She flew home alone? My stomach rolls knowing how anxious she must have been by herself boarding that plane. I tilt my head back toward the ceiling, eyes shut. God, I really did fuck this up. The fact she didn't even want to leave together...

"You were the man she needed. The man she *loved*. You had to give up something you loved very much, and that breaks my heart that you did but you have to stop using it as a crutch to push people away," he says, ripping straight into my chest. "It is a weapon you wield. It shouldn't be."

"I didn't want this," I snap. "I didn't want to come home and do this."

"You are acting like a child!" he roars. "We are adults. We must grow up. Life is unfair. It always is, but you have been given a gift. A beautiful, precious, wonderful gift, and you wasted it." I flinch, lowering my eyes. "I love you like my own child, Roman but this..."

The disappointment in his eyes makes me want to vomit. "I had expected more."

"Yeah, well," I mutter, "so did everyone else."

His eyes are mutinous as he turns on his heel, leaving me alone.

I deserve it. I deserve every bit of his disdain, his disappointment. I deserve Andy's rage and soul-crushing silence.

I wish I could go back. I would have dropped to my knees in the sand. I would have owned it, swallowed my fear, allowed myself a chance at happiness. He's right, I know he is. I've been so bitter, so jaded over coming to New York that I let it get in the way of the very best thing to happen to me.

Midway through packing, I drop to my knees in the bathroom and empty the contents of my stomach into the toilet over and over and over again. My legs are shaking as I slide to the floor, the tile cool against my sweat-slicked skin.

I scrub my hand over my face and lean back against the tub. My hand lands on something soft and small and I bring it to my tired eyes.

Andy's father's wedding ring falls into my hand and out of the pouch.

My laugh is dry, broken, when it comes.

"Of course," I mutter. "Why wouldn't she have left you behind?"

I twirl the ring between my fingers and slip it over the ring finger of my left hand. It fits me like a glove.

I don't cry until I see the little heart staring up at me.

I broke her heart and in doing so, broke my own in the process.

***

The ride between us is tense as Sergei drives me back to Rome. The car is silent. I miss her singing, her humming. I miss the way she and Sergei would poke at each other. It felt like we became a family during this trip. We did, I think sadly. We did, but then I went ahead and ruined it.

When Sergei drops me off, he hands me my bag without a word.

"I'm sorry," I say simply. His dark eyes are still angry when they meet mine. "I've been acting like a coward. I just... I was so dead set on making it all mean something that I didn't see what was in front of me."

The tension around his mouth dissolves.

"It does mean something," he insists. "Love is everything. It is the reason we breathe, the reason we rise day in and day out. She is your meaning. Football will be there. Cin Cin will keep standing but Andy... She is the pillar. She is the reason, Roman. Did you ever think that everything in your life that's happened up until right now has been to bring you here? To her?"

I stare at him, dumbstruck.

"Your career ended so you could come home. Imagine if you had not come when you did. If you had not gone to the bar that evening. You would have missed each other. You would have maybe only ever worked together, been passing friends or acquaintances. Imagine if you did not come at all. You never would have met her."

A world without Andy seems incomprehensible to me. I can't imagine existing without knowing who she is. Not knowing her heart, her soul, the way that I do.

"Your road has led you here, Roman. Now the question is, what are you going to do about it?"

"Jesus," I mutter. I pull him against my chest, hugging him hard. "I'm going to get her back."

Sergei's smile is pleased when it comes.

"Good man. You are worthy," he says, cupping my cheek. "You have always been worthy. Now go and get your girl."

It's the longest flight of my life. I catch a few fitful hours of sleep on the plane before landing in New York around ten. When I check my phone, I have a dozen missed calls and texts.

Seeing Willow's name on my phone makes me want to shrivel up and die. I can't read her texts right now. Like the coward I am, I duck my head and go home.

Wes calls me for the sixth time and I send it to voicemail. I need to get my head on straight, work through the mess of scar tissue around my heart before I start returning phone calls. My email is exploding with payroll, meetings, label choices, more meetings, and contract updates as we begin to sort through the next steps.

Everything is overwhelming and loud.

I collapse into bed, face down.

Tomorrow, I think to myself. I'll make it right tomorrow.

I fall asleep with the lights on, still fully clothed.

Chapter 27

Andy

Willow curls up on my couch, drawing her knees to her chest. She sips her wine, eyeing me warily.

I haven't moved from my spot on the couch in hours.

Neither of us have.

"If you're going to sink," she'd said, "then I'm going to do it with you."

Against my request, she was waiting for me when I landed, arms folded against the baggage claim wall. I've never been more thankful in my life that she chose now to refuse to listen to me.

Her blue eyes were filled with concern when I raced through JFK toward her. She pulled me against her and I collapsed into her arms, sobbing into her chest.

She held me for a long time while the baggage carousel spun around and around behind us. Wes was kind enough to give us space, but when she finally grabbed my bag and took my hand leading me outside, he was leaning against his car waiting for us.

His normal sea-glass eyes were dimmer than I've ever seen them. He and I have become friends over the last year, but it still shocked me to my core when he pulled me into a hard hug, banding me to his chest.

I stained his shirt with my leftover mascara.

When we got back to my place, Willow pulled her own bag from the trunk. She kissed Wes lightly on the lips and told him to go home—she'd be back in a few days.

I feel only a little guilty that she's here.

The movie credits roll across the screen and I lift my head from the pillow.

"What are you going to do about the gala?" Willow asks.

I groan, dropping my head back into the pillow. My dress arrived yesterday, care of Dior and Roman. I was expecting a card, a note, anything, but there was nothing. My phone has been silent where it rests on my coffee table.

Two days and nothing.

No calls, no texts.

Sadness burns up my throat.

Willow, of course, made me unbox the dress and try it on. It fits like a glove. The shoes are perfect. All together, I felt like cinderella.

When Willow saw the price tags for both items, she screeched.

"Why is that *so hot*?" she complained, flopping back on the floor of my bedroom. "Ugh!" She threw her hands up in the air, exasperated.

We do begrudgingly add it to our Hot or Not list.

The gala looms ahead of me. George has sent a few follow up emails with instructions. The limo will come to collect me at six sharp, not a second later.

Brooks worked his magic a second time for me and was able to invite Wes and Willow. I emailed George back, saying I already had a ride and I would meet him there.

The silence that followed was very passive aggressive, but he's the least of my concerns right now.

"I don't want to think about it," I say, face down on the pillow. "I don't want to think about anything at all except when we're ordering dinner."

Her chuckle is light, airy. Ever since Wes came into her life, she's been happier, freer than I've ever seen her. It's like they changed each other's lives in the span of a few breaths.

"We just had pizza."

"And?"

"Well, when you put it like that..."

I blindly reach for her, flicking her in what I think is her knee. I love having her here. After spending hours on FaceTime when she was halfway across the world, I love being able to see her all the time. My place feels like a home when she's here.

I always wondered what Roman would think about it. The last time I saw his place, it was empty and cold. I wonder what it looks like now. I hate that I let myself dream of the image of him on my ivy-green couch, feet propped up on my coffee table with all of New York hanging over his shoulder.

I imagined him bare-chested in my kitchen in the morning, wrestling with my coffee pot and pulling breakfast from the fridge. My eyes burn against the pillow beneath my face.

It's a life full of 'what ifs' once more. I think of Verona and the letter I wrote to Juliet. I never asked Roman what he wrote, but I wondered for days what caused the tension around his mouth and eyes. For a moment there, I thought she granted my wish. I thought I had him.

I clench my fingers into the blanket.

Somewhere, she's laughing at me.

"Well, what if we think about something happy," she suggests, breaking up my internal spiral. "Would that distract you?"

"Like what?" I grumble. "Give me your best shot."

"We set a date for the wedding."

"WHAT?!" My head flies off the pillow, blonde hair falling into my eyes.

I scramble over my sectional and practically throw myself into her lap, wrapping my arms around her.

"You did?" I ask, joy exploding through my hollow chest. "When? Why didn't you tell me?"

She laughs, wrestling me off her.

"You're crushing me," she wheezes, prying my arms from her neck.

"It's your punishment," I admonish. "I can't believe you didn't tell me!"

"You were away and I wanted to be able to surprise you!"

"When?" I gasp, shaking her. "When?"

"We thought maybe in the spring," she says sheepishly, cheeks flushing. "April tenth. The vineyards will be pushing flowers then."

"The grapes for champagne," I say, heart threatening to shred itself apart within my chest. "The first crush."

She nods, biting her lip. "It's a special time for us."

I wave my hand by my face, blinking the moisture from my eyes.

"You don't need to explain it to me," I say. "I know."

I think of Roman's request to Dom. The champagne he ordered should be arriving soon. Willow and Wes will be thrilled. My eyes fill with tears.

"I'm sorry," she says weakly when she sees the sheen in my eyes. "I shouldn't have told you."

"Please," I snort. "I'm so thrilled for you, Will." I take her hands in mine. "I can't wait. You're going to be the most beautiful bride in the entire world."

Her eyes mist over. "I don't know about that."

"I do," I say fiercely. "Wes is the luckiest man. I'm so happy for you both."

"I know it's not the best moment but…"

I grin so broadly my cheeks ache.

"Go ahead," I say haughtily. "Ask me to be your best woman. I dare you."

She rolls her eyes at me. "You are," she snipes, "insufferable."

"I am, but it's why you love me so much."

She shakes her head, exasperated.

"Will you be my maid of honor?"

I squeal, crushing her to my chest.

"God, yes. I already have my speech written."

She stares at me. "You do not."

"I do! I wrote it when Wes created his *Master Chef* date for you. I knew right then he was your person."

"Damnit, Andy," she says, sniffling. "Knock it off."

I fall back beside her and wrap my arm around her shoulders.

"I did," I insist. "If I'm being honest, I started thinking about it that first day you walked in the conference room and knocked him on his ass."

"Now you're being ridiculous," she chides, resting her head on my shoulder.

I shrug. "I don't know. I think I'm pretty good at predicting these things. Well," I say, cutting myself off. "I thought I was."

We sober up for a moment, smiles faltering. Willow's phone buzzes on the coffee table.

"That's probably Wes. Maybe I can see if he can pick us up Thai?"

"Sounds good to me."

When she reaches for her phone, we both freeze.

I stare at the name on the screen, palms dampening on the blanket.

"Why is he calling you?" I whisper.

Anxiety grips me by the throat.

"I don't know," she says inaudibly. "Should I answer it?"

"Yes. Put it on speaker."

She licks her lips and answers the call, transferring it to speaker mode.

"Hello?"

"Willow."

I have to stop myself from sobbing as his voice floats through the phone. My body prickles in goosebumps. Two days is too long to go without hearing his voice. I miss him so badly my body is aching. I'm desperate to crawl through the phone and curl up on his lap.

The grief of losing him is all-consuming. I'm dreading going to work next week and seeing him, forced to pretend the last three weeks didn't happen. I'm dreading seeing him at the gala, beautiful in a suit. It'll be a new circle of hell, forced to look at him but unable to go to him.

"What can I do for you, Roman?" she asks coolly.

I stare at her in surprise. There's real rage in her eyes as she glares down at her phone. I don't know if I've ever seen Willow angry before in my life.

There's a long silence from his side of the phone. I hear his sigh and press my eyes shut. Willow's hand threads through mine.

"Have you seen her?"

Her eyes flick to mine. I nod, telling her to answer him.

"Yes."

"And?" he asks expectantly.

"What do you think, Roman?"

"I know," he mumbles, sounding so unsure. "Do you think... Do you think she'd see me? I want to apologize. I want to— no, I need to make it right."

I shake my head. I'm not ready for that conversation yet. My heart can't handle it.

"Not right now," Willow says. "She needs time."

"Of course," he says, chastised. "Of course. I just... I'm going out of my mind, Willow."

"Roman," she says, and sighs. "You gave me some great advice at one point in my life. You asked me what I wanted to believe, the voices in my head or the man that loved me. I think you need to ask yourself the same thing."

My eyes cut to her face. She told me very little about their conversation from last year. Every time I asked, she shut me down. This is the first time she's mentioned it.

"Yes, you're right," he says curtly. "Thank you for answering my call. There should be a few boxes arriving for you. Let me know when you get them, okay?"

"All right," she says uneasily. "I will."

"Thank you. I'll see you at the gala?"

"Yes, I'll see you then."

The line goes dead. I stare down at her phone through a fog.

"Oh, God," I moan, falling back onto the couch. "I'm going to have to see him in four days."

"We can figure it out," she says, transferring right into mom mode. "We can keep you away from each other all night."

"Oh, my GOD!" I scream up to my ceiling. "What am I going to do? What if he wants to apologize? What if he wants to make it work? What am I supposed to *do*?!"

"Well," she says hesitantly, "is that something you'd think about?"

I huff. "Well, considering he's curb stomped my heart twice now, I don't know."

"It's something you need to prepare for."

"I miss him," I whisper. "I miss him so much I think it's going to kill me." She takes my hand again. "I can't trust myself when it comes to him. My heart is going to want to run right back to him."

"Then maybe that's what's meant to happen."

"What if he just shakes my hand and says it's good to see me?" I lift my head from the back of the couch. "I can't do this. I'm going to hurl. Text your man. Tell him to bring me two containers of Chubby Hubby on the double." I push from the couch and pace. "I think I'm having a life crisis."

Willow already has her phone to her ear.

"Hi, Wes," she says in that sweet little voice she reserves only for him. "Alexandra is having a life crisis. Can you bring us ice cream?"

"TWO CARTONS!" I bellow, pressing my hand to my temple.

She stares at me like I'm crazy.

"Yes, two cartons. Okay, thank you. I love you. See you soon."

"Oh, fuck," I groan.

Could I take him back? Could I ever trust him again? Hope is running the control panel in my mind and I brush it away. I don't need hope right now. I need logic. I need sense. I need...Fuck, I don't know what I need.

When Wes arrives with ice cream, he enters the room cautiously. I still haven't made sense of my mind, my heart. I drown my thoughts out with enough ice cream to last me a good long while. It's not until I'm drifting off, Willow snoring beside me, that I have my answer.

If he calls, I'll always come running.

Chapter 28

ROMAN

I STARE DOWN AT my phone, Willow's words lingering in my mind.

Damn. I do give good advice but it tastes bitter as I'm force-fed my own medicine. I've been pacing my apartment for two days. Nothing seems right. Nothing seems like it's *enough* to make up for what I've done.

I want to respect her wishes, give her space. I want to explain, tell her I'm an idiot and a coward and I'll do anything I can to make it right.

I'm still wearing her dad's wedding band like some sort of pathetic idiot.

I can't bring myself to take it off. It belongs there, just like she belongs with me. Anxiety grips me by my internal organs and shakes for all its worth.

I need to fix this and I need to fix it right now.

I do the only thing I can think of.

I call my brother.

I hear his surprise when he answers the phone. I know he would probably expect me to call Wes or Brooks if I needed something, but right now, I need my brother.

"Roman?" he asks hesitantly. "What's up?"

"Are you around?" I ask, pinching the bridge of my nose.

"Sure," he says, sounding anything but. "I can be there in twenty. I'll bring pizza?"

"Yeah, that sounds great."

"Okay, I'll see you in a bit."

He clicks off without a goodbye and I take in the disaster that is my apartment. I keep things neat, tidy. I like order, rules. I like control, and my life has none right now.

I scoop up my dirty clothes and drop them in the hamper in my bedroom. I scroll through a playlist and send it to my speaker. I straighten up the living room and discard the takeout containers that have built up on my coffee table.

I head to my bar cart for a bottle of whiskey, but think better of it. In the light, it's almost the exact shade of her eyes.

I grab a cold bottle of rosé from the fridge and pour myself a big glass. I settle in at the kitchen table and wait for Nic to arrive.

He lets himself in with his key twenty-minutes later, two pizzas stacked in his arms. He glances around my apartment, searching for something— quite possibly an answer for why I called him. He takes in the half drank bottle of rosé and the misery on my face.

"Are you day drunk on rosé?" he asks, setting down the pizzas.

"Yup."

He turns his head to the speaker.

"Is that Michael Bolton?" he asks, really alarmed now.

"Mmmm," I murmur, downing the last three ounces of wine. I wince against the burn. "Deep tracks only," I say.

He shucks his jacket and drops it on a barstool.

"What the fuck is happening?" he asks, approaching me like a wounded animal.

My laugh is bitter when it comes. That's what I feel like.

"Sit." I gesture to the seat next to me with my wine glass.

He does as I ask, fingers drumming over the table. I take a moment to study him. His black hair is an inch or two shorter than mine. His eyes are a touch bluer than my own. They remind me of the water in Cinque Terre. I can spot the black ink peeking out from the collar of his henley. He's broad across the chest now. He never used to be. When did he grow up?

"Roman." He snaps his fingers in front of my face. "What's going on? Did something happen in Italy?" The blood drains from his face. "Fuck, did something happen to —"

"No, she's fine," I say quickly. The relief on his face is palpable.

"Okay, then," he says on a heavy breath. "What's wrong?"

"I need your help."

"My help? What are you, the fucking crypt keeper?" he asks, splaying his hands wide.

"Do you think I've changed since coming back from Italy? When I left the league?" I ask abruptly.

He shakes his head. "What is going on?" he asks more to himself than to me.

"I'm in love with Andy," I say simply.

The words hang between us. He bangs his fist on the table, mouth twisting into a grin.

"I *knew* it. I knew you were being some alpha hole idiot for a reason. Dude, that's great. I'm happy for you."

My smile is tight. "I messed up."

His face falls. "Of course. Why else would I be here?"

"I needed my brother," I say plainly. "I need you to help me. I need you to give it to me straight. No one else will. Well, Sergei laid into me a little bit. But I'm asking you."

He eyes me suspiciously. "This feels like a test."

"It's not," I murmur honestly. "Promise."

He sighs. "I need a drink. Hang on." He grabs a glass and pours himself a few ounces of rosé, grimacing. "This is really more of a hard alcohol sort of conversation."

"Help yourself if you want."

He studies me for a long moment.

"Nah, if you're drinking rosé and crying to Michael Bolton then I'm doing it with you."

I feel the first smile in days split my face. I love my brother. I don't say it nearly enough.

He downs the glass and straightens up in his chair.

"Yes," he finally says. "You've changed. You were so much lighter when you played for the league. From the second you got to New York, it was like a stranger took over your body. You shut everyone out. You stopped laughing. You were acting like if you couldn't do this job right, you'd die."

"That's what it felt like."

"Why?" he asks, genuinely puzzled. "We all have your back. You're doing a great job."

"I didn't want to come home. I know it's old news, everyone knows this. It became vital to me that I make it mean something. I needed to do the job well. I was dedicated to that and that alone."

"So, how does Andy fit into all of this?"

I sigh, and tell him everything. His eyes widen, his face pales. He cracks up laughing halfway through, and then falls silent.

"She said she'd leave Cin Cin if that's what it took. I can't ask her to do that."

He shrugs a broad shoulder. "Doesn't sound like you are. Sounds like she's offering."

"How can I let her do it? She loves her job. She works with her best friend. It's everything she's wanted."

"Things change," he says, like it's that easy. "Something more important has come into her life. Her priorities have shifted."

"It's that easy?"

He nods. "It's that easy. I don't understand why you won't just tell Dad. It's not like he can't see that there's something between you. Everyone can."

"I'm her boss," I say. "She's going to be on my payroll."

"It's not like you're the only person in power at Cin Cin," he reminds me dryly. "Or have you forgotten the ax hanging over *my* head, as well?"

"Of course not."

"Then I process her pay. People work and date all the time. Besides, Dad has a year left until retirement. It gives us plenty of time to find a solution."

Something nags in my chest.

"Why does it feel too easy?" I groan. "Why is it so complicated in my head?"

He sighs and gives me the truth.

"Because you're a rule follower, Roman. You take things in stride. You adjust, adapt, problem solve at an annoying rate. You led your team in Verona. *You* took care of them. You shouldered the responsibility of captain, keeping your guys in line. You're doing it here, too. Stepping out of line for you is like... operating backwards. Control is *everything*. You're a by-the-books sort of guy, and this relationship with Andy tests every rule you live by."

"So... I'm stubborn?" I ask, lips twitching.

"The *most* stubborn person I've ever met. You're so stubborn you can't get out of your own way." He rests his elbows on his knees and leans forward earnestly. "It was never this job or your happiness. Both can exist. Both can be true. You act like you left Verona and could never play again. No one told you that, but that's what happened. It was Cin Cin or football. It's Cin Cin *or* Andy. It can be all three. Break a rule, Roman, and let yourself be happy."

"You don't think he'd be upset?"

"He's probably going to be more pissed that you've been half in love with her for three years and never told him."

"Damn," I sigh. "Probably."

"Why are you wearing a wedding band?" he asks, staring at my hand. "Oh, my God. Did you *elope*?" He pushes from his chair.

"No, sit down. Jesus. It's her dad's. She left it behind in Italy. I wanted to keep it safe."

"So you just put it on like some sort of weirdo?"

I shrug. "Pretty much."

"When are you going to give it back to her?"

"I'll see her at the gala on Thursday. I was going to return it then. She left in such a rush she probably doesn't even know she dropped it."

He winces. "That bad?"

"The worst thing I've ever seen," I confess. Every time I close my eyes, I see the haunted look on her face. Missing her feels like a physical punch to the gut. "She scared the shit out of me. She's so brave, you know? She just looked me dead in the eye and laid it out for me and I... panicked. Even as I was talking, I couldn't get myself to stop. I operate off order, structure— control. We had an agreement. She pulled the rug out from under me."

"Rule follower," he mouths, eyes sparkling.

"Yeah," I chuckle. "Rule follower."

"Why didn't you go after her?"

"That is the million dollar question," I groan, sucking my tongue back against my teeth. "I didn't know what to do. I couldn't even process. By the time I got back, she was gone. Courtesy of Brooks Harper."

"Don't break his face," Nic warns. "He's a good guy."

"Oh, I'm aware."

I stand and grab the two boxes of pizza from the kitchen island and set them on the table before us. I flip the lid, the smell of grease and cheese assaulting my nose.

"It's shit, isn't it?" I ask, glancing up at him.

He shrugs and rips into a slice.

"Well, considering you've spent three weeks eating the real thing, I'd say so."

I help myself to a piece of pepperoni.

"I missed you," he says suddenly. I pause, pizza midway to my mouth. "We used to be close. Well, closer than we are now."

"I'm sorry," I say, and I genuinely mean it. "I'll do better."

"It's okay, I get it. I know it rocked your life. I saw the clippings though," he says. "I watched the game and saw you in the stands. You looked happy."

"I was," I admit. "I was surprised how happy I was and how okay I was with leaving. Matteo and Christian want to come visit."

"Good. They should. Matteo needs an ego check. Let him get rejected by a few American girls. He'll be bearable again in no time."

I laugh. "Were you always this funny?"

"And getting better with age," he quips.

Despite it not being as good as what I just left, we polish off most of the pizzas. He hangs for a long time and we talk, just catching up. Before he gets ready to go, he hesitates. He raps his knuckles on my counter.

"You saw her?" he asks, barely meeting my gaze.

"I did," I say, tucking my hands into my pockets.

"How... How is she?"

I smile a little. "She's good. The same old Rora."

He nods thoughtfully. "That's what I was afraid of."

"She wants to come visit," I say. "She asked to come for New Year's Eve."

"Oh." He nods, lost in thought. "Well, she should. New York is beautiful during Christmas."

"Will you be okay if she does?"

His laugh is mirthless, and I get it.

"I guess I'll have to be."

"How long has it been again? Remind me."

His eyes narrow. "Don't be a dick."

I hold up my hands. "Just saying."

"You know what you're going to do?" he asks, walking to the door.

I nod. "I'm going to talk to her at the gala. Apologize. Tell her I love her like I should have. I'll tell Dad, figure it out. I don't want to exist without her, Nic. I know that now more than ever."

His smile is tender. He claps a hand to my shoulder and gives it a little shake.

"Good," he says, and I can feel his happiness. "Be happy, Roman. You deserve it."

He slips out, tossing me one final smile over his shoulder before he disappears.

I feel lighter than I have in days.

Three days, I think to myself.

Three days, and I'll have her back in my arms, in my life, where she belongs.

Chapter 29

Andy

Willow and I get ready for the gala in my apartment Thursday night.

Wes will come and meet us in a little bit and together, we'll head over. I owe him an unthinkable amount of wine for giving me Willow for an entire week. I know she misses him, but she's been the steadiest and most hilarious rock for me over these last few days.

She forced me to go outside last night. We walked Central Park, arm in arm. I finally stopped crying some time Wednesday afternoon.

I'm dying for her to meet all of my Italian cousins. I choke up again, telling her about my surprise reunion with Luca and then seeing Gio for the first time in over a decade. Happy tears streamed down her face.

"I don't know how you're standing, honestly," she'd said. "That's a big three weeks."

I tell her that they've invited me for Christmas. She immediately tells me that I should go. I tell her that Rora wants to visit.

"Tell her to come. I want to meet her," she said firmly. "I want to meet the woman who charmed Nic off his feet."

I laughed. "She's something, all right."

Now, as she twists my hair back from my face, I feel ready to collapse. I haven't been able to eat anything all day. My stomach rolls through another wave of nausea. I feel like I've been simultaneously living for and dreading this day. I'm desperate for even a glimpse of him.

Missing him feels like a part of me now. Like it'll always be a noose around my neck.

I haven't been able to sleep. I can't stop running through the hundreds of scenarios of what could happen when we see each other for the first time.

"Breathe," she commands, slipping another pin into place. "I'm serious, Andy. You're turning blue."

I twist the ring he gave me around my finger. I haven't been able to take it off. The twin hearts he bought me rest in a comforting weight between my breasts. The pictures I took of us are drilled into my mind. I stare at them endlessly, seeing the joy in his eyes.

It's bittersweet. I finally got all of my questions answered, I just wasn't prepared for what happened after.

"Okay," Willow says, brushing her hands on her jeans. "All done."

She pulls me from my thoughts and I glance in the mirror. She's braided my hair back from my face in a loose crown, the rest falling down my back in loose curls.

"It looks beautiful. Thank you."

She gives me a soft little smile. Her own hair is pulled back into a sleek ponytail, highlighting her heart-shaped face and blue eyes. Wes knocks at the door and she practically skips to answer it.

I smile, even though my heart aches. I hear their whispering, the quiet laughter. I'm happy for her. I really, really am.

I tug my dress from the hanger and run my fingers across the silk. I debated for a long time if I'd wear it or not. I think of how he looked at me in the mirror, the heat in his gaze.

His words echo in my mind.

When you put it on, remember who you're wearing it for.

I tell myself I'm wearing it for me, like a badge of honor. I strip while Willow is in the living room with Wes and shimmy it on. I fumble with the zipper, getting it only halfway up before I call for help.

"What do you— oh, shit. *Andy!*" Willow exclaims, looking me up and down. "You look amazing."

She rounds my body, working the zipper the rest of the way up and fastening the buttons. I slip on my Louboutins and turn in the full length mirror by my closet.

I wish I didn't look so Goddamn sad. My eyes are bleak, the circles below them deep enough to rival the Grand Canyon. She did a great job with my hair and makeup, but it's not enough to disguise how broken my heart is.

"Go show Wes," she says, shoving me out of my room. "I'll be right out."

I step into my living room and find Wes staring out the windows, eyes thoughtful on the city below.

"You look nice," I say, gesturing to his black tux.

He turns and grins at me. His dark hair falls across his brow in soft waves.

"You look beautiful, Andy."

"Thank you," I whisper, so Willow doesn't hear. "I needed her so much this week. I can't even tell you."

His eyes are so infinitely tender when they flick to the door she's walking out of.

"That's what she does," he says softly. "She makes everything better."

My eyes are misty when she joins us, the deep forest green of her dress setting off her blue eyes. I turn away when he kisses her.

We ride together silently in the car. The gala is being held at the Waldorf Astoria in Midtown. We inch along in traffic and I coach myself to keep breathing.

When we pull up out front, Wes tosses his keys to the valet driver and takes Willow's hand. We present our invitations at the door and are ushered inside.

I can't help my head from swiveling, scanning the crowd for any sign of him. Willow and Wes head to the bar to get us a drink and I find a hightop table on the side of the dance floor and take up residence there.

The room is beautiful with its rounded stage and balconies hovering on each wall. The chandelier overhead drips like raindrops from the center of the ceiling, casting a warm glow over the walls and marble floor. The band strikes up another song.

Each table is covered in fine china and fresh flowers. Corks are popped behind the bar. The amount of wealth floating around the room like it's nothing… It makes me sick to my stomach.

There was a time in my childhood when we truly had nothing. Seeing this now…

It almost doesn't feel real.

"Alexandra, there you are."

The hope in my chest dies in a fiery inferno. I turn, plastering on my very best smile.

My mother and George stand behind me, arm in arm.

George's hair is thinning. It's the first thing I notice. He's put on a little weight around the middle, but he's mostly the same. Straight and perfect nose, frosty blue eyes, and a strong jaw.

It's painful to see my mom sometimes. Being in Italy, seeing my family, hearing about my father… I want to pull her to the side. Ask her if she's happy. Ask her if she's trapped. Ask if there's anything I can do.

She's just a girl, after all. A girl who lost the man of her dreams and had to raise a little baby, all alone. My eyes burn painfully.

"Andy?" she says, reaching for my arm. "Are you all right?"

"I'm fine," I choke out, my smile edging on insane. "You look beautiful."

She does. Her blonde hair just swings against her chin now. She's never worn it so short before, but it suits her. Her eyes are caramel-ice-cream-brown. Her perfume hits me and I'm aching to lay my head on her chest like I used to.

"I'm glad to see you've made it," George says stiffly.

I want to tell him to pull the stick out of his ass more than I want to take my next breath.

"As requested," I say, hands falling against my thighs. "Where are Grandma and Grandpa?"

My mother gestures to the far side of the room where George Senior and Linda, his wife, mingle with the mayor and a few other politicians.

"Ah, the usual rounds I see."

"This is a big night," George warns. "I need you to behave."

I laugh. "Oh, George. Don't worry. I wouldn't dream of messing this up for you."

I can feel my mother staring a hole into the side of my face. Wes and Willow return with drinks.

"Mom, George. You remember Willow, don't you? This is her fiancé, Wes. He and his brother run MacFadden Designs."

"Oh, you built the tasting room for the little winery Alexandra works in," George says, shaking his hand.

Wes and Willow exchange a silent glance.

"It's not a little winery," Wes says, clearly annoyed. "It's the largest wine import company in the world. Your stepdaughter handles a lot of that."

George's answering smile is polite and razor thin.

"Quite."

"It's good to see you, Mrs. McNeil," Willow says, cutting the tension. "You look lovely."

My mom and Willow chat for a bit while George and Wes size each other up. A prickle breaks out on the back of my neck and I know instantly what it means

Roman is here.

I tune them out, eyes scanning the crowd in quick sweeps. My heart gallops against my ribs. I feel dizzy enough to faint.

"Andy."

When I turn again, Brooks Harper is staring down at me.

"Hey, Brooks."

"Brooks Harper," George practically whimpers. "How do you know my stepdaughter?"

Brooks' smile is nothing but acid.

"We're friends," he says, not bothering to turn and look at him. "Right, Andy?"

"Yup," I say sweetly.

"Alexandra," George mutters, "you never told us you were friends with the Harpers."

I shrug. "You never ask."

All he wants is the connection. A bragging right amongst his friends. Brooks is a powerful man— and all at the age of thirty-four.

"How are you?" he asks, tuning out George and his gaping eyes.

"I'm fine," I mutter. "I'm—"

My eyes pull hard to the right, like an invisible string yanking my gaze away.

He's here. Roman is ten feet away from me.

Seeing him is a visceral thing. My lungs can barely bring in enough oxygen. His dark navy-blue suit hugs his arms and thighs perfectly. I slept in those arms, clawed them, bit them. I sat on his lap curled against him. I see all the places I belong.

Seeing him... I suck in a sharp breath. I'm going to pass out, I just know it.

Again, he hasn't seen me. I'm afforded a few minutes of openly staring at him. There are circles beneath his eyes, too. The thought brings me a little satisfaction.

His head is tilted down and there's a little smile playing on his lips. I follow his line of sight, the smile slipping off my face. A beautiful woman stands next to him, her hand delicately placed on his forearm.

"Oh, God," I say out loud.

He brought a date.

He brought a *date*.

I need to get out of here.

When I turn to run, I slam into Brooks' chest.

"Don't run," he says, eyes staring hard over my head. "Don't run, Andy. It'll only make it worse."

How can it possibly be worse?

"He's looking," he says, looking down his nose at me. "You and I are going to dance."

"If you spin me around I'm going to puke on your very expensive shoes."

He shrugs, unbothered. "Then I'll buy another pair. Let's go."

He doesn't give me time to argue as he drags me to the dance floor. He grips my hand and drops the other to my waist. I can feel Roman's eyes on me everywhere.

"He brought a date." I'm practically hyperventilating in his arms.

"We don't know that," he says, eyes calm behind his mask.

"But we do," I say, a little breathless. "Is she still with him?"

He grinds his molars together.

"Yes."

"Oh, God. Oh, God." I'm dizzy. "Brooks—"

"Inhale, for the love of God. If you pass out this is going to be infinitely worse."

"I can't run, I can't pass out. What can I do?"

"Breathe," he reminds me drolly. "Please."

We dance in silence for a few minutes. When Brooks spins me, Roman and I lock eyes. Once more, all the oxygen in the room leaves me in a sweep. It's been a long time since he looked at me like that. Frustration, rage, lust, indifference. It flicks over his face like a slideshow. His eyes are shadowed, sad. The woman beside him tugs on his arm, drawing his attention away.

I know at that instant what I need to do.

I can't live like this, tortured day in and day out. I'll never be able to find closure, move on if I stay.

I glance up at my dance partner.

"I need to leave Cin Cin."

He nearly stumbles over his own feet.

"What?"

"I can't stay there, Brooks. Not like this. I'm just supposed to pretend nothing happened between us and move on? Watch him date someone else? Fall in love?" My throat is closing up. "I can't watch it happen. It'll kill me. It's already killing me."

"Fuck," he grumbles. "What about Willow?"

I glance to where she stands with my parents, her arm threaded through Wes'. Leaving her will rip me in half, but I'll never be able to heal if I stay here. I know she'll understand. She'll be sad, but she'll get it.

"Willow will understand," I say, voicing my thoughts. "It will be tough, but we'll figure it out."

"Where will you go?"

"I don't know. I have a lot of experience on my resume. I'll start applying for jobs tonight. I'll figure something out."

I'm mentally cataloging how long it would take to pack up the essentials in my apartment and move. I could put it into storage, sublet my place until the lease ends in January.

"Beckett and Bennet have been scouting out the West Coast for another set of offices," he finally says, albeit begrudgingly. "We'll be getting ready to start hiring for a Portland location." I gape up at him. He's offering me a lifeline. "We need someone to head up the marketing department."

"Done," I said immediately.

"We'd need you out there in a few weeks."

My laugh is humorless. "I'll put in my resignation tomorrow."

"Andy, take a minute to think about this, yeah? You don't need to decide right now. I'll hold the job for you until you're ready if that's what you really want."

"I do. Why would I stay? Send me the paperwork, Brooks."

He presses his lips together, swallowing down his remark.

"I'll send it in the morning," is all he says.

When the song finishes, he lets me go. I feel slightly more stable now that I have a plan in place.

Roman cuts across the floor toward me the same moment Mayor Townsend steps in front of me. Roman stops abruptly and turns on his heel.

"Alexandra," Mayor Townsend says, air kissing me on each cheek. "It's so lovely to see you. I was thrilled when I heard you were coming."

"It's good to see you, too," I say, and I've never meant anything less.

"You remember my wife, Marie."

I do remember Marie. She was the only one who ever bothered with me at these functions when I was small. She'd sit and talk to me and sneak me desserts when George wasn't looking. She was the only reason these things were bearable.

"Yes, of course," I say, giving her my most winning smile. "How are you?"

"You look beautiful, Alexandra. I can't believe it." She studies my dress. "You've turned into quite a woman."

I cringe, uncomfortable. I feel like a trussed up show pony.

"George and Annalisa must be so proud."

My smile is brittle.

"I'm sure they are."

They walk me over to where my family waits. Willow and Wes are introduced. Willow's eyes dart to me and away again.

I chug my drink while the pleasantries are exchanged. When I finish mine, I pick up Willow's and drink that, too. I feel her urgently tapping me on the arm, but I ignore it.

"Alexandra, darling," George says, eyeing my two empty drinks, "we were hoping you'd regale us with your many talents and sing for us tonight."

I snort. "No, thank you."

"It's Marie's mother's birthday," Mayor Townsend says. "We've told her all about you. She's anxious to hear you sing."

Mayor Townsend waves at an elderly woman seated toward the middle of the room. The woman is ancient. I don't think she can hear anything at all, but I don't say it.

"Oh, well if it's for grandma," I say sweetly, "sign me up. Wes, could you grab me another drink? Thank you."

Wes lumbers off, tossing me a worried glance over his shoulder.

"We don't want to impose," Marie says, hesitating.

"Not at all," I reassure. I'm having an out of body experience. I'm watching myself from far, far away. Nothing else matters right now. He brought a date. I'm leaving Cin Cin. "Happy to do it. It's why George removes me from my cage, right?"

"Andy," Willow murmurs from beside me.

"What has gotten into you?" George asks, cheeks flushing with embarrassment. "I'm sorry, Mayor."

"Not at all," he says stiffly, clearly uncomfortable.

"Don't worry, George. I'll go sing my song and you can put me back on the shelf for when you need me next." I turn to the mayor. "What song?"

Wes presses a fresh drink into my hand.

"Andy, you're clearly not well. Maybe let's go sit down for a little while," my mother says, gently circling her fingers around my wrist.

I rip it from her grasp.

"Oh, I'm just fine. I just have nothing left to lose. The love of my life is gone, and I'm stuck staring at a life without him. What's the song?"

Her eyes widen in surprise.

"'Moon River' is her favorite," Mayor Townsend says.

My laugh is cold, maniacal, downright unhinged when it comes.

"Of fucking course it is." I take two deep sips of my drink.

"Alexandra," George growls.

His hand clamps down on my arm almost painfully.

The vodka rushes through my system. It's at this moment I realize I haven't eaten anything all day. My body is finally perfectly and completely numb.

"Well?" I ask, yanking my arm from George's bruising grip. "Lead the way." I gesture toward the front of the stage.

Hesitantly, the mayor waves for me to follow him.

I feel Roman track my movements. When I look over my shoulder, he's there. His eyes are heavy with concern as I follow the mayor to the front of the room. He grabs the microphone when the band finishes their song and quiets the room.

"Good evening, ladies and gentleman," he calls, and waits for the polite applause to die down. "I thank you again for joining me in such an amazing cause. Every dollar of your generous donations tonight will go right back to the children's hospital for supplies, toys, and other life-saving technologies." Another round of applause. "We have a special guest this evening. Many of you know this lovely lady next to me," he says, waving an arm toward where I stand. "As a special gift for my wife's mother, Miss Alexandra has agreed to sing for us." Whoops and cheers go up as I step forward on the stage.

Just like in the karaoke bar, I find Roman beneath the lights. His fingers are white-knuckled on his tumbler and his eyes are only on me.

"Take it away, Alexandra."

Mayor Townsend passes me the mic and the starting strings for 'Moon River' begin. I see it, the moment Roman recognizes the song. His mouth tightens at the corners. I want to laugh. He can hide where no one can see him. His heartbreak is cloaked in the shadows, but I don't have the luxury to hide.

Once again, I'm an exposed nerve for all the world to see.

When my cue comes, I open my mouth and sing.

Chapter 30

Roman

I'M IN MY OWN circle of hell watching Andy sing our song, tears in her eyes.

She looks like a fucking dream in that dress, her hair brushing softly against her shoulders in those thick curls I love so much. My eyes are glued to the amethyst ring on her left hand.

She hasn't taken it off.

Hope surges through me.

It's been painful being away from her for so long.

I can barely sleep without her. I reach for her as soon as my eyes open. My bed— my life, feels empty without her in it.

I came up with a plan before I left. I'd find her in the room, pull her to the side and return her father's ring. I'll get on my knees and apologize and give her every word in my heart.

Instead, I'm stuck here, watching her drift further and further away from me.

Her eyes are soul-crushingly sad as they skim over me.

I want to climb on the stage and pull her into my arms.

I want to take her from this place, where they can't parade her around like some little doll. It took every ounce of my self control not to snap her stepfather's arm when he gripped her up.

I've been trying to get to her all night. Each time I get close, I'm tugged to the side.

Mariah sneaks to my side, smiling up at me.

I've been trying to get away from her. I've brought her as a date for these events in the past, but not this time. I only want to get to Andy.

I ran into her at the bar and I stood impatiently, politely catching up with her. I think she took it as an invitation to stay close. She's trailed me around the room since. She's a beautiful woman, smart, funny, but she's not mine.

Andy's eyes fall to where Mariah drops her hand on my arm, voice wavering.

I want to shout, scream, tell her it's not what she thinks it is.

I see the hurt, the betrayal in her eyes when she looks back to me.

'Moon River' has never sounded so sad before.

When the last note leaves her mouth, she drops the microphone and runs. There's stilted, confused applause as she books it off stage.

I'm moving before I can think about it.

"Alexandra!" I shout, weaving through the crowd. "Stop!"

She ignores me, banking right out of the ballroom and running through the hallway. I can hear her sobs, her labored breathing.

I catch up to her by the elevator banks. The hallway is covered in mirrors, and I'm forced to look at the devastation on her face from every angle possible.

"Andy, wait, please."

"No," she sobs, hitting the elevator button. "No. Leave me alone."

"It's not what you think," I say, reaching for her.

She physically recoils from me.

"You brought a date."

"It's not a date. I've brought her to these functions in the past, but not tonight. Not after everything. We ran into each other at the bar."

"Is that why she was falling all over you like a love sick puppy? You let her *touch* you, Roman. Right in front of me." Her eyes are hard when they swing to mine. "You *smiled* at her in the way that you do."

"I've been trying to get to you all night," I say a little desperately. "You have to know that, baby. Please. I came here only for you."

She shrugs me off when I take another step closer.

"I don't know that. I don't know anything anymore."

"I told you I would be here for you, and I meant it. I came here *for you* and nothing else."

"I know all too well that you say everything you mean," she says inaudibly, shoulders rounding in.

"Andy, please. Let's talk. Let me explain. I can fix it."

"Fix what?" she asks. Tears stream down her face. "I told you, Roman. If you let me walk off that beach, I wasn't going to come back."

The elevator dings and I slap my hand against it, blocking her from it.

"I've regretted it ever since," I plead. "Every moment of it. I should have chased you down. I should have *begged* you to stay with me." My voice breaks.

"But you didn't," she reminds me. "You never came home."

"Another thing in the long list of regrets I have. You scared the shit out of me, Alexandra. I wasn't expecting you to say that to me."

"That's not an excuse," she says, eyes hard.

"It's not," I agree. "Not at all."

"Where did you go?"

God, I hate the insecurity in her eyes and in her voice.

"I didn't know what to do. I walked back to the village and found a bar in the piazza. I went and got a few drinks and tried to make sense of my head. I couldn't bring myself to go back to the villa. I fell asleep in a beach lounger."

Her eyes shut. "Do you know how that sounds? How it looks?"

"Fuck, yes I do. I do know," I implore. "Nothing, nothing on this earth could ever make me unfaithful to you, Alexandra. You own me, heart and soul."

She says nothing. She worries her ring around her finger. I missed seeing it. Missed her little idiosyncrasies that make her, her.

"How did you think it was going to end?" she finally asks, folding her arms across her chest. "What would have happened if I didn't say anything?"

"I—" I suck in a sharp breath. It's now or never. "I think I would have broken down as soon as we hit New York. I think I would have been desperate, half out of my mind. I don't know what would have happened, but I know I wouldn't have been able to walk away. I still can't."

Her eyes shift from my face to the hand holding the elevator door open. The blood drains from my face.

"What is that?" she whispers, staring at my hand. "Roman. What is that?"

I follow her gaze to the gold band around my left ring finger.

"I found it in the villa." I let the elevator doors shut. I twist the band around my finger. "You dropped it when you were packing. I wanted to return it to you tonight."

"It fits." Her eyes are locked onto my hand.

"It fits," I say softly.

"Why— why wear it?" She glances up at me. "Why put it on?"

I look down at the band. "I wanted to keep it safe so I could return it to you."

She shakes her head. "No, that's not why."

She knows me too well.

"All I could think of was what you told me in Piedmont. I wanted to see if it would fit," I confess. "I wanted to see if I was the man your father sent you."

She shudders.

My body revolts as I slide the gold band from my finger and press it into her waiting palm.

"Don't, Roman. Don't use that against me. Not now."

"I'm not trying to," I explain. "Andy, please." I dip my head to meet her eyes. "Let's talk."

"And say what? You told me everything you needed to on the beach. That was all it was ever going to be, right?"

"No, I was wrong. It's more. It's so much more," I murmur, heart breaking open inside my chest.

"I'm leaving Cin Cin," she says, and every thought rushes from my head.

"What?" I whisper, panic-stricken.

"Brooks offered me a job for his soon-to-be Portland location. I'm going to submit my resignation tomorrow. I'll stay until you find my replacement, but I need to be out there in a few weeks."

This can't be it. I'm blowing it all over again.

"Don't go," I plead. "Don't."

Her tear soaked face lifts to meet mine.

"Tell me why," she demands. "Tell me honestly, Roman. Right now."

She slips the gold band over her thumb for safe keeping. She's offering me a second chance. This brilliant, wonderful woman...

I know I don't deserve it, but fuck if I'm not going to take it.

"Because I'm in love with you," I say brokenly.

A fresh wave of tears floods her eyes.

"Roman."

God, I love the way my name sounds and tastes and looks coming out of her mouth.

"I have loved you everyday for three years. Every. Single. Day. Even when I was too stubborn and arrogant to get out of my own way. I loved you before we even stepped foot in Italy, but God, I've fallen deeper and deeper every day since then."

She stares at me, unblinkingly. She lets me take her hands in mine. I can feel how badly I'm shaking, but I can't stop. This is it, my very last chance. I have to give her everything I am. She deserves nothing less.

"It's not one or the other, I know that now. It can be both. It can be everything. I'm so sorry, Andy," I breathe, pressing her fingers to my lips. "I'm more sorry than I can ever say. I was so desperate to make this work I gave up the only thing that truly made life worth living. That made me happy. That helped me see my future. I gave *you* up. Nothing is more important than you. Nothing. Tell me you'll forgive me. Tell me we can try again."

Her throat works on a heavy swallow.

"What if things get hard?" she asks. "How do I know you won't run on me again? That you won't— change your mind?"

"I will never, ever, make this mistake again," I say, staring right into her eyes. "I can't do it without you."

"Do what?"

"Any of it. Life. Existing. Being happy. You're the cornerstone of my life, Alexandra. These last few days have been unbearable without you next to me. Sergei *yelled* at me. For the first time in my entire life."

Her lips twitch a little bit. "He did?"

I nod, grinning. "Like I was ten again. And then I called my brother, and he helped me get some sense. Between the two of them, I was able to get my head out of my ass. My brother is wise— way more than anyone gives him credit for. He helped me see what I couldn't over these last three years. Nothing on this earth is worth losing you over," I murmur. "Come *home*," I plead, drawing her closer. "Come home to me. Be with me. Let me love you in all the ways you deserve. We'll figure out whatever comes our way. You don't need to leave Cin Cin. We'll make a plan but God, please, come back to me. *You're* my dream, Andy. Everything else is secondary."

She's silent for a long time, working out what she wants to say. If she rejects me, I'll know I gave it everything I had.

"Roman," she says. She presses her head to my chest and I think my heart may beat right out of it. "I spent all this time trying to figure out where I belonged, where my home was. All this time... It's been with you."

My relief, my gratitude, my tears, are endless as I crush her to my chest.

I can't believe it. This beautiful, gracious, kind, forgiving woman.

My hands are uncontrollably shaking as I lift her face to mine.

"You mean it?" I breathe. I don't bother to wipe the tears clinging to my jaw. "Really?"

"I love you," she says, and everything clicks into place.

"God," I choke out. "*Andy*."

I drop my head, bruising her mouth with mine. Her fingers sink into my hair and tug. The moan building in the back of my throat is raw, unhinged, when it comes.

"Take me home, Roman," she pants against my mouth. "Right now."

I press the elevator button blindly, my hands still tangled up in her dress.

We fall into the elevator car together, our hands moving in a frenzy over each other. I suck the skin of her neck into my mouth and she grinds against me, desperate.

When we reach the lobby, I take her hand and we race to the valet. I call for my car and we turn to look at each other, bursting into laughter.

I hug her against me, legs quaking.

"You should tell Willow you left," I say. "She'll worry."

When she reaches for her phone, there's already a text waiting for her.

> WILLOW: Go get him, Andy. Be happy. Forgive each other. Learn and grow. It's all worth it, in the end. I love you.

> WILLOW: P.S. the make up sex is great ;)

"Should we see if she's right?" I ask, bending to kiss her jaw.

She laughs, and it's the most amazing sound I've ever heard.

"Yes, please."

Chapter 31

Andy

We crash into Roman's apartment, already tearing each other's clothes off.

I feel like I'm dreaming. My hands slide up his neck and into his hair.

Seeing him chase after me down the hall, the *anguish* on his face as he stopped the elevator...

I was done for right then and there.

Listening to him tell me he loved me... It will be forever imprinted in my brain. The joy, the longing, the hope that crashed into me was enough to make my knees weak.

He loves me. He loves me. He loves me.

I'm home now. We're together.

I can feel his joy, his relief, as he cups my face with the utmost tenderness. His mouth moves over mine with urgency, but his hands are soft everywhere he touches me.

I've never shaken so badly in my life as I try to undo the buttons on his shirt without ripping them off.

"Rip them," he grunts, reaching for the buttons on my dress. "I don't give a fuck, Andy. Take it off."

I do as he says. I tug, scattering them all over the floor. His answering grin is dark and dangerous. I run my fingers across his bare chest, reveling in the feel of his muscles under my hands again.

His eyes take it all in. My fingers dip down his chest, over his stomach. I palm him through his pants and he groans, thrusting into my hand. When I squeeze him, he bats my hand away.

He boosts me up on the countertop and hikes my skirt up my legs. He knocks over a stack of mail and his fruit bowl, sending apples everywhere on the floor.

"God," I pant, watching his big hands move up my skin.

It feels so good, having him pressed against me again after so many days apart. My body rises to his touch, just as it always has.

"It's only me in this room with you, baby," he says against my throat. His tongue licks up my neck. "He's not the one making you feel this good."

"I've missed you. I've missed you so much," I gush. "Roman, please."

His hands work down my zipper with care. He tugs the neckline of my dress down and his mouth descends, kissing and sucking my nipples into his mouth. My eyes flutter shut, my fingers work through his hair as he yanks me to the edge of the counter. He thrusts between my legs, letting me feel how hard he is.

I can't stop the little laugh that slips past me.

He lifts his dark head, eyes molten in the light.

"Something funny?" he asks, fingers slipping high between my thighs. When he presses his index finger against my thong, my eyes roll back into my head. "Hmmm? I asked you a question, baby."

"We— we just—" His finger moves in a slow little circle. "We're back where we started," I say, wiggling against him.

His lips curve into the smile I adore so much.

"It's different this time, Andy," he says. "This time, no one walks away."

His finger nudges the material between my legs to the side and he slips a finger inside me.

"Yes," he hisses, pumping slowly. "So wet for me, aren't you?"

I hum, deep in my throat. I arch my back when he adds a second finger, stretching me deliciously.

"Right here on the counter, sweetheart? Is this where you want it?"

I can only nod, hips moving in time with his hand. The bed, the couch, the floor, it can all come later. I need him right now. He must see it on my face, because he slides his fingers out of me and undoes his belt. His eyes stay on mine as he unzips his dress pants and steps out of them.

"Wait," I say, slipping the wedding band off my thumb "I need to put this somewhere safe. Where can I put it?"

He studies me and the little gold band for a long time before he says, "You can put it back on my finger, Alexandra. We both know that's where it belongs."

My heart rises to my throat as I slip the band back on his left ring finger.

"I do," he says, cupping the back of my neck and dropping his mouth to mine.

He kisses me with abandon, tongue working against mine until I can't see straight.

"Roman," I say.

Does he know what he just said? He pulls away, staring me deep in my eyes.

"For the rest of my life, I do."

I hold his gaze as I remove the amethyst ring from my left middle finger and slide it to my ring finger.

"Alexandra," he grits out.

"I do, too," I murmur, reaching for him again.

"Goddamn," he pants. "Going to give it to you so good for that, baby. Come on. Right now."

He lifts my hips and I help him drag my dress down, discarding it on the floor. He tears my thong and sets me back down, naked on the counter. He shoves his briefs down and pulls me to the edge of the counter. I watch him stroke himself, a desperate little moan coming from my throat. I spread my legs and reach for him.

He sinks inside me in one hard thrust. I go limp on the counter, head falling back. The marble is cold against my skin and I shiver. He stares down at me, pumping in and out with exquisite slowness. He watches us move, his cock covered in my arousal. I know it turns him on to watch, to see it.

"So good," I say. "Baby. It's so good."

"Oh, fuck," he groans at my nickname. "You're made for me, aren't you?" He grips my hips and picks up the pace, slamming to the hilt with each thrust. "Me and only me. My *wife*," he practically snarls the word.

I flutter around him, my orgasm hanging out of the corner of my eye.

"You like that, don't you?" he asks, mouth hitching up. "You like me calling you my wife, sweetheart? You want to belong to me?"

"Yes, yes, yes," I chant. I reach for him, but this angle keeps me flat on my back. "Let me up. Let me touch you. Roman."

He slides from between my legs, though I think it kills both of us. He grabs a chair from the kitchen table and drops into it. I swing my legs over his hips and seat him back inside me.

"Ride me, wife," he says against my ear. "Let me see it."

I rock against him, hips bouncing up and down. I wrap my arms around his neck and kiss him with all I've got. His fingers dig into my ass, spurring me on.

I whimper against his lips and I can feel his smile.

"Come, Alexandra. Come on your future husband's cock right the fuck now."

I explode around him, head thrown back. He roars my name, hips slamming into mine as he comes. We roll against each other, drawing it out as much as possible. His eyes are locked on mine as he spills himself deep inside me.

I can barely breathe, barely think straight. He brings my left hand to his lips and kisses my ring.

"I mean it," he says. "This stays." He holds up his left hand. "I'll get you something better, but this belongs to me now."

I nod, because it does. It was only ever going to belong to him.

He kisses me again, mouth moving over mine.

"Come to bed," he says. "Let me hold you."

He leads me up the stairs and into his bedroom. It looks a little different than when I was here last. He wraps his arms around me and sinks us onto the mattress, already knocking my knees apart.

"I'll never get enough," he says, pressing his lips to my heart. "Forever, Alexandra. I want it all."

"Forever," I echo, holding him tight against me.

***

I wake up in Roman Bendetti's bed for just the second time in my life— but I know there will be a hundred mornings ahead of me where

I'll be here with him. When I roll over to face him, he's already staring at me.

"Morning," he says, kissing my knuckles.

"Morning," I say, curling against him.

"So I didn't dream it?" he says. His voice is so hopeful it makes my chest ache. "You love me?"

"I love you," I say.

His answering smile is dazzling.

We lay in bed for a long time, just holding each other. I trace the patches of sunlight over his skin. This time, no one has to run out the door.

"Tell me something real," I say against his chest.

I feel his smile.

"I hate spinach, but I eat it anyway. I'm jealous of anyone you've ever smiled at. I think my brother is my best friend. I watched your *27 Dresses* rom-com over and over again all week, just to find a way to be close to you. I love spending time with Wes and Brooks. I hate cantaloupe. I sleep on airplanes all the time."

I gasp, lifting my head to glare at him.

"But you said—"

"I know what I said." He rolls me onto my back. His eyes are wicked when they meet mine. He spreads my legs and rubs himself against me. He hitches his hand behind my knee and lifts it high on his waist. He pushes against me and I gasp. As he sinks into me, he says, "I lied."

"Why?" I ask, trying to hold onto the conversation.

"Because," he grunts, thrusting until he bottoms out, "you needed me. And there isn't anything I wouldn't do for you."

The next minutes pass in a blur. His hands and mouth are everywhere. He's tender and gentle but absolutely filthy as he whispers into my ear. I love the contrast of it. It makes me feel beautiful, desired, empowered, and loved, all at the same time.

We're still grinning like two idiots in love as we walk to Cin Cin.

"What are you going to tell him?" I ask as we enter the lobby.

He shrugs. "The truth."

I'm nervous when we reach our floor. The gold band on his hand looks so damn good, I'm having a hard time concentrating. His father is in his office and Roman lets himself in, his hand still in mine. He shuts the door behind me.

Mr. Bendetti looks up from his computer. His eyes dart from me, to Roman, to our joined hands before repeating the cycle all over again.

"Roman?"

Roman takes a deep breath.

"I haven't been honest with you," he begins without preamble.

Mr. Bendetti sets down the stack of papers in his hand and sits up taller in his chair.

"Sit down."

Roman and I drop into the chairs in front of his desk. My pulse flutters wildly against my ribs.

"About what?" Mr. Bendetti asks.

"Everything. How I felt about leaving Italy, feeling forced to come home and into a job I didn't want but none of that matters now." He smiles over at me and takes my hand again. He rubs his thumb over my ring. "You've given me a gift, whether you know it or not. If you never called me to come home, I never would have met Andy. Thinking about a life where that didn't happen..." He shakes his head. "I can't fathom what it looks like. I'd like to tell you I wasn't in love with her before we went, but I was. Nothing happened between us until we got there, but I just needed you to know."

His father stares at him, flummoxed.

"I'll sign whatever papers you need me to," Roman continues. "I'll do whatever is necessary to make this work between us." He squeezes my hand. "If it comes at the price of my resignation, I'll pay it."

My eyes widen. Would it really come to that?

"Roman," I begin.

"There's nothing more important to me than her," he says, staring only at me. "I know that now. Whatever dreams I thought I had, they don't compare. She's everything to me. I love her," he says baldly. "I love her more than anything."

When I glance back at Mr. Bendetti, there are tears in his eyes.

"Finally," he whispers, and crosses the room to hug his son.

Roman hesitates for only a moment before hugging his father back.

"I am so proud," he says, arms trembling. "It's all I wanted for you, Roman." He pulls away and cups his face. "I watched you try to work through the change for years. I'm sorry for the pain I caused you," he says sadly. "I knew it hurt you to leave the league, but I had no idea how much until right now. I am sorry, Roman."

"It all worked out," Roman says. "It's okay."

"I can see that now. Life has a way of working out exactly how it's meant to. With *who* it's meant to be with."

His eyes are kind when they meet mine.

"Come here, Andy."

He hugs me the same way, and I feel my tears sink into his very expensive Italian suit. When he lets me go, he kisses my forehead.

"Why did you think you couldn't tell me? I think of Alexandra as one of my own. Seeing you two together... It brings me great joy."

"He won't need to resign?" I ask hopefully. "We can both stay at Cin Cin?"

Mr. Bendetti huffs. "Like I'd ever let either of you leave. No, he doesn't need to resign. We'll need to draw some documents together, but those are easy enough. I can have our lawyers take care of that this afternoon."

Roman takes my hand. I watch the weight slide off his shoulders. He pulls me to his side.

"Rings?" Mr. Bendetti asks, noting the band on his son's hand.

"Yeah," Roman says, leaning down to kiss me. "Rings."

***

We have one more stop to make when we leave Cin Cin. Roman drives us north through Manhattan. My mother and George own a condo in Marble Hill. It keeps them close to city life, but offers them the quaintness of a small-town neighborhood.

Roman pulls up at the curb and kills the engine.

"Ready for this?" he asks.

I nod, because I finally feel like I am.

"Ready."

We walk inside the complex and take the elevator to the top floor. They're not expecting us, but it's almost better this way.

My mother answers the door when I knock.

"Andy!" she exclaims, throwing her arms around my neck. "Are you okay? You left so quickly last night."

"I'm okay, mom," I say, squeezing her. "Things worked out."

I pull away from her and reach back for Roman. Her eyes lift to the man behind me. Her mouth forms the smallest 'oh' shape I've ever seen.

"Mom, this is Roman. My— well, we never did quite decide."

"I think the word you're looking for, sweetheart, is fiancé," he says, grinning down at me.

"I don't recall receiving a marriage proposal," I say dryly.

"No? I didn't propose to you yet? Shame," he teases. "I think I need a ring for that," he says, looking right at my mom.

She watches our exchange with the happiest little smile on her face. When I meet her eyes, they're filled with tears.

"Come inside, please. Roman, it's so nice to meet you."

We follow her into the living room. She's redecorated since I've been here last. It feels more like her and less like the McNeil's. She looks happy for the first time in a long time.

We take a seat on the couch.

"Where's George?" I ask.

"Work. Don't worry about him," she says. "Tell me everything."

I do.

I walk her through the last three years, mourning Nonna, and starting up at Cin Cin. I tell her about our recent trip to Italy, meeting Lena and Rora and reconnecting with Luca and Gio and all of Dad's family.

"He loved them so much," she says. "They were his joy. And then you came along, Andy. I've never seen anyone love something so much in their life."

Roman wraps a strong arm around me.

"Are you happy, mom?" I ask the question I've wanted to ask for years. "I feel like you married George because of me and now you're trapped here."

"Honey, no," she admonishes, reaching for my hands. "There was certainly a bit of security he offered me, but I fell in love with him. He's not all bad, I promise. We've had our moments, but I'm happy. He's given me a good life. I have no complaints."

I nod, unconvinced.

"Do you really feel that way?" she asks. "Like a little bird in a cage, waiting to be let out?"

I sigh. "Sometimes, yes. He seems to only want me around when he can get something from it. It put a rift between us," I say, gesturing to the space between us. "It almost felt like choosing sides. I know he never really wanted kids, but I feel like a fixture and less like a stepdaughter. He doesn't need to love me," I say. "I just wish he cared a little."

"He does," she says quickly. "And nothing could ever keep me from you. I'm sorry if I ever made you feel that way. You are my joy, Alexandra. You always have been. Sometimes I think it's still you and me against the world in that little hovel in the projects, but I see now you've found someone to take care of you, too."

"I have." I beam up at Roman and he brushes a kiss across my forehead.

Her eyes drop to his left hand.

"Where did you get that?" she whispers.

I touch the band I slid on his finger last night.

"I've had it all this time," I say, glancing up at her. "After the morgue. You gave me his things. I carry it with me all the time."

She's utterly mute before us. She stands up without a word and disappears up the stairs.

"Roman," I whisper nervously. "What did I just do?"

"Nothing, sweetheart," he reassures, brushing another kiss across my temple. "She's okay."

She comes back down a moment later, a light pink box in her hands. When she lifts the lid, my vision blurs with tears. There's dozens of photos and letters and cards shoved inside. She sorts through them, digging for the little velvet box buried in the bottom. She cracks the lid and spins it my way. Nestled in the black velvet is the engagement and wedding ring my father gave her.

Her engagement ring is beautiful and simple. A large circular diamond sits in the middle of a gold band, a few diamonds wrapped underneath creating a hidden halo below the stone.

"I miss him all the time," she says, brushing a finger across the diamond. "I will love him every day for the rest of my life. We didn't have the time I had hoped for, but they were the greatest years of my life. I always wonder where we'd be if he wasn't taken from us. What life would look like."

"I think about that, too," I confess.

"He was the very best man. Always laughing, always smiling. He would be proud of you, Andy," she says, touching my cheek. "He would be thrilled to see you in love and so happy. He'd be honored that you chose his ring, Roman. I'm touched that you would even want it."

She hands me the box. I swear I can feel him next to me, smiling, his laugh echoing in my ears.

"I can't take both from you," Roman says. "It doesn't feel right. You should have something to hold on to."

Her smile is tender. "I do." She rests her hands over her heart. "I have him right here."

She pushes the box into his hand.

"Marry my daughter. Be happy, love each other. Make as many memories as you can. This life is precious."

We stay for a long time, just talking. When we leave, I feel lighter than I have in years. She hugs me hard, whispering to me again to be happy. I promise her that I will.

As long as we're together, we have everything we need.

When we get back to Roman's place, he stops me in the kitchen.

He pulls me into his arms and kisses me long and slow until he's got my heart galloping in my chest.

"I sat right here when I realized my life was about to change in the very best way," he says, dropping into the chair he sat on all those years ago when he asked me to take off my dress for the first time. "It feels only fitting that I sit here again when I ask you to be my wife."

He holds up my mother's ring between his forefinger and thumb.

"Roman." I press my hands to my lips. I can't believe that this is real. That he's here, grinning up at me in that chair after all this time. That we found our way back here, together.

"Marry me, Alexandra," he murmurs, slipping my amethyst ring off my finger and setting it to the side. "I've belonged to you since that very first night and I want it to be forever. You and me, this is it. You're the dream of my life. Marry me," he says again.

A hysterical laugh escapes me as I nod over and over and over again.

"Say it," he taunts. "I want to hear it."

"So bossy," I tease, throwing my own words back at him, but I give him what he asks for. "Yes! Yes, I'll marry you, Roman."

He slides the ring home on my finger and lifts me off my feet, spinning me around his apartment.

"I love you," he says against my mouth. "I love you. I love you. Let's get married tomorrow."

"So impatient," I say between kisses.

He nips my lower lip. "Oh, baby. You have *no* idea how long I've waited for this."

I can't stop the smile that splits my face as I kiss him back with everything I have.

Home, I think.

As long as he's with me, I know exactly where I belong.

Epilogue

Roman

I marry Andy in a little courthouse on New Year's Eve, surrounded by our friends and family.

I wear my best suit, and she finds a white silk dress that makes my pulse go a little crazy at the base of my neck.

I cry through every second of my vows. It feels like a miracle to be here, staring at her like this. I promise to dance with her in the kitchen as much as possible and always make her laugh. I promise to love her, cherish her, honor her, all the days of my life.

She promises herself to me forever, and I'm speechless.

This woman, my home, my life.

It's everything.

She's everything.

I haven't taken her father's wedding band off since she slid it over the knuckle of my fourth finger back in October. For the sake of the ceremony, she lifts it up and slides it back down, grinning up at me.

When I slide her mother's wedding band down on her finger, I swear I can feel a hand drop down on my shoulder as morning sunlight filters through the courthouse windows.

When I kiss her, I give her everything I've got. She's breathless when I pull away. Nic sticks his fingers in his mouth and whistles, sending us all into fits of laughter. Willow wipes at her eyes, staring up at Wes in adoration.

Their wedding is only a few short months away. When we got engaged, we knew we didn't want to wait. We wasted enough time as it was. Andy and I went to both of them and explained everything.

Willow launched herself at me, pressing a smacking kiss to my cheek.

"Don't worry about us," she says, slipping her hand into Wes'. "We have our first crush to look forward to. And Roman," she'd said softly, "thank you for the gift."

As promised, four cases of custom labeled champagne arrived from Italy for them a few days after the gala. Wes was misty eyed when he hugged me.

"This is incredible," he'd said, shaking his head. "I can't believe you did this for us."

It was another reminder for me, just how far I've kept everyone for so long. I think I surprised everyone when I pulled him into another hug.

"We can age this!" Willow had shouted. "Wes!"

Andy turned into my chest, grinning. I have to pinch myself most days that this is real, she's here, in my arms. That I can turn my head and brush a kiss to her temple, jaw, lips...

A beautiful, perfect dream.

We did go to Italy, but not during Christmas. Once we decided on a date, we needed to be home to get our marriage license. We spent the first two weeks of December trapezing through a very snowy and beautiful Piedmont. Sergei came, practically weeping when he saw Andy's engagement ring and the band on my finger.

"I am so proud," he said, hugging me. "Congratulations, Roman."

I had to turn my face away, tears threatening to swallow me whole.

Her entire family made the drive and had a reunion on Lena's beautiful property. I watched it all, chest tight. Her cousins, nieces and nephews, swarmed her. Her aunts and uncles fussed over her. The smile she threw at me was absolutely radiant.

When it was time to go, Aurora had her bags packed and met us at the front door.

"Harvest is done," she'd said, shrugging. "I have a few months of free time ahead of me."

"Are you sure?" I had asked her. "Nic will be there."

"I'm ready," she'd said, eyes hard. "It's time."

I didn't tell him she was coming.

Maybe I should have.

Since we've come back from Italy, Andy has spoken to Luca and Gio nearly every day. They FaceTime regularly and they plan to visit in the spring after Willow and Wes' wedding. Aurora moved into Andy's old place since she moved in with me the day after the gala. Aurora signed a lease for an entire year. My brows had risen in surprise at that.

My mother made her usual pilgrimage back from Italy for the holidays. Andy fretted endlessly about meeting her for the first time but as soon as my mother landed and took one look at my future wife, she burst into tears. Mom hugged Andy for a long, long time, just rocking her back and forth. When they finally pulled away, Andy's eyes were misty. They've been joined at the hip ever since.

Two days after Christmas, Matteo and Christian showed up on my doorstep. I remember standing there, blinking in shock at the sight of them.

Matteo hoisted a case of beer over his shoulder like a battle ax while Christian spun a soccer ball around his finger.

"What's up, asshole?" Matteo had said, grinning.

Christian's usual storm cloud eyes were sparkling with joy when I turned to look at him.

Andy cackled behind me, training the camera my way. I'd rewarded her very thoroughly for that surprise.

We found a field and had a pick up game, inviting Wes, Brooks, Beckett, Bennet, and Nic. Andy and Willow cheered from the sidelines. This time when we won, Andy threw herself into my arms, kissing me in a way that was not suitable for the public eye. I ignored the catcalls and whistles and lifted her right into my chest, wrapping her legs around my waist.

When the Justice of the Peace announces us as husband and wife, Matteo and Christian break into *Un'Estate Italiana,* which is the fight song for all the soccer teams in Italy.

As a wedding gift, Brooks rents out an entire ballroom at the Plaza for the fifteen of us, complete with a massive brunch, dance floor, and private DJ.

Andy and I ride separately in the limo to the plaza.

When we get in the back seat, she rides me in her wedding dress. It's an image I'll never forget as long as I live. The gold bands on her fingers have me finishing in seconds; both of us exhausted and smiling and deliriously, incandescently happy.

I glance around the room, heart uncomfortably full at the sight of my family around me. My parents spin around the dance floor. My mom is flushed and laughing while my dad grins at her. Hope riots in my chest. Maybe they can make it work, after all.

I watch my brother across the ballroom, nursing a beer and talking to Wes and Brooks. His eyes dart across the room to where Aurora stands, head bent in conversation with Willow.

I feel a smile pull across my face.

To say he was surprised...

Aurora settled in at Andy's place and met us at my brownstone Upstate. Andy and I didn't move from the kitchen when the doorbell rang. Maybe it was a dick move, but I'd called for Nic to answer it.

He grumbled something about not being a damn butler and threw open the door. I stuck my head around the corner and watched the shock register on his face.

"Aurora," he said, almost strangled.

She grinned up at him. "Hey, Nic."

She brushed right past him as if he were a piece of furniture in the living room. I'll never forget the look on his face as she pushed past him and made herself at home in my kitchen. Andy and I exchanged a secret glance. She acted tough and aloof but when she picked up her wine glass, her hands were shaking.

They've danced around each other for the last two weeks but I have a feeling the dance will end. And soon.

"Time for the first dance," the DJ calls into the mic.

I set my champagne down and whisk Andy into my arms. 'Moon River' erupts from the speakers and she smiles, linking her arms around my neck.

"Happy?" I ask.

The flush on her face is the most beautiful thing I've ever seen.

"There aren't even words," she whispers, pressing up to kiss me.

When we turn on the dance floor, I glance over to her mom.

George remains stoic, but the time Andy has had to reconnect with her mother has been a beautiful thing to witness. They grab lunch together once a week and are closer than ever. My girl is happy, and it's my favorite thing to see.

"New deal," I say, smiling when she chuckles. "We love each other forever. When we go, we go together. We promise to find each other in every life after." Her eyes well with tears. "I'll love you just as much as I do right now. Every life, every timeline, Andy. We'll be together. Promise me."

"I promise," she whispers, eyes tender on my face.

"You accept?"

"Yeah," she says, kissing me again. "I do."

Acknowledgements

Andy and Roman's story was something that flowed out of me akin to a landslide. Even as I was writing *First Crush,* Andy and Roman were begging to be written.

I'd no sooner finished *First Crush* before I was opening a clean Google Doc and dumping Roman and Andy's story into it. I knew exactly what I wanted this book to be and it was so much fun to write. Both of them leapt off the page and right into my heart. This story is so, so special to me.

I have so many thanks to give and hardly enough space to get them all down on. So, thank you to those who took a chance on me, who beta read and ARC read for me— *thank you*. It's a big leap to invest your time into an indie author with no real following, and I'm so thankful you took a chance on this book *and* on me. It's been such a joy to be able to bring this world and these characters to you.

For Ryan, who decided to go round two on this cover for me. Let's do this forever, yeah? Thank you for investing your time and energy into all my crazy requests.

For Sandy and Joe, who let me into their own Massey/Matranga family the same way Andy belongs in hers. It's an extraordinary honor to have such an amazing second set of parents.

For Amanda, always, who stands by my side and offers up the most unwavering and unrelenting support. You've made my life what it is. You've shared your bravery and your joy, and I am so much better for it.

For my sister, who keeps me moving forward and reaching for more. Thank you for always helping me to find new ways to be brave.

For my mommom, the safe place of my life. Thank you for helping to raise this incurable romantic heart and fostering the stories you did. The days watching the classics with you are a part of my DNA forever. My very own kindred spirit.

For Zach, my husband, who leaned into this dream just as hard as I have. For the long nights and early mornings, for your love and support. For the laughter you bring day in and day out. You are always my new and constant dream.

Lastly, to you, dear reader. Thank you for allowing me to take you on this journey. To share my dream with you. I hope these characters meant as much to you as they did to me. Thank you, thank you, thank you.

Made in United States
Orlando, FL
02 March 2025